Jake McPherson
Editor
Writersliterary.com

Dear Mr. Deshayes,

I am so happy that you allowed me to edit your manuscript "Gene." You've accomplished a lot, and I'm excited about the prospects for the piece.

I give it that strong emotion, because I truly believe that you have the elements necessary for a book to see print. Those elements are not difficult to delineate:
- an easily recognizable protagonist
- thrust into quick action
- forcing him/her to face challenges from understandable antagonists
- that lead him/her through a series of highly emotionally charged scenes
- that propel him/her to a breath taking climax and denouement.

You've got all that and so much more. The more is your writing style. You use it well. Dialogue is used in appropriate scenes avoiding boring exposition. Dialogue is active and keeps the reader involved. I believe all the events you put your characters through in the book serve the all-important purpose of pushing them to the climax. In my opinion, nothing needs to be cut.

I liked all the action surrounding the scene. You milked it well! That's the climax of the book. You don't just let it slip by as the simple physical action that it is. The characters have time, energy, emotions, and more invested in this. The readers have time, energy, emotions, and their imagined place next to Gene invested in this. Your readers aren't sitting in chairs holding books. They're not sitting up in bed reading before lights out. They are in the words. They are tied up with Gene, and their hearts are pounding. Your readers will love this book, and they will love the surprise ending.

My hat's off to you. Good job.

Truly,

Jake McPherson

Order this book online at www.trafford.com
or email orders@trafford.com

Most Trafford titles are also available at major online book retailers.

Note for Librarians: A cataloguing record for this book is available from Library
and Archives Canada at www.collectionscanada.ca/amicus/index-e.html

Printed in Victoria, BC, Canada.

ISBN: 9781-4251-5627-5 (soft cover)
ISBN: 9781-4251-5628-2 (eBook)

*Our mission is to efficiently provide the world's finest, most comprehensive book publishing
service, enabling every author to experience success. To find out how to publish your book, your
way, and have it available worldwide, visit us online at www.trafford.com*

Trafford rev. 10/14/09

 www.trafford.com

North America & international
toll-free: 1 888 232 4444 (USA & Canada)
phone: 250 383 6864 ♦ fax: 812 355 4082

GENE

Gerald Deshayes

The author would like to thank the following: Michael Jackson Music Inc. (MJJ Productions) and Sony/ATV Music Corporation for the use of a verse in the song, *Getting Better*, Rolling Stones Music Inc. (Colgems-EMI music INC.) for lyrics in their songs, *(I can't get no) Satisfaction* and *You Can't Always Get What You Want*, as well as the musical group, Trooper, for quoting lyrics from their song, *Raise a Little Hell*.

Special mention goes out to Dr. Robert White for his pioneering efforts and research as well as the late Christopher Reeve and his family.

The author would like to thank Jake McPherson (Writersliterary.com) for the initial editing of the novel as well as Robert Daniel for his many hours in helping 'fine tune' the story. Also, special thanks to Yolande Daniel RN for her medical input.

Although the manuscript is a work of fiction, it is based on medical experimentation and achievements that are considered highly controversial. There is little doubt that this type of research continues today.

Dedicated to my beautiful sister,

Jeannette King.

Your inspiration and love will never

be forgotten.

1953 – 2001

Me used to be an angry young man

Me hiding me head in the sand

You gave me the word, I finally heard

I'm doing the best that I can

Getting Better – The Beatles

He suspected he was having a nervous breakdown. Why else would one of the hospital counselors show up in his room? Gene wasn't quite sure. His mind was elsewhere. He knew that Doctor Klein had made the appointment soon after he'd left his bedside. He wondered what the good doctor had told the counselor; that his young patient was on the verge of—losing it? Perhaps he was.

The counselor introduced himself as Bruce somebody-or-other and looked to be in his mid-fifties. It was hard to tell. The shaved head and small diamond earring appeared to make him look younger. He had an easy manner, nothing what Gene would have expected in a shrink. He was also short.

He smiled as he casually pulled a chair up beside Gene's bed.

Gene smiled back. "Sorry I can't shake your hand, Bruce."

"Yeah, I know. You've suffered a terrible accident. I can only imagine how you feel, my man."

Gene tried to nod as Bruce continued, still standing beside the chair he had pulled up.

"You know, Gene, I've talked to a lot of patients who are in the same situation as you. It's never easy. I do want you to know that I have a lot of experience with this sort of thing."

"How many?"

"Pardon?"

"How many people have you talked to that are like me?"

He slowly sat down, giving the question some thought. "Well, no one is like you, Gene, but … there are many similarities." He leaned back, looking up at the ceiling. "You know, I'm guessing maybe one hundred people. I've never really counted until you asked."

Gene liked him. He was honest, short and answered questions with facts. He smiled, noticing how Bruce waved his hands while speaking.

"There have been some unique cases, some worse than others. The bottom line is I truly feel I've helped them help themselves."

Gene was becoming angry. He could feel his cheeks flush. He couldn't help but think, *"Yeah, you're just another one of those doctors with a healthy body who's preaching to me."* He decided not to go in that direction. He knew that he was angry and frustrated. He'd had enough for now. He was going to try and keep an open mind instead.

Bruce sensed what was going on and was ready for it. He wanted Gene to talk as well. He wanted some feedback. He quickly stood up. Gene noticed the guy couldn't keep still. He decided to nickname him 'Warp' as in 'Warp Speed.'

"So, you must be wondering how I do it, right? How do I, Bruce Whitman, help people—people like you?" He waved his hands, palms out.

Gene was wondering the same thing. He tried to stay positive. It was hard to do.

"The answer is we do it together. You and me." He pointed toward Gene and then to himself. "Let me take some of the pain away, Gene. I mean, why not? I'm your friend. I know we've just met but I'm not here to hurt you. I like you. I was eighteen once. Yeah, I know it's hard to believe, looking at me now." He smiled. Gene couldn't help himself. He smiled back, now listening intently.

"I used to think I could do anything." He paused, trying to think of the right word. "I was, hmmm, invincible. Yes, that's what I thought I was, invincible! I've got some crazy stories to tell you." Bruce looked up at the ceiling, thinking back to a time years ago. He was also waiting for Gene to respond. He had given him a hook, waiting to see if he'd take it. He sat back down, crossing his short legs.

"Uh, like what?"

Bruce smiled to himself, pretending he was still far away. "What? Oh yeah. Well, the time I was playing in this blues band. Yeah, I used to play bass guitar in this blues band. Know what it was called?" He stood up again, leaning over toward Gene as he asked the question, not expecting an answer. "The 'Strange Movies.' That was the name that we called ourselves." His face broke into a broad grin. Now he was really thinking of the past.

"The *what*?"

Bruce shook his head and chuckled, straightening. "Yeah, I know. Stupid name, huh?" He was having fun. He hadn't thought of those days in years.

"Hey, no, that's kinda cool! So like, what happened?" Gene had momentarily forgotten his problems. He wanted to hear everything Bruce had to say about the band. He loved that sort of stuff.

"We wanted to enhance the show a little, you know? We wanted to perform with a strobe light so our stage presence would be better. We'd seen a few acts that had done that sort of thing so we thought, well, it would be cool to do. Know what I'm talking about?" He raised his eyebrows.

"Uh, I guess so." Gene trailed off, not quite sure, waiting for more of an explanation.

"Well, back then there was this movement, this"—he held up his hands once more—"thing called a 'Psychedelic' movement." He had two fingers extended, indicting he was quoting as he spoke. "That's what it was. Yeah ...." He was lost in his own thoughts for a second or two but then came back, seeing the confused looked on Gene's face. He smiled, knowing Gene had no idea what he was talking about. He needed to have been there to fully understand the movement back in the sixties.

"Yeah." He was getting excited as he spoke. "People wanted to be free and expressive. It was an era that was very visual, right?" He nodded, agreeing with himself, walking around the chair as he continued. "Yeah. So, in the music business somehow someone had thought of combining color with music, creating a light show." He again quoted with his fingers. He couldn't keep still, walking back and forth from Gene's bed to the window, sometimes circling the chair as he spoke.

Gene was mesmerized. *Yes, the guy's name should have been 'Warp.'*

"What a lot of bands were using for the visual experience was a backdrop with colored lights. There weren't any giant video screens back then, only projectors and two or three bed sheets sewn together. Different colored plasma gels or whatever would be displayed behind the band on the sheets resulting in an explosion of ... color!"

Bruce smiled at the thought. He visualized an old bed sheet stretched out behind the band with lights projected onto it, knowing how archaic it was compared to today's technology. He looked at Gene, thinking that if the kid could jump out of bed so he could hear him better, he would. Gene was all ears.

"So ... one of the things introduced in the light show was the strobe light. It was made up of a very bright light that flashed on and off several times a second producing a visual effect that was very cool. Very cool indeed! When it was on, you could see people in the crowd moving, appearing to be in slow motion. The movements seemed ... choppy, because you'd only see the crowd when the light was on. The problem was it cost too much to buy. One of our buddies told us he'd built a strobe light and wanted to know if we would use it."

"Yeah, so ... what happened?"

Bruce looked at the young man lying on the bed paralyzed from the neck down. He thought Doctor Klein was wrong; he wasn't having a nervous breakdown. He needed to get his mind off his problems, even for a few minutes. The kid would be all right.

"Well, it was nothing more than an electric motor with a fan belt that turned this plywood wheel, see? The wheel was about three feet in diameter. It had a hole cut out near the edge. The hole was around six inches across. As the motor turned the plywood wheel, a light would shine through the hole with every revolution of the wheel. It was like turning the light switch off and on about ten times a second. It did have the strobe effect so ... we set it up on stage and started playing songs to about two hundred people. That's when all hell broke loose."

He paused, relishing the moment, seeing the look of anticipation on Gene's face. He liked the kid. He thought, "*Good. It's working.*" He figured the last thing Gene was thinking about at that moment was his hopeless situation.

"What happened?" Gene wanted to shake the answer out of him.

Bruce pretended he was in deep thought. "Huh ...? Oh yeah. We were playing like crazy, playing the blues and grooving, man, enjoying the strobe effect." He was getting great pleasure in bringing back the old jargon. Words he no longer used. "Yeah, the crowd was grooving too, man. They were really getting into it. They loved it. They thought we were cool. C-O-O-L!" He spelt the word out. "The problem was—" He smiled at the thought. "The problem was the plywood wheel. It would make a bit of a 'flap-flap' sound as it spun around at a high speed. We knew how to handle the noise it made. All we had to do was turn up the volume on our amplifiers. That was our solution to everything back then." He smiled again, thinking about the high decibels he had subjected himself to in his younger years.

Gene was smiling too, thinking about the old technology. He imagined being there, taking in the scene.

Bruce continued. "So, we're in the middle of our tenth song. I think it was 'Satisfaction' by the Rolling Stones when we heard this crashing noise. All four of us—Don, Jim, Bill and myself—looked over to the side of the stage where this marvelous piece of equipment was positioned. The plywood wheel had come loose, flying across the stage, barely missing us. Several people in the audience screamed as the wheel spun out of control, racing across the dance floor."

His hands were held up high, reaching for the ceiling to illustrate. "By the way, that was the *only* time fans ever screamed at us while we were on stage." He winked as he said it.

Gene was laughing. He could see the band standing on stage with stunned looks on their faces, the crowd looking on in disbelief, all wondering what the hell was going on. Was this part of the act? He kept on laughing. This Bruce guy was C-O-O-L!

Bruce laughed with him. It was funny indeed. They stopped after a few minutes, Bruce pretending he was playing the guitar, humming a few notes to 'Satisfaction' as he danced around the chair. This set them both off into another fit of laughter.

After a minute or so they stopped and looked at each other. Both took in a deep breath. Bruce knew the bond had been made. He liked Gene. He had to choose the next few sentences very carefully. "So … what about you, Gene? Have you ever played in a band?"

"Naw. I wanted to, but—" His cheeks were sore from laughing. It had been a long time since that had happened.

"But what?"

"My dad and mom, they—"

"They, what?" Bruce came closer to him, this time sitting still on the edge of the bed.

"They never supported me. I—they—well, it just didn't work out."

"Yeah, I hear you. My mom and dad were like that, too."

"Really?" Gene was surprised. He hadn't given much thought to other people's problems.

Bruce was drawing Gene out of his shell as he kept on talking. "I couldn't stand being with them in the same house. They were so un-cool, man. I had nothing in common with them, even the music. They didn't even know who the Rolling Stones were."

"Yeah, I know what you mean." Even though he was only eighteen, Gene knew who the Stones were. He and his buddy Dan were mostly into rap but did like some of the older music. "I was never close to Mom *or* Dad. I wanted to be, but—" He stumbled with what he was trying to say. Bruce sat there, patiently waiting for him to continue. He smiled and nodded, encouraging him to go on.

"I loved them both. They didn't love me back!" He spoke with defiance, no longer smiling.

Bruce wanted to reassure him both parents probably loved him but stopped short, letting Gene continue.

"Anyhow, no, Doctor. I never played in a band."

He could sense Gene was shutting down, not wanting to talk. He tried changing the subject.

"So, what *did* you do for fun, and please, my name isn't 'Doctor.' Call me Bruce, okay?"

"Yeah. Okay, Bruce. Hmm, what did I do for fun? Good question. Nothing really. I hung out with some of the guys down at the gym."

"Did you want to build up your body?"

"Yeah, I wanted to be a muscle man."

"Why?"

Gene was staring at the ceiling, thinking about the question. He felt like he was squirming. He knew that was impossible. He couldn't move from the neck down. "Why? I dunno. I guess I wanted to be popular."

They talked for over an hour, Gene opening up a little more, telling Bruce how he wanted to be a hero. Bruce would nod and encourage him, sensing the disappointment and anger below the surface. He tried coaxing him into talking about his social life. In particular, he wanted him to talk about girlfriends but sensed a strong reluctance on Gene's part.

Doctor Klein had been right in arranging the interview. Bruce was starting to build a pretty good profile of Gene. He saw two immediate issues. One was Gene's hurt and anger with his parents. The other was his frustration with the opposite sex.

As he talked, Bruce wondered about the parents. They certainly sounded dysfunctional. He wasn't sure if they cared about their son. The hospital could call the parents once more, asking them to come and visit, but they couldn't force them to.

The other issue was more intriguing, the issue on how he handled the opposite sex. He knew that a young man such as Gene would have problems with girls, no matter if his parents were supportive or not. That was normal. What wasn't normal was his anger toward them, not only his anger toward females but also his anger toward himself.

He tried to get the interview on to a more positive note but it was proving too difficult. In the end, Bruce told him how much fun he'd had. He really meant it, saying he'd be back again soon. He started to walk away, stopped, turned and faced Gene, pretending to play the bass guitar, humming 'Satisfaction' one more time while dancing.

It didn't take long for Gene to break up and laugh again. He had tears in his eyes, especially when, unbeknownst to Bruce, Doctor Klein entered the room behind him, witnessing the crazy performance.

Bruce looked at Gene, wondering why he was laughing so hard. Surely, what he was doing wasn't that funny, was it? He continued to dance while pretending to play the guitar. He finally turned, bumping into Klein.

He blurted out, "Oops! Sorry, Doctor."

Gene thought he was going to pee the bed. Bruce had a sheepish look on his face as he quickly left the room.

Doctor Klein couldn't help but chuckle, a rarity for him. He was glad he had called Bruce. He was one of the best. He was anxious to read the counselor's report.

PART I

Chapter 1

He opened up the yearbook while walking down the front steps of Irvine High. He started reading the glossy front page—IRVINE HIGH, CLASS OF 2005. It was the last day of school. Most students were both happy and sad. They were setting off on a new adventure, not needing to attend class anymore, yet knowing they would not be seeing some of their school friends or teachers again. Gene wasn't sad. He was only happy.

Thank God I don't have to deal with those idiots anymore.

He slipped into his black Mazda 626, quickly rolling down the windows. This June was hotter than normal. The car's interior was baking. He would have burned his legs on the vinyl seat if he had been wearing shorts. Of course, none of the students were allowed to wear shorts at Irvine High.

He decided to get back out of the car and wait for the interior to cool. Besides, he wanted to meet with his so-called friend, Dan. He wondered if they were still going swimming. Dan had told him he would be right out after he talked to a few of his friends. Gene didn't have any real friends. He didn't much care. He knew he was a loner.

He heard someone shout from behind him. Turning, he saw Chad McVie's fat ass get into the back seat of Jason LaPointe's Mustang. Chad looked over and gave him the finger as Jason squealed out of the parking lot. Three other guys were in the car, all laughing, as they tore down the street.

Gene shook his head, thinking they were a bunch of losers. Chad had been taunting him all through his senior year, trying to pick a fight. He knew better than to get suckered in. After all, Chad was six feet tall, almost seven inches taller than him. That made things somewhat difficult. No, it would have been suicide on Gene's part if he had gotten into a fight with Chad except ... it wasn't.

It had been over two weeks since Chad had stopped him in the school hallway. There were several kids hanging around the lockers, including Lindsey. Gene was talking to her. They had gone out to a movie the week before.

He stood by his car, thinking about her, how they had kissed, how he felt he was falling for her until she had told him. He was choked at what she had said, telling him he was cute but it was too bad—too bad he was so short.

He clinched his fists at the thought. He had been humiliated. He wondered if that was the reason why he had lost it when Chad stopped him in the hallway.

It was the wrong time and place for Chad to do something so stupid. Lindsey and he had been talking when Chad walked up, sticking his fat finger in his chest, giving him a slight push. Chad had a smirk on his face, taunting him, telling him he had heard that Gene wore elevator shoes. Gene didn't know what to say. He looked at Chad, focusing on his gold earring. Jason LaPointe and his buddies stood nearby, smirking. Everyone was waiting for him to deny it.

He remembered glancing toward Lindsey, seeing her look down at the floor, embarrassed for him. He, too, was embarrassed, wondering how Chad knew about the elevator shoes. The manufacturer had claimed their product would discreetly add two inches to the user's height. He wondered if Chad had closely looked at them while they were in the gym changing room. It didn't matter. His secret was out.

His cheeks reddened as he began to turn away like he usually did, but … this time it was different. This time he had had enough. He was backed into a corner and he needed to save face, what little face he had left, especially in front of Lindsey.

As he started to turn away, Chad's guard went down. Gene saw an opportunity so quickly brought his left fist up, hitting him squarely on the nose, not believing what he had just done. Since Chad was taller, the punch was more like an under-cut. His nose split as he started to fall back. The punch had come as a complete surprise to both of them, a complete surprise to everyone witnessing the event. Gene stood in front of him, seeing him clutch his nose with both hands as his knees buckled.

Chad made a nasal sound while looking up with incredulous and teary eyes. He took his hands away from his face, staring at the blood on his fingers, his blood. He slowly glared back at Gene, regaining his composure, getting ready to rip him apart. Gene had the momentum, hitting him on the nose again, this time with his right fist. The meaty sound of the punch could be heard down the hall. The metallic 'bang' of the steel lockers followed as Chad fell back against them.

LaPointe and his gang cheered them on, yelling, "Fight! Fight! Fight!" He couldn't stop. The adrenaline had kicked in. He kept hitting him, again and again until he felt strong arms pull him off. Chad was on the floor, crying, covering his head with his arms. Gene was standing over him with his fists still clenched.

Mr. Gibson, the science teacher, demanded to know what was going on as he gripped Gene's arms. No one said a word. There was silence, except for Chad's whimpering. Mr. Gibson glared at the students, one by one, waiting for an explanation. Finally, Lindsey piped up, pointing toward Chad, claiming *he* was the one who started it.

They were both marched off to the office. It wasn't until he had sat down, waiting for the principal, that he realized his fists were still clenched. That's when he noticed Chad's earring in his hand. He had ripped it from his ear during the fight. He smiled, deciding to keep it as a trophy.

Gene stood by his Mazda, thinking about the finger Chad had given him. He smiled. He had shown that bag of shit how he could take care of himself. He had hoped that his reputation at school would improve because of the fight, but unfortunately it was too late. School was now finished. The students would still think of him as a loser, a short loser. He felt that they were probably right.

Everyone else's parents were most likely getting ready to take their kids out to a graduation supper, maybe later a summer vacation, perhaps college in the fall. He knew his dad was likely drunk right about now and God only knew where his mother was. He, on the other hand, had a wonderful career to look forward to, pumping gas at the Irvine Exxon for the rest of his life.

He could feel the intense heat from the sun on his head. He decided to take another chance, slowly sliding back into the car. This time it was bearable. He looked at his watch, thinking he would give Dan five more minutes. If he didn't show by then, well … he wasn't sure what he would do, maybe head on down to the gym for an hour.

He flipped through the yearbook. Most students had a caption of some sort under their picture—'Voted most likely to succeed,' 'Most likely to marry and have five kids.' When he got to his picture the caption simply read—'A nice guy.' They didn't know what to write about him so chose something that said nothing. He knew he wasn't a nice guy. He hated some of the students, guys like Cory Klein, the self-appointed jock. Not only was he good looking but also tall. The girls had nicknamed him 'Calvin Klein.'

Gene knew he was only being jealous. He wished he were taller. Taller and more popular. He needed to get his anger under control. *Yes, I'm glad to get out of school, away from all those fucking idiots! Outside of Dan and Lindsey, I never want to see anyone from school again. And speaking of Dan, where the hell is he?* He decided to give him another five minutes. He didn't want to go swimming alone. He'd rather go home and listen to what his mother labeled 'Devil's Music.'

Chapter 2

He looked up from the yearbook when he heard Dan yell, "Hey, Dickface."

Gene yelled back, "Hey, Bonehead." Dan could be so stubborn at times. "It's about time you left that fucking place. I couldn't wait to get out the door. What's up?" He smiled inwardly. Dan was wearing those stupid wrap-around sunglasses. Dan thought he looked cool. Gene thought he looked like a dork.

"I had to talk to Dale about something. Looks like a few of us are going swimming after all."

"Like, who?"

"Well, like Lindsey. *That's* who." He said it in a teasing fashion.

Gene smiled at him while his stomach churned. The thought of being in a bathing suit in front of Lindsey made him feel uncomfortable. Besides, he wasn't sure how he felt about her after the stupid comment she had made, saying it was too bad he was so short. And, what about the other guys who might show up to go swimming? They would all be taller. There was no doubt about that.

"So, who else besides Lindsey?"

"Well, ah ..., let me see ..." He started to lean against the car but quickly jumped back.

"Jeeze! That's *hot*, man. Anyway, who gives a shit? Are you coming or what?" Dan was getting impatient.

"Yeah ..., I guess so."

"Good. Look, why don't I meet you at the lookout in half an hour? I'll head on home and steal a couple of beers. Besides, I've got some good grass we can smoke."

"Sounds like a deal. I'll get my towel and stuff and meet you there."

Gene started toward home. He was both excited and nervous, thinking about being with Lindsey with only her bathing suit on. It brought back memories of Amber, his previous girlfriend.

"*Ah yes, Amber,*" he thought. He was five inches taller than her. He loved looking down at her and having control. He loved the power. Amber was rather stupid as far as he was concerned. In fact, the more he thought about it, they were all rather stupid, even Lindsey.

The relationship with Amber only lasted a month. He finally tired of her. He wanted to do his own thing. She was becoming a nuisance. He didn't need that kind of shit so broke it off. She had cried, begging him to stay. Again, he loved the power. He couldn't have cared less about her feelings. His only concern was for himself, no one else.

Chapter 3

He thought back to several months previous. It had been cold and rainy when his dad finally came home. Gene was in his room with the headphones on, listening to music, facing the window, his eyes half-closed. He saw the glitter of car lights as his dad pulled into the driveway. When his dad drank, Gene and his mother needed to be careful. Phil was a volatile man.

He suspected his mother must have had enough. He wondered why she wouldn't leave Phil alone. Gladys kept pushing and belittling not only Phil but also Gene. She always had snide remarks for both of them. Her tone would intentionally hold a double meaning. She was simply a bitch.

That night she had been drinking by herself at the kitchen table. She had sat for over an hour with the bottle of bourbon. Gene would leave his room from time to time, noticing she was still at the table, the bourbon getting lower. He stuck his head out just before Phil pulled into the driveway, seeing she had placed a steak knife on the table beside her drink.

He wasn't too alarmed. She had pulled that sort of stunt before, pretending she would stab Phil if he threatened to hurt her anymore. Gene knew it was only talk, drunken talk. She was too weak to follow through with her threats.

He heard him half-walk, half-stumble up the front steps of the porch, turning the door handle one way and then the other until, a second or two later, he began pounding on the door. It was locked. Gene wondered why his mother had done that. It was all Phil needed to set him off. Sure enough, Phil started yelling while kicking at the door. It didn't take much for him to lose it. She, in turn, yelled back that she didn't want him in the house or in her life anymore.

Gene didn't want to get involved. He knew from past experience it was best that he stayed out of their arguments. He kept to his room.

Phil threatened her through the door. He promised he would strangle her scrawny neck until her eyes popped out of her ugly fucking head. She told him he was not going to be let in until he cooled off. That upset him even more. The yelling and banging grew louder.

"How dare you tell me what to do! I pay the fucking bills here. Do you hear me you dumb, stupid, bitch? You let me in, now!" He had had enough of her brainless stunt.

She answered back in that squeaky voice of hers, "Phil? Just promise me you won't hit me again. Please!" She couldn't care less if Phil hit Gene. She was only worried about her own stupid ass.

"Gladys?" His voice raised several decibels. "Open up this fucking door, now!" The commotion was beginning to disturb the neighborhood. Big George, who lived beside them, angrily pushed open his front door.

"What's with you two?" He made his way to the side of his porch, facing Phil. "If you want to fight inside your house that's your business but not when you take it outside. I'm fucking tired of listening to both of you fighting every night!"

Phil glared at him, ready to snap back. He was planning on saying something smart but caught himself. It was one thing to slap his tiny wife. It was an entirely different matter getting involved with his neighbor who was the size of a Mack truck. He wisely held his tongue and, instead, half-whispered to his charming wife to please open the door.

She wouldn't let up. She knew he was in an awkward position, standing on the porch with George looking on, ready to take care of business. She wanted to push him further. She loved to humiliate him. She taunted him.

"Phil?" She spoke in a quiet tone, putting him off guard. She unlocked the door, opening it a little. The safety chain was on, the door now ajar. She quickly yelled through the gap, making sure the entire neighborhood could hear. "Do you promise you won't hit me anymore?" Her voice carried out over the rainfall. Sure enough, another neighbor across the street opened his front door, wondering what was going on. Phil was steaming.

She did it again, yelling "Do you promise not to hurt me or the boy?" She couldn't give a damn about Gene. She only wanted to rub the salt deeper into the wound. She made sure the neighbors heard every word.

"Gladys. Open the fucking door, would you?"

"Phil, will you promise?" She asked the question, no longer shouting, standing behind the door with the knife clutched in her right hand.

"Okay, okay. Open this fucking door!" Phil looked over his shoulder and saw George take a few threatening steps toward him, waiting ..., waiting for him to say something, anything. Gene could hear everything from inside his room.

"Phil? Do you promise?"

"Okay, Gladys. I promise." Phil's voice lowered.

"Okay what, Phil?"

Gene finally peeked out from his bedroom. He could feel the tension and anger emanating from his dad. Phil surprised both of them by speaking in a soft voice.

"Okay, dear. I promise I won't hurt you."

"Phil? Do you love me?"

He finally lost it. Phil pushed his way through the door, snapping the security chain in the process, quickly slamming it shut behind him.

"You fucking bitch! I've had enough of this shit!" He was yelling as he lunged forward, trying to grab her. She stepped back, still clutching the knife. Phil didn't see it. He was targeting her neck. He was fast. Fast for a drunk. In a flash he had both hands around her throat, pushing her backwards. As he began to squeeze, she brought it up, stabbing him in the upper leg. His eyes bulged as he slowly let go. She backed away, taking in the bizarre scene. He stood there, puzzled, looking down at the knife—the knife that was now stuck deep in his left thigh.

He didn't scream, he moaned instead. He was drunk, not quite comprehending what had just happened. Gladys stood aghast in the middle of the living room, hands on her face. She was staring at him, waiting for him to continue with his attack. His mind was no longer focused on her throat. Instead, he looked down at his leg, still not understanding. He slowly lowered his hand, trying to grasp the handle. He started to pull, trying to remove the knife but … had trouble. It was in deep.

His knees weakened. She had done a good job, thrusting it into the soft tissue of the upper thigh. A dark stain was quickly appearing around the entry point. His khaki pants began to turn a darker brown from the blood that was now flowing from the wound.

Phil made another attempt at trying to pull it out but was quickly going into shock. He shuffled sideways, slowly making his way toward a kitchen chair, groaning all the while. He eased himself into it, extending the injured left leg. He tried to focus, perspiration now appearing on his brow. Blood was running down his leg, soaking his white sock. Gladys made no attempt to help. Instead, she stood with her hands up to her face, still not believing what she had done.

Gene witnessed all of this, standing just outside his room, frozen in shock. Finally, he slowly moved toward the scene, not knowing what to say or do.

"Dad?"

Phil's glazed eyes slowly turned toward him. Gladys moved to the side, out of the way, as Gene came closer, looking at the knife in disbelief. Phil moaned as he looked up.

"Help me, son," came the shaky and weak request.

Gene was stunned, not only because of the stabbing but also because his dad had called him 'son.' It was the very first time he had called him that. He turned his head, looking at his mother, questioning her with his eyes. She shot back an indignant stare, snapped her head toward the bedroom and walked away, leaving her sixteen-year-old son to tend to her now bleeding husband.

Gene instinctively reached for the knife, wanting to pull it out. His dad put his shaky hand on Gene's and grimaced.

"No," Phil whispered hoarsely, "leave it." Dark blood was now dripping down from under his injured leg, creating a small pool on the linoleum floor.

He stared at his dad, confused, not knowing what to do and then realized he needed to get help. As he dialed 911, his mother came walking out of the bedroom, this time with her coat on, clutching a suitcase that she must have packed earlier in the evening. She passed her son and husband as she marched toward the front door. She stopped and turned, looking at both of them for the last time. She seemed at a loss for words. She opened her mouth, wanting to say something, but thought better of it. She turned her back to her family, quickly walking out.

Chapter 4

Sitting in his car in the driveway, he couldn't recall what she looked like anymore. He had blocked her out of his mind. He hated her for leaving him and his dad. He hated her for the cold-hearted way she had done it.

He remembered calling for an ambulance, standing by, waiting with his dad. Neither had said a word—Phil partially out of shock, he partially out of disbelief.

The police arrived a few minutes after the ambulance. They had questions for them. Phil claimed it was an accident. He had stumbled while holding the knife. Gene kept saying he didn't know what had happened. He was in his bedroom listening to music and then came out to go to the bathroom. That's when he saw his dad sitting on the kitchen chair with a knife stuck in him. He didn't know how it happened.

They asked about his mother, where she was. Gene told them she hadn't been home. They thought that was strange. The neighbor next door said he had seen her inside the house. Had there had been some kind of dispute?

He stuck to his story claiming he knew nothing. One policeman, Sergeant Frank Morgan, gave him his card, telling him to call if he remembered anything. Frank Morgan also gave Phil his card, telling him that he didn't buy the story about him stabbing himself. He wanted answers. He threatened he would be back again next week. Phil would be wise to answer his questions with the truth the next time they met.

The ambulance took Phil to the emergency room at Irvine General Hospital. He was treated for a severe stab wound and blood loss. He was kept under observation for several days.

It was awkward visiting him. Gene hated hospitals. He didn't know what to talk about when he was there. Neither displayed any love for the other. It didn't happen in the household so why should it happen in the hospital? The closest thing to love was when Phil had called him 'son,' asking for his help. They barely spoke. What could Gene say?

He thought of what he would like to say. *So, Dad, good ole Mom finally had enough of you, huh? Stuck you good like a fat piece of pork. And you …, just look at you, trying to strangle her in the process. What model parents. And, oh yes, by the way, I love you.* No, that wouldn't work, maybe in a movie but not in real life, at least not in his.

He remembered getting on his bike and pedaling the ten or so blocks to the hospital, deep in thought, wondering what he should say. He dreaded the visit, feeling sick as he walked into the main lobby. He could smell the strong antiseptic stench, but it wasn't the smell that upset his stomach. It was the thought of what he should say to his dad.

He glanced at his watch while in the lobby, deciding on giving himself twenty minutes tops for the visit. He had to do it. It was his dad who was lying there, thanks to his stupid, fucking mother. He cursed her again as he stepped into Phil's room, seeing him in bed with bandages around his thigh. He was watching TV.

Gene tried to smile while saying, "Hey, how's it going?"

His dad looked toward him and grunted, then quickly turned away.

Gene managed to ask if he was still hurting.

Phil said, "Yeah," staring intently at the TV, indicating he had better things to do than talk to his son.

Ten minutes of silence later he said, "Well, I gotta go." Another grunt from his dad and that was it. He sarcastically thought, *"What a nice visit."* He was out of the hospital in seventeen minutes flat.

Several days later, when Phil was back at the house, things were awkward. Each was trying to tolerate the other. For a short time it appeared to work. Gene had hoped his dad would thank him for helping, for calling the ambulance. Phil wouldn't bring himself to acknowledge the incident. He acted as though nothing had happened. He went back to work selling used cars two days after being released from Irvine General. Neither one talked about Gladys or the stabbing.

It wasn't long before Phil stumbled home, drunk once more, taking his anger out on his son, telling him he was no good and that when he was sixteen he already had two jobs. Gene was confused. He didn't understand why his father was so angry with him. He had thought that, once Gladys was out of the way, he and his dad could bond. Why was he acting that way? Gene felt like a failure. Even his own father didn't like him.

He had decided the sooner he moved away the better it would be for both of them. Meanwhile, he had to stick it out, wishing for the day when he would graduate from high school and move on.

He had discovered long ago he could easily escape into another world when his parents fought. He was doing it again, this time with only his dad at home. He would spend hours in his room, dreaming about how things should have been so much different in his life. He should have had two wonderful parents, he should have been popular at school, he should have been taller and he should have had more respect from the girls. He should have, he should have and he should have. That was the story of his life. That was what he thought life should be like.

Instead he grudgingly admitted he was short. He would never be a real man, only a shadow of one. He sensed disrespect from both his teachers and parents. He was also failing his grades, not caring.

Most of the girls dismissed him and his so-called friends were few. Besides, they were all losers. He was angry with everyone around him. More importantly, he was annoyed and frustrated with himself. He was in a downward spiral and didn't know how to break the fall. Instead, he tried to escape.

He got out of his car and walked toward his porch, knowing he was feeling sorry for himself. He felt that perhaps it was justified. At a time when he should be celebrating graduation he was feeling miserable and confused. He was also apprehensive, worried about seeing Lindsey at the beach. He wondered who else would be there. He was glad Dan was bringing beer and a little smoke. He needed to get high. Today he felt more stress than he had ever felt.

He unlocked the front door and went in, going straight to his room, getting his bathing suit. He loved to escape in his room, putting on the headphones, listening to his iPod. He would fantasize that he was the lead guitar player for whatever group he was listening to at the time, the girls screaming for him. He had downloaded hundreds of music files over the past few months. Most were what his dear mother labeled 'Devil's Music.'

When he wasn't listening to his Devil's Music he would dream he was a football star at school. They wouldn't laugh at him anymore. He remembered trying out for the team.

The coach approached him after their first practice session, telling him he didn't have what it took. He hadn't had the common decency in taking him aside, away from the rest of the guys, when he made the announcement. He looked around the field while the coach spoke. He could see a few of the other players looking back his way, snickering. The coach elaborated even though he didn't need to. He spoke in a loud voice telling Gene that being a team player was very important. He informed him he didn't seem to have the team spirit. As an afterthought, he also advised him he had too much anger. Too much anger to be playing a group sport, a group sport that required team effort.

He knew the coach was talking in a loud voice intentionally, letting everyone know he would and could cut players if need be. He was making an example.

Gene wanted to yell out, "Isn't playing football and being on the attack what it's all about or do you want some pansy in there holding back all the time?" He knew he had to be aggressive or he'd get pulverized because of his size. Hadn't the coach told them the best defense was a good offense? He was humiliated once more.

He went back into the locker room, hating who he was. Frustrated, he made a fist, punching the wall in front of him. Unfortunately he had chosen a brick wall. It might have been funny if it weren't so damned pitiful. He sat alone, holding his badly cut knuckles, shaking with anger and humiliation. He saw clothes lying on a bench. He walked over, noticing a pair of jeans and white tee-shirt that belonged to one of the jocks. He adjusted his hand so that a nice pattern of blood would drip over them. He enjoyed the moment immensely while thinking about what the coach had told him. Maybe, just maybe, there was some truth in what he said. Perhaps he was too angry to be playing a team sport.

He came out of his bedroom with his bathing suit on and headed toward the laundry room, still deep in thought. He wasn't prepared to take the blame, not for that, not for his anger. "No," he told himself. He knew it was his poor upbringing. That's what it was. His parents were to blame. He was sure of it.

His mind wandered back to Lindsey. It was too bad she was taller by two inches. That was a problem. He wondered if there was any correlation between how short the girls were compared to how much he liked them. It seemed the same with the guys. The taller they were, the less he cared for them. Dan was an exception. They connected in a weird sort of way. Dan was like a brother, the brother he never had. He wished he had a family with brothers and sisters.

No, I don't have family, not even a decent father or mother.

He finally found a clean towel and quickly left, locking the front door behind him. He was glad to get out of the house.

Chapter 5

He met Dan twenty minutes later at the lookout. Dan was already out of his car, sitting on a log, the lake below him. There was another car in the small parking lot but they didn't notice anyone nearby. They sat together, each having a beer, smoking a little pot. Before too long he was feeling much better, sitting with his friend, knowing school was finally over, thinking of working at the gas station for the summer and then ... what?

He came out of his daydream, half-listening to what Dan was saying. He was talking about little Marcy from the gym. He listened to his friend speak, all the while knowing Dan would love to have a girl like her. Dan was also a loser with girls. He might be taller than Gene, but so what? He looked over, seeing Dan's stomach start to hang out over his bathing suit. In a couple of more years Dan would have a beer gut. In fact, it was already happening. *"Besides,"* he thought, *"Dan has no class."*

They were sitting on a log near the path that headed down to the beach. Dan kept talking about Marcy and how hot she was. Gene would love to take her out. *"Hell,"* he thought, *"who wouldn't?"* She always wore a pair of tight little gym pants and tee-shirt while lying on the bench doing presses. All the guys kept looking. She knew it. She loved to show off her little body. She had that real bitch attitude, pretending to be offended when guys looked her way. Gene would try not to stare so he could show her. *"Show her what,"* he wondered? Show her he didn't care, that's what! Unfortunately she couldn't care less about him. He was out of the equation. She wanted the big he-man type.

That's why he worked out, to be a he-man. He wanted to have a muscular body. He knew, no matter how hard he worked at it, he would never get taller. He hoped women would look at him if he at least had a good build. There was nothing he could do about being short. Well, maybe the elevator shoes might have helped, but that had backfired.

The gym was a good way to release anger and frustration. There was also the competition between him and Dan. He knew it bothered Dan that he had more muscle. He could see the results from working out. He tried harder than Dan because he was shorter. He worked twice as hard at building his body. It was Gene's nature. He needed to prove himself.

He closed his eyes, visualizing Marcy, looking down at her. In his dreams he's at least six feet tall, always looking down at the girl, his girl. He has his way with them and then when he's done, well, he moves on. *Kind of like the 'catch and release' program the fishermen use at the lake. Ah yes, the lake. Man is it hot!*

He vaguely heard Dan mumble. "What? What did you say?"

Dan had a puzzled look on his face as he replied. "Huh? What?" He was still holding the marijuana, wearing those stupid wrap-around sunglasses.

Gene asked again, "What the fuck were you just talking about?"

"Huh? I dunno. Was I just talking?" He had a stupid grin on his face.

They both started laughing. The more they laughed, the harder it was for them to stop. They were bent over, now in tears. They were having a great time, two buddies who would change the world. They might even kick a little ass. They continued to chuckle while finishing their beer.

He thought about last summer when Dan and he used to jump off the cliff. They would fall nearly thirty feet into the cool water, going instantly from hot to being totally alive.

Yes, that's what it was ... being totally alive! Hitting the cold water on a hot summer's day would certainly make you become aware, every sense in tune, waking you up. If you didn't hit it just right it could hurt.

He remembered last year, the angry red welt on Dan's stomach when he screwed up, hitting the water at a bad angle. He had a good laugh over that one, especially when Dan pretended it didn't hurt. Dan had tried not to grimace but it was obvious he was in pain. Of course Gene wouldn't let it go, teasing him for hours. Gene knew he was a better jumper. He had always hit the water perfectly when he either jumped or, on occasion, when he dove.

They heard a boat in the distance and looked toward it. Neither said a word, not wanting to end the moment. Finally, they decided on making their way down the path to the beach. It was time to go swimming.

They had only walked a few feet when they heard voices. They stopped and listened closer. They heard female voices from below. They peered over the edge. It looked like Lindsey and her girlfriend. Gene had completely forgotten she might be there. His stomach began to act up. He was nervous, thinking, *"What if she doesn't like me in my bathing suit?"* He looked over the edge once more. He couldn't see them. They were behind some trees near the beach.

He still liked her, even after what she had said. At least she had stuck up for him when he had the fight with Chad. She was the one who told old 'Gibby' Gibson that Chad had started it.

He was kidding himself. He more than just liked her. He hoped they could develop some sort of relationship, maybe a long-term dating thing. He wasn't sure. His only other experience with girls had been with Amber and only for a month. He wondered if he was good enough for Lindsey. He knew it would be easy for some jock to take her away from him.

A childish urge came over him. He felt the need to prove himself once more. She and her girlfriend were down below. He tried to convince Dan into jumping off the cliff together, scaring the girls as well as showing off.

"Fuck you, Midget," was the quick and loud response. Sometimes Dan could be such a jerk. Gene held his tongue.

The girls heard the voices and looked up. They noticed the boys and waved. Dan started walking down the path to meet them. Gene stood still, not sure what to do. He didn't want to appear too eager to see Lindsey so decided to hike to the top of the bluff and sit for a while. He needed to think. He turned and made his way upwards. It really wasn't that high, maybe thirty feet at the most.

He began to feel better once on top, enjoying the moment, deciding not to think about her. His body soon felt in tune. He could hear the whispering of the wind as it blew past his ears, blowing his longish hair. He made his way to the edge and looked down. He heard Dan yell up toward him.

"Hey, Dickface. Lindsey wants to talk to you."

He heard her giggling. He raised his hand up in order to give Dan the finger but instead, kept lifting it, lifting both hands until … his arms formed an inverted 'V' over his head.

Dan commented to the girls in a loud voice, making sure Gene could hear. "Look at him. He's too chicken-shit to dive." The girls giggled. Dan stepped forward, Lindsey and her friend now behind him. He was having fun teasing his friend. "Come on, Gene. I dare you!" All three were looking up, waiting, anticipating.

He couldn't help it. He was born to show off. He arced his body into what he thought would make a perfect dive.

Chapter 6

The curtains must have been drawn tight. They had to be very thick because they stopped all light. He had never been in a darker place. There was absolutely no light. He had hoped his eyes would adjust, picking out at least a few details. He wondered if he might be outside. This wasn't natural. There wasn't any moonlight. No stars, no anything. He opened his eyes wider, trying to see, to see something. They still wouldn't adjust. They gathered no light.

He wasn't sure if he was lying or sitting. He wondered if perhaps he was floating. There was something wrong with his eyes. He thought they were open but quickly realized that, no, they weren't responding. They didn't want to open. He tried willing them to but it was hopeless. They seemed to be welded closed. They would never open again.

He felt a wave of panic wash over him. His heart raced, his breathing rapid and shallow. He tried to calm down. He was trapped. He was buried alive. Buried alive!

They thought I was dead and put me in this coffin, six feet under! He tried desperately to remain calm. *It's all starting to make sense. It's dark and quiet. I can't hear a thing. It's deathly quiet.*

He wondered how long it would take before he died. How long would it take before the air ran out? He needed to slow his breathing. He had to conserve the little air he had so that ….

So that, what? So that I die a little later than sooner? And why did they put me here? Why did they fucking bury me? Was it Chad who did this? Was it Chad and fucking Jason LaPointe?

He tried opening his mouth, wanting to scream. It wouldn't open. He tried to move his arms and legs, thinking that if he could at least kick and scratch and make noise, someone would hear him from up above. Someone would realize he was buried alive and start digging, frantically digging, trying to save their boy.

Yes, that's right. Dad would save me. I know he would.

He knew he was only kidding himself. His dad couldn't care less. In fact, he was the one who probably buried him in the first place.

Yeah, I'm only a pain in his ass. He's finally gotten rid of me. Maybe I'm buried under a tree. Dan will come. Yeah, Dan will wonder why I didn't show up at the gym.

He knew nobody would come. No one would want to save him because he really didn't have any friends. He certainly didn't have any family.

Wait a minute, the air isn't stale. I can still breathe. If I were buried I'd be dead by now. I'm still breathing! At least I think I'm breathing.

He was angry, knowing he should get a grip. He decided to concentrate on kicking and punching, trying to get out of this … what?

It's a nightmare, that's what it is, only a nightmare.

He made an attempt at kicking but this time it wasn't working. He panicked again as he asked himself, *Why? Okay. Okay! Calm down. Take a deep breath. Try opening your eyes.*

He tried to yell. *Help! Please!* He knew he was yelling but couldn't hear himself. It was only in his mind. He kicked again and again but couldn't feel his legs move. He wanted to get out of this terrible dream. He had to wake up. He needed to wake up, wake up and leave this dark place, this place where he had no control. He bounced from panic, to anger, to exhaustion. He could feel himself falling, falling into an abyss.

It's a foggy day. He's standing, but not sure where. He notices his grandfather coming out of a field of some sort. It looks like a cornfield. He'd always been Gene's real hero though he barely remembers him, a tall man who looked magnificent in his service uniform.

He had found Grandpa's picture hidden away in one of his dad's drawers, wondering why he would hide it. He always wanted to ask but was afraid. He would often sneak into the bedroom, pulling out the picture from deep within the nightstand drawer. He loved the way Grandpa looked, tall and commanding. He wanted to be just like him.

He dreams that he and his Grandpa are together, surrounded by women. He, too, is in uniform. They look at each other and smile their mutual approval. Grandpa is proud of his young grandson. They look down at the bitches, knowing they are both so much more superior to the women. One has the nerve to look up at them. She tells Gene it's too bad he's short.

He wonders what she's talking about. In his dream he's tall, as tall as his grandfather. He looks down at where he's been standing. He tries to see his boots but can't. He is so very close to the ground. He wonders what happened. He tries to focus, looking at his legs. They appear to be cut off at the knees. He's standing as tall as he can but the lower parts of his legs are missing. He can't feel his toes.

Panic sets in. He can't feel his legs! Everything is going numb. Things aren't quite right. He screams. Things have changed for the worse. The bitches are now looking down at him. He sees a blonde, a brunette and a red head. All three are surrounding him. They smirk, ridiculing him. They laugh at him. Grandpa is laughing, too.

Gene feels betrayed. He tries to scream but he is mute. He can't feel himself. He can't hear himself. He is nothing, only a shell floating helplessly away from light into darkness.

Chapter 7

Doctor Klein was in his office at Irvine General Hospital thinking about the phone call he had just received. He was sitting in his chair, long legs up on the Formica desk, cleaning his glasses. It was Mr. Lincoln calling him from the lab once again.

Doctor Klein worked part-time for Irvine General Hospital. The remainder of his time was spent at a company called Bosch Research, an organization funded by individuals as well as by government. Mr. Lincoln was the major contributor.

Bosch Research had evolved from a smaller company, one that had developed several promising drugs ranging from reducing menstrual ache to a quicker healing process in skin grafting. Bosch Research took up most of a wing in the long-term care center called Edgehill Clinic, a building several miles away from the Irvine General Hospital.

Mr. Lincoln had spent a good portion of his life at Edgehill, suffering a major injury years ago. He had suffered spinal cord damage resulting in paralysis from the waist down.

Doctor Klein knew that was where the patients suffering from paralysis always ended up, at Edgehill. The staff tried to make their lives as pleasant as possible but everyone knew it was only a holding area, a place to languish until death eventually took them.

There were a few fortunate ones who were wealthy enough to live at home. They could pay for health care visits or even have a live-in nurse take care of them. Mr. Lincoln would certainly fit into that category. He could buy the whole clinic if he wanted to. He stayed at Edgehill because he was in charge of Bosch Research. He had his own private living quarters on site and could easily move back and forth in his electric wheelchair, through the glass doors from Edgehill Clinic to the adjoining research area of Bosch Research Inc.

Doctor Klein glanced over his desk at the wall across from him while still cleaning his glasses. His eyes scanned the different diplomas and awards that hung there, coming to rest on his beloved picture once more. Not a day went by that he didn't see the photo, either with his eyes or his heart. He looked at his young daughter's and wife's image. He missed them both very much. Even now he still loved Elise though he knew she had never truly loved him.

He understood why. He wasn't an affectionate man. His real passion was in his work. He had spent many, many long hours away from his home, being drawn into scientific and medical research.

He knew Elise had married him out of convenience. He wasn't a foolish man. They were born and raised in Germany. Both families had an influence on their marriage. Her mother and father wanted her to be cared for by a professional, someone who would pamper her just like they had done in her earlier years. He and his family simply loved her even though they knew she had a troubled side to her. Elise wanted the status and security of marrying an up-and-coming doctor. They both wanted a family. When the timing was right they immigrated to Canada, ending up in the United States where Sarah was born.

They loved her very much, hoping a son would soon follow. They even had a name picked out for their phantom boy, 'Joseph.' *Yes. Joseph Junior.* He had dreamed of the day he could mold Joseph into being a truly great doctor, a doctor on the leading edge of science, just like him. His own father had never been in his life. Joseph wanted so much to have a son that would follow in his foot steps.

She wasn't quite four years old when he found her in their swimming pool. Elise had been out shopping at the time. He had stepped away from the pool, only for a few minutes, not very far, just to the kitchen to answer the phone. They had a cordless phone they usually brought out by the pool. This time it was left in the house. He came back five minutes later, finding her floating face-down.

He jumped in, quickly picking her up, turning her over. He shook her, sobbing her name. He leaned forward, feeling her shallow breath on his cheek. She was still breathing, barely. He carried her out as fast as he could, gently laying her down on the cement deck. He performed artificial respiration while he prayed. Oh, how he prayed. She was turning blue but still breathing. He worked on her several more minutes, oblivious to Elise entering the house.

He still remembered the terrible scream she uttered when she came upon the scene. It was almost animal. They both kept chanting, "Sarah, Sarah, *Sarah*," desperately trying to bring their beautiful and innocent little girl back to consciousness. Elise kept talking to her while he tried to keep her breathing. Her little eyelids fluttered on occasion. The rest of her was returning to a healthier pinkish color but her lips were still blue. She was simply not coming out of her coma.

He told Elise to run to the phone and call 911 immediately. She wouldn't listen. He grabbed his wife and shook her, looking into her eyes, trying to bring her out of her shock. Again, he yelled for her to call. Her mouth was wide open. There was drool hanging down her lower lip, some clinging to her chin. Her eyes had a look of disbelief.

She slowly nodded, getting the message. She scrambled, half-slipping, half-sliding on the pool deck, trying to run as fast as she could to get to the phone. He heard her crying and sobbing, speaking incoherently to the person on the other end of the line.

She came back several minutes later, walking slowly toward them. He had to look twice because, for a moment, he didn't recognize her. She was in so much pain her face was contorted, twisted, her eyes vacant. He would never forget the moment. He would carry it with him to his grave.

They came minutes later. The medics took over, trying to keep the doctor's and good wife's little girl alive. They put her in the ambulance, taking her away with Elise and him at her side. They never did bring their beautiful daughter back home. She had suffered irreparable brain damage, dying four months later.

Many times since her death, Doctor Klein had asked the same question over and over. "How could that have happened, especially to a man who dedicated his life to the caring of others?" To have their only child die because of his neglect was unforgivable.

He and Elise finally came home after many hours at the hospital. Their home was no longer a home but now an empty house. They eventually went to bed, holding each other, both sobbing uncontrollably. She hadn't blamed him, yet. She was still in shock. She only wanted to be held. She needed to be held. They both did. They tried to comfort each other as best they could. Several days passed as each tried to give one another love and support.

When told their daughter would probably never regain consciousness, Elise turned on him. She started to blame him. Of course he was to blame! He knew it more than anyone. He should never have left their daughter alone by the pool. Never. Never!

Elise very quickly cut off all ties. She couldn't forgive him. He remembered hearing it over and over, again and again. She hated him. In her eyes he was to blame. He was put into a position of trust and failed. He had failed miserably.

She finally couldn't take it any longer. She couldn't look at him. She wouldn't talk to him. She despised him. She soon left, forever blaming him for the murder of their only child. That's what she considered it—a murder. No medication or therapy would help. She was beyond help. She took her own life three months later.

He sighed, shaking his head, thinking of how long ago it had been, more than twelve years. Now in his mid-fifties, he still felt as if it had happened only last week.

He kept the picture on his wall because he missed and loved both Sarah and Elise. He also kept it out in the open, hanging in the midst of all his awards and diplomas, to remind himself of his failure as a father, husband and doctor. He had let himself down as well as the people close to him. He felt a tremendous amount of guilt for being irresponsible.

He knew, in his heart, he had indirectly killed *both* his daughter and wife. Perhaps he quite possibly killed himself as well? He thought about the last part. Was he ready to simply give up? He questioned if he could still be redeemed, perhaps somehow give life back.

He secretly thanked the team at Bosch Research. It had become his support group. They had helped him get through the worst of it.

"Ah, yes, the team," he thought. All members were carefully chosen not only because of their expertise but also their dedication. The biggest concern was security. Team members with little or no social life had been chosen first, ensuring minimal security leaks. Dedication and long hours were essential in making Bosch Research a leading medical research company.

Some did have families of course, including Doctor Klein at the time he had joined. Those few were carefully interviewed and asked to make a pledge, an oath to secrecy and dedication, akin to joining the military service. The industry was vulnerable to patent thefts as well as the selling of industrial secrets. Secrecy was essential.

Unbeknownst to Elise, he had made the commitment. She never questioned him. She understood that he, being a doctor, would require many late nights of devoted service.

Perhaps she was happier when I did spend countless hours away. He pondered the thought, finally pulling his mind back to the present.

He reviewed the recent phone conversation with Mr. Lincoln as he took his legs off the desk, focusing on what was said about the present and future and Lincoln asking Joseph to increase his hours at Bosch. Mr. Lincoln wanted all members of the team to increase their hours. He was excited about new developments taking place and wanted to continue 'moving forward' as he put it, 'moving forward with their latest discoveries!' He had reiterated that everyone needed to put renewed vigor into the project in order for it to succeed.

Joseph Klein opened up his briefcase, pulling out a schedule, checking his agenda once more. Tomorrow morning he was headed back to Irvine General for a half-day and then, he wondered, could he put in at least eight hours with Bosch.

The phone rang, bringing him out of his planning strategy.

"Doctor, please come to Emergency. There's been an accident."

Chapter 8

He felt a hand on his face. Fingers were trying to pry open his right eye. He wanted to tell them the eye was welded shut; that it couldn't open. They'd break it if they kept prying. They'd rip the eyelid off.

They must have succeeded in opening it for he was now looking into a blinding light. He tried to sit up but couldn't move. They must have had him tied down. They must have numbed his body. They must have loaded him with painkillers because he couldn't feel. He couldn't feel a thing except for the fingers that kept his eye open.

He asked himself, "Who are they?" He tried to focus but couldn't, he was too groggy. He thought, "*Are those voices? It sounds like a far off conversation, a conversation between a man and a woman, an older man and a younger woman nearby.*"

He wondered where his buddy, Dan, was. He started to remember a little, being stoned, being with Dan and getting ready for a swim. He tried very hard to remember it all. Yes, he remembered now. He did jump.

He stopped himself, thinking, "*Wait a minute, wasn't it a dive? I must have come close to drowning. That's what it was. They found me floating face down and gave me CPR or something.*" He tried to put the pieces together, but no, the pieces didn't fit. It was far too crazy for him to accept.

He began to drift once again, trying to stay awake, fighting the drug. *Man, this dope is powerful.* He believed he was still sitting on the log, smoking with Dan. At times, he wasn't sure if he were awake or not. He kept telling himself it was bizarre. He didn't know what to think, trying not to panic. He felt as though he were in limbo. *No, more like suspended animation. That's it!*

He made a concerted effort in trying to kick. In his mind it felt like he was kicking but something was wrong, terribly wrong. He couldn't feel his legs. He couldn't feel anything except for the dope in his blood. He slowly realized that it wasn't cannabis but something completely different.

He fell back into a deep dreamless sleep, waking up several hours later, feeling the sun on his face. He thought he was lying on the cliff with his good buddy, Dan, beside him, but something wasn't quite right.

He tried to open his eyes but that proved to be too difficult. He felt groggy, telling himself he'd never drink that much booze again. He wakened a little more, thinking, "*No, just a minute, I'm not hung-over.*" He still didn't have an answer to why he was so dazed. The only thing he was sure of was the sun on his face.

With that realization he concentrated on his eyes. He could see the white glow of the sun behind his eyelids. All he had to do now was open one, just a crack. Slowly, his right lid became unlocked. He could see the sun shining. He started to focus, understanding that he was feeling and seeing the rays coming through a window. It felt good. He hadn't felt anything like it in hours.

He heard a female voice in the background. He heard something fall and clatter on the floor nearby. He heard other voices, thinking it was his mother. *What the fuck! No, thank God it's not her.*

He closed his eye, giving himself a break, knowing he needed to rest. It took a tremendous amount of energy to open one eye. Now, he needed to rest a little. His mind slowly traveled back to his mother.

He remembered her yelling at him when he was a child. He tried to recall happy times with her but his mind went blank. He would never forget the time she told him she had wanted an abortion rather than have a child. He would always carry the pain of that terrible statement with him. She had cried, telling him it really wasn't true, she did love him! She had tried to explain that her life had been frustrating at the time. He didn't care how 'frustrating' it had been. He would never forgive nor forget.

He heard more voices and smelled the antiseptic in the air, which made him realize he was in a hospital. He thought of his dad—the time he had gone to visit him and how the hospital smell, coupled with anxiety, made him sick.

He wondered how bad the damage really was. He figured he must have swallowed a hell of a lot of water. *Enough! Get me out of here.*

The female voice sounded closer. He slowly opened one eye, this time the other. He caught a glimpse of a person, a nurse. As she leaned over, he had a better look. She wasn't bad looking.

"Good morning, Gene."

"Yeah," he mumbled.

She looked at him with a bright smile, saying, "I hope you're feeling better."

He wondered how she knew his name. *Oh yeah, there must be some kind of medical chart with all that info on it.*

She fussed with the bed a little, smiling at him one more time, saying, "I'll be right back."

He slowly tried to open up the other eye, trying to focus. His whole body was numb. He wondered what kind of medication they had given him and why they gave him so much. Did he break his legs? He tried to move one leg and then the other. Nothing happened. He tried to lift his head off the pillow but couldn't. He wondered if they had strapped him down.

He remembered seeing something on TV about how they sometimes tied the patient down. He tried to relax, concentrating on the ceiling. He heard a fan blowing warm or cool air into the room. He wasn't sure which.

He struggled, trying to come to grips with his predicament but became distracted, having difficulty concentrating. He noticed a clock on the wall. He began to stare at the minute hand as it slowly moved. He tried to turn his head but found it impossible to do. He noticed a mirror and sink to the right of his vision. He saw a window with curtains to his left. The window was partially open. The curtains were fluttering in the breeze.

There was a post of some sort to his extreme left. He could barely make it out with his peripheral vision. He wondered if it was a coat hanger sort of thing or a place to hang hats. He wasn't sure. He couldn't think straight.

A few minutes later he heard more people. They walked into the room. There were two of them. One was the nurse. She seemed too young to be a nurse, looking only a couple of years older than him. She was a little on the plump side but still pretty. The other was a tall guy with gray hair, wearing glasses. They came up to the side of the bed. The tall guy smiled. He carried a clipboard. The nurse stood behind him. He leaned forward, looking at him reassuringly.

"Hello, Gene. I'm Doctor Klein." He spoke rather loudly and with an accent. Gene wasn't sure what kind. "Are you comfortable?"

He tried to talk but needed water.

Doctor Klein turned to the nurse, saying, "Cynthia, would you please be so kind as to get Gene some water."

"Yes, Doctor." She looked at Gene and smiled as she left the room.

Doctor Klein looked back at him, still smiling. Gene was not fully alert and tried to smile in return.

Where am I? Why am I here? What in the fuck am I smiling for? He tried to shrug. *Why not smile, everyone else seems to be.*

Doctor Klein looked as though he could read his mind. He leaned over, looking into Gene's eyes. After a minute he spoke.

"Gene, you are a patient here at dee Irvine General Hospital. You were admitted five days ago."

Gene thought he had misunderstood. *Five days? How could that be?*

Doctor Klein paused, not sure on how to continue. He decided to tell him the truth, or at least part of it.

"You have suffered a serious injury. You are lucky to be alive."

Gene tried to yell, "What? What are you talking about?" He managed a groan, instead.

The doctor paused once more, seeing the look of astonishment on his young patient's face. He noticed Gene becoming more alert and focused, wondering perhaps if it was from fear or apprehension. He decided to continue.

"The ambulance brought you here after your accident at dee lake."

Dee Lake? I wasn't at Dee Lake. Hell, that's over fifty miles away! I haven't been there since I was a kid. What are you talking about, Doctor? Maybe you have the wrong patient.

Cynthia appeared, handing the doctor the water, again smiling at Gene. He could smell her perfume along with the antiseptic scent of the hospital. It was bothering him. He tried to take his mind off it.

Instead, he wondered how tall she was. Hopefully she was shorter than him. It occurred to him once again, the taller the people, the more he disliked them, especially women. She was still smiling at him, making him feel a little more uncomfortable.

The doctor carefully placed the straw from the glass of water between Gene's lips. Gene attempted to raise his head a little, trying to reach for the glass. He couldn't. He sucked on the straw, feeling the cool liquid slide down his throat. It felt good. He wondered how long it had been since he'd had any liquids. His throat felt raw and sore. He tried to speak.

All he could say was, "Doctor?" in a raspy sounding voice he couldn't believe was his.

Doctor Klein looked at him and answered.

"Yes, Gene?"

Gene's eyes filled with tears. He couldn't help it. He glanced over the doctor's shoulder and saw the nurse looking at him, this time with pity. He didn't want to be pitied. He felt himself getting angry. He wanted to tell that bitch to "Fuck off!" He wanted to tell both of them to leave him alone. He was embarrassed that a woman had seen him cry. How dare she look at him that way!

The doctor could see his agitation so suggested to Cynthia to please leave them alone for a while. She gave them a look of disappointment as she left the room.

The doctor looked down at his patient and saw a poor frightened boy. His heart went out to him. He wondered how he could break the news with the least possible damage. There was no way around it. He'd try to be as tactful as possible but he still had to tell his patient the truth. It was going to be very difficult. This was one of the very few times he hated his job.

He looked at the young man, the young man who seemed to be full of anger and defiance, wondering about his history, wondering about his parents.

Why aren't they here beside him, now? Especially now? The poor boy needs family support.

The hospital had phoned the parents several times with no response. They eventually left a message, letting them know their seventeen-year-old son had been involved in a serious diving accident and that they should please contact Irvine General Hospital as soon as possible.

Unfortunately, he had seen it too many times before—a young person coming in with an injury or drug overdose with no support from family or friends. It seemed to be getting worse. His new patient appeared to be another one of those sad cases.

"Gene? Please relax. Let me tell you vat has happened, yah?" He paused, waiting for Gene to absorb what he was about to say.

Hearing the doctor's accent made Gene wonder if, in fact, he had misunderstood what he had previously said about Dee Lake. Maybe he had meant 'the' lake instead.

"First of all, you are in very good hands. You were under dee water for only a short period of time. You can thank your friend for jumping in and pulling you to safety."

Klein had also wanted to tell him that he could thank his young friend for aggravating the injury by picking Gene up the way he did, dragging him to the beach over some rocks, but he held his tongue. The young man that saved him had no way of knowing the severity of the injuries and, besides, the only other alternative would have been to let Gene drown. It was a bad situation but at least he was alive.

Doctor Klein gathered his thoughts. "You ingested a large amount of water and were floating face-down in dee lake when," he consulted his clipboard, "your friend, Dan, jumped in to save you."

Telling Gene he was floating face-down brought back those terrible memories of poor Sarah. He put the memory into the back of his mind, knowing full well that later on that night he would be dealing with it again and again. It was the same thing every night for the past twelve years. He put the thought aside. Right now he had a job to do.

Gene stared at him, trying to remember what had actually happened. He remembered the sun. He remembered Dan being there with him at the lake. He couldn't remember anything else. He was confused. He couldn't believe he was lying in a hospital bed, listening to a doctor who seemed to be struggling with what he needed to say. He knew it wasn't good. *"In fact,"* he thought, *"it's bad, very bad."* He hoped it was a dream but no, he was conscious enough to realize it was the truth. He waited for the doctor to continue.

"Vee have tried to contact your parents but haven't got a reply. Are dey out right now?"

Gene thought about *that* one. He wanted to say, "Well, Doc, you could say they are 'out.' In fact, my sweet mother is fucking out to lunch and Daddy, well, he's out, too, you see, probably lying flat on his back on the kitchen floor right now, drunk out of his mind. Yeah, Doc, they're both 'out' right now."

He blinked instead, partly trying to stop the tears. Klein could see anger flash in his young patient's eyes. He decided to leave that one alone for now and, instead, continued to explain.

"Vee managed to pump dee water out of your stomach. Your throat is probably still sore from that, yah?" He tried to smile. Gene tried to smile back.

"You know, Gene, you have to remember you are very lucky to be alive."

Gene repeated the last sentence in his mind.

I have to remember I'm lucky to be alive. What the fuck does he mean by that?

Then it hit him. The guy was trying to soften things up a little, make him appreciate he was lucky to be alive. No, very lucky to be alive. He wanted to ask, "So, Doctor, cut the bullshit and come clean. What the fuck is going on? I'm a big boy. I can take it." He looked at the doctor but could only mumble, desperately trying to speak. He managed two words.

"Tell me."

His eyes were focused on Klein, pleading. The doctor sighed, wishing he were a million miles away rather than here, beside this bed, telling his young patient that his life, the life he had known, had come to an end.

Klein looked at him and, without thinking, took his hand. Gene saw him do it but was puzzled as to why he couldn't feel it. He couldn't feel the doctor's hand holding his. Then, he slowly began to understand.

He looked at Klein, noticing the doctor had a tear forming in his left eye.

"I'll make it quick and simple, yah." His voice was choked. He reached over and pulled out a Kleenex. He took off his glasses and wiped his eyes, thinking all along that he was being very unprofessional at this moment, but he couldn't help himself. This was affecting him more than it normally should. He wondered why as he continued.

"You have suffered a terrible injury. Your spinal cord has been damaged in several places. At dis time," he paused, taking a deep breath, "dair is nothing vee can do."

The doctor's voice was becoming thicker with the accent. That's when Gene realized he was German. Gene was trying to block out the terrible news by focusing on the doctor's accent. He was doing everything he could in order to escape from what he was being told.

Yes, German. Just like Grandpa! He wondered if the doctor had also been in the war. His mind drifted wildly, trying to focus on anything except what the doctor was awkwardly trying to tell him.

Before he left, Doctor Klein told him Cynthia would be nearby if he needed anything. He smiled one more time as he got up, reassuring Gene that he was in good hands. They would be doing some more tests during the course of the next few days. He didn't want to leave his patient with a complete feeling of hopelessness, so instead said they would be looking at his injuries more closely over the next several weeks.

He conferred with Cynthia in the hallway, asking her to stay nearby, telling her the patient would need time alone. He had just been told the terrible news. He would never walk again. He would never be able to use his hands again.

"Please be nearby, just in case. A patient in such a predicament usually needs company a little later, once the news has sunk in, someone to talk to. Perhaps someone to open up to?" He was well aware that Cynthia was only a temporary employee at Irvine General Hospital and lacked experience in communicating with patients. He shrugged, thinking back in time to when he, too, was young and also inexperienced. He knew that the only way for her to learn was in a real life situation like she was now in. He suspected she would do just fine.

Once the doctor left, Gene thought about what he had last said. *If there is anything I need, let Cynthia know. That's what the doctor said.* He wanted to yell, "Fuck you, Doctor Klein! Yeah, there is something I need. How about the use of my legs and arms you stupid fucking German asshole. And, oh yeah, don't let that stupid smiley bitch come back into my room again!" Of course he couldn't speak. His throat was still too sore and besides, he was too angry for words. He tried to recap what was said only a few minutes earlier.

Doctor Klein had told him he was in a bad accident and had been unconscious for several days. He had also told him he was lucky to be alive. He had injured his spinal cord in several places and that was why he couldn't feel anything below his neck. He had almost drowned as well and, oh yes, there was nothing they could do.

Gene played that last part over and over. There was nothing they could do. There was nothing they could do! He would never forget the moment he was told it was pretty much all over for him. He could look forward to several years of nothing until what, until he died?

He wanted to scream, "Fuck you and your luck, Klein! Don't be telling me I'm lucky just because you're tall and have two good arms and legs!" No, he couldn't say that because he began to cry instead. He couldn't stop, letting the tears flow. All his life he had wanted to be a man's man—someone who was big, tall, handsome, rugged and respected. He didn't want to be like this, a seventeen-year-old midget who would never use his shitty little legs or arms again.

He cried, feeling self-pity and anger, his tears running down both cheeks. He tried wiping his face, realizing he couldn't. He tried to kick his feet in frustration and fury. That made it worse. They didn't move. He had never felt so helpless in his life. He lay there, sobbing uncontrollably.

Minutes later he opened his eyes and saw that nurse looking down at him like she really cared. She put her hand on his forehead. He felt embarrassed. He'd never cried in front of anyone before. He felt defenseless and vulnerable. She took a wet towel, wiping the tears away. He wanted her to go. He wanted to be left alone. He found himself asking how it could have happened. How could he be paralyzed?

He looked at her and croaked, "Why? I don't understand."

She softly whispered back, "It's okay, Gene. Everything will be all right. We're here to help you. You're in good hands."

She put her hand on his brow, patting and rubbing it, telling him everything would turn out just fine. He cried harder. He couldn't stop, continuing to sob for several more minutes. He was out of control but didn't care. After spending most of his life with a tough man attitude he was now reduced to jelly—a bowl of hopeless, quivering, pitiful jelly.

He kept his eyes closed so he wouldn't have to look at her, hoping she would go away but glad she was still there. He felt her breath on his face. A few moments later he felt a drop on his forehead. He looked up to see her crying. He never had anybody cry over him before. He knew it was a cry of pity, nothing more. He started to get angry. He had had enough of this. With his eyes closed he uttered one word.

"Go!"

Chapter 9

He cried himself into a deep sleep, waking up several hours later. He tried to listen, to hear if there was anyone else in the room. No, all he heard was the rain outside his window. He wished he could stand in it, feel it on his face. He was beginning to understand that he was trapped. Yes, trapped—in his body. He was stuck in a shell. He felt he had been punished again, just like he had been punished all his miserable life, only this time it was the ultimate sentence.

Things were hopeless. He couldn't walk, he couldn't move his arms, he couldn't sit up on his own and he had no control over his bladder or bowels. Thank God a male nurse helped him in the middle of the night. He was humiliated. The nurse made light of it, trying to comfort Gene by telling him it was no big deal and not to worry.

Gene told himself, "Shit happens," and laughed a little despite the situation. Finally, the nurse left, leaving Gene to his thoughts. He couldn't help it. He began to cry, again losing all self-control. For the first time in his life he wondered about his future. There wasn't any. None. He considered suicide. He had never given his life a second thought until now, until the accident. All he wanted to do back then was be with as many girls as possible and get stoned with Dan. He was invincible! He would give anything to go back in time before the accident, to have things the way they once were, but it was too late. What he once had was now gone.

A few hours later another nurse came in, giving him more medication before leaving. He wasn't sure what the drug was except it was powerful. He fell back into a deep sleep, this time with a much better attitude.

The sun's bright glare woke him. He wondered where he was. He thought he was in his room at home and had slept in. He would be late for school. He heard activity in the hall just outside his door. He tried to turn his head. He heard footsteps, the sound getting closer. A voice greeted him.

"Hello, Gene."

He still couldn't see who it was. It was a male voice that was vaguely familiar. A face finally appeared in his field of view. He thought, *It's our neighbor, George!* He tried to smile back at the big guy standing awkwardly beside the bed.

He croaked "Hi, George." His throat was ten times better than yesterday. Good. The only time he ever really talked to George was when he came home after school. George would be in his driveway working on his '56 Chevy. George loved the car, telling Gene it was his baby.

He also loved growing his roses by the side of the house. Gene had seen him out there many times before, carefully pruning, talking to them as though they were his children. The big guy did have a soft side to him, especially when he had called Gene last month, telling him they needed help at the gas station and would he like to work there for the summer.

"Uh, I'm sorry 'bout your accident, Gene. Uh, the doctors let me come in to see you before I go to work. I know it's kind of early but um, I wanted to come and see how you're doin' and stuff. I sure hope you get better."

Gene looked at him, realizing he meant what he said. George had taken his baseball cap off, holding it with both hands in front of him as he spoke. Gene could see he was nervous by the way he squeezed the brim. He was worried about Gene and cared for him. Gene never knew he felt that way. He had always thought that George didn't like any of them, especially his dad.

"The doctor told me there's nothing he can do for me. I damaged my spine and will never walk or use my hands again." His voice was hoarse.

"Jeeze, Gene! I'm so sorry to hear that."

Gene closed his eyes while saying, "Yeah, I know, George. Thanks." He was trying not to cry.

"Listen, Gene. Uh, like, is there anything I can do for you? You know, like get some stuff for you from home or anything? I haven't seen your dad in awhile but I'd be glad to go pounding on his door if you like."

Gene thought for a minute. What would he want from home and where the fuck was his father?

"You haven't seen my dad, at all?" It was starting to hurt when he talked.

"Well, yeah, I have seen him. He's been kinda drunk and all so I haven't talked to him. We don't get along, Gene. I kinda hoped he would come here to see you but I think your dad has trouble doin' that sort of thing, right? Like, I'm sure he loves you and all but he doesn't know how to show it. Know what I mean?"

Gene smiled, whispering, "Yeah, I know exactly what you mean."

"If it makes you feel any better, my dad was like that, too. Never gave us kids the time of day and always yelled at Ma. I know what 'cha goin' through buddy and, like I said, if I can help you, don't hesitate to call. Ya hear?"

"Can you get me water ... please?" He was groaning now.

"Yeah, here you go." George put the straw to Gene's lips. He took a long pull.

"Yes, I hear you, George." The water helped immensely. "Thank you, I do appreciate it. Hey, George, there is one thing I would like from home."

"What's that?"

"Could you get my iPod and headphones, please? They're in my room."

"Sure, Gene, you got it."

George was wondering if Gene wanted any pictures of family or friends and was about to ask but hesitated, knowing what the answer would probably be.

"Oh, and George?"

"Yeah, Gene?"

"Could you tell my dad that I love him and not to worry about coming to see me?" He blurted it out without really thinking, surprised at what he had said.

George nodded. Gene could see a tear forming in the big guy's eye.

Aw shit, now why did I have to go and say something stupid like that? I don't give a shit if the old man ever comes and sees me. Maybe it's better he stays away. It would be too awkward for both of us.

He wanted to tell George to forget the last request, but it was too late.

Chapter 10

Gene wasn't hungry when a nurse came in with breakfast. He was surprised since he hadn't eaten real food in six days.

He finally saw the object that had been next to him that he previously couldn't quite see. It was an intravenous hook-up. He laughed a little about what he had first thought; that it might be some kind of coat rack.

The nurse fed him porridge after coaxing him to at least eat a little. She did all the talking, explaining that his doctor would be coming in to see how he was around noon once he had finished working at the research center. Gene didn't say anything. He was busy eating. His appetite had quickly come back.

After breakfast she gave him more medication, claiming it would help him to relax. He noted she hadn't said, "To take away the pain" because, he didn't have any pain. *In fact, I can't feel a fucking thing*! He desperately wanted to feel something, anything; but no, he couldn't feel a thing.

Just after noon Doctor Klein walked in with another man. Gene knew exactly what time they arrived. His eyes were never far from the clock on the wall. He found himself becoming somewhat obsessed with the time of day. It gave him a small sense of control.

"Good afternoon, Gene." He said it with a bright smile. "I want you to meet Doctor Morin."

They both approached on the same side of his bed. Doctor Morin was slightly shorter than Klein and balding. He, too, wore glasses.

He had a sincere smile on his face as he spoke. "It's a pleasure to meet you, Gene."

Gene pegged him at around fifty years old. He didn't have an accent. He wondered if he was a local doctor here at Irvine.

Gene heard himself saying, "Good morning." His voice sounded better than yesterday. He thought that at least part of him was healing.

He didn't want to see the doctors. If he could avoid the meeting, he would. Seeing them reinforced the hopelessness of his condition but he did want to know what was going on with his body. He wondered if it could be saved. Was there anything they could do to bring back at least some feeling?

Doctor Klein continued by asking, "How are you today?"

"I'm okay." Gene knew it was only small talk. The doctor probably didn't want to hear about him feeling sad and frustrated.

"Good. We're glad to hear it." He paused, looking at his colleague before continuing.

"As you know, you severely damaged your spinal cord with your diving accident. We have taken numerous X-rays while you were unconscious. Doctor Morin is a specialist in dat sort of ting." He paused again, looking at Doctor Morin, waiting for him to continue. Doctor Morin was no longer smiling.

"Well, Gene. Yes. As Doctor Klein has pointed out, we took X-rays and a CAT scan, focusing on your lower back, neck and head area. There was and still is a lot of swelling so we need to conduct more tests. We do know, however, that your spinal cord is damaged in two separate areas, near the base of the neck as well as your lower back." He pointed to the lower portion of his own neck and back to illustrate.

"Now, the cord is not completely severed and sometimes, over a period of time, patients have been known to regain some sensation in their extremities. The possibility of that, however, is rather remote."

As Doctor Morin spoke, Doctor Klein still wondered about Gene's parents. They should have been here to support him. The young man was facing this news alone. The hospital had finally contacted the father. They told him about the accident and how his son was doing. They had also explained that, since he was immediate family, he could ignore the visiting hours. He was allowed to come and see his son at anytime he chose. He never showed. Staff also wondered about the mother. Nobody knew where she was.

Doctor Klein looked away, pretending to study the clipboard in his hands. He was both angry and sad. He had seen similar cases in the past but nothing as bad as this. At least some family member would be there for support. Not this time. He listened as Doctor Morin continued.

"You'll probably feel what we call 'phantom stimuli.' You may feel an itch on your foot or an ache in your back but that is strictly psychological. Do you understand what I'm saying, Gene?" Doctor Morin looked at the young man. Even though he'd made the same speech to so many others, it was never easy for him, especially with one so young.

"Yeah, I guess so. Like, I'll never feel anything for real, again?"

"Well, I don't like using the word 'never.' We don't know that for sure."

Doctor Klein quickly looked up from the clipboard. Both doctors glanced at each other. Doctor Klein felt the need to interrupt his colleague. He thought Doctor Morin could sometimes say more than needed.

Doctor Klein cleared his throat. Gene could hear the accent come back. He suspected Klein's accent grew thicker when he became more excited. It was now very thick.

"Excuse me, gentlemen, yah? Let me just say dat"—he paused, looking toward Doctor Morin—"the vord 'never' is not in our vocabulary." He looked at Gene. "Vee feel vee have been fooled before widt dat vord, yah? Some tings do happen dat surprise even us."

Doctor Morin jumped in. "Now, Gene, don't misunderstand us. We are practical men of science and know that miracles rarely happen so we do not want to give you false hope." He turned and looked at Doctor Klein. Nothing more was said.

Gene had been witnessing this—what would it be—sparring?

Is that it, sparring between the doctors? They seemed very uncomfortable with what they were saying. It was as though the words were being very carefully orchestrated. And, the stare they had given each other. What was that all about?

Gene was confused with all of it. "So, Doctor, you're telling me there is hope, maybe, and there is probably no hope, maybe? What is it?"

Doctor Morin thought, *"Well said, Gene. Under the circumstances I couldn't have said it better. Yes, what is it?"* He tried to suppress a smile even though the circumstances were far from funny. This young man wanted some answers.

"Gene, before we can even begin to answer the question, let's give it some time. We need to wait for the swelling to go down so we at least have a better idea of the, hmm, situation. Okay? Will you be patient with us, until we can give you some better answers later when we accumulate more data?"

Gene closed his eyes. They could see tears forming, slowly running down his cheeks. The doctors looked at each other. There was nothing more to be said.

Doctor Klein finally spoke up, the accent almost gone. "Okay, Gene. We have said enough for now. Let us do some more tests in the next few days and vee'll talk again, yah?" He found himself putting his hand on Gene's brow, slowly brushing his hair. He usually didn't do that sort of thing. He looked back at Doctor Morin and saw that he, too, had a tear in his eye.

As they left the room he cursed both himself and his colleague, muttering under his breath, "Damn, it is difficult to remain professional under dees circumstances, yah?"

Gene lay there, pondering what had just taken place. He tried to understand the difficulty in what they needed to do, telling their patient there was no hope for recovery but not to give up hope. He wondered what it was all about, just a bunch of smoke and mirrors?

He was still in shock, trying to adjust to his predicament. He was becoming very tired of lying in bed like a lump of meat, dead meat. He realized he was exhausted, emotionally exhausted. He closed his eyes, feeling the medication take effect, and finally fell into a deep sleep.

He dreamed of Marcy, the hot little item from the gym. He had never taken her out. Now, in his dream, he does.

She is only five feet tall and madly in love with him. She tells him how much she adores him—how she likes the way he treats her. She loves abuse. The more she gets, the more she wants. Weird, he likes it, too.

They're at a beach party, along with thirty kids from his class. Even though it's dark out he's easily spotted because he's the tallest. He's also the center of attention. Everybody loves Gene. He feels Marcy at his side. He's so much taller. She only comes up to his chest. All the other girls are eyeing him with desire while his buddies wish they could be more like him. He's got it made.

He makes his way to an area that is hidden behind some rocks near the water. Marcy is with him. They lie down on a blanket and start to hug and kiss. Soon they have their clothes off. They hear the pounding of the surf nearby. He can smell the salt air and feel the coolness of the night. He can feel her warm body against his.

He tries to hold her tighter but she leaps away, teasing. She tells him she wants to go swimming and, before he can respond, she runs toward the surf.

He picks himself up and follows. He hears her laughter above the pounding waves. He catches a glimpse of her in the moonlight, already shoulder deep in the ocean. He doesn't want to go in. He's not having fun. He should be in control of the situation but he's not. He was close to having her and now she's slipped away, taunting and teasing him.

He finds himself neck deep in the cool water, hearing her laugh from the deeper waters beyond, beckoning him toward her.

A wave comes out of nowhere, pulling him under. He holds his breath, keeping his eyes tightly closed as the water surrounds him, pushing him farther away from shore. He tries to swim up towards the surface but can't. He wonders why. He panics. He opens his eyes and sees the moon's image from beneath the water. He's only a few feet below the surface, now quickly running out of air. Why can't he swim? Why can't he move his arms and legs? He can't hold his breath any longer. His lungs are aching. He opens his mouth, trying to breathe but gets nothing but salt water. He starts to choke. He's drowning.

He woke up sputtering, choking on his own saliva. His face was hot and covered in sweat. He could hear his heart pounding in the back of his head. He had panicked and was now trying to catch his breath. It took several minutes for him to clear his throat.

The smiley nurse, Cynthia, came running into the room. She heard him screaming in his sleep. He was still not fully awake as she leaned over.

"There, there, Gene. Are you okay?"

She's talking to me like I'm a fucking baby. She's only a few years older and yet she's trying to act like a mother to me. Besides, I can smell her perfume. The same fucking perfume Mom used to wear.

He tried to settle himself down, slowly realizing that it was only a nightmare, nothing more. He took a few deep breaths. He couldn't get enough air. He wondered if he'd been holding his breath in his dream. He slowly relaxed, listening to her pampering him.

He half-smiled, sarcastically thinking, *"Of all the fucking people that could come and rescue me from a nightmare, it had to be that stupid bitch."* He didn't like her. Besides, she looked tall, at least five feet eight inches.

She placed a cool towel on his face, wiping away the perspiration. It did feel good. She looked at him and again asked, "Are you okay?"

He mentally answered, *Yeah, you stupid bitch, I'm okay. All I wanted to do was escape from this shitty life of mine by dreaming. You know? Dreaming! Not any old dream but a nice warm dream where I'm the king. And do you know what happened you stupid bitch? It turned out to be the worst nightmare of my fucking life. I just about died in my sleep. It's bad enough I have to live a nightmare let alone dream one, too.*

He grunted, "Water!"

She nodded, feeding him from the straw in the glass. He closed his eyes and sipped until the liquid was drained.

As he drank, Cynthia raised his bed up a little, making it easier for him, all the while telling him everything would be all right. He opened his eyes, seeing part of her cleavage four inches from his face. He wondered what her tits looked like. He wondered if he was getting sicker thinking of her in that way. He also wondered if she were breaking hospital rules. He couldn't recall any other nurse that showed that amount of cleavage. Was she doing it just for him?

She asked if there was anything else he needed. He realized what she was getting at. He could smell himself. He must have crapped himself in his sleep.

My God! Can it get any worse than this? He answered "yes," to her question. They both knew what they were talking about. She quickly left, feeling embarrassed for him, trying to find a male nurse that could help.

He lay with his eyes closed, trying to settle down from the nightmare.

How fucking humiliating. Shitting your pants and having someone clean it for you. He had never felt so small in his life.

A few minutes later he heard noise in the room, the sound of footsteps. He automatically tried to turn his head but his neck was too sore. It was the first time he realized he could feel his neck muscles, albeit sore neck muscles. He thought the doctors had anchored his head down to minimize movement. He slowly realized he did have feeling in his neck but nothing lower.

"Hey, Gene. I hear you need my services."

Gene saw the male nurse come into his field of view and grimaced. The guy just ignored him, getting down to business, talking to Gene while cleaning him.

The nurse's named was Harry. He loved to talk. Gene found it comforting because he didn't know what to say. He was totally humiliated by what was going on down there. He tried to block out the next few minutes, waiting for the nurse to finish. He couldn't help but listen to what Harry was saying while he was busy.

It turned out that Harry had been working at the hospital for several years. In fact, he started out at the Edgehill Clinic when it used to be the General Hospital. Evidently, the community built Irvine General a few years later and now Edgehill was a care center for the long-term patients. A wing of the building housed a research facility called Bosch Research. He told Gene he was going to like it better at Edgehill. There were fewer patients and the staff and facilities were geared to a more pleasant environment.

"Hell, they even have high-speed Internet for the patients."

As if that will help me. I can't even turn on a computer.

Harry seemed to have read his mind. "They've got all these peripheral gadgets that you can use to browse the Web. It's really cool!"

He was listening, warming up to the idea, wondering when they planned on moving him out. The sooner the better; he was starting to get fed up with being where he was.

As Harry left the room he thought about Gene. He knew from the medical charts that he was another one of those hopeless victims who would never get better. He shook his head, wondering when they were going to transfer him to Edgehill. *The little guy has nothing to live for.*

He passed a young man in the hallway that was walking toward Gene's room. Harry shook his head again, deep in thought, wondering about Gene's future, or lack of it. He made his way to another patient.

Gene was staring at the ceiling when he heard the familiar voice.

"Hey, Dickface."

Smiling, he tried to turn his head to respond.

"Hey, Bonehead." He waited for Dan to come into his field of view.

Five seconds later he appeared with a big smile.

"Well, well, *well!* Look at the patient lying there nice and cozy. At least you've got a private room. How are you doing?"

"I hate this fucking place. Get me out." Gene was thankful Dan hadn't appeared a few minutes earlier when Harry was cleaning him.

"Yeah, well, I can't or I would. Believe me."

There was an awkward silence between them and then they both talked at once, laughing in the process. Everything was sort of back to normal again.

Gene said, "I want to thank you for getting your feet wet when you were saving my ass."

"That was the shittiest attempt at a dive I have ever seen! What the fuck were you thinking, my man?"

"I dunno. Guess I was trying to show off ... again. What did Lindsey have to say about it?"

"Well, she called you a dumb-ass but I think you're her hero." He didn't want to tell Gene that Lindsey was now seeing Jason LaPointe. He continued by saying, "She would never say it but she's worried about you and wants to come and visit sometime."

That made Gene smile. "Tell her to come by anytime, okay?"

"Yeah, sure." Dan was anxious to talk about something else, knowing how Gene felt about her.

"So, you were sure laid out face down in the lake, buddy. I got in as fast as I could but it was tough getting to you. Did you know you hit some rocks about four feet under?" Gene tried to shake his head. It barely moved.

Dan continued. "So ... how bad is it? When are you getting out?"

Gene looked at him. Dan could see tears form in his eyes. He thought, *"Aw shit, I don't need that sort of thing. Man, it must be bad. Why did I ask?"*

He tried to recover by saying, "Hey, I know it will get better and you'll be out in no time." Suddenly he felt very uncomfortable being there. He didn't know what to do or say. He decided on trying to cheer him up. "Hey, Dickface."

Gene raised his eyebrows.

"On the way up here I was thinking of all the good times we've had." He smiled, all the while talking. "Do you remember when you got so drunk that one night?"

Gene started to smile as Dan kept talking. He knew what was coming.

"You were in love with—what's her name?"

Gene kept listening, remembering the time a couple of years back.

"Well, buddy, we were at this party when you started drinking vodka, straight!"

Gene thought he could feel his stomach churn from the memory. He had gotten terribly sick that night. Dan was enjoying the recount.

"Yeah. We brought you back to the car and put you in the back seat. Ten minutes later you were hollerin' at us to stop the car 'cause you were going to get sick. Remember?"

Dan knew damn well he remembered. Gene smiled as he listened to Dan relish.

"So, you were yelling, 'Stop the car! Stop the car! I'm going to get sick!' That's when I turned around, seeing you lying there on the back seat. I said, 'Gene, the car's not moving! We haven't hit the road yet.' You were looking pretty green—spread out on the back seat like that."

They started laughing, Gene remembering it all too well.

Dan was having fun. "Then, we let you out and you start running down the road, ranting and raving. We thought you were going to get sick but no, you were saving the best for last, right?" He winked.

"We get you back in the car and head out to another party. We no sooner walk into the house when you make a dash for the bathroom because now you *are* going to get sick. Then, next thing we know, you're screaming, 'Help me! Help me! Someone's trying to drown me!' We run into the bathroom and there you are, on your knees with your head stuck in the toilet bowl. The lid had dropped down and you had mistaken it for someone's hands, thinking they were trying to push you in."

They were both laughing hysterically now. Gene loved the way Dan laughed with that 'yuk-yuk' sound. They spent a few more minutes together. Gene was wondering if he would ever have the opportunity to party again, or had his life come to an end. A tear slowly crept down his left cheek. He thought about how things had changed.

Just then, Doctor Klein arrived. Dan looked at the doctor then back at Gene. "Ah, look, I gotta go. I'm heading over to the gym to meet with the guys. They all say 'Hi' and miss you. I'll be back real soon, okay? I promise. See ya, Gene."

Gene was surprised that Dan had used his name. It was usually just 'Dickface.' He wondered if he'd ever see his friend again.

Chapter 11

Doctor Klein studied Dan as he left the room, wondering the same thing. It wasn't unusual for people, young and old, to feel uncomfortable when visiting patients, especially the severely injured. He hoped Gene's friend would come back soon. He looked at Gene and tried to give him an encouraging smile.

"I vant you to know we are scheduling you for another CAT scan a little later on. We still vant to give your injuries more time to settle down before we take any more pictures, yah?"

Gene tried to nod.

"Vee are also scheduling you for some physiotherapy in the next few weeks. I think dat, before you know it, we'll be able to have you in a veelchair so you can get out and see the rest of the vard, but right now vee have to be patient."

"When will they transfer me out to this 'Edgehill Clinic,' Doctor?"

Doctor Klein raised his eyebrows, startled, wondering who had already been talking to Gene about moving him to the long-term care facility.

"Vell, yes, vee will be transferring you out of the hospital to a more home-like environment. Vee vant to monitor your condition a little longer but it appears dat dee plan right now is to move you in a week or so."

"Can I get the Internet there?"

"Yes, you can, yah? We've got dee Internet as vell as a communal TV room, a swimming pool and spa, and an exercise room. Dair are workshops, a kitchen where you can help prepare your own meals, classes on most anyting and even a library, yah?" He left the room a few minutes later, assuring Gene they had not forgotten about him.

Thinking about the Edgehill facility made Gene feel a little better, knowing there were people looking after him, helping him. He was in a reasonably good mood, thinking about the move as well as getting his iPod from George, when Cynthia walked in.

He could smell her before she came into view. He thought, *"Maybe not. Maybe her perfume isn't that strong."* He wondered if it only smelled strong because it was the same type of perfume his mother had worn.

He made a mental note to try and be a little more pleasant with her. He understood she was only trying to help and, besides, he was in no position to be making enemies. If he could just tolerate her, she might be of some use to him later.

"Hello, Gene. How is your day so far?" She spoke in a high, squeaky voice. She had lipstick on. Again he wondered if she were breaking hospital rules. Gene held back his true feelings and tried to smile in return.

"It's been good, thank you."

"My, oh my, you seem to be in a better mood today! That's good, Gene. I've got some supper for you. Would you like that?"

He wanted to quip, "No, you fucking bitch, I like starving to death. What the fuck do you think?" He held his tongue.

"Yes, I'm hungry."

"Good boy!" She blurted it out without even thinking, simply happy that he was feeling better. "Open wide. Here we go!" She loved the idea that she could feed him.

Gene had a fleeting thought of putting his hands around her fucking neck and squeezing. She called him a 'good boy!' That bitch. He opened his mouth while closing his eyes, trying to taste the mush she was spoon-feeding him. She couldn't stop smiling.

Dan was almost out the main door of the hospital when he realized he had forgotten one of the reasons why he had chosen today to visit poor Gene. He made an about face, ran back to the elevator, and re-entered Gene's room a few minutes later.

Gene heard the familiar voice as he opened his eyes. Dan was standing behind Cynthia, watching her spoon-feed him. He felt humiliated as he looked over at Dan with his mouth full. He knew some of the mush has fallen onto his chin and hoped Cynthia would wipe it off before Dan could see it. Too late!

He wondered why he had come back up to his room when Dan blurted out, "Oh yeah, Mid—" He caught himself. He had almost called his buddy, 'Midget.' Gene looked at him quizzically as Dan tried to recover from his mistake.

"Oh yeah, *midway* down the stairs I remembered something. I forgot to tell you. Happy birthday! See ya later." He patted Gene's head and quickly left the room, feeling more awkward than ever.

Cynthia purred, "Aw … that is so sweet!" She started singing "Happy Birthday."

He wondered how he could get his hands around that fat neck of hers. He had mentally choked her ten times since she had come into his life. This would now be number eleven. He remembered the food that had dribbled on his chin. He closed his eyes, feeling helpless.

What a fucking way to celebrate an eighteenth birthday.

Chapter 12

George pulled into his driveway. The warmth of the day was slowly leaving. Stars were beginning to appear in the evening sky but his mind wasn't on stars. It had been on Gene most of the day. He wished he could do something more for him than just get his stuff. He was choked when Gene had asked him to tell his dad not to worry and that he loved him. George felt the kid deserved so much more. He figured Gene should have had decent parents and now, with the accident, well, the kid was again dealt a terrible hand.

He noticed lights on in Phil's house so decided to get down to business and go over there. He hated talking to him. The father was an idiot. Before he got out of the car he told himself to calm down, to get the iPod without making too much of a fuss. He walked over to Phil's house, realizing his fists were clenched. He shook his hands, hoping his fingers would loosen up, trying very hard not to be angry.

He knocked and waited. No answer. He knocked again, shouting, "Phil, are you in there?"

He heard someone mumble, "Go away."

A minute later Phil opened the door. He had a white tee-shirt on with what appeared to be several interesting patterns of ketchup down the front. One of the patterns looked similar to a rose petal. George was mesmerized for a moment or two.

"Yeah? Wadda ya want?" He looked like he'd been sleeping. His hair was tussled and he was unshaven.

George came out of his momentary trance. "Hey, Phil. Can I come in?"

Phil looked at him and shrugged, turning back into the living room. George followed. Phil was drunk. He turned around, looked at George in a belligerent way and snorted, "So, whatzzup?"

George unconsciously clenched his fists. "Look, Phil. I came here because your son wanted me to get his music and stuff. You *do* know he's in the hospital, don't you?"

"Lookee here, George!" Phil walked up to him, pointing a finger at his chest. "Don't be telling me shit like that with that tone of voice! I know he's in the hospital. That was his fucking fault, not mine! Once again Geneo does somtin' stupid."

When he said 'stupid,' George could see spittle drip down Phil's lower lip. George kept his fists clenched, thinking how easy it would be to hit the motherfucker. He took a deep breath instead.

"Look, Phil. Can I go get Gene's stuff?"

"Yeah, sure. I don't give a fuck. Just take it and leave." Phil turned around, wobbling, grabbing for the arm of the couch for stability. He slowly sat down, reaching out to a full glass of booze on the coffee table.

George wanted to leave. He was disgusted with the whole situation. He focused on getting the things and walking out. He went into Gene's room and looked around. He saw his skateboard by the bed. That shook him up. He knew Gene would never be using it again. He found the iPod and power pack as well as the headphones on the desk. He took one last look before closing the door behind him. He couldn't help but think Gene would never be back in this room. More importantly, he would never be back to his past way of life.

Walking into the living room, he heard Phil slur, "Yur happy now?"

"No, Phil. I'm *not* happy now! What's with you?" George had had enough. "Can't you go and visit your only fucking son in the hospital?"

Phil stood up and walked as quickly as his drunken legs could carry him toward George, again pointing an angry finger at his chest. "Look, mishter. Dis is none of yur fucking business. I'll never go and see my son!" His voice grew louder until he was shouting. "Ya wanna know *why* I won't see that fuckin' kid? Ya wanna know? I'll fuckin tell you why. 'Cause he ain't mine, dat's why! I got hoodwinked by that stupid bitch I used to call a wife. She told me that we was goin' to have a child. Yah, I found out later that it wasn't mine. And you know what, George? I'm fuckin' glad. Now, get the fuck out and leave me alone!"

For a moment George stood there, stunned. Thoughts of when he was a young boy went through his mind. He had pretty much experienced the same situation when he was growing up. He had the same kind of step-dad who never accepted him. At least he always knew he wasn't his real dad.

His thoughts went back to Gene. He wondered if this would be good news for the boy. Maybe that would explain why his so-called dad and mother treated him the way they did. Maybe it would make Gene feel better to know that Phil was not related to him, at least not in blood. He decided it would be best to keep the secret. He wouldn't tell a soul.

He walked to the door, stopped and turned, looking back at Phil, meeting his eyes. "One other thing, Phil. Gene told me to tell you he loves you." He said it in a quiet voice, the anger now gone.

"Get out. Get out. Get out!"

George walked out the door, hearing a glass smash against the wall behind him. He stopped on Phil's porch, shaking his head in disgust.

He walked back to his driveway, standing in the middle of it for a moment or two. That's when it hit him. He couldn't help it. He quickly made his way to the side of his house, throwing up all over his roses.

Chapter 13

Gene woke up early the following morning. After being fed, he was wheeled into the X-ray room where he met Doctor Morin. The doctor explained what he was going to do. Soon he was subjected to more tests that continued for most of the morning. He was back in his room by lunchtime, five minutes before George walked in.

"Hey, Gene. How are ya doing, today?"

Gene smiled, wishing George were his dad instead of Phil. He told George he'd been on his back, sides, every which way while they did more tests.

"That's good. You're in good hands." He paused for a minute, staring at the floor, thinking of what to say next. "You know, I got your stuff here." He pulled out the iPod and headphones from a bag as he looked up. He wasn't sure how to continue for a second or two, finally deciding on lying, instead.

"I saw your dad and he says to tell you he loves you, too. I guess he's too stressed to come in and see you right now, but he *does* love you."

Gene didn't believe it. He knew George was full of shit. He knew the old man wouldn't say anything like that. He pretended to listen.

George rambled on and, the longer he talked, the less believable things became. He told Gene his dad was doing great and wanted Gene back home as soon as possible. George's voice trailed off. Even *he* knew he had gone too far.

Gene thanked him and asked if he would please come and visit again soon. George said he would.

As he walked out the room he paused, thinking perhaps Gene could come and live with him and his wife. "No, that wouldn't do," he told himself. They both worked and, besides, Phil would only make trouble for all of them. He knew Gene was better off at Edgehill.

A nurse brought in lunch several minutes later. He still didn't have an appetite. He thought perhaps he'd be hungry later on in the afternoon. He wasn't sure. He was still thinking of his dad. He no longer wanted to be like him. He was ashamed of not only his dad but also his mother. He knew he shouldn't kid himself anymore. Everyone in his whole fucking family was a loser. He knew he was, too.

He closed his eyes, thinking about how long he had to live. *Let's see, I've just turned eighteen. I figure someone like me probably lives up to twenty years after the injury. There are three hundred and sixty-five days in a year. Multiply that by twenty years. Hmm, that comes to around seven thousand days. That's seven thousand times I'll be cleaned by a male nurse and twenty-one thousand times that I'll be spoon-fed. That's seven thousand days of either sitting or being on my back. That's seven thousand days of nothing. Seven thousand days of emptiness, of hell. If only I could die sooner. How can I kill myself? I can't hang myself. I can't shoot myself. I can't drug myself. I can't fucking live and I can't fucking die!*

In desperation he cried himself to sleep, waking an hour later, still not believing his situation. He couldn't accept it. He was too young to be paralyzed. It wasn't fair.

The room was too dark to make out the clock on the wall. He had no idea what the time was. He was transfixed with knowing the time of day, thinking it gave him a sense of purpose. He snorted. *Who cares? Will I be late for my date or football practice? Yeah, right!* He fell back into a self-pity mode.

Cynthia came into his room an hour later. He pretended to be asleep. He could sense her looking at him. He could feel her leaning over him. He heard a rustle as she pulled his bed sheet down off his chest. He wondered what she was doing. Should he steal a look? He felt her breath on his face and then sensed that she had turned her head, looking toward the end of the bed. He chanced a glance, noticing she was holding his hand. He quickly closed his eyes as she turned her head back up toward his. She was giving him the creeps. He pretended he was deep in sleep, not knowing what to do, hearing her whisper.

"I'm so sorry, Gene. I'm so, so, sorry. I'll take care of you. Don't worry. You're in good hands."

After she left, he spent most of the night staring at the ceiling, wondering how he could kill himself, maybe take that Cynthia nurse with him. She was becoming attached to him. He had mixed feelings. One part of him liked the idea that he could use her. He loved to take advantage of women. Another part made him feel totally in her control. He wanted to die. He knew he was powerless, no matter what he thought or said.

Doctor Klein came in at noon the following day after completing his shift at Bosch Research. He told Gene the test results were not good—his spinal cord was severely damaged. He looked at Gene intently while he carried on, becoming very clinical in explaining the injuries.

"As far as we can tell, your spinal injuries will never heal properly. The surrounding tissue and muscle are healing but ... it's the spinal cord dat is the problem. Because of the injury, you will have no feeling in your body below your neck. With the restrictions that have been imposed upon us from society and the government, all vee can do right now is make you feel as comfortable as possible." Doctor Klein was becoming frustrated as he continued with his speech.

"Believe me, Gene, I vould like nothing better than to see a young man such as yourself walk again. Here are dee facts. Under current medical procedures at this point in time, you vill not have the use of your arms or legs."

There it is—the death warrant. There goes my life ... right from the good doctor's mouth. That's it. Just shoot me, please.

He was starting to drift far away, wanting to die. He was becoming very pale. Doctor Klein could see he was going into shock. He lightly tapped Gene on the face, trying to get his attention. He gave him some water as he continued.

"Gene. Listen to me. I'm not finished."

Gene slowly focused back, preparing for more bad news. Doctor Klein fed him another sip while he continued. He didn't want to tell Gene anymore at this time but he felt he couldn't leave him hanging. He carefully prepared what he needed to say.

"Gene. I want you to do something for me, please. Vill you do dat for me, yah?" Gene tried to nod, noticing the doctor's accent was becoming thicker.

Doctor Klein could see that he now had Gene's full attention.

"I'm choosing my words carefully for several reasons. For one, I do not vant to give you false hope. Perhaps dair is no hope at all. I vant you to know I vill personally continue in trying to find a solution to dis. Please do not give up hope. Vill you do dat for me?"

Gene tuned him out. It was a dead end. He barely heard the doctor ramble on about life and shit and hope and no hope.

Doctor Klein left a few minutes later. Gene was thankful for that. He knew the doctor was very frustrated with the whole situation. He understood the doctor's position. He actually felt for him. He chuckled a little, thinking he had been given a sentence worse than death and yet he felt sorry for the doctor—the doctor who had to tell a patient that he was a hopeless case. That had to be the toughest job in the world. As usual, he cried himself to sleep.

Chapter 14

When he saw Doctor Klein the following morning he asked him the question. "Is there any hope? Any hope at all?" Gene wouldn't and couldn't accept his condition.

Doctor Klein looked pained and stressed. This was not easy for him. Bruce Whitman, the counselor, was also in the room. Doctor Klein was thankful for that.

Gene's anger had left him. He was exhausted. Doctor Klein stared at him, trying to again gather his thoughts on how to respond to this most delicate matter. He looked over at Bruce for support. Bruce shrugged, knowing how difficult this was for all of them. He had told Doctor Klein the best way to handle it was with the truth.

Doctor Klein slowly looked back toward Gene and sighed. A funny look came over his face as he sat down beside his bed. The doctor appeared defeated.

Yes, that's what it is. He's given up hope. Man, even my own doctor has lost hope. And what about the counselor? He's certainly no help.

Normally, Bruce would be talking a mile a minute, not being able to keep still. This was not the time for any of that. Bruce waited patiently while Doctor Klein explained.

He took Gene's hand, telling him a little about himself, all the while his accent growing thicker. He tried to make things sound better by downplaying life, telling him it wasn't that great in the first place. He began to open up, letting Gene know that being whole did not guarantee a good life.

"Yes, it would be nice to have it all. Money, health, happiness. I do have part of it, Gene ... a part of dee triangle, yah. Money and health, but ... happiness? No. I have my demons as well. I do not have it all. In fact, I live through people like you. It's important for me dat you know this, yah?"

Gene wanted to say, "Yes Doctor, it would be nice for me to have my fucking body back. Fuck you and the triangle!" Instead, he didn't say a word, trying to suppress his anger. He thought it rather odd, his feelings for Doctor Klein. He began to feel sorry for him. *"Can you believe that one,"* he thought. His emotions were all over the place as he chuckled.

Doctor Klein looked at him, puzzled as to what was going on in his young patient's mind. Gene was now laughing. The doctor couldn't understand why. He finally asked Gene what was so funny.

The baffled look on his face made Gene laugh even harder. The stress and anger plus the absurdity of the whole situation made it difficult to understand. Laughter became the release mechanism. He felt he was coming undone, thread by thread. It was all too much for him. He stopped laughing long enough to try explaining to the perplexed doctor that he had been feeling sorry for himself and then, when he saw Doctor Klein come in looking defeated and unhappy, he started to feel sorry for him instead!

"Can you believe it, Doctor? Here you are with health, money and success while I have absolutely nothing. I'm lying here, paralyzed, with news that things are hopeless for the rest of my life and yet I feel sorry for you! Isn't life funny?"

The mood quickly changed after he spoke. Once put into words, it didn't seem funny at all. In fact, it seemed rather sad.

Chapter 15

Cynthia stepped out of the shower, getting ready for work. She glanced at the clock. It was four-fifteen in the afternoon. She started work at five. The hospital was only three blocks away.

She studied her naked body in the mirror, liking what she saw. She used to be a fat kid while growing up on the farm, especially through her teen years. She found herself pretty but boys never wanted to date her. She thought the problem was her weight so went on a diet. She lost forty pounds but that didn't seem to help with her social life. The boys thought she was too … too what? She was trying to think of the word.

Ah, yes, 'intimidating.' They thought she was too intimidating. She shrugged it off. They didn't understand. All she wanted was a good man, someone she could take care of, someone who needed her, someone who she could love and watch over. The men she dated wanted things their way. They thought they could grab her anytime they damn well wanted to.

No, that's not happening in my lifetime. I'll decide if and when they can touch me. She felt they didn't appreciate her for who she really was so, instead, channeled her affection toward her two pets.

She was an accident, an only child. Her folks were in their early fifties when she was born. They were both loners. She kept to herself as well. She had read hundreds of romance novels, knowing, if she were patient enough, she would eventually find that perfect partner.

As she began to dress, her thoughts once again turned toward Gene. He was so cute and helpless. She could see the hurt and pain come through in his beautiful eyes. She suspected he had suffered much in his past. He came across as being mean-spirited.

She saw herself smiling in the mirror. Yes, she could change his outlook with a little bit of loving care. She felt goose bumps sweep over her with the thought.

She knew she was born to be a nurse. That was her calling. She loved helping people. With Gene, well that was different. She felt compelled to make up for the misery he had suffered in the past as well as the present, and perhaps, maybe into the future?

He had no friends to speak of. She felt sorry for him. He hadn't had any visits from a girlfriend. She had wanted to ask him if he had a girlfriend. She needed to be careful. After all, she was only there on a temporary basis.

Kaleb was sitting, watching her. She could see him in the mirror. She loved the dog with all her heart. She wished she could have several more. She simply loved animals. She grew up on a farm, wanting to be either a veterinarian or a secret agent. Neither career had quite turned out as planned but that was okay. She wished she could live in the country again.

She cupped her breasts, thinking of Gene, wondering what kind of bra she should wear for him. She giggled, knowing she was being silly. She turned sideways and looked at herself, enjoying the view.

Kaleb barked, startling her. Savannah had walked into the room and was rubbing herself against him. For cats and dogs, they usually got along. This time he decided to voice his displeasure.

Cynthia glanced at the clock, realizing she had better get dressed. She started putting on her perfume. She knew she had to be careful. She could get into trouble at work if she put too much on. She also had to be careful about the lipstick and cleavage, making sure to button up and wipe it off before leaving Gene's room. She liked the excitement. She suspected Gene did, too.

She walked into the bedroom to turn off the TV. The local news was on, catching her attention. There was another pro-life demonstration outside the doors of Irvine General. That seemed to happen on a regular basis. The hospital was performing abortions again. She hated the idea. They were murderers! How could the staff condone the murdering of innocent babies?

She wanted to be there, on the line, protesting. She would if she could but she understood the situation all too well. She could easily get fired if she did. She watched the news report, her heart going out to all those unborn children.

There were perhaps ten protestors walking back and forth in front of the main entrance. A few minutes later hospital security came along with the police, successfully disbanding them once more.

She looked up at the clock. She would be late if she didn't hurry. She decided on the black one with no straps.

Chapter 16

Gene had been in the hospital several weeks, going through more and more tests. He could now be lifted off the bed into a wheelchair. In doing so, they needed to limit his head and neck movements by anchoring them with a mechanical halo.

Doctor Morin and his partner, a Doctor Schultz, conducted several tests with Gene over the course of an afternoon. Doctor Schultz was totally academic. Gene had trouble relating to him. Doctor Morin, on the other hand, seemed to be a gentle soul, very sympathetic to Gene's predicament.

He was wheeled in and out of different rooms and labs, being X-rayed, CAT scanned and injected here and there with different chemicals and drugs. He hated it but knew they were at least working on the problem and hoped that perhaps they might find something that could possibly help him. He didn't want to give up hope, even if it seemed to him that his own doctor had.

Later on in the afternoon Dr. Morin took the time to explain Gene's injuries in more detail, helping him develop a better understanding. He sketched a rough diagram of the spinal cord on his clipboard, explaining that the adult vertebral spinal column consisted of twenty-six bones. Out of those twenty-six, the neck was made up of seven cervical vertebrae separated by discs. Those seven were referred to as C1 through to C7, counting from the top of the neck down. Unlike the rest of the spine, the segments in the cervical spine contained openings in each vertebral body for arteries to carry blood to the brain and spinal cord.

He continued to explain. Gene's spinal cord was not severed but damaged in several locations—the C7 area as well as other areas in his lower back. The multiple injuries were the straws that 'broke the camel's back.'

He also explained that, when Gene dove into the lake, his outstretched arms and inverted V formation served to protect his body only a little. His arms probably helped him glance off a submerged rock. The problem was his head had been very likely forward of his shoulders, like any typical dive, when he hit the water. His lower neck and vertebrae were vulnerable in that position.

Doctor Morin demonstrated by placing his chin on his own chest while pointing to the bumps his vertebrae made at the base of the neck and lower back. To make matters worse, the impact of the dive had also crushed several vertebrae in Gene's lower back, damaging the spinal cord in that area beyond repair.

Later that afternoon they were done. Gene was wheeled back into his room and lifted into bed. Lying there, thinking about what Doctor Morin had said and how he had described the injuries, had put C7 on his mind.

What did Doctor Morin say about my injuries? The straw that broke the camel's back. Yeah, that pretty much summed it up, didn't it?

He was tired of being tested. He was also depressed with the results when Cynthia came into his room, ready to feed him supper. He noticed her stupid smile as she sauntered in. She cranked the bed up so he would be in a slightly upright position and wheeled a serving tray closer to him. She was all bubbly and happy. It made him sick.

No, maybe the word 'smothered' is a better way of describing how I feel.

He wanted to tell his doctor to not have her come into his room any more. He didn't want to see her. He should have mentioned it before but there were too many other things on his mind. Besides, they were going to move him soon. He decided to put up with it, thinking that maybe it wasn't so bad after all.

She was jabbering about what she had read in a magazine concerning similar patients in the same situation. She looked at him closely while explaining they had found alternative treatments. She let the statement hang, waiting to see what his response would be. She loved the control.

Wait a minute. Alternative treatments? What does she mean by that? He was getting excited.

"Does that mean there are other ways of curing me?" His mind was reeling with the thought that there might be possibilities that Dr. Klein hadn't mentioned but what this dumb-ass nurse could explain. He couldn't wait to hear the good news. Perhaps it was only a simple matter and he could very well be walking in no time. Even if it took a year he could do it. His mind was racing. *Anything, just give me anything!*

She sat down on the edge of the bed, smiling. She knew she had him. He was waiting for more of an explanation and she was taking her sweet time in giving it. She bent forward more than necessary, wiping his brow with a cloth, making sure he had a good look at her cleavage and black bra.

He held his tongue, not wanting to shout, thinking, *"Tell me you dumb bitch. Tell me more about this alternative thing."*

She smiled, looking at him in a rather sick and adoring way, doling out more information, enjoying his attention on her.

It soon became apparent that what she was saying was useless. He heard her yakking about herbs and oils and spirituality and finally he decided he had had enough. He wanted to scream.

That fucking bitch has gotten my hopes up and now she's talking about rubbing oil on my useless fucking body?

He did scream. "Give me a fucking break!"

He tried to hit her, quickly realizing how helpless he was. He was furious with her for leading him on with false hope.

She looked at him uncomprehendingly. She couldn't figure out what the problem was. It made the situation even worse in his mind. She thought she was actually helping him.

He lost all control. Tears began flowing down his face. He felt sick to his stomach. Another false hope like so many others he'd had in his life. She started to cry as well. He knew she wasn't crying for the same reasons. She was crying because he had yelled at her.

Not only that, she feels fucking sorry for me! He hated her and he hated himself for being so eager and ready to jump at anything. He hadn't known how desperate he was until then.

He tried to hit her again, strictly acting out of instinct. That was the kind of person he was. He was choked with the whole scenario, not being able to speak. Feeling totally defeated he closed his eyes and, in a weak voice, finally managed to utter, "Get out."

She quickly left the room, buttoning up her blouse and wiping off her lipstick. Deep down she felt rather pleased. For a few moments she had had the control, loving the attention he was giving her.

He wished he were dead. He had never felt so low in his life. He wished he had never been so preoccupied with his height when he was healthy. He wished he could have his arms and legs back. He wished, he wished, he wished! If only he could go back in time and change everything.

He opened his eyes a few minutes later. He immediately felt sorry for the way he had handled it. He had once again lost control. He hated himself for reacting that way. He thought she was only trying to help. He knew he had to be more considerate. It wasn't her fault he was in here—it was his fault, caused by his own stupidity. He did it to himself. No one else should be blamed for what he did. No one had forced him into diving. Now, he realized, he had the rest of his life to pay for his mistake.

Chapter 17

Gene was to be moved to the Edgehill Clinic the following morning. Doctor Klein had met earlier with Doctors Morin and Schultz as well as the counselor, Bruce Whitman. Based on their findings, they all agreed Gene was ready to be transferred. Besides, he was excited about it. There was nothing more they could do for him at Irvine General. It would be easier to treat Gene at Edgehill. It was next door to Bosch Research Incorporated where they worked on a part-time basis. They would be on site a good portion of the day and so could easily monitor his condition. It was time for Gene to make Edgehill his home.

They called his friend, Dan, and let him know where they were taking Gene. The hospital also called his father one more time, telling him about the move. The nurse who had made the call reported he had hung up on her.

Doctor Klein had read Bruce's report with interest and suggested that Gene would benefit by confiding in a friend. Bruce agreed, saying Gene had a lot of anger and frustration that he needed to vent providing it was with the right person. He added that Gene was also a loner, having only one so-called friend and virtually no parents, a bad combination. It was agreed that Bruce would visit several times a week on a professional and social level. After all, he did like Gene. A part of him loved telling the young man stories that were long forgotten.

Physiotherapy would begin as soon as they finished with the move. Weeks had gone by since the accident and Gene was now ready for it. It was essential for Gene's muscles and limbs to be regularly exercised. Doctor Klein insisted that Gene be given a private room at Edgehill. He understood Gene could be easily agitated and needed time alone to work things out. He was thinking about the incident that had taken place with the young nurse and the way Gene had shouted at her. She was only trying to help but, alas, things didn't quite work out that way.

All three doctors, along with Bruce, agreed that Gene was an intelligent young man with several emotional problems exacerbated by his accident. They also agreed he had potential but needed to be persuaded into a more positive direction.

Doctor Klein signed the necessary release papers. Gene's life would once again change direction.

Gene made a promise to himself, a promise to be a little more tolerant of Cynthia if he saw her again. He knew she liked him. He could feel there was something more to it than just being his nurse.

Maybe that's what it is. That's the problem. She's starting to fall for me or at least act like a mother to me. He flinched at the thought.

He looked at the clock as he lay on his back. It was only seven-thirty in the evening and yet he was ready for bed. He laughed at that one.

Ready for bed? Yeah, sure, ready for bed for the rest of my miserable life. Okay, maybe a wheelchair for a few hours each day as well. No, I'm not ready for bed. I want to get out of bed. I want to walk again!

He settled down, trying not to get too upset. His mind wandered, thinking of Cynthia, feeling sorry for her.

"What the fuck is going on here?" He was getting into the habit of speaking to himself, finding that the sound of his words gave his thoughts more credibility. "I'm the pitiful one. No, wait a minute." He had to admit she was also pretty pitiful.

He wondered what kind of life she had outside of nursing. *And, why, for God's sake, does she bathe in that stinking perfume?* It smelled like the same shit his mother used. 'Liz Claire'—something or other. He wondered why the doctors didn't notice like he did. He questioned if he was the only one bothered by the smell. If so, why was it affecting him so much? Was she wearing the perfume because she felt insecure? He knew all about being insecure. Maybe, just maybe, he and Cynthia had a lot more in common than he had originally thought. Besides, he was sure she would be back. She felt pity for him. He knew she also cared for him. He fell into a deep sleep, dreaming of her.

Cynthia sneaks into his room in the middle of the night. She holds up a finger to her mouth, whispering for him to be very quiet because they are going somewhere special. He tries to speak but he's completely paralyzed. He doesn't want to go but he can't stop her. She has total control.

She gets him in the wheelchair and pushes him out of the hospital, into her van. He can see her face lit up by the dash lights as she drives him down a maze of streets. He doesn't know where she's taking him. He can't speak. She keeps talking, telling him it's for his own good. She'll take care of him at her house. No one will know. It will be their secret.

He tries to protest but she interrupts him by saying, "Now, Gene, your daddy and mom don't care about you and you have no friends. Who's going to miss you, right?"

She smiles wickedly, her mouth partially open. He notices she has long fangs. He's in trouble, deep trouble. He's terrified! She's a blood sucking vampire. She's going to feed on him, drain his life out of him. He starts to breathe faster and harder. He hears his heart pounding, knowing it might burst at any moment. He tries to scream, "Help me! Help me!" but he can't. He chokes instead.

"Gene. Gene! Wake up."

No. He could hear her yelling. She was still after him! He mumbled, "Go away. Don't take me with you."

"It's okay, Gene. You were having nightmares again. Here, drink this."

He opened his eyes, finally understanding that he had indeed been dreaming. He looked at the clock. It was only eleven p.m. He sucked on the straw, draining the glass. She refilled it and he drank again, looking at her as she cooled his forehead with a wet facecloth. He finally smiled, relaxing, thankful it was only a dream. She smiled back.

"Uh, Cynthia?"

"Yes, Gene?" She was looking at him almost adoringly. She was happy he was okay.

"Uh, thank you and I'm sorry for how I acted at supper."

She had tears in her eyes as she kissed him on the forehead. She whispered, "That's okay, Gene. That's okay." She thought that was the best thing that had ever happened to her. He had apologized!

He was thankful she liked him yet he was slightly nervous about her. His life was in her hands when they were alone. The situation made him feel somewhat uneasy. He decided that the best thing he could do right now was treat her a little better even though he didn't like the power she had over him.

An hour later he was in another deep sleep—this time, dreamless.

Chapter 18

He woke up early. It was Saturday. Pancakes were on the menu. He could now start to eat real food instead of the mush they'd been serving him in the past. He had two servings. An hour later he heard a knock on his door.

He still couldn't turn his head but did say, "Come in."

"Hi, Gene." It was Lindsey. What a surprise! He wasn't ready for that. He wondered how he looked. Was his hair combed? Too late—she'd already seen him.

"Hi, Lindsey."

She looked great. He was excited to see her although he felt uncomfortable lying there, wishing he could at least get out of bed.

"Hey, how are you doing?" Before he could answer she said, "I was talking to Dan and he told me you were going to be moving today so I thought I'd better come in while I still had a chance at seeing you."

"Uh, yes, they're planning on moving me to the Edgehill Clinic. You can still come and see me there. It's only five miles away." He was cursing himself for saying it the way he did. It sounded … too eager.

Lindsey smiled, saying, "Yes, I'd love to visit you there. So …, how are you doing?"

"Well, I … ah … guess okay. No, not really okay. I will never use my arms and legs again. I'm paralyzed." He hadn't wanted to tell her about being an invalid. He was worried she would feel sorry for him, thinking that if she did, it would change their relationship. Of course she already knew.

"Jeeze, Gene. I'm so sorry." She leaned over and gave him a kiss on the forehead. He wanted to put his arms around her. He tried to smile but he was too choked. He had a lump in his throat.

Now she feels sorry for me. I didn't want that. I don't want her to pity me!

They talked for a while about Dan and school and stuff, just small talk until Gene finally blurted out, "I want to tell you something, Lindsey."

She looked at him with interest as she put her hand on his cheek.

"I really care for you and—" He was surprised at what he was saying. He did mean what he said but now he felt like a bowl of Jell-O quivering in front of her. He sensed their relationship was changing.

"It's okay, Gene." She felt uncomfortable as well. She had only wanted to come and say "Hi." She knew they would never be an item, especially after his accident. Besides, now she was seeing Jason LaPointe.

"Are we still friends?" He decided to try from the beginning. At least being friends was better than nothing.

"Of course, Gene. I like you."

She bent over and kissed him on the lips. He wanted to hold her so much. He loved her smell and her touch. He closed his eyes, feeling her lips on his, more so than he had ever felt in the past. He immediately gave himself false hope that things could get back to the way they used to be. For the moment, he had forgotten all about his accident. He quickly came back to reality, wondering if the sense of touch on his face had been enhanced because he'd lost it elsewhere. He reminded himself to ask Doctor Klein about it later.

She sat upright, stroking his hair. They looked at each other without speaking. He wondered if she felt the same about him.

Finally she said, "I guess I better get going. I've got a lot of running around to do."

"Will you visit me, soon?" Again he sounded out of control. He cursed himself for pleading with her.

"Yes, I will."

"Do you promise?"

He did it again! *Why the fuck don't I just get down on my knees and beg like a dog. I mean, I probably would if I could! What's wrong with me? Have I lost my pride?*

"Of course I will. I'll see you in a few days, okay?" She knew she shouldn't have kissed him. She had wanted to because—she wasn't sure why. Maybe it was because she felt sorry for him.

"Okay, Lindsey." They looked at each other, smiling. She left a few minutes later.

He was shaken. He knew he hadn't handled the visit very well.

Under the circumstances, what else could I have done? If I acted aloof would that have been better?

As the elevator doors opened for Lindsey to go down to the main floor, Cynthia walked out, giving her a passing glance as she made her way toward Gene's room. A minute later she was at his door, undoing a button on her blouse and putting lipstick on. She walked in, asking how he was.

Gene tried to smile; his mind was still on Lindsey's kiss.

"Oh, hi. I'm feeling good. Thanks for asking. What are you doing here so early? You don't start your shift until five, right?" He didn't want her here, especially now. He was nervous. He felt as though he was cheating on her. He was talking too fast.

Cynthia noticed he was—what? Glowing, that's what. He looked very happy. She wondered about the girl she had seen in the elevator but dismissed her, thinking that perhaps he was happy to be getting out of the hospital. "*Or,*" she thought, "*maybe he's happy to see me.*"

"Uh, yes. I do work at five but I didn't want to miss seeing you so I came to say 'Hi' before you left."

This was making Gene feel very uneasy. He thought she had stepped over the line from nurse to—what?

Does she think she's my girlfriend? It sounds like she thinks we're dating! He didn't like it. He was not sure how to handle the situation so, instead, decided it didn't matter anymore. He would be gone in an hour.

She leaned over, partially revealing her large breasts, as she gave him a kiss on the cheek. He couldn't help but groan. She heard it, thinking he was groaning for her.

"I'm going to miss you, Mr. Gene. I'll make a point of coming and visiting you as much as possible, okay? After all, I want them to treat my favorite patient just right." She winked.

He weakly smiled back. She was thinking that he wanted her. She had an urge to put her hand under the sheet and see how he was reacting but quickly put it out of her mind. She had goose bumps again. She loved his smell and his eyes and his smile and ....

Two aides came into the room interrupting their visit. They had come to put him in a wheelchair, to prepare him for the move to where he hoped would be a better place—Edgehill.

"Uh, thanks for coming by and seeing me, Cynthia." He was thankful other people were in the room.

"Not a problem, Gene." She winked again, thinking about the groan he had let out when they had kissed. "Besides, I've got an appointment with Miss Hazel from personnel in a few minutes. I'm curious about that. She just called me out of the blue. Maybe now I've got a full-time job here."

He said, "Good luck, Cynthia," smiling sweetly, hoping she was offered a full-time job a hundred miles away.

While the aides were getting ready to lift him into the wheelchair, Cynthia winked at him once more. This time one of the aides saw her do it and smiled knowingly back at Gene. Gene wanted to tell him to fuck off. There was nothing to smile about.

Chapter 19

She left feeling very excited—not about the visit to personnel, but because of Gene. She couldn't explain it. She had always been leery of men but this time it was different. She was in charge. She controlled the play. She liked the position she was in.

She went into the administration office, making sure her blouse was buttoned up and her lipstick wiped off. She only had to wait a few minutes before Miss Hazel met with her.

Hazel Worandowski was close to sixty-five years old and she looked every bit of it despite the orange dyed hair. Miss Hazel had seen a lot at both Edgehill and Irvine General over the years. She was one of the original nurses at Irvine General when it first opened. She had also been a nurse at Edgehill for many years previously. Her peers called her 'Miss War.'

Her long earrings dangled as she put on her glasses, looking at some papers on her desk while speaking to Cynthia. She didn't bother with small talk. She was all business.

"I've got some good and bad news for you, dear. Your term here at Irvine General will be finished within two weeks from today."

Cynthia's mouth dropped open. "But Miss Hazel, I can't—"

Miss Hazel put up her hand to stop her and continued. "Yes, yes, I know, dear. Let me explain. The nurse that you were filling in for will be coming back from maternity leave. I'm sorry but we have our hands tied. After all, you *are* only a temporary employee." The way she spoke to her made Cynthia feel like trash.

She waited for Miss Hazel to finish up. She could feel her cheeks turning red.

"The good news is there are two jobs that are full time and will become available in a month from now. The job postings are closed as of midnight, tonight. Judging by your qualifications, seniority and the way you take care of your patients, it looks to me like you could have a choice of either one … if you applied today."

Miss Hazel smiled as she looked up. She remembered the day when she was just as eager as the young nurse in front of her. It seemed like only yesterday. All she had to do was look in a mirror to be reminded that many years had passed since then.

"Now, I know both jobs won't be officially available until next month, however"—she looked down, her earrings bouncing, as she shuffled more papers on her desk—"I know they could use help now." Miss Hazel was in charge of personnel and had made her decision. If no other applicants applied by midnight, Cynthia could have the choice of either position. She had the seniority and qualifications. "We do need help now. You could be temporarily placed in either position on Monday … if you like." She half-smiled, her eyebrows rose when she spoke the last part of the sentence. Cynthia smiled back. Someone was looking out for her.

"Yes. Good! I can start Monday."

Before she had a chance to speak any further, Miss Hazel continued. "Okay, now, let's get back to the two available positions." She picked up another batch of papers and looked at them while speaking. "There is an opening at Edgehill Clinic as well as one at the Kelowna General, which is forty miles from here. The one at Edgehill is a position Four while the one in Kelowna is a position Two. That means the Kelowna posting pays more than Edgehill. If you look at the Nurse's Union Collective Agreement you'll be making"—she punched some numbers on her calculator—"uh, close to five thousand dollars a year more at Kelowna General than Edgehill." She looked up, smiling once more, knowing what job she would take if she were Cynthia.

"Besides, the shifts are better." She had already filled out the required fields on the application form for Kelowna General. She handed the paper over to Cynthia, waiting for her to read and sign.

Cynthia held the paper without looking at it. She was deep in thought. Miss Hazel wondered what the problem was.

Jobs are few and far between and now this nurse has a choice of two jobs, one being much better than the other. Miss Hazel was puzzled with the nurse's behavior.

"Uh, Miss Hazel? Would my duties be the same at both locations?"

"Yes. The Kelowna job would give you more of an opportunity for advancement than the Edgehill position, but both jobs are essentially the same."

"Yes, good. I'll take it!"

Miss Hazel could see Cynthia was getting excited. Good! She would be too—more money, more opportunity. Good for her!

Cynthia handed the form back.

"No, dear, you need to sign the form before you give it back to me."

"It's the wrong form, Miss Hazel. I want the Edgehill position."

Chapter 20

Doctor Morin walked into Gene's room, wondering how things were going with the move. One of the aides had packed Gene's personal possessions in a small box. Doctor Morin was concerned, wanting to be sure there were no issues. Most patients felt mortified at the thought of going to a long-term care facility. They would hold on to the belief that being in a hospital meant there was still hope for recovery. Gene seemed to be more than happy to leave.

They took him down to the main floor and quickly shuttled him the several miles to Edgehill. Gene was glad to be out of the building. He took several deep breaths, getting some much needed fresh air. He still had the smell of hospital antiseptic in his nostrils. Worse, he also had the smell of what's-her-name's perfume. He was happy to leave her behind. He figured he had gotten out in the nick of time, a clean getaway.

It was a sunny day. It had been close to ten weeks since the accident. As they approached Edgehill Clinic, Gene could see the grounds and the old three-story institutional building from the van window. He had pedaled past the building many times before when he was younger, never giving it a second thought. He remembered seeing nurses push patients in wheelchairs around the grounds when the weather was nice. He had always thought it to be a place where old people went to die, never thinking that he might one day call this place 'home.'

Now things had changed. Oh *how* they'd changed. He was telling himself to take it one step at a time as they pulled up in front of the main entrance.

He was quickly transported through the lobby, down several halls, finally reaching his room. He looked at the room number as he was being wheeled in. He couldn't believe it. It was C-7.

In the middle of the room was a single bed, nothing more, not even a TV. He was immediately disappointed. The aides asked if there was anything he needed before the orientation nurse came in to visit. He thought for a moment. *Yes, maybe this is the time to put on headphones and listen to music.*

They placed the iPod on his lap, turned it on and, in a few minutes, with their help, he was listening to some of his favorite stuff. He closed his eyes, trying to get into the music but couldn't. His mind drifted. He couldn't help but look out the window into what appeared to be a courtyard surrounded by the building and high chain-link fence. He could see friends and relatives visiting with some of the patients. He was thinking of Lindsey, hoping she would come and see him. He wondered if there was a chance she and he could get together again.

"Yeah, right," he muttered. "What would she want with me? She's just sorry, that's all. She's sorry for me and feels obligated, nothing more. She probably did like me at one time but … that's all changed now. Come on, man, think about it. Do you think she would be happy pushing you around in a wheelchair the rest of your life? Do you think she would love to go to work every day to support you while you sit there all fucking day, staring at the walls, shitting your pants, until she comes home from work only to have to clean and feed you? Come on, my man. Give your hat a spin. No one would want that. The best thing for me is to be here, placed in a room for the rest of my life, hopefully a short life."

The music from the headphones blared in his ears but he wasn't listening. He was becoming more and more depressed. He had hoped that moving would make things better. Maybe he could finally accept his predicament. No, that wasn't working. Looking at the patients outside made him feel worse.

He cried. He tried to stop but that proved impossible. He needed to let his emotions go. He sobbed uncontrollably. His nose ran and tears freely flowed down his cheeks. He felt so alone, so cheated with life. He hated to rely on anyone. He kept crying, realizing he wished Cynthia was in the room with him.

"What! Are you out of your fucking mind? You wish that Cynthia were here? You can't stand her. Besides, you're actually afraid of her. She gives you the creeps!" His throat was feeling sore from his one-sided conversation.

He laughed, knowing he was mixed up. What he wanted he couldn't have and what he didn't want, well, he could have.

He kept talking. "And here's the kicker, Mr. Gene." That's what she had called him this morning—Mr. Gene. He kind of liked it. "Anyhow, here's the kicker. Maybe I *do* want what I can have. Maybe Cynthia would be good for me. She's like a mother and a puppy dog all rolled up into one. She could willingly be my hands and feet—if I played my cards right."

Chapter 21

She enjoyed walking the dog, getting away from her apartment. It gave her time to think. She loved her dog like a mother a child. The dog and cat were her family. She loved animals and nature. She thought of nature as living proof of God's work.

It was early Saturday night and she was off work. She didn't know what to do with herself. She felt restless. She tried to get in as much walking with Kaleb as she could. It kept her body fairly trim although she admitted she could still lose a few more pounds. *That doesn't matter. He seems to like me just the way I am.* She had noticed him looking down her cleavage. That was good.

It started to rain a little. She liked that. Kaleb seemed to like it, too. Her mind went back to Gene. She couldn't help it. She felt they were meant for each other. She wondered what it would be like living with him. He could become a teacher, writer, or anything he desired and she would be by his side, nursing him along. They could have a little house in the country.

She also wondered what it would be like to sleep with him. Could he still do it? She had a feeling that, yes, he was still a healthy young man. He sure felt good to kiss and … that smile!

She couldn't help but smile herself as she walked down the street—Kaleb running slightly ahead of her on a leash. She was getting goose bumps thinking of him. As she turned a corner she realized Edgehill was only a block away. She had already known that. She didn't even think of where she was going when she left her apartment. She followed her feelings, trying to get closer to him.

She thought about Miss Hazel, her employer, as she approached the clinic. She smiled, remembering the look on the old girl's face when she told her she wanted the job at Edgehill instead of Kelowna. She had just blurted it out. Normally she would have chosen the better paying job. It was all because of Gene, of course.

That young man owes me big-time and I'm going to take it out of his hide. She smiled at the thought as she stood in front of the main doors to the clinic. She looked over to her left, to the side of the building. She saw a sidewalk leading toward another entrance. The sign overhead read 'Bosch Research Inc.' She wondered if they were still using test animals. They had been accused of doing so only a few months earlier.

She remembered the news. The lady she had met at the S.P.C.A. was being interviewed on TV. *What was her name? Sheila? Yes, Sheila.* She was the spokesperson for the animal rights group.

They had stormed the building, claiming Bosch Research was using not only rats but also rabbits and dogs. The allegations were investigated but, according to the courts, there was no evidence of such. She wondered if someone had paid off a few judges. She found part of that hard to believe. She knew Doctors' Klein and Morin worked there. They didn't seem to be the type to torture animals. She became ill with the thought. If they ever did anything like that to her babies she would shoot and ask questions later!

Her thoughts turned back to Gene. She smiled and wondered what room he was in. She couldn't wait to see him. She wanted to tell him the news. She planned on a surprise visit tomorrow, Sunday.

"Come on, Kaleb. Let's turn around and go back home." There was a light skip to her walk. She was in love.

Chapter 22

Gene met with Karol, the administration nurse at Edgehill Clinic. In her late fifties, she looked like the motherly type, someone with a caring heart. He supposed that was good. It appeared patients needed a lot of caring hearts here at Edgehill. On his way in he noticed many people seemingly worse off than him. It made him feel sorry for them until he caught himself, realizing he was no better off. He was now one of them.

Karol went over the many things that Edgehill could offer its residents. She talked about the pool and spa, great meals, a workshop, library and, yes, Internet service. She said the staff encouraged the residents to leave their rooms for most of the day. That's why there was no TV in his room. He would need to go to the communal TV or Internet room instead. Nothing much was in the actual patient's room except a bed and washroom. She asked if he was ready for the tour. He tried to nod. He was ready.

She brought him into a large lunchroom. He chose a hamburger and fries from the menu. He couldn't remember the last time he had eaten a burger. Karol put the mustard and mayonnaise on, holding it up to his mouth as he ate, dripping some of the mayo on his chin in the process. He didn't mind. Karol didn't intimidate him. In fact, she seemed to enjoy seeing him eat. She was busy talking about the facilities while she grabbed a napkin and dabbed at his chin.

On occasion she would wave or greet a patient as he or she passed by. To Gene, most seemed old. Several moved about with the aid of either a cane or a walker. The majority were in wheelchairs. He noticed many of the patients had vacant stares—lost.

After he took the last bite, Karol wiped his face and wheeled him down a hallway toward the pool area. Gene could immediately smell the chlorine. A few patients were with therapists playing water polo.

While he was being shown the library and woodworking shop, Karol's beeper went off. She parked him in the TV room saying she'd be back in an hour. That was fine with him. He had seen enough for now. He looked around, counting six other patients, all in wheelchairs. A couple of them were way out to lunch, some still in pajamas. A few smiled and nodded in Gene's general direction. Everyone was watching 'Wheel of Fortune.'

Shit, I wanted to watch MTV. He made a mental note to ask if there was another TV room for guys his age. *Were* there guys his age?

Later, once he was wheeled back to his room, Gene had a nurse put his headphones on. This time he really did listen to the music, badly needing to escape from what he had seen.

Around five-thirty he was brought back into the dining room for supper, sharing a table with three other 'residents.' They would be his regular dinner companions from now on. He needed to adjust to his new life, wondering if he ever could.

Looking at them made him lose his appetite. One of the patients was bent over in her wheelchair, moaning and groaning throughout the supper. Her name was Susannah. The fellow sitting next to Gene was named Karl. Karl laughed when he heard Susannah's name mentioned. He started singing 'Oh Susannah' over and over, stopping several times so he could tell Gene that his name was Karl, Karl with a capital 'K.'

It was going to take a while for him to become comfortable with Edgehill if, indeed, he ever could.

PART II

Chapter 1

Doctor Klein finished reviewing the previous night's test results at Bosch Research. He was pleased. The printout lying on his desk indicated they were on the right track. Once again they were moving forward. Doctor Schultz was clearly the leader in the research part of the program. He was doing a marvelous job.

Doctor Klein was thinking, "*The old saying is indeed true. One step back and two forward. Or is it the other way around?*" He wasn't sure. He was tired from working long hours like the rest of them here at Bosch.

He decided on having supper in the communal staff cafeteria, shared by both Bosch and Edgehill employees. Later, he walked into section C and then on to room seven, wondering how his young patient was doing. They had removed the halo apparatus from his head a few days previously. His neck muscles were healing nicely and it was time for some physiotherapy. That would start in the morning. Doctor Klein was glad Gene was a fast healer.

He was very much concerned with Gene's attitude and outlook. He knew and understood the young man's frustration. He sympathized, hoping he and his team could eventually do more for him.

Gene was in a sitting position in bed when he entered.

"Hello, Gene. Welcome to your new home."

"Hi, Doctor. Thanks."

"I hope you like it here."

Gene didn't reply. Doctor Klein kept talking. He wanted to let Gene know that he wasn't forgotten and put away. The doctor had plans for him.

"Tomorrow morning you're going to have physiotherapy. Your muscles and tendons are no doubt becoming stiff so we need to work on that, yah?"

Gene nodded, feeling the ache in his neck.

"We're going to set up a schedule for you. Several times during the week you'll be having physiotherapy. Bruce would like to come and visit you, too. Perhaps he vants to play the guitar for you once again?" He smiled as he said it, trying to make a joke. It was unusual to see the doctor display any kind of humor.

Gene couldn't help but smile back at the remark. He thought about Bruce playing in the—what was the name of that blues group? He thought about the strobe light and smiled.

"Doctor Morin wants to see you again, as well."

"Doctor?"

"Yes, Gene."

"What does my future hold?" Gene said it with a pleading voice. He cursed himself for asking that kind of question. It sounded stupid. He really wanted to ask if anything had come up. Were there any new developments that might make him better?

Doctor Klein chose to sidestep the question, the real question.

"No one knows vat his future will be of course, but I must say what we can do today in medical science would have been considered science fiction only five years ago. Without giving you any false hope, dee future holds—" he was trying hard to think of the right word. He wondered, *"What does the future hold?"*

"Dee future holds surprises, Gene. You're lucky to be here today as opposed to say twenty or even ten years ago, yah? Science has grown leaps and bounds in only dee last few years. Vat vee need to do is adopt a vait-and-zee attitude. Vee need to be patient. Who knows vat is around dee corner, yah?"

Gene nodded to himself without even realizing he was capable of such a thing. *A good answer to a difficult question, Doctor. Well done.*

Later on, just before he drifted off to sleep, he again thought about the future and what it might hold for him.

Yes, the doctor was right about the fast pace of medical and scientific developments. Maybe I could have some kind of bionic limb or limbs within a few years?

He completely forgot about Cynthia as he fell into a deep sleep.

Chapter 2

At exactly seven-thirty Sunday morning he awoke to a clatter in the hallway. It sounded like someone had dropped dishes on the floor a few doors down. They had put a clock on his wall opposite his bed. That was the first thing he looked at when he woke.

He heard voices and then laughter. He instinctively turned his head toward the door. He noticed the neck movement for the first time. It ached but he was willing to put up with the pain. He tried to experiment, turning his head left and then right, very slowly. It was tender but still felt good. He moved his head slightly forward, looking down toward his feet. He was startled. He could see the outline of an erection through the sheets—*his* erection.

How could that be? He thought he was paralyzed from the neck down. He had a thousand questions. Did that mean he was getting better? Was he healing? Was his spinal cord repairing itself? He had to find out. Who could he ask? He wasn't sure if he should ask Doctor Klein. He seemed so stuffy about that sort of thing.

He kept looking down at it, mesmerized. It didn't seem to belong to him. He couldn't feel it. He looked farther down to his feet. They didn't seem to be his, either. He tried to wriggle his toes. He could do it in his mind but nothing moved.

A nurse came into his room a minute later. The name 'Sharon' was on her name tag. He was terribly embarrassed. *God, please don't let her see me like this.*

As she spoke, he took another chance at looking down, noticing his condition had changed. Nothing was visible. She told him he had a busy day ahead. After breakfast he was going to see a physiotherapist named Harold who would be working with him for most of the morning. Gene was looking forward to it. He wanted to get his body back on the road to recovery. Maybe it wouldn't be a complete recovery but at least he would try to keep his body in shape.

He had spent many hours at the gym before the accident and didn't want to lose any more of his muscle tone. He needed his body to start working again even though he didn't have control over it. He'd be getting help. This Harold guy would bend his legs and arms, hopefully making his body flexible again. He ate quickly, anticipating the workout.

After breakfast Harold came in and introduced himself. He stood beside the bed, asking a few questions but doing most of the talking. He wasn't interested in Gene, only in himself. He was single and had been doing physiotherapy for over twenty years. Before that he was involved in the National Hockey League as a physiotherapist. He had gotten tired of being on the road so decided to settle down here in Irvine.

Gene figured Harold to be around forty years old. He was short, chunky and mostly bald. He also had a bit of a smell to him. Gene suspected Harold probably wanted to be a hockey star when he was younger but ended up being the team's physiotherapist instead. There was something about him that Gene didn't like. He caught Harold looking at some of the younger nurses. The guy was a sleaze ball.

Harold wheeled him into an exercise room. The next hour was a blur. He was rubbed and stretched and twisted. He knew that if he could feel anything, it would be pain. Harold had worked him hard, exactly what he needed.

Just before noon, Harold brought him back to his room. Cynthia was waiting for him.

What the fuck? What's she doing here?

She jumped up off the chair as they entered. She had a low cut blouse on and tight fitting pants. Gene could sense Harold staring and, for some reason, became jealous.

"Hi, Gene."

She stood there smiling with her hands clasped in front of her. It made her cleavage show even more. Gene had to smile, not only at her eagerness in seeing him but also at the greeting. He was constantly teased in school with those same two words. Were the kids really saying 'Hygiene?'

He could sense the feeling of power surge through his body. It wasn't because of the physical workout he just had. No, it wasn't that at all. It was because he knew she was hot for him. He liked it. He liked to control the play. He only wished Lindsey would feel the same.

"Hey, Cynthia. This *is* a surprise!" He meant it.

Harold had his eyes all over her as he wheeled Gene into the room, accidentally bumping the wheelchair on the corner of the bed.

She smiled, all the while focusing on Gene. "Yes, I wanted to surprise you." She had wanted to say, "You look so damned cute, glowing like that after your workout!" She held her tongue, sensing it wasn't an appropriate time to say that sort of thing, especially with that weird guy in the room.

Harold looked at Gene and winked. Gene decided right then and there that Harold was definitely a pervert.

"Well, you did that!"

"Huh?"

"You surprised me, Cyn."

She stood there, glowing. She was absolutely thrilled with what he had just called her.

Finally, after an awkward silence, Harold introduced himself. Gene had forgotten all about him. Harold kept looking at her, hanging around as if he were waiting for a tip.

Cynthia ignored him, leaned over and gave Gene a kiss on the lips. She looked deep into his eyes. It might have been a look of concern but Gene knew it was more than that. He decided to play along, thinking he could use her.

Besides, he rather enjoyed the kiss, especially with Harold staring at them. He smiled. Harold was standing behind them, no doubt looking at her ass.

Gene knew Harold was watching and listening closely so said, "I just love your company, Cyn." He just had to show off in front of Harold. Show him that even though he was a quadriplegic, women still wanted him.

She came close to fainting. She thought she was in heaven. All she heard was the word 'love' coming from those beautiful lips. *Yes Gene, I love you, too!*

Gene asked without looking at him, "Is there anything else, Harold?"

"Uh … no. I'll let the nurse know you're back here so she can bathe you."

"Thanks." He said it in a dismissive fashion.

Harold mumbled, "Nice to meet you, Cynthia," giving her another once-over before leaving.

They were alone. Cynthia ran her fingers through his hair. "Ummm, you're sweaty." She was totally excited about him saying that he loved her.

"Yeah. Harold had me working out."

"That's great, Gene." She leaned closer. She wanted to hold him, tell him how much she loved him, too, but decided not to get carried away. Besides, she had some very exciting information to share. She couldn't contain herself any longer. Hopping up and down, bouncing her breasts, she exclaimed, "Guess what. I've got some great news!"

"What?" Alarm bells went off in his head. Great news for her was probably bad news for him.

"I've got a full-time job here at Edgehill starting tomorrow." She moved a little closer, sitting on a chair, leaning forward as she spoke. She knew she was exaggerating a little. The full-time job wasn't hers just yet.

"Wow. That's great." His mind was reeling. *Did she do that for me? Maybe she's a little sicker than I thought?*

He was feeling uncomfortable, feeling smothered once more. He could smell the perfume. He found it interesting he hadn't detected it while Harold was in the room. He felt his control over her diminish. In fact, he thought she was the one who now had the control. He wondered if he should have said he 'loved' her company.

"Uh, Cynthia? Can you sit back in the chair because I smell—" He had wanted to say, "Because I smell that fucking perfume of yours," but caught himself. Instead, he said, "Because I smell … sweaty."

She looked at him, still smiling like a puppy, finally cooing, "You are so, so, sweet, Mr. Gene. Worried about what I would think of you! There's nothing to worry about. Maybe I can help the nurse bathe you?" She smiled, teasing him with the last remark.

He formed what he hoped was a smile. He was quickly getting tired of this. He had mixed feelings for her. She had crossed the line with him once more. He knew he had crossed the line with her, too, saying he loved her company and calling her 'Cyn.'

Yeah, Cyn—more like 'Sin.'

She sat up, pulling her tight blouse down, trying to tuck it into her pants. It had come out while leaning over him.

Sharon, his nurse, walked into the room just then, announcing, "Okay, Gene, time for your bath." He secretly thanked her for coming into the room and breaking this—. *This what? This stupid display of twisted affection, that's what!* He knew he was as much to blame as her.

Cynthia smiled at Sharon. She would have smiled at Osama bin Laden at that moment, she was so happy. She very much wanted to say, "That's okay. I'll be working here, soon. I can bathe him." She knew she would be overstepping her boundaries with Sharon and perhaps also with Gene. She had to be more professional or else people would soon start to talk. She didn't want to start off on the wrong foot here at Edgehill.

"Well, Gene, I'd better be going. I'm glad you're doing okay." She was worried she might do or say the wrong thing. She knew that, if she showed any feelings toward Gene, the staff would quickly find out. That might risk her chances of looking after him, of being his personal nurse in the future.

She introduced herself to Sharon, explaining she was starting work at Edgehill the next day. They chatted on a professional level for a few minutes while Gene half-listened to their conversation. When Sharon looked away, Cynthia winked at him one more time before leaving.

On the way out she wondered about the nurse. Did Sharon sense how she felt about Gene? She had to keep her emotions in check. She smiled inwardly, bursting with happiness. She couldn't help how she felt about him.

Poor Gene, lying there with no one to love him. Not any more!

Chapter 3

Harold walked over to the staff cafeteria for lunch, noticing Mr. Lincoln in his wheelchair at one of the tables. That always bothered him. He thought, *"The guy is getting worse. He always gets into one of those coughing spells, spitting up his fucking food. He's supposed to be a patient here and yet he works next door at Bosch."* Harold simply didn't like the man. He was also slightly afraid of him. Mr. Lincoln was very wealthy and rumor had it that he had some powerful friends in Washington.

Harold remembered having a discussion with that skinny nurse, Sharon, about him and his ideas. She had told him that Lincoln had little faith in the contemporary way of doing things when it came to treating injured spinal cords. Harold agreed. In fact, there was nothing that could be done except make the patient as comfortable as possible. She said Mr. Lincoln believed the government was not putting enough money into a more radical approach in research. Harold wasn't sure what she had meant by that.

She had explained. Mr. Lincoln felt bitter about the foot dragging Washington had been doing and had taken it upon himself to help fund the different programs that were needed in developing stem cell research. He felt that perhaps the cultivation of specific cells could regenerate damaged spinal cords. He was also involved in other types of research, all similar in nature.

Harold had asked her why Lincoln was so interested in injured spinal cords. Sharon replied that the answers were obvious. There were several reasons. One was because he had lost all feeling in his lower extremities over twenty years ago. Another was he had the connections and money to perhaps find a solution. As an afterthought she had added he was doing it for himself although he liked to preach it was for the good of all mankind. She continued by saying he also had a big ego and would love to have the recognition if he ever did find a solution.

Harold asked about people like Klein and Morin who worked for Bosch next door. They seemed to be too nice to be working for Mr. Lincoln and his self-interests.

Sharon said that the doctors wanted to find solutions for the good of all mankind, not only for their own interests. Doctors Klein and Morin were dedicated in helping others, not themselves. They did have their own personal motives in wanting to help patients but it was all for the common good. Lincoln was different—his interests were purely selfish, nothing more.

He still had a begrudging respect for the man even though Lincoln's purpose was self-serving. Harold hated to see the waste of human lives because of injury or disease. He thought about the young kid, Gene, and what he had to look forward to.

Mind you, he did have one hot tamale waiting for him in his room when we came back from therapy this morning. He smiled at the thought, his mind wandering.

He sat down near Mr. Lincoln with a plate full of food. He nodded toward Lincoln's general direction. Lincoln had another bout of coughing. Everyone tolerated him because of who he was. Harold still didn't like the idea of a patient eating with him.

Even though management encouraged staff to 'dine' with the residents in their cafeteria, Harold didn't want any part of it. He had a job from nine to five and he'd be damned if he'd spend his unpaid lunch hour eating with patients. Besides, he liked looking at the young nurses as they bounced in and out of the staff cafeteria.

Lincoln finally stopped coughing long enough to take a gulp from his inhaler. He maneuvered himself out of the cafeteria in his electric wheelchair and through the glass doors leading back into Bosch Research.

Harold was looking at him as he left, thinking he could see the fucker coming or going from miles away. He always had that stupid red plaid blanket covering his legs. He could see Lincoln going through the glass doors, passing by the nurse at the front desk of Bosch Research, finally entering his office just beyond.

Chapter 4

Mr. Lincoln drank a couple of glasses of water. The coughing finally subsided. He knew he didn't have long to live. Pneumonia usually set in after a few years, depending on how young and healthy you were. He was neither.

He was scheduled to meet with Klein, Morin and Schultz as well as another surgeon named Doctor Adams in a few minutes. They wanted to discuss the current situation. It looked as though things were improving. Two months earlier an important discovery had been made totally by accident at Bosch Research. He was at his desk, reflecting that most discoveries were usually accidental. This seemed to be one of those unexpected bonuses.

They were careful, doing more testing to verify, deciding not to have any news releases. Only the L-Team knew. That was short for 'Lincoln Team.' He didn't mind. In fact, he was rather proud of it. His mind went back to thinking of the discovery.

Ah yes, the discovery. It was turning into another stepping-stone for more possible successes. This latest development stemmed from a chain of events that happened many months earlier.

He had learned through experience that, if a breakthrough had been made in science, government red tape would hold the discovery up indefinitely, sometimes holding back the momentum, stifling more research. Bureaucratic policies were to be avoided at all costs if they wanted to excel. There was a lot the government didn't know. Bosch Research had, to a certain degree, gone underground.

Public pressure and corporate backstabbing were other pitfalls that had to be avoided. They needed secrecy and that's what they had. After all, everyone was playing for keeps. They were talking about a billion-dollar business—if things went right.

They also needed security. It was decided a few years earlier to have a system installed throughout the wing at Bosch. For the most part it was only an intrusion alarm. They didn't want to draw attention to themselves by having a high level security system. The intent was to keep a low profile. They did apply higher security measures, such as electronic door locks, in some of the more sensitive areas. They also had two security guards patrolling in twelve-hour shifts. Some of the windows had ancient grilles attached from the outside, going back to the days when part of the building had been used as a sanitarium. The problem at the time was keeping patients in rather than keeping people out.

The one thing concerning all of them was the animal activist group. Bosch Research had already been accused of animal abuse.

Not that long ago a group stormed through the entrance to Bosch demanding they stop their terrible experiments. Lincoln never could figure out where they had come up with that idea. He chuckled at the thought. He glanced up from his desk, thinking he heard the four doctors outside his door. "Come in. Come in!" Instead, it was Manuel, the heating and air conditioning guy.

"Meester Lincoln, I have to tell you the air conditioning unit is on its last legs. I believe that we had talked about this before, si?"

Mr. Lincoln only nodded. He had no time for such mundane issues. Besides, the temperature in the wing wasn't that warm. Manuel kept talking.

"Eets not so much thee unit, Mr. Lincoln." He paused for effect, still standing in the doorway.

"Yes. Yes! What? I'm busy, Manuel."

"Eets thee electrical panel next to the unit … in the crawl space." He put out his hands, palms up, hoping that would help him to better explain in his broken English. "There is only a one hundred amp panel feeding it and when the temperature outside gets hot, well—thee breaker trips and thee compressor stops. It then needs to be reset for thee fan." He shrugged, waiting for a response. There was none.

He continued. "I've shown Emil how to re-set everything but there needs to be new wiring."

Just then all four doctors were at the door, standing behind Manuel, waiting to enter the small, stuffy office.

"Yes. Yes. Okay, Manuel. I'll talk with Emil later. In the meantime, you do what's necessary to get this thing fixed." Emil was the older security guy who fancied himself as being a jack-of-all-trades. Mr. Lincoln was glad Emil knew what to do if the air conditioning stopped again. He'd talk to him when he came in on his regular shift later in the evening. "Leave it with me and thank you for coming out so promptly."

As Manuel walked out, the doctors entered. Three of them took their regular seats. Lincoln had to smile, thinking the human being could be such a predictable creature. Ever since they had formed a team, all three doctors claimed their own chairs in his office out of habit. Doctor Adams was the new kid on the block and was delegated to the remaining chair. He would be the last acquisition for the team. He came highly recommended.

Mr. Lincoln was all business. "I've got good news, gentlemen."

Chapter 5

Gene was back in the TV room, resting after his lunch. It had been a busy morning with Harold and then Cynthia's unexpected visit. She was going a little overboard with him but he had to admit he liked it. If anything, it was entertaining.

He wished he could sit where he wanted, get up when he wanted, grab her when he wanted, and more importantly, walk out when he wanted. He could play and use her a little but … then what? What happened when he became tired of her and she still hung around? He could picture it, her hanging around, like a puppy at his feet. Maybe she would get transferred out to another location. He mentally shrugged. He wasn't sure what was going on. He knew he should never have said he loved her company.

He knew who he really wanted. Without a doubt it was Lindsey. He was making a mental comparison between Cynthia and her, knowing that Lindsey was younger than him. He liked that. *Besides, we have … history. Uh, well that was true, if you wanted to call three or so weeks of dating 'history.'*

He was still very angry and hurt at what she had told him—"You're so cute, Gene. If only you were a little taller."

Those fucking bitches! Never mind. I still really like her. Then there's Cynthia. I've really got to think about that one. Okay, at first I couldn't stand her. I hated her perfume and her smile. As I got to know her a little better I thought maybe she was okay.

Even though he wouldn't admit it, he was only looking at what she could do for him. He knew Lindsey would soon be long gone. She wouldn't bother with an invalid but … Cynthia might. He smiled at the thought, but no, he had to admit that he became excited when he saw Lindsey, apprehensive when he saw Cynthia. She was too bold for him. She was intimidating. She was older than him and had a good profession. She was self-supporting. She was everything he wasn't.

Maybe that's what he liked about her, because his mother never …! He quickly stopped that line of thought. He'd be damned if he would compare Cynthia to the likes of his fucking mother!

He decided he wanted Lindsey but he'd still play the game with Cynthia. He had nothing to lose and, anyhow, it was out of his control. He laughed, realizing he was still pissed with Lindsey making the remark about him being short.

Isn't it funny? It doesn't matter anymore. It wouldn't matter if I were eight fucking feet tall! It just doesn't matter.

He looked around at the other patients in the TV room, thinking, *"Some new faces?"* Most of them were old fucks who had suffered strokes or whatever. He could smell one of them. How disgusting. He wished he were older so he could die sooner. He thought of all the years he had left, stuck in a wheelchair. He knew he was still too young to die from natural causes.

Today they had decided to watch the fucking news. How boring! Same old shit. This time some pro-choicer got shot in his home a few miles away. The news continued, explaining the suspected radicals were becoming bolder and more aggressive. Gene knew all about pro-choice thanks to his mother. Thank God for his sake abortion was illegal back then or he wouldn't be around today.

News of the abortion protest rally in front of Irvine General was next. People were screaming at each other. Two groups were involved, the pro-life and pro-choice camps. Things started to get out of hand just before the police arrived. Several scuffles had broken out. The cops quickly got the situation under control.

The female newscaster commented it was the second time this year Irvine General had been targeted by the pro-life group. On the same topic, about protesters in Irvine, she reported Bosch Research had also been in the news not too long ago when an animal rights group stormed the building claiming the company had used lab animals for testing purposes.

She wound up by saying, "No evidence of animal abuse was ever found. According to Sheila Stringer, a spokesperson for the animal rights group, Bosch Research would pay dearly for their moral and ethical sins if they were found to be in violation of animal abuse. Bosch Research had no comment on the allegations.

"From the hot spot, here in Irvine, this is Nancy Inaba for NBC News."

Chapter 6

After Lincoln explained the good news of how Bosch research was moving forward in its discoveries at an exponential rate, Doctor Klein had some news as well. His wasn't so good. He was sweating; part of the reason was because it was warm in the room. The other reason was because he was upset.

"Gentlemen, I don't vant to be an alarmist but I have some disturbing news." Everyone gave him a questioning look.

"Between us und only us, I vant you to know"—his voice was getting thick from his accent—"I received a death threat in the mail this mornink!"

There was a hush. Nobody spoke for a second or two and then everyone tried to speak at once. Mr. Lincoln took over.

"Joseph, what did it say? Do you have it with you?"

"Yah, let me read it to you."

Doctor Klein opened the letter, his hands shaking as he began to read. "We are watching you closely. You are nothing but a killer of babies. You and your staff. Beware! We wish you death, Doctor Joseph Klein."

There was silence. Joseph put the letter down on the desk. The words had been cut out of various magazines and pasted on a blank piece of paper.

Doctor Klein asked, while pointing to the note, "Well, what do you make of dis, gentlemen?" He was looking for support. He felt terrible. It was an ethical question that had always troubled him. Should a mother have the right to end her child's life? His heart said no, but there were always extenuating circumstances.

When he first became a doctor, he had pledged to save lives and was rather naïve in his thinking. He still wanted to save lives. This time it was saving the life of perhaps a young would-be mother who had been raped by her father or brother or stranger and had become pregnant. She could possibly have another chance. He shrugged. He didn't want to think about it anymore.

Doctor Morin was deep in thought as well, finally speaking. "Joseph. It sounds like the work of a nut-case. I wonder how many other doctors will be getting the same letter. I would suggest we keep this to ourselves, especially at this time." He looked around the room. Everyone nodded. They did not need any attention right now.

Doctor Schultz spoke up. "I think we should keep our eyes and ears open. Perhaps, as you said, Henry, other doctors have received similar threats. I know I haven't—yet."

Mr. Lincoln was next. "Yes, let's all be careful. Joseph, do you want to stay here for a few days instead of going home? Just in case? You spend most nights here anyhow." Doctor Klein nodded. He didn't have anything to go home to. This would now be his home.

Mr. Lincoln took a sip of water and continued. "Okay, so they are accusing you of doing abortions. Obviously they are watching Irvine General. Someone is leaking information. Perhaps it would be best if you stay away from Irvine for a few weeks. You only have five or six patients there, correct? We can shuffle things around a little. We can always use you here. It would be safer for you. You wouldn't need to travel back and forth. You could work at Edgehill in the mornings instead of Irvine. I can fix it for you."

Joseph Klein agreed. He smiled inwardly. Mr. Lincoln could always 'fix' things—he had connections. He would miss working with the staff at Irvine. He liked being a doctor, a healer, but ... perhaps it was time for a change. He was afraid someone would shoot him. It was all very unnerving.

All five got back to talking about the advancements they had been making with the research. The death threat wasn't far from their thoughts. When the meeting adjourned several minutes later, the four doctors left Mr. Lincoln's office. He sat alone at his desk, pondering. He didn't take the threat lightly, especially in light of the recent shooting of a pro-choicer.

He unlocked his bottom desk drawer and carefully pulled out the small .22 caliber handgun. He took out a box of shells and loaded all six chambers. He put the safety on, slipping the gun into a deep side pocket in his wheelchair. He pledged to carry it with him because of the death threat on Doctor Klein. He hoped he wouldn't need to use it.

He made a phone call to Mr. Whitman, telling him it was time for the visit. After hanging up, he sat for a minute, contemplating. He heard the air-conditioning unit hum once more. It jogged his memory. He made a mental note to talk to Emil later.

Finally, he wheeled himself to the side door of his office and sliced his security card through the reader. He heard a click as the door's deadbolt unlocked. He pushed his way through, heading down the hallway toward what they fondly called the 'McDonald' room.

Chapter 7

Gene soon tired of watching the news. He looked around, trying to get a nurse's attention so he could leave. He slowly turned his head, feeling his neck creak. It was sore but getting better. He could see Bruce walking up behind him from the reflection in the window.

"Hey, Bruce."

"Wow, you've got eyes in the back of your head, my man! How are you doing?"

"Okay, I guess."

"This is better than Irvine, right? I mean, look around you. There are some nice looking nurses here, right?" He winked.

"What are you doing here?"

"I was in the neighborhood so thought I'd drop by."

"Hey, that's great." Gene looked at him questioningly. "Uh, Bruce? Can I talk to you?"

"Yeah, sure, talk to me, my man." He had his hands turned out toward Gene.

"Can we go somewhere … private?"

"Tell you what. Let me wheel you out to the garden, okay? It's a beautiful day." He didn't want to wheel Gene out through the front doors because of the security check. Security was looking for any type of weapon or bomb. Everyone was on high alert since the shooting of the pro-choicer.

They left the building through a side door used for staff and patients, entering a fenced garden area. Several other patients were there with visitors, enjoying the sunshine. There was a fountain in the center. Bruce wheeled Gene up near it and sat down on a bench facing him.

Bruce prompted him by asking, "Isn't this nice?"

"Yeah, it is. It feels good to be outside, away from all those old fuckers."

Bruce laughed while slapping his hand on his leg. "Yup, well spoken, my man. I bet you none of them know who Mick Jagger is, right?" They both chuckled.

"So, Bruce, I've got a question for you. It's a medical question and I don't know how to ask Doctor Klein so I thought you might be able to answer it for me, okay?"

Bruce wasn't a medical doctor. He was thinking about the question. Was it about Gene's condition? If he was wondering about walking again, well, he couldn't answer that one. It would be best to ask Klein.

"Okay, shoot. Ask me."

"I, uh, looked down at myself this morning you know, and well, I was … uh, stiff."

He smiled. "Well, Gene, that's normal. You haven't moved your neck for so long that, yeah, it would be stiff!" He wondered about the question, thinking the kid should know better.

Gene saw the puzzled expression on Bruce's face and laughed.

"No. No. No! You know, I was … *stiff*!"

Bruce was completely taken by surprise.

"Oh. *That* stiff." They both laughed. "I'm sorry, Gene. I guess I didn't expect that kind of question. Hey, that's good, right?"

"Well, that's what I'm trying to ask you. Is that normal? I mean, with my condition. Is that normal? Am I getting better? Am I getting feeling down there? Like—what's going on? Nobody told me about this. I'm not sure what to make of it."

Bruce looked at him and nodded. "Yes, it could be confusing. I've got an idea. Let's go back in and get on the Internet, all right? I know a few great sites that can give you a better answer than I can. I'm not trying to avoid answering you but it's best to get the complete and correct picture as to what is going on."

Gene nodded. Bruce was up in a flash, wheeling him back into the building. Gene thought of the nickname 'Warp' once more.

Within minutes they were on-line, hoping to get their answer. They both read the Web page. It described in great detail how intimacy had little to do with the actual sex act compared to caring touch. The act of loving was so much more powerful than raw sex and could be demonstrated in many different ways. Once the ability to perform sex was lost, the focus changed, often to a more intimate and fulfilling experience.

Gene wasn't impressed with the site, however, it did answer part of his question—would the sense of touch be enhanced elsewhere when lost from other parts of the body? He still wanted an answer to the immediate question concerning his stiffness. Bruce sensed his annoyance so suggested they check out another site. They finally found what they were looking for.

This site again reiterated the strong emotions associated with love rather than with the actual sex act. It was possible for the sense of touch to be transferred and sometimes enhanced when limited or eliminated elsewhere in the body.

They clicked on the bulletin board and read posted notes from several male quadriplegics, all indicating that it was indeed possible for arousal. Some needed various drugs in order to overcome the physical restrictions, but there were moments when they and their partners did achieve sexual climax.

He thought back to when he had kissed Lindsey last and how beautiful it had been. He couldn't remember it ever being so good. He had wondered at the time if his sense of touch on his face and lips had been enhanced because he had lost it elsewhere. From what he was reading, that could very well be.

While Gene was thinking that he was finally getting some answers, Bruce was also thinking, "*The poor kid. That should be the least of his worries.*"

Chapter 8

They logged off and headed back outside to the garden. Gene had some time to digest all the information and was getting depressed. He wasn't so much concerned about the erection and sex as he was with the hope of getting better. He had thought it was a sign he was slowly getting some feeling back. No, that wasn't the case. It was probably similar to his heart still beating or his bowels still working. It was simply another involuntary body function—nothing more.

They were in the garden, sitting in the sun by the water fountain, both deep in thought. Gene finally spoke. He was close to tears. "That's all it was, just an involuntary action." He was whining. He hated the sound of his voice. He was falling apart. He had never known that side of himself. He had always thought of himself as a tough guy, not a wimpy kid who seemed to cry all the time.

Bruce looked at him for a moment while rubbing his chin, sitting with his legs crossed. Finally he said, "Yeah, involuntary action, speaking of which, listening to this fountain makes me want to go pee."

Gene had to smile through his tears. Bruce was a funny guy. This time Bruce wasn't laughing. He looked at Gene very closely, very seriously.

"What? Why are you looking at me like that?" Gene was becoming apprehensive. Bruce didn't say a word, still staring at Gene. He seemed to stare through him.

"Bruce? Bruce! What is it? What are you doing?"

He came back, focusing on Gene as if this were the first time he had noticed him. "Look, Gene ..." He uncrossed his legs and leaned toward him, rubbing his hands together. "How bad do you want to—? Ah, let me rephrase the question." He leaned back, straightening, holding his hands out, palms up, thinking for a minute. It was clear he was agitated. He couldn't sit still. Gene was both anxious and angry. He had no idea what Bruce was thinking, let alone what he was trying to say.

Bruce moved closer until his face was only inches away, speaking in a low and self-righteous voice. "Look, I work closely with the doctors. It wasn't a fluke that I was called in to talk to you. They wanted me to. I'm hired by both Irvine General *and* Bosch Research. Okay? I'm the best in the field. I don't pull any punches. I say what I have to and it works for me. Most people like me and I like most people."

Gene was slightly dumbfounded. "Yeah, so what are you getting at?"

"Here's what I'm getting at. I'll tell you but I want you to know that I will deny what I've said if this ever gets out, okay? You got it?" His voice had an angry edge to it.

Gene felt a cold sweat run down his body even though it wasn't possible. He was wondering what Bruce was talking about. He had never seen this side of him, so serious and intense. He trusted him. He knew he was a friend.   He was puzzled as to what was going on. With his eyes wide open, he nodded "yes," to the question, unaware of the pain in his neck.

"Okay, now here's the deal." Bruce paused, lowering his voice. He chose his words very carefully. "I've been asked," he was whispering, "to see if you would consider exploring some ... possibilities, okay?"

"What the fuck are you talking about?" Gene had an alarmed look on his face. "What the fuck is going on?" He was getting agitated. He raised his voice.

"Shhh. Calm down, man! Don't make a scene here." Bruce quickly looked around. No one was close enough to hear.

Gene wanted to scream, wanting to yell, "What are you talking about, telling me not to make a scene." He wished he could grab Bruce and shake him. Before he could get another word out, Bruce began whispering again.

"Like I said, there are some possibilities for you to explore. I can't say much more right now, okay? I was asked, when the time was right, to approach you with a proposition."

"Like, do you mean that I can be healed? They can operate? Or, maybe there are new techniques? I could have a bionic arm? What? *What*?"

"Shhh, please, Gene! Keep it down, okay? Work with me here, all right?"

Gene's eyes were glazed. He was looking past Bruce, his mind racing. He could see himself throwing a football. Throwing it farther than he could have ever dreamed possible because ... he now had a bionic arm!

"Gene. Gene!"

"Huh? What?"

"Listen to me, okay?" Bruce's face was beside his as he whispered into his ear.

"Yeah, sure."

"Okay. First of all, promise me that you won't talk to *anybody* about our conversation, okay? Promise?"

"Yeah, I promise, Bruce. I promise. You know that I would do anything man, anything for another chance. Please believe me. Please!" Gene was crying, pleading. "Please, Bruce, I'll be good. I'll do what you say. I just want another chance. I'll be happy with anything that you can give me. Please, give me another chance!"

Bruce was becoming embarrassed with the emotional display as he pulled his head back. He looked at Gene, watching him break down in front of him. He couldn't fault the kid. Instead, he felt sorry for him. He'd given him a small ray of hope and now the boy was turning into putty.

"It's okay, Gene. We'll work together on this. It's our secret." He got up off the bench and squatted beside Gene, his hand on Gene's head, brushing his hair, trying to soothe him.

Some of the patients and visitors were looking their way. Bruce wasn't concerned. He knew that kind of outburst happened all the time, especially around here.

"Now listen to me, Gene. Let's leave this alone for a while. We'll talk about it later." He spoke in a soft voice, trying to calm him down. Gene nodded. Bruce wiped away his tears for him. His heart went out to the young man, wondering if he should have said anything.

He stood up and wheeled him back to his room, neither of them speaking. Gene was both puzzled and shocked. He was also starting to get very excited about the possibilities. He had a million questions to ask but had promised Bruce they would not talk about any of this until the right time. He needed to be patient. There was nothing more to be said.

Bruce hooked up his headphones for him and selected the songs Gene wanted to listen to. "I'll talk to you as soon as I know anything else, okay? That's a promise." Bruce left the room a minute later and quickly made his way toward Bosch Research. He was feeling very uncomfortable, wondering if he had said more than he should have. He needed to talk to Mr. Lincoln.

Gene sat in his room with the lights out, his headphones blaring, but he wasn't listening to the music. He was lost in thought, his mind drifting miles away, throwing one football after another, farther than he had ever done before.

Chapter 9

It was close to four o'clock when Lindsey came in. He instinctively tried to reach up and remove his headphones. He caught himself. He had forgotten where and what he now was. Lindsey removed the headphones for him.

"Did I surprise you?"

"Did you ever!"

She leaned over and gave him a kiss on the lips. He wanted to put his arms around her. After what seemed like an eternity she pulled her head back. They looked at each other, both smiling. The intensity of her kiss felt very powerful to him.

"Hey, can I wheel you around in this thing?" She decided to keep things light. Her feelings had changed for him. She wasn't sure if it was pity or—? She had to admit she did feel sorry for him. The way he talked to her on their last visit wasn't the Gene she once knew. He sounded like he had been pleading with her. The balance of power had shifted.

"Yeah, take me out of here. There's a beautiful courtyard and fountain out back. Let me show you the way." She wheeled him out toward the garden.

By chance, Cynthia was walking fifty feet behind them. They hadn't seen her. She had flowers and a Teddy bear in her hands. She looked at their backs, hearing them laugh. She quickly made an about-face, her vision becoming blurred. She started to run down the hallway. Near the end, she noticed a trashcan. She threw away the flowers and stuffed bear. She knew she was going to be sick. She quickly found the ladies room.

Lindsey told Gene how she had gone through a security checkpoint, similar to one in an airport, at Edgehill's main entrance. "Apparently, some nut shot a pro-choicer yesterday so security is now elevated."

Gene said he had seen it on the news. While she was talking, he wanted more than ever to tell her about his visit with Bruce. He wanted to let her know what happened and that perhaps he had a chance at—*at what, at being somewhat normal again?* He wasn't quite sure. He was sure that being given any chance was at least a step in the right direction.

She wheeled him to the same spot where he and Bruce had been only a few hours before. Sitting together, they both looked at the fountain, feeling the sun on their face. She needed to talk, wondering how to begin. He solved her problem by speaking first.

"Uh, Lindsey?"

"Yes?"

He wanted to tell her about Bruce's visit but stopped short, remembering his promise to keep it confidential. "Uh, thank you for coming to visit me."

She smiled and took his hand. He wished he could have felt his hand in hers. She told him she was starting a job at Barney's Grocery. She was going to work as a cashier for the rest of the summer. She wanted to save enough money for university.

"University? Where did that idea come from?"

"I've always wanted to become a nurse, Gene, a registered nurse." She told him she was planning on attending a university several hundred miles away this fall. Gene felt like he had been slapped. He wanted to ask, "What about us?" but quickly realized there probably wasn't an 'us.'

He was getting angry, thinking about those fucking bitches. They didn't give a fuck about anyone else. He wondered why she hadn't told him this before. She couldn't care less about him. He didn't blame her. He told himself he was nothing.

He pretended to listen, feeling his cheeks turn red. He wanted to slap the stupid bitch but couldn't. He felt she had been leading him on. He broke his fucking neck for her and for what—for her to go to university? He knew he was out of control. He had to get a grip but talked himself out of it, thinking, *"Get a grip? What for? Who cares? This is how I really feel so why should I try to hide it?"*

"Gene. What's wrong?" She was looking at him with a stupid expression.

He thought of what he wanted to say. *"What's wrong? I'll fucking tell you what's wrong. I really care for you, you stupid bitch. I risked my life to show you and you couldn't care less, could you? You're so fucking involved in going to some university. Did you ever think about me? Did you ever think about us?"*

No, he didn't say a word, except, "Take me back in. I don't feel very good."

"But Gene, what's wrong?"

Now she was starting to sound like his mother. That did it!

He spoke slowly and loudly. "I said take – me – back – in – the – fucking – building!"

Some of the same people who were outside when Bruce was with him were still there. A few looked his way. He glared back, daring them to say something. They all looked away.

She did as she was told, knowing full well why he was angry. She didn't know how else she could break it off except by telling him some story about going to university. She had hoped they could still be friends but that was up to him. She had to admit she did love the way he could treat her. He could take control like he was doing right now and she didn't mind one bit.

She wheeled him into his room. They looked at each other. He was very angry. She was going to speak but thought better of it. Instead, she turned and walked out.

Gene thought, *"Just like my mother did, turning her back and walking out. Go, you stupid whore. Go!"*

Chapter 10

Cynthia couldn't keep her mind off Gene or his girlfriend. She had gone home after being sick in the ladies room. She went straight to bed. Kaleb and Savannah were with her. She hugged them as she sobbed. They were her best friends. They never gave her any trouble, always there beside her. She loved animals, especially those two.

She hated men. They wanted just one thing. No one ever cared about her. She thought perhaps Gene would be different, especially with his situation. She wondered how long he and that girl were friends. She lay with her eyes closed, fantasizing about stalking her, following her at night, and—and what? She wasn't sure. She had to think about it. She did have her small hand gun in the drawer and knew how to use it. Maybe she could force that bitch—. She stopped herself.

No! Don't say that word. Don't swear. It's not nice. She kept thinking. *Force that woman into an alley and then shoot her? No, maybe I should shoot him, instead? Yes! That's a better idea. I could walk right into his room and bam! No, that wouldn't work. I'd kill him but he isn't worth the jail time. I can't get caught.*

Maybe take him out past the loading docks. Shoot him there? No, I would most certainly be seen wheeling him around just before the shooting. It would be easier to kill the girlfriend.

Why hadn't he told me? Why was he leading me on? Didn't he say that he loved me? She asked the questions but already knew some of the answers. He hadn't led her on—had he? She played it back in her mind.

I was the one that jumped all over him, but … he looked so sweet and helpless. Not only that, but he has a bit of an attitude. I like that fire in him. I love the way he calls me 'Cyn.' Maybe I could still be with him. After all, I'm sure he and the girlfriend aren't doing it. Maybe she just feels sorry for him and that's why she came to visit. I would treat him right. I could look after him. It's only a matter of time before he sees how good it can be together.

She decided that, no matter what, she would still try to be with him. "After all," she told herself, "I love him." She closed her eyes, dreaming of a time when he would be totally in her care. They would have a nice small house together, perhaps in the country. She could have it all. She dreamed of the four of them, Kaleb, Savannah, Gene and her, living together happily ever after.

Chapter 11

Monday morning found Doctor Klein sitting in his usual spot. He was in Mr. Lincoln's office along with Doctors Morin, Adams and Schultz. They were listening to Bruce Whitman as they sipped their coffee. They had already gone through one pot. Doctor Schultz had just finished pouring more water into Mr. Coffee, getting ready to make another, listening as Bruce spoke.

He had taken it upon himself to make the coffee. Watching Bruce speak made him somewhat dizzy. He shook his head as he listened.

The man can't keep still when he's talking, moving his arms and legs while he gets up and sits down and gets up and—.

"So, without saying more than I needed to, I left Gene after suggesting that something could possibly be done to help him. I understand what we need to do here." He looked at Mr. Lincoln as he spoke. "This is an extremely touchy situation but I think it went as well as it possibly could. He's had nearly twenty-four hours to think about it. What we now need is a follow-up visit." He turned, looking at Doctor Klein.

Mr. Lincoln cleared his throat. "Joseph, are you ready to speak with him today?"

Doctor Klein knew what he was referring to. He felt like an Olympic runner who had been passed the torch. Now he had to continue with the race. "Yes, as vee discussed several days ago, our plan is now in motion. Vee have to be extremely careful. Fortunately, he is eighteen years old so is of legal age to sign dee appropriate forms if ... he is agreeable."

Everyone realized that 'signing the forms' was only a figure of speech. He would be asked to sign with a special pen he would hold in his mouth. The signature would be notarized in the process.

Doctor Klein continued. "He's also young enough to benefit if the procedure works. The trouble, of course, is not saying too much and yet describing dee situation as fully as possible. The fact is, vee have to be very careful in explaining the circumstances without leaving ourselves vulnerable and exposed."

They all nodded in agreement as he stood up, pressing onwards. "The key word is 'receptive.' We are not surprised by his initial reaction." He smiled as he spoke. "Who wouldn't react dat way? I tink dat you," his accent was starting to kick in as he looked at Bruce, "did a marvelous job in a most difficult situation, yah?

"You've got dee young man's trust. It was perfect the way it was handled, especially when he wanted to confide in you about his, ah, stiffness." He raised his eyebrows while looking at all four of them. Everyone was smiling.

"So, now my plan is to communicate to him dee possibility that dair might be a future, a better future for him. Again, let us see how receptive he is, yah?"

Everyone nodded in agreement. They would all be notified later on as to how it went. Bruce was to stand by and, if need be, do a follow up visit. This had been well thought out several months before they had ever met Gene.

Mr. Lincoln took his hands out from under his blanket saying, "Very well, Joseph. Is there anything else anyone would like to add?" He coughed. They waited patiently until he was done.

Doctor Schultz spoke next, holding a fresh cup of coffee. "Gentlemen," he paused, gathering his thoughts. "I believe that both the team members and the … uh … situation is in perfect harmony. Uh … what I mean is …," he was fumbling, searching for the right words. "We still don't need to commit ourselves." He continued, his voice becoming stronger. "We can deny everything if the patient doesn't agree to our offer. The timing however is perfect and the members of the team have all been briefed. Everyone is waiting to see how the next few days will turn out."

He made eye contact with each person as he summed up his thoughts, making sure they all understood what he was saying. "This might become the perfect window of opportunity for everyone involved. Our side is ready. Let's see how the candidate feels about it."

Doctor Morin leaned forward in his chair. He, too, looked at each person in the room, one by one, as he began to speak. He looked at Doctor Schultz first and explained.

"There are no 'sides,' Doctor Schultz. Mankind is in this together." He raised his eyebrows and paused. Doctor Schultz started to interrupt him but Doctor Morin cut him off by raising his hand. "No, let me speak. We are not here to do anything against anybody's will. You're inferring that 'our side' is ready contradicts that statement. Now, we all know you didn't mean it that way—but we need to be very careful in choosing our words, not only amongst ourselves but also with the rest of the team members.

"Another thing we must be careful of is appearing too eager. Yes, we are ready to begin but we need to make sure our candidate is comfortable with all of this. After all, he *is* the patient. We cannot hide anything from him once he agrees but we do need to do it in carefully planned stages. I know we've discussed this again and again but when it comes to the real thing, well—" he paused, looking at Mr. Lincoln for a second and then shrugged. He finished by saying, "It can easily backfire if we are not careful."

Doctor Schultz was getting tired of Morin's preaching. They all knew the rules and, yes, he had to agree that he did indeed slip up with the 'our side is ready' comment but everyone knew what he had really meant. He thought Morin could be so self-righteous at times. He stopped, realizing that everyone, including himself, was getting edgy.

They adjourned a few minutes later. Doctor Klein was deep in thought, thinking about his young patient. He decided he would wait and discuss the situation with Gene after the physiotherapist had visited. Physical exercise had a way of easing the mind, removing frustration and anger.

Chapter 12

Gene had finished breakfast but was still at the table thinking about Lindsey. He knew he was being foolish in dreaming about her. He should have been deep in thought about the possibilities that Bruce had alluded to yesterday. His mind was blank with that one. It was on overload. He couldn't go there. He was afraid of putting too much hope in what Bruce had said and then becoming very disappointed if things didn't pan out.

Instead, he turned his attention toward Lindsey, wondering if he really was in love with her, telling himself that she was only a girl. *Who needs that kind of shit?* Deep down he knew he wouldn't mind 'that kind of shit,' if it were reciprocated.

That was the problem. She treated him like someone who wasn't important to her. It hurt even more because she did it without realizing it. He had to get her out of his mind. Again, he thought it to be one of those paradoxes in life— what you can't have you want and what you can have, you don't want.

Had it been only several weeks ago when he was rather indifferent to her? Now, because he was physically vulnerable, she looked at him with pity and he looked at her with—desperation?

He heard the moaning again so looked to his right. The woman was staring at the wall across the table from him. He tried to remember. *What was her fucking name? Not that it mattered. Oh yeah, Susannah.*

To him, she looked old. He guessed she had to be around forty. Her hands were in her lap, all twisted. Her mouth was open, drool running down her chin. It was a low deep moan. He wondered what her problem was. Was she like that since birth? She probably never had a chance. He couldn't help but think he was so lucky. It could have been worse. He caught himself. *What the fuck am I lucky about? I'm fucking paralyzed!*

He whispered, "Get that through your thick fucking skull, Mr. Gene. You are paralyzed! Don't ever forget that."

He looked over at her again. Thank God he wasn't in such bad shape, at least not yet. Maybe when he got old like her he would be in the same predicament. Then, there was his buddy, Karl, beside him, fucking Karl with a capital 'K!'

He started thinking, wondering if he really was lucky, all things considered. After all, maybe there was hope for him. He wanted more information from anybody about this thing Bruce had talked about. He knew he had to do what was required in order to regain some semblance of normality. Who wanted to sit here at breakfast and listen to some old broad moan?

A minute later, Harold, the scumbag, walked in. "Hey, Gene. You about ready for some torture?"

Gene smiled a little and nodded. He needed to get his anxiety out. Yes, he was ready for the torture, more than ready.

Off they went to the exercise room. Minutes later he could feel the sweat on his face as they exercised on the mats. They worked as a team. Gene told him he wanted to get his heart pumping again. He wanted a good workout.

During a break, Harold decided to do a little fishing. "So, I hear that hot tamale is starting work here today." He had read the job-posting announcement on the Union bulletin board just that morning.

Gene stared at him, wondering what he was talking about.

"You know—your girlfriend!"

Gene wondered if Harold was talking about Lindsey and had she gotten a job here at Edgehill. He slowly nodded when it occurred to him that Scumbag was talking about Cynthia. He hadn't thought about her since Lindsey came to visit yesterday. He was becoming annoyed with Harold. He didn't like the way he was talking.

"She's *not* my girlfriend."

Harold thought, *"My, my, my, aren't we testy. All right, Mr. Schmuck, if she ain't your girl I'm going to have me a little bit of fun."*

"Uh, sorry, Gene. I just assumed. I thought you two were an item."

"Well, we're not."

There was silence. Harold hoped Gene would say a little more but he didn't. Harold went back to thinking about Cynthia, how he would love to jump her bones. She was a little chunky with nice big tits. That was perfect for him. He was going to make his move. After all, what woman could resist him? He smiled.

Gene was thinking of her as well. He was also wondering why he reacted the way he did to Scumbag. He almost felt like he would be cheating on Lindsey if Cynthia came into the picture. No, with Cynthia it was different. He had no real feelings for her. He just wanted to give her enough so she would stay interested in him. He could maybe use her down the road. Besides, Lindsey was now history. She wasn't worth it. He could repeat that last part in his mind a thousand times but it didn't matter. He was still hurt by her.

They went back to doing the exercises. The workout was more intense than ever. He was angry with both Lindsey and Scumbag. He hated Lindsey. He hated women. He hated all of them. They gave a man nothing but pain and misery. You could never please them.

His anger had Harold sweating. He was lifting and lowering Gene's legs on the mat again and again while Gene told him to go faster. Gene was looking at him, thinking, *"That fat son-of-a-bitch needs to lose fifty fucking pounds."*

Harold was looking back at him, thinking, *"I'll show the kid a thing or two. I'm going to stretch that fucker's limbs more than they've ever been stretched before. It's too bad he can't feel any pain."*

Thirty minutes later they both lay on the mats, exhausted. It felt good. Harold was still puffing. He finally got up and wiped his face with a towel. He grabbed another and wiped Gene's face. He reached over for a bottle of water and stuck a straw in it. He pulled Gene up into a sitting position, holding his arms, offering him the water. Gene took a long drink, feeling his neck muscles ache. It was a good ache. He moved his head up and down, turning it slightly left and right. He was still extremely limited in his movements but each day seemed to be getting a little better.

Within the hour he was in a special bathtub being scrubbed by a male nurse. He looked in the mirror, happy with what he saw. The exercise made him look healthy.

After he had lunch and was ready to be moved to the TV room, Doctor Klein dropped by. "Gene, how did Harold treat you this morning?" He sat down on a chair beside Gene as he spoke.

"Good, Doctor. Yes, really good! I'm glad that Scum—uh, I mean Harold, worked me hard. I'm also finding that my neck isn't so stiff and sore anymore."

"Good. The swelling is almost all gone."

There was an awkward silence. Doctor Klein was never good at opening up a delicate subject so instead asked if he could take Gene out to the fountain for a breath of fresh air.

The alarm bells went off in Gene's head. He thought, *"Okay, here it is. The doctor is going to do some 'splainin' to me."*

For some weird reason he was thinking about the 'I Love Lucy' reruns and how Ricky would always say, "Lucy! You got some 'splainin' to do." Maybe it was an escape mechanism because he knew this talk with the doctor would be the most important one he would ever have in his entire life.

Chapter 13

Gene felt it surreal—being wheeled down the hallway, going through the doors to the garden, the sun on his face. He was in hyper-aware mode, his mind taking it all in, even the sound of the crickets in the background. His senses were totally in tune with the world. He could feel the adrenalin kick in. He found himself breathing fast, telling himself to slow down.

Doctor Klein wasn't aware of any of this. He was lost in his own thoughts. He sat across from Gene on the now familiar bench, the same bench that Lindsey and Bruce sat on only yesterday. Gene could have sworn it had been months ago.

Doctor Klein nonchalantly looked around. He made sure they were far enough away so no one could hear them. He looked at the fountain, taking in a deep breath before beginning. "I know you're wondering what this is all about, yah?"

Gene nodded. The doctor, sitting the way he did, reminded Gene of a spy movie—two spies sitting together at a park bench, both pretending they didn't know each other while they spoke. Gene wondered if there was anything illegal going on. *Why the cloak-and-dagger routine?*

"Well, perhaps Mr. Whitman, uh, I mean Bruce, left you rather puzzled, yah?" The doctor realized he was fudging with the conversation and needed to get to the point. He still wasn't looking at Gene.

Finally, after another minute of silence, while leaving the question hang, Doctor Klein turned his head and looked directly at him. "You know, Gene, I've been involved with dis kind of work for years. I mean, being a doctor, and being a good doctor! My goal is to help patients, to help them enjoy a better quality of life. Sometimes I can cure them … sometimes I can't." He paused, looking away, planning on what to say next.

He swallowed hard, turning back towards Gene. He leaned forward as he continued. "Many tings have changed since I first started as a doctor. In fact, some tings are changing so quickly it's difficult to keep up, yah?" Without waiting for a response, he pushed on. "For example, the lab where I work—Bosch Research." He stopped, again thinking, trying to better compose what he needed to say.

"Yes, Bosch Research. Well, vee have gone forward with many new developments. New possibilities! Each new discovery building from dee last one, yah?"

Gene was still breathing fast, feeling the perspiration on his brow. He knew he needed to slow down a notch but couldn't. He was waiting for the bomb to drop. He was not sure what kind of bomb, but *"Oh yes,"* he thought, *"there definitely is a bomb coming my way."*

"Dee trouble we are having is—vee need to be very careful." He was waving his finger at Gene as he spoke, as if he were lecturing him. Perhaps he was.

"Vee need to be careful of our competitors and … other tings as well."

He let the last part of the sentence hang—allowing Gene to consider what he had really meant by saying 'other tings as well.' Joseph Klein was becoming slightly flustered because he couldn't explain any more, at least not at this time. He looked around to make sure they were still out of earshot. Gene didn't think the doctor would make a very good spy.

Doctor Klein was satisfied with their location. They were far enough away from prying ears. It was now time for him to ask his patient some very serious questions.

"Uh, Gene? Are you following me with dis?"

Gene hesitated in answering, his mind on the movies, thinking of a spy thriller. He was escaping from reality. He couldn't afford to do that right now. He focused, getting back to the question.

"I'm not sure. I don't know what this all means. Can I be cured? Is that it? That's what I really want, Doctor. I know it's probably impossible to be fully cured but maybe partially cured? Get me out of here, please. Get me out of here!" It was all becoming too much for him. He sobbed, grasping at straws. He was a desperate young man.

"Uh, Gene. It's all right, yah? Please, settle down and let me ask you a few questions, yah?"

Gene nodded, feeling tears run down his cheeks. He took a deep breath.

"Okay, now—dis is very important. I vant you to tell me if you tink you can keep this all confidential." He had wanted to ask if Gene could keep a secret but that sounded too sneaky, too juvenile. He chose the word 'confidential' instead, like they had planned many weeks earlier.

Gene nodded, not feeling the stiffness in his neck.

Doctor Klein said, "No, Gene, you must *tell* me your answer."

"Yes, I can keep this confidential."

"Good! You must realize sometink here." He was again pointing his finger at Gene as he raised his voice. "Vee are not playing a game. You are not to discuss dis with anyone, yah?" He looked at Gene with such intensity that Gene could feel himself squirm even though he couldn't move. He felt as though he were being scolded. Tears were running down his cheeks.

"Yes, Doctor," he sobbed, "I will not discuss this with anyone."

Doctor Klein looked around one more time before continuing. He pulled out a Kleenex and wiped away Gene's tears as he spoke. "Good. Now, the second question I need to ask is are you ready to take dee necessary risks in perhaps improving your quality of life?"

Gene had a blank look on his face, not sure on how to respond.

Doctor Klein leaned back. "Please, take all dee time you need to answer. It is a very important question."

Gene still couldn't believe this was happening to him. He thought about his quality of life now and the possibility of it improving. He would do anything. Yes, he would risk everything for this, including his life.

It was his turn to ask a question. He slowly regained his composure, looking at Joseph Klein directly in the eyes. "What kind of necessary risks?"

Doctor Klein turned his head, looking away. It was becoming unbearable for him.

Gene repeated the question, this time louder. "Doctor! What kind of risks?"

Joseph Klein swallowed hard and whispered, "Possibly risking your life. You could die in the process, Gene." He couldn't say it while facing the young man. He was looking down at the ground. He waited another minute. There was silence. He slowly turned his head, looking at Gene, studying his response.

A few people walked by as they quietly sat together. They looked at each other, neither wanting to speak. They had both said enough for the moment. The only sounds were the water fountain—the water fountain and crickets.

Gene had been studying the doctor all this time, thinking on how to respond, trying to find the right words, ending up by softly saying, "But Doctor … I'm already dead."

Doctor Klein slowly nodded in understanding. He swallowed hard, holding back his tears. He couldn't help but think that this young man in front of him was remarkable. He was a good candidate after all. They had made a very good choice. In his mind, Gene had passed the test.

"Doctor, what is this exactly about? I mean—what are the procedures? What are you going to do to me?" Gene needed some answers. His patience was running out.

"Please, have faith in us, Gene." Joseph sighed. "Vee cannot tell you anymore at dis time, okay? You vill be briefed later on, believe me. Now, again, are you ready to take dee necessary risks in order to improve your quality of life?" He wanted to be sure—sure that Gene knew they were playing for keeps.

This time Gene didn't ask any questions. Instead, he quickly replied, "Yes, Doctor. Without a doubt in my mind, I am ready to take any risks necessary for the possibility of improving my quality of life." His voice was strong and firm as he made the statement.

He heard himself saying it but knew it wasn't totally true. He had doubts. He had big-time doubts. He needed to think about it some more but that would come later. Right now he had to keep the ball rolling with Doctor Klein. He needed to keep him talking.

"Okay, that is good, Gene. Vee have the necessary papers for you to sign so vee can continue with dis. Of course you cannot really sign with your hands so you vill sign widt a pen in your mouth and it vill be witnessed and notarized. Dee form is an agreement between you and us, yah?" He lifted his hand up, extending three fingers, touching each one with his other hand as he went down the list.

"One, it states dat you agree to keep dis confidential. Two, dat you are giving us permission to operate and do all necessary procedures dat we see fit in order to improve your situation, yah? And," he took a deep breath, "three, it vill state dat vee will not be held responsible if anytink goes wrong." He paused, making sure Gene understood.

He did. He understood perfectly.

Doctor Klein carried on. "It is a legal contract between you and Bosch Research. It protects us from any recourse if sometink unforeseen happens. Do you understand?"

Gene was thinking of the alternatives. He thought of the old lady at the lunch table. *What was her name? Susannah?* She kept moaning and slobbering all over herself. He thought of Karl with a capital 'K.'

A disturbing thought crept into his mind. *Am I selling my soul to the devil?* He quickly came back to reality, answering the doctor's question. "Yes, Doctor. I understand."

"Good, Gene. Now, dair is one udder tink." The doctor's accent was now very thick. "Vonz you sign dee agreement dair is no turnink back." He was again shaking his finger in front of Gene's face. "Vee can't have dat because, vonz you sign, vee have to take you out of dee picture, yah?"

Gene was puzzled. He wondered again—about selling his soul to the devil. "What do you mean, 'picture'? "

Here it comes. There are always strings attached. This is too good to be true. What does the doctor mean by taking me out of the picture?

"Vell, you have to understand dat dis procedure has to be kept secret. Vee do not want our competitors to find out about our techniques."

Gene was speculating on how they could cover up a bionic leg or arm from the patients and staff at Edgehill. In fact, he wondered how they could cover it up from the entire world. He understood their predicament.

No, he couldn't be operated on and then be slipped back into a bed at Edgehill. They needed him to be isolated from the rest of the world until the arm or leg started to function properly. And—what if it didn't function? It didn't much matter. No one would know what had transpired and perhaps he would mysteriously appear back at Edgehill no worse off than he now was. He wasn't sure how that would work.

He was thinking about what his stupid mother used to say, "Nothing ventured, nothing gained." He had nothing to loose and everything to gain.

"I understand this has got to be kept quiet. How long before I can come out of hiding?"

"Oh no, Gene. You wouldn't be in hiding." Doctor Klein put a hand up to his chest and smiled. He took his glasses off, suddenly deciding on cleaning them. "No, no. Not at all. Vee just need to keep you away in isolation, so to speak, until vee feel that you are fine and we can show de world, yah? Vee are not sure how long dat vill be but you cannot have visitors anymore vonz vee start, yah?"

For the first time in their relationship, Doctor Klein found himself lying. He was thinking that they couldn't very well announce to the world they had performed a radically new procedure even if it was or wasn't a success. For one thing, they would have the government on their backs. They would be accused of overstepping the boundaries on medical procedures.

The Food and Drug Administration would find them guilty of performing secret medical operations without being given prior approval. That was only the beginning.

The plan had always been to keep their discoveries secret until they needed to be divulged. Time was of the essence. They could not afford to wait for the required government approvals before they forged onward. They had to act immediately in their research and hope that, in the meantime, their successes would be filed and patented as quickly as possible.

Gene closed his eyes, thinking, *"Okay, now I'll be in isolation and can't have any visitors. What next?"*

Doctor Klein was also thinking. He was thinking about the lie he had just told his young patient.

Chapter 14

The rest of the day was a blur. He remembered spending part of the afternoon on the Internet. He had a pointer similar to a pen that hung in front of his face. It wasn't easy for him to grab it with his mouth, bending his neck down slightly, trying to click and point on a large touch pad to his right. It took patience and skill to press the right spot so he could navigate the screen. There was also a small keyboard attached above the touch pad. He could type out characters with the pointer.

He was finally able to maneuver around the Web, searching for spinal cord sites. Most of them were already in the 'Favorites' section of the browser. It seemed that spinal cord research was a popular topic here at Edgehill.

He read and re-read articles ranging from stem cell research to bionics—the science of using electro-mechanical devices to enhance a patient's quality of life in many different ways. He quickly became bogged down with scientific and medical jargon. The more he learned, the more confusing it became. He had to talk to Doctor Klein face-to-face. He needed answers.

He was becoming more and more frustrated with his search, eventually giving up. He daydreamed, thinking about walking again, this time with two artificial legs and arms. Could that be possible? Yes, he was sure of it. They had experimented as far back as the seventies with stuff like that. They had artificial limbs attached to amputee stumps that could do marvelous things. His life would never be the same as before but at least he would be able to get out of the wheelchair, away from the care facility.

And, what about stem cell research? Perhaps they weren't too far off in regenerating the spinal cord. The articles he had read were promising, but they mentioned 'in the future,' not now.

He asked a nurse if she could wheel him back to his room. He needed to be alone. He was feeling tired and worn out. He knew part of the fatigue was because of the exercise he had done earlier with Harold. That was one of the reasons. The other was because of his meeting with Doctor Klein. He felt drained.

He was settling comfortably in his room when Cynthia peeked in. He noticed her and smiled. "Cynthia! Come in."

"Hi, Gene."

"Hey, how are you doing? Is it true you're already working here?"

"Yes, I'm so excited!" She wanted to tell him all about her orientation, working in Unit A, not too far from him, but her brain froze. She stood in front of him and smiled stupidly instead.

Gene had to smile, too. He kept thinking of the puppy waiting for her master. It was so obvious. He needed to be careful with her.

"Come in and sit down. Come visit with me for awhile." He was actually happy to see her and almost told her again how he loved her company. He needed to talk, to get his mind off things. Besides, he liked the effect that he had on her. He was the master, she the puppy—at least for the time being.

She sat down, blurting out, "Gene, I didn't realize you had a girlfriend and I saw you with her yesterday and—"

"Whoa. Whoa. *Whoa!* You must be talking about Lindsey. Yeah, we've dated but I don't know where that's going." He didn't know what else to say. He didn't want to tell her anymore than he had to.

He thought he might have said the right thing because she stayed. They had a good visit even though it was too short. It helped Gene get his mind off things. He needed a friend in the worst way. She said she had to get back to work and would see him tomorrow. She leaned over and gave him a wet kiss on the lips. He almost gagged. It wasn't at all like Lindsey's.

Chapter 15

It was early Tuesday morning. It was going to be another hot day. He was still in his room, waiting for someone to take him to breakfast. He was in no hurry and, besides, he didn't have much of an appetite. He had spent most of the night awake, thinking about all kinds of possibilities. He knew that, for whatever reason, he was being given a second chance. He didn't know what kind of chance. That made him nervous; that and also being told he would be kept in isolation. He couldn't have any visitors. He had to make up his mind. What if he never saw Lindsey or Dan or his dad again? Hell, after the visit from Cynthia last night, what about not even seeing her?

He was going through a mental checklist. With Dan, well, he could get over it if he never saw him again. Then there was his dad. Ha, that was a joke. Forget it! What about Lindsey? No, she was going to university. She would probably never come and see him again anyhow. Fucking bitches! And with everything he had done for her. He put his fucking life on the line to show her how much of a man he was and that was how she repaid him? Fuck them all!

And what about Cynthia? She was becoming a bit of a friend. He came very close in telling her about the meeting with Doctor Klein but had held back. It could complicate things immensely.

He knew what the problem was. He was afraid. He was terrified. He couldn't help but think he was signing his life away. They wanted him to donate his body so they could do what they deemed as necessary? No, he decided that he wasn't going to sign anything until he found out more about the procedure.

Bruce had come in the night before to see if everything was all right. Gene told him he wanted more information. He knew he didn't have much to lose but it concerned him. He needed to know more. All of this was still very unclear to him.

Bruce admitted he'd been thinking about it, too. He told Gene that if he were in his position he would jump at the opportunity. There was no doubt in his mind. He knew the doctors better than Gene did. He knew what they could do and he was confident in their abilities. For him, this narrowed the risks considerably. He tried to assure Gene he would see things differently in the next few days, once things were made clearer to him. He asked if Gene felt up to meeting the doctors the following morning.

"Yes, the sooner the better. I want answers."

After Bruce's visit, Gene felt somewhat more comfortable. He still couldn't help being frightened. Maybe Bruce was right. Once he knew a little more, then perhaps he would begin to feel at ease with the doctors. Until then, he had a lot of questions that needed answering. He fell into a deep sleep.

Doctor Klein walked into the TV room and spotted him.

"Good morning, Gene."

Gene was struggling with his emotions. He wanted this whole thing to be over with. "Good morning, Doctor Klein."

He felt like he was playing poker with the doctor and his group. The poker pot was his life. He didn't like it. No, he didn't like it at all. He noticed a few dark stains on the front of Doctor Klein's smock, wondering if it was coffee or something worse. Perhaps dried blood? His mind wandered with the thought.

Doctor Klein wheeled him into a small office down the hall, saying they should talk some more. There was a lot to talk about. He parked Gene and pulled up a chair across the desk from him.

"So, Gene, you have some questions, yah?" He slowly sat down.

"Uh, yes, I have some questions, lots of questions."

"I'll try to answer as many as I can."

"For starters, I want to know what you plan on doing to me."

Doctor Klein shifted in his chair. He was becoming uncomfortable. He recited the statement that he and the L-Team had worked on earlier. "I can't answer that due to the corporate and legal consequences. I would put the whole project at risk if I were to tell you anything more than I already have. Dair is nothing more I can say about it at dis time."

He looked at Gene stone faced. The thought of a poker game once again entered Gene's mind. The doctor would not show his hand.

Gene stared back, making Doctor Klein feel extremely uneasy.

Joseph Klein decided on using a different tact. "Look, Gene—"

"No, *you* look, Doctor!" His voice had risen. He was close to shouting but caught himself. Doctor Klein stared back at him, startled. He could not help but notice Gene was a very frightened and angry young man. He also knew Gene was in no position to bargain.

Gene continued, trying to calm himself as he spoke. "I'm tired of this cloak-and-dagger scene. I want some answers. The main question again is what are you planning on doing to me?"

Klein decided on giving it to him, straight. "We plan on operating on you, Gene." He raised his hands, revealing his palms, showing Gene he had nothing up his sleeve, nothing to hide. "Vee plan on making your life better. Vee plan on you being dee first patient that will have dis procedure and I'll tell you vhy we chose you!" Doctor Klein told himself to remain calm. He had been slamming his hand on the desk as he spoke the last part of the sentence.

Gene thought, *"Okay, keep talking."*

"First of all, you are a bright young man who has had his future robbed from him, yah? You are still young and have a healthy body. Second, you are legally old enough to make your own decisions. Third, your body is near or at the end of its growing period. This is crucial as you are now at the peak of your physical and neurological development. Fourth, you have no close family so are a prime candidate to be put into isolation." He also wanted to tell him he had no friends to speak of but stopped short.

"Fifth," he took a deep breath, "your blood type is not rare and you are a fast healer. Sixth, your mental attitude is aggressive. You are angry but yet you are a fighter! You vant to live! And ..., maybe dee most important reason is"—he caught his breath—"you are talking to a doctor and scientist who represents a team dat is capable of performing dee operation with a very high success rate!" He stopped at that, taking in another deep breath. There were many more reasons but he had covered the more significant ones.

Gene was silent, his lower lip quivering. Doctor Klein thought he might have gone too far. *No, Gene needs to know how lucky he really is.*

"You have got to realize dat you are dispensable, Gene, yah? Vee are on your side here, but"—he held up his hands, waving them in a take it or leave it fashion—"if you do not vish to do it den vee vill look elsewhere." He shrugged, suggesting it didn't really matter to him if Gene was onboard with them or not.

Gene turned pale, slowly understanding the position he was in. His throat was terribly dry. He gulped. *Between a rock and a hard place. I'm screwed if I don't take this opportunity. I would kick my ass the rest of my miserable life if I didn't take it. It's my only chance.*

He hadn't wanted the meeting to go that way. He had many more questions but they didn't seem to matter anymore. He knew he was in no position to negotiate. The doctor was right. They could go elsewhere.

He sat there, dumbfounded. He still didn't feel right about it. He hesitated for a moment and then slowly moved his head back and forth, oblivious to the pain, going with his gut instinct. "No. No. No. It's not right! I demand some answers."

Doctor Klein had had enough. It was coming down to the wire. He stood up, arms on his hips, looking down at Gene in frustration. Thoughts of his beloved Sarah crept into his mind. She hadn't had the opportunity for a second chance. Gene did. For a moment he put one hand to his chin, looking down at the floor, deep in thought. He looked back up, unaware that his fingers were now nervously drumming on his desktop. He looked at Gene while taking another deep breath. Gene stared back, defiant.

He understood Gene's position all too well. He began to soften, wanting this to work. Not only did he want this to work, he knew the whole team did as well. Mr. Lincoln would be very disappointed in him if he let Gene slip through his fingers. No, he realized, it was best he try a little harder. Gene certainly was an ideal candidate worth pursuing. There was only one other thing to do, throw some of his cards down. If that wasn't enough, well, then they would need to look elsewhere. He sighed, looking away, taking off his glasses, deciding on cleaning them once more.

"Gene," his voice softened, "dair is something I am prepared to do ... if you like?" He raised his eyebrows while speaking the last part of the sentence.

"What?" Gene had his mouth open, like a dog anticipating a bone.

He whispered, "I can show you dee results of some of our tests, yah?" He was becoming upset, knowing he was being forced to give up more than he wanted to. Before Gene had a chance to respond, he quickly spoke, his voice growing louder. "But again, you are putting us in an extremely vulnerable position. Do you understand? You need to sign a non-disclosure agreement before I show you anyting! This will legally protect us, yah?" He angrily crossed his arms and leaned back in his chair, staring at Gene.

Gene was intrigued. Of course he would sign. The doctor was giving him a little tidbit. It was better than nothing. "Okay, Doctor. I'll sign the agreement—only the non-disclosure agreement."

Doctor Klein was annoyed. He did not like negotiating yet Mr. Lincoln had chosen him to speak to Gene. Doctor Klein was uncomfortable with Lincoln's decision. He was a surgeon, certainly not a salesman. In his mind Doctor Morin would have been the better choice. Still, Mr. Lincoln had insisted, claiming that Doctor Klein was closer to Gene which would make his young patient feel more at ease.

He knew he had gone too far by promising to divulge anything. He felt the young man drove a hard bargain. They did not want to do this—to give away their secrets. In fact, this was as far as it could go. Mr. Lincoln would not be pleased.

Chapter 16

He was furious. He told him as much. He asked with an incredulous tone, "Joseph! You almost had him ready to agree and then you told him you would show him some of our work?"

Doctor Klein sputtered, attempting to defend himself, but Lincoln wouldn't listen.

"Don't give me excuses, Joseph! You've been out-maneuvered by an eighteen-year-old."

Bruce decided to step into the discussion before it got out of hand. He tried to reason with Mr. Lincoln. "Doctor Klein had no other option. You have to give him that much."

"I don't have to give him anything! This is my project. I have spent a king's ransom so far and I will not allow it to fall apart because of someone's poor negotiating skills." Mr. Lincoln was yelling.

Bruce persisted. "Do you think you or I could have done any better?"

Lincoln started coughing while glaring at him.

Bruce took the opportunity and kept talking. He was getting annoyed with Lincoln and his narrow-mindedness. "Look. Gene is an intelligent young man. If you feel that this is not working out with him then we stop it right here. We go no further! We don't have to tell or show him anything." He had his hands up in surrender.

Lincoln knew Bruce was right. They could stop now and no harm would be done. He didn't want that to happen. He was getting old, his coughing becoming worse. His time was running out. He needed Gene. He was the perfect candidate. It was becoming an all-or-nothing situation.

"All right," he barked, trying to suppress another coughing bout. "Perhaps I—perhaps I should be a little more reasonable with this." He looked at Doctor Klein. "Joseph, I apologize. I suppose your back was up against the wall and, yes, we had discussed this very same problem before."

They had met several weeks previously, discussing several 'what ifs.' They had all agreed that, if the subject was worth the effort, they would take a chance and show some of their test results in order to make him more comfortable. They all knew they could not ask a patient to risk his life for something he didn't have the faintest idea about.

Doctor Klein told him the apology was accepted. He felt foolish about the whole incident. Still, he understood the stress Mr. Lincoln was going through. He felt stressed as well.

Bruce agreed to go back to Gene later in the evening and set up an appointment with him and the doctors for the following morning. This time, if need be, they would take him into Bosch Research and show him a little of what had been achieved over the past several months.

Bosch Research had, on occasion, brought patients into their research center. They were willing candidates who wanted to participate in various programs. Bosch had developed several types of medication and it was not uncommon, after being cleared by the FDA, to discuss the benefits and side effects of each one. Patients would be given either the real thing or a placebo, usually on a daily basis, administered at the research center. Bringing Gene into Bosch Research would not raise any eyebrows.

Chapter 17

Gene was not only excited, he was thrilled. The meeting had gone better than he had hoped. He hadn't expected the doctor to offer him anything. In fact, he thought the doctor would have said he was sorry it hadn't worked out and move on.

No, they thought he was a good candidate after all. He had them over a barrel as much as they had him. He decided he wasn't going to back down. If what they showed him tomorrow wasn't good enough, then he'd tell them he wasn't interested. He was feeling very confident and proud of the way he handled things. He had a fleeting thought of his mother and how proud she would have been.

He was in the woodworking shop. There were four of them plus the instructor. The project today was making a model airplane. His job was to place some of the spars, which had been previously cut, into the wing assembly for gluing. He was slowly learning how to hold a pair of tweezers in his mouth so he could carefully place the wing spars in the right location.

He wasn't much into it. He had trouble focusing on something so mundane. It was marvelous what could be achieved with only one's mouth but patience was required, a lot of patience. His patience had run out. Finally, the instructor told them it was time to break for lunch. They could come back tomorrow to continue.

Gene was at his normal spot at the dinner table when Cynthia walked by. She gave him a quick smile and kept on going. It was like they were having an affair and she was afraid they would get caught. He smiled. He'd play the game as long as it was good for him. He was getting his life back under control.

She walked around a corner and accidentally bumped into Harold. It wasn't an accident on Harold's part. He had planned it that way.

"Oops, I'm sorry. Uhh—Cynthia, right?" He had his finger up, pointing at her.

"Yes and your Gene's physio. Uhh—" She couldn't remember his name.

"Harold, that's me! So, I hear that you've recently started here, right?"

"Yes, on Monday."

They kept talking. Harold finally convinced her to join him in the staff cafeteria for lunch. He knew she was from Irvine General and he wanted to get information as to what it was like working there. That was only an excuse to get to know her.

They were sitting across from each other, having a coffee, when he blurted out, "So you and Gene aren't seeing each other?"

She blushed but quickly regained her composure. "Why do you ask that?"

"Well, I dunno. I was talking to Gene and said he was lucky to have that hot tamale waiting for him and he said you were not his girlfriend."

Her mouth dropped open, partly because it was none of Harold's business and partly because Gene had denied they were seeing each other. In her mind they were in love.

He kept talking, hoping to shock her even more. "Besides, I saw him with a young lady the other day." As an afterthought he added, "They were having a lot of fun. That must have been his girlfriend."

Rather than making friends with her, the opposite was occurring. She held her tongue, not knowing how she was going to handle all of this.

He looked at her while reaching across the table, putting his hand on hers. He sweetly said, "I'm sorry if I've upset you, Cynthia. You seem to be too nice a person to have that kind of thing happen to you."

She wanted to scream at him but smiled instead, saying, "I think you're jumping to conclusions, Harold." She pulled her hand away and said with an equally sweet smile, "Besides, it's none of your fucking business."

He was the one that was now flustered as she got up and walked out.

Chapter 18

He joined the rest of them after lunch in what they called the 'Gathering Room.' It was a large meeting area where patients would sometimes be treated to local performers. Today three young ladies were singing in what was close to perfect harmony while someone played the piano. They were good, singing a little bit of country as well as blues. Gene would have stomped his feet to the music if he could.

He felt someone behind him but still couldn't turn his head enough to see. It didn't matter. He could smell her perfume. It gave him the creeps. He felt like she was stalking him.

"Hey, handsome, are you enjoying this?"

"Uh , hi, Cynthia. Yeah, they're pretty good. And you?"

"I wish I could dance with you."

Again, that feeling of being out of control; he didn't know what to say. He was actually afraid of her.

She kept it up. "I had a wonderful visit from someone you know today."

"Yeah, who?"

"Harold."

"That scumbag?" Oops, he had to be careful. Harold could be in earshot for all he knew.

"Yes, that scumbag. He tried to get me jealous about you and your old girlfriend."

He didn't say anything. She was standing behind him, her hands on the wheelchair handles.

"She *is* your old girlfriend, isn't she?" She shook his wheelchair as she said it.

That annoyed him immensely. She was now definitely threatening him. He wanted her to leave him alone. He didn't need that shit, especially with what had been going on lately. He didn't respond. She grunted, shaking the wheelchair one more time before stomping down the hallway like a child throwing a temper tantrum.

He wanted to keep his distance from her for a while. She was far too freaky. He continued trying to watch the show but his mind wasn't on it. No, it wasn't working. He'd seen enough. It was time to go.

Bruce appeared out of nowhere and asked if he was ready to leave. He brought him back to his room, closing the door behind them.

"We've got a problem here, buddy." Bruce was the type that would not hold back on what was bothering him. "That nurse is getting too close to you. It might make things very complicated."

Gene was getting angry. "Now Big Brother is telling me who I should and shouldn't see, right? Bosch Research is going to take over all of me, right?" His voice was growing louder. "I won't even get to call the shots on who the hell I want to sleep with!"

Bruce looked at him for a few seconds and then shrugged, saying, "That's right. You've got it."

Gene was flustered with the response. He didn't know what to say.

Bruce pulled up a chair and sat down across from him. "This is not a game, Gene. This is for real. We do give a damn about not only your health but also your social life. Don't make it more complicated. If you decide to go ahead with this you've got to clear your life of everyone. Your family will now be the team at Bosch Research, no one else."

He paused, looking at Gene, hoping that the message was sinking in. He decided to try a different tactic.

"Gene, please listen to me. If Klein and the others ever thought you were involved with anyone they would cut you out of the deal without hesitating. That's part of the reason why you were chosen." He paused, wondering if he should go any further with an explanation then decided not to hold back. It didn't matter anymore if feelings were hurt. "You have no ties. You have no family! You are essentially a loner. That's perfect!" His voice had risen in pitch and his arms waved in the air as if he had just scored a goal. He quickly brought them back down.

"Don't complicate it." He was pointing a finger at him as he said the last sentence. It was a borderline warning.

Gene was silent. He knew Bruce was right. He knew he was walking on thin ice with Cynthia. Besides, he didn't really care much for her anyway. She was too creepy. Yet, he needed a friend. He was afraid. Deep down he hoped he could use her in case things went wrong. He felt his life was being split, moving from one side of an imaginary line to another. She was a link to this side. He didn't want to lose that. He was terrified of the other side.

He knew it was already too late. The team was now aware of the supposed connection he and Cynthia had. He had to get rid of her—get her off his back.

"Well, what do you say?" Bruce could see he was in deep thought. "Do you have any ideas?"

"Yeah. You're right, Bruce. Look, I'm not going to justify myself, okay, but she seemed like she could help me if things went wrong. You know, like I feel that she's a safety net for me. Do you understand?"

"Gene, listen to me. If you have the procedure, odds are you will not be coming back here. I mean, you probably won't be coming back to Irvine." He read Gene's face. Before Gene could respond, he continued. "They don't want you back here. They don't want publicity. If things go according to plan you'll be in isolation for an indeterminate amount of time and then eventually moved away to some place where you won't be recognized. You'll be given a new identity. In exchange for the new lease on life you will be relocated and monitored for the rest of your life." He thought he might have gone too far. He tried to bring a positive note into the conversation.

"Now, the good news is there *is* a future for you. It won't be a normal future, but at least it will be a future. You don't have that right now. You are a very lucky man to be given a second chance, if … they are still willing to do so."

Bruce smiled to himself. He was good. It hadn't taken him long to put the fear of God into him. Gene needed a wake-up call.

"Do you think they still want to work on me after what's been going on?"

"I don't know. I do feel compelled to tell them."

"They don't already know?" His voice had risen. "I'll take care of it, Bruce. I really will. In fact, I don't really like her all that much."

"Let's think about this, okay?" He paused for a minute, making it look as if he was really thinking about it. In actuality, he wanted to show Gene how serious this was, how serious they all were with him.

"No, I won't tell the doctors about it if … you work with me. We might be able to fix this … together. Have you told her or anyone else about the conversations that have taken place recently?"

"No. No one!" Gene was thinking about how he almost told Cynthia but decided at the last minute not to.

"Okay, good. Now, is there anyone else you might be close to that we're not aware of?"

"Uh, yes … sort of. Her name is Lindsey. She and I were friends. She came to visit me. Cynthia was really jealous about her but now she's no longer my girlfriend. She's going to university this fall." He was talking fast and with a high pitched voice. Bruce knew he had frightened him. That was good.

"Okay. Does Cynthia know Lindsey's no longer your girlfriend?"

"Well, she asked me about her again, just before you saw me. I didn't answer her."

"Good, Gene. Maybe the best way to fix this is to tell Cynthia you're in love with Lindsey, right?"

Gene almost groaned. He hesitated, finally saying, "Okay, I'll do that." Deep down he was afraid of Cynthia and what she might do when he told her. He still wasn't sure if that was the right thing to do. He had to be careful from now on. He was being watched.

Chapter 19

They had another meeting later on in the day. Doctors Klein, Schultz and Morin were sitting across from Mr. Lincoln and Bruce Whitman.

Doctor Adams was a little late. He had to finish up his rounds at Irvine General. He was the chief surgeon and needed to tend to another accident victim. It seemed there were more and more vehicle accidents happening, especially in the summer. That was understandable. After all, traffic volume was at its highest this time of year.

Mr. Lincoln took charge once everyone was present. "So, Gene says he's going to take care of the problem, right?"

Bruce slowly nodded. He felt bad for suckering Gene into believing he would keep it confidential. The project was far too important to keep anything a secret from the team members.

Mr. Lincoln continued, "Good! I don't think we'll need to worry about her anymore." He smiled, thinking of the young and innocent nurse deeply in love with a helpless young man. It was almost Shakespearean. "Once he tells her he loves another girl she'll probably leave him alone. The good news is he doesn't care about her."

Doctor Klein didn't like the way they could manipulate people and their lives. They were playing with people so they could have their way with them. He was beginning to feel guilty.

"Now, I have a proposal for the meeting tomorrow, Joseph."

Doctor Klein quickly came to attention, wondering what Mr. Lincoln meant.

"The original plan was we would all meet with Gene in order to address any concerns he might have and then show him some of our results, right?"

"Yes, that is correct."

"I suggest that tomorrow Bruce brings him back here to my office. He's got the closest bond with Gene right now. That would make him feel a little more comfortable with all of this. You, Joseph, should meet with him as well."

Doctor Klein nodded in agreement as Lincoln continued.

"Now, we still don't have to show our cards to the young man, right? I mean he doesn't have to see any of our results if it's handled carefully." As he spoke, Mr. Lincoln was thinking about how Joseph Klein had managed the last meeting with Gene. He still wasn't happy with the way it turned out. *Perhaps Bruce could negotiate better?*

Doctor Morin spoke up, clearly agitated. "He will need to know more before he signs anything." He raised his voice. "You can't expect someone to sign their life away without knowing what's going on."

"Yes, yes, yes! I know that!" Mr. Lincoln turned his wheelchair toward Doctor Morin, facing the barrage. He defended himself by saying, "That is not what I'm implying. If we can convince Gene without showing him too much then it's all the better for us. I do not want to put this opportunity at risk by having him back out of the deal, not sign the proper agreements and then talk to the general public or worse, the media."

Doctor Schultz responded. "Perhaps, if he does see our work and decides he does not want to … participate, we might be prudent in having him transferred somewhere many miles from here. A place where anything he says will fall on deaf ears."

They all knew what he was talking about. The government had many institutions where someone like Gene could be placed and forgotten. This was not a new idea. Everyone had thought of the possibility but no one had discussed it until now.

Mr. Lincoln was pleased with what Doctor Schultz was saying. Now, if anything went wrong and they had to move him, he wouldn't be blamed as the person who originally suggested it.

No one spoke for a few minutes while Mr. Lincoln finished a coughing spell. Once it subsided, Mr. Lincoln continued. "Okay. Do all of you agree that we should still try to hold back and not divulge anything? This would be for the good of both Bosch and the patient." No one objected.

As an afterthought, he looked at Doctor Morin and said, "Henry, perhaps you should be there with Joseph as well. After all … there is supposed to be a team behind all of this. Your presence would give him a better understanding of how prepared and serious we really are." He also thought that Henry was a good communicator and negotiator. He would keep Joseph in check if necessary.

It was agreed that the following morning, after Gene had his time with the physiotherapist, Doctor Joseph Klein, Doctor Henry Morin and Bruce Whitman were to meet with him in this office.

Doctors Adams and Morin both quickly left after the meeting was adjourned. They were needed in performing more corrective surgery on the latest accident victim back at Irvine General. Doctor Klein wished he could be there. He and Doctor Schultz were equally capable but unfortunately they both needed to stay here at Bosch. Doctor Schultz was needed in the research lab and he had to stay because of the death threats.

After everyone left, Mr. Lincoln made his way back into the lab. He wheeled himself through another door after running his card through the keyless entry, entering the McDonald Room once more.

Chapter 20

The next morning Harold showed up right on time, ready to take Gene down to the exercise room. Gene was wondering how to handle Mr. Scumbag but decided to leave things alone. He smiled as they worked out. Harold made a comment or two about Cynthia but Gene pretended to be detached from the whole scene. He knew Harold would try to bait him, get him to talk about her. He never gave Scumbag the pleasure.

Harold brought him to the bathing area after they were done. A male nurse took over and, after he had been washed, Bruce came in and asked if he was ready. He was ready, more than ready. The adrenalin from his workout was still in his system.

Bruce wheeled him down the hall to Mr. Lincoln's office. At first it was only the two of them in the room. Neither spoke for several minutes. Gene finally asked how many doctors would attend the meeting. Bruce shrugged, saying he didn't know. As if on queue, Doctor Joseph Klein and Doctor Henry Morin walked in.

Bruce quickly stood up, addressing the doctors. "Good morning, gentlemen. You remember Doctor Morin, don't you, Gene?"

Gene nodded.

Bruce and Doctor Morin took their self-appointed chairs while Doctor Klein kept standing, taking charge. "Good, now how are you feeling today?"

Gene told him he was fine. He didn't want the small talk but knew it was a requirement.

"Good, good. Your neck muscles are virtually healed and I'm impressed widt your neck movements. Dat's very good."

They all smiled as Doctor Klein finally sat down, putting his briefcase on the desk. He continued. "Now, everyone here is aware of dee discussion that you and I had yesterday, yah?"

Doctor Morin and Bruce nodded.

"Good. Now, I told you I would show you some of our results as long as you signed a non-disclosure agreement, yah?" He was all business. Gene had never seen that side of him before.

Gene nodded, feeling the need to be very careful with what was taking place.

"Good. Okay, before I do, let me tell you a little about what we've been doink here at Bosch Research."

He began by suggesting that the medical world should be looking at damaged spinal cords from a different angle. Gene thought, *"Yeah, what are you getting at, Doc?"*

Klein was being very delicate in explaining a little about the new marvels of medical science. He was watching Gene closely, trying to get some feedback from him. Gene was playing the game as well, concentrating on staying calm and poker faced.

Klein talked about advances in genetic research, cloning, new therapy and stem cell research. He elaborated with a prepared statement that he began to read.

"Stem cell research is one of the most fascinating areas of biology today. These cells have the remarkable potential of developing into many different types of cells in the body. Serving as a sort of repair system for the body, they can theoretically divide without limit, regenerating other cells, as long as dee person or animal is still alive." His accent thickened as he pushed his glasses back on his nose, continuing.

"Ven a stem cell divides, each new cell hazz dee potential to eider remain a stem cell or become another type of cell widt a more specialized function, zuch as a muscle cell, a red blood cell or a brain cell."

He paused, waiting for Gene to ask questions. He did.

"How does that apply to my injuries, Doctor?"

Doctor Klein continued. "Vee are getting closer and closer everyday in learning how stem cells work with the spinal cord, yah? Dis promising area of medical research is also leading scientists into investigating dee possibility of cell-based therapies in treating diseases, vich is often referred to as regenerative or reparative medicine."

Gene wanted to ask Klein to quit skirting the issue and tell him straight up if this could help him but Klein kept on talking.

"Zoe far, science has made tremendous strides in stem cell research but as var as vee know, stem cells are still not capable of repairing dee spinal cord." He paused, letting this sink in. "Don't be discouraged with dis, Gene, because tings are changing dramatically in the medical vorld. Vhen I say dramatically, I do mean dramatically! Dee near future is exciting, yah? I feel very privileged in being a part of dat."

Doctor Klein looked at Doctor Morin, giving him a slight nod. Doctor Morin nodded back, silently giving him the go ahead. Doctor Klein quickly continued, not wanting to lose the momentum.

"Now, Gene, if you are villing, vee have the required forms for you to sign. Dees forms vill give us your permission to go ahead widt dee procedure."

He pulled out some papers from his briefcase and placed them in front of Gene. He reached back in while shifting in his seat and pulled out a pen that Gene could hold in his mouth. He spoke quickly. "Here you are, Gene. I vill put dee pen in your mouth, yah?" Bruce Whitman stood, getting ready to notarize the signature. He had been a notary several years before becoming a counselor.

It felt to Gene as though the doctor were forcing something more down his throat than just the pen. The doctor was sweating and excited. Bruce appeared nervous. It heightened Gene's suspicions. He was very wary with what was going on.

"No."

Everyone froze.

"Vat do you mean!" He spoke with astonishment, his mouth wide open.

"I mean … no! I told you I would sign a non-disclosure agreement only if you showed me some of your research. Have you forgotten, Doctor?"

Doctor Klein felt his face flush. "No, no, most certainly not," he sputtered while raising both hands, palms facing out. "I didn't forget, Gene. Please forgive me, yah. I got carried avay with dee moment."

Gene had one word to say to him but said it under his breath instead. "Bullshit!"

There was an awkward pause while Doctor Klein tried to compose himself. Bruce decided to quickly step in and do damage control.

"You know, Doctor Klein, Gene is right. That was the deal." He was playing the good-cop routine, hoping to dissolve the tension in the room.

Doctor Morin spoke up as well, sensing things might be getting more out of control. "Here are the facts once again. First of all, forgive my colleague's excitement and over exuberance." He glared at Doctor Klein, silently cursing him for how he was handling things, before looking back toward Gene. "No one can blame the good doctor for that. The fact is we really can't afford to put our organization at risk."

For the first time, Gene noticed they used the term 'organization.' He wondered how big this whole thing really was. If they could take him and place him anywhere without questions being asked, was the government involved in this as well?

This revelation gave him mixed feelings. He felt glad he wasn't dealing with some local quacks but he also felt frightened, knowing they had so much power over him. Unless he saw some physical evidence on what they could do, he decided he wanted no part in any of it.

"I've heard enough. Please take me back to my room. You people scare me. I feel you're trying to manipulate me. You're not completely honest. You told me you would show me some results, some evidence on how you could make my life better. You're not doing that. Take me back, now!"

Doctor Klein looked at both Doctor Morin and Bruce. They slowly nodded. They were all in agreement. He sighed while taking out some other papers, holding them in front of Gene. He spoke very softly, in a defeated fashion.

"Here are the non-disclosure papers. You need to sign on the bottom. Vee vill vitness dem and date dem. Bruce vill stamp them, yah? Once dat is done vee vill keep our end of dee bargain and show you tings … I promise."

He looked at Gene, his eyes and facial expressions silently speaking, telling his young patient in so many words, "This is it. Take it or leave it. We can't give you anymore." The room was silent. Everyone held their breath.

Chapter 21

Gene knew they were at the end of their rope. He was convinced that the doctors would indeed hold up their end of the bargain and show him 'tings.' He signed the papers and was given a copy. He wondered where he could put it for safe keeping. He questioned if he had any legal recourse if things didn't go according to plan. He still had the upper hand. They were worried about him and what he might do. Would he keep his word and not speak about what he was going to witness at Bosch Research? He had every intention of honoring the agreement—so far.

All four made their way out of Mr. Lincoln's office. Directly across from it was a door labeled 'Security.' They continued down the hallway to the next room on the right. It was the boardroom which doubled as a classroom.

As they entered, Gene noticed a large blackboard on one wall and an overhead projector mounted on the ceiling. The right wall had a window that looked into Mr. Lincoln's office. The left wall had another window that looked into what appeared to be a laboratory. A large table and several chairs took up the middle of the room. Doctor Morin explained.

"This is our meeting room that also serves as a multimedia room. Our team meets here on a regular basis. We go over the projects that we are currently involved in. To the left, as you can see, is our laboratory. We can monitor the activities through that window." He pointed as he continued.

"This is where we do most of our research. You can see several people working on various processes. Behind them is another door that is hermitically sealed. Anyone entering that particular room needs to be equipped with a laboratory suit. The room has to be free of contaminates."

They left the boardroom and moved farther down the hall. Doctor Morin pointed to two doors on the left. Both were living quarters. One was for Mr. Lincoln and the other was open to whoever needed it. Right now Doctor Klein was using it.

They went farther down the hall. To their left was a closed door labeled 'Utility Room.' It housed electrical panels as well as the alarm system and communications panel. To their right was an anteroom that held several office desks and lockers. Two sealed swinging doors were on the far wall of the anteroom, each equipped with a window. Gene could see, just beyond the swinging doors, what appeared to be an operating theatre. He caught a glimpse of an operating table with overhanging lights as well as several small tables loaded with electronic equipment. Next door to the operating room was another similar room. Both rooms were divided by a glass partition.

Doctor Morin once again explained as he stood in front of the two swinging doors leading to the operating theaters. "As you might have already guessed, these are our operating rooms. Both are identical, divided by a large glass window. As you can see through the doors behind me, we have the latest in equipment from respirators to heart monitors.

"We have several team members that work with us. Most are from leading universities and hospitals. We have carefully recruited the 'cream of the crop,' so to speak. We are a cohesive team, Gene. We are all here to achieve a common goal in making life better for everyone." He said it with such conviction that Gene felt he was very privileged indeed to be there.

They made their way out of the anteroom and back into the hallway. They passed by another large room, again on the right, next to the two operating rooms. In it were several cubicles with a bed in each one. Doctor Klein took over, explaining this was a recovery area. The patient would be monitored twenty-four hours a day by the best medical team in the world.

Gene had to ask the obvious. "So, who are and where are the patients?"

Doctor Morin anticipated the question, already having an answer. "Well, they come and go whenever there is a need for a special procedure, Gene. They are brought here from all over the country because of their circumstances." This was partially true.

He continued. "Right now things have been rather slow and that's why we've approached you. We have the facilities waiting as you can see. It's only a matter of time, under the right circumstances, when we can proceed." He caught himself. He had said the wrong thing and couldn't take it back.

"What are the 'right' circumstances, Doctor?"

Doctor Klein took over.

"The 'right' circumstances are a number of variables dat need to come together, Gene. It is dee paper work dat needs to be done. It is dee blood work. It is dee health condition of dee patient. It is his age. It is many tings."

"So, what about this stem cell thing? How does that work for me?"

Doctor Morin looked at Doctor Klein. It was time. They could not get around it any longer. It was time to show him the rest. If he could accept that, then they were half-way there.

Doctor Klein looked at Bruce and asked, "Are you ready?"

Bruce nodded.

Gene was very concerned. His mind was again racing through a myriad of possibilities. He kept thinking, "Ready? Ready for what?" He didn't ask. He couldn't speak.

Chapter 22

They wheeled him down the hallway at Bosch. They had decided, rather than give Gene a quick lecture on the medical procedures, it would be best to show him some results first. Once he understood the facts, they could better explain how their successes had evolved.

Doctor Morin turned to Gene. "We want to make sure that you keep an open mind, Gene—an open mind from now on."

Gene looked at him quizzically, wondering if he was entering a phase in their relationship where there would be no turning back. They had secrets they were being forced to give up. He was beginning to have doubts.

"We are going to show you the results of what we have been working on for the past while. We are very proud of what we've achieved." Doctor Morin squatted down in front of Gene, his face only inches away.

"Because of our hard work and dedication, along with some luck and answered prayers—" he paused. Gene could see perspiration on his brow as he continued. It seemed rather warm in the hallway. "It might be very possible that you could be given the chance at walking and feeding yourself again, to be somewhat ... normal again." He whispered the last part of the sentence.

Gene's mouth dropped. He had speculated and now the doctor had confirmed it. They were going to do something that would get some or part of his limbs to function again. He knew that his suspicions had been on the right track all along.

It could be some bionic device they could implant to make me at least—what did the doctor say, somewhat normal again? That's what he said. Yes!

Gene was breathing faster with this confirmation. He was overwhelmed and found all of this unbelievable, absolutely, positively, unbelievable.

Doctor Morin could sense Gene's mind racing, his young patient thinking of all the possibilities. He wanted to continue in preparing Gene for what he was about to see but decided that saying too much right now might make things more difficult. Instead, he stood up, looking at both Doctor Klein and Bruce. They looked back and nodded in silent agreement. They continued to wheel Gene down the hallway.

Things were spinning in Gene's mind as they stopped outside a door that had another security lock. Doctor Morin explained, telling Gene they called this room the 'McDonald' room. Bruce had been there once before and still had trouble dealing with it. They all had trouble dealing with it.

Bruce squatted down in front of the wheelchair, his face only inches from Gene's. He spoke very slowly and softly. "What you are about to see will be disturbing. There is no doubt about it. It will take you a while to actually grasp the implications. That's a perfectly normal reaction. The handful of people who have witnessed this have all felt deeply troubled at first. You have to understand. This is being done in the interest of science. We are in a new age, a new beginning. We have to be strong in order to move forward."

Gene's throat was dry. He was breathing hard. He was terrified. He felt helpless. It had come to this. He had asked for it. This opportunity had to be taken. There would be no turning back. He needed to be normal again.

Bruce continued, "Remember, we are with you. We are here to help you. Keep in mind that things will become easier after the initial shock." He patted Gene on the shoulder. "Okay?"

Gene gulped and nodded.

Doctor Klein cleared his throat, saying, "Gene, vee ask dat you do not make any loud sounds, yah? Also, it is dark in dair. Vee need to keep dee lights low, yah? Okay?" Gene nodded again.

"Okay, shhh. Keep as quiet as you can, yah?"

Chapter 23

Doctor Klein ran his security card through the card lock. There was a metallic click as the lock was released. They were ready to enter the room. He went in first, followed by Morin. Bruce entered last, pushing Gene in the wheelchair.

The room was dark—dark with a peculiar odor. Gene couldn't quite place it. It didn't belong with the antiseptic smell of the research center. It was ... musty? The smell became stronger as he was wheeled deeper into the room.

What is it? It's so out of place. It smells like ... hay! That's what it is—hay. Fresh cut hay. Not only hay, there's also a manure smell mixed in it as well.

He was startled by a low moan. His eyes tried to focus toward the source. It was coming from the back of the room. He heard another moan from a different direction, to the right of the first. His eyes were gradually adjusting to the darkness. Bruce pushed the wheelchair farther into the room until Gene was in front of what looked like a pen.

It's a pen. It's a fucking pig pen! They're experimenting with animals! What have they done?

It suddenly dawned on him. *No wonder they call this room the 'McDonald' room. It's not about fast fucking food. It's about animals.* A long forgotten song sprung into his mind. *Old McDonald had a farm—.* He thought he was going crazy.

Doctor Morin whispered, "Hello, Harley. Hello, Farley. How are you guys doing, hmmm?"

There was another moan. Gene finally made out a large pig in each of the two pens, both lying on their sides in a bed of straw. He kept looking, trying to see them more clearly. His eyes were still not fully adjusted to the dark.

They both appeared ill. They couldn't get up. One of them, Harley, was moaning, his right rear leg twitching, his tail wiggling. Farley also had a twitching leg. They seemed to be getting agitated, the moaning becoming louder.

Doctor Morin attempted to soothe the animals while Doctor Klein squatted down beside Gene, whispering in his ear. "Look closely, Gene. Focus on the nearer one. His name is Harley. Vee named him dat because one of our team members loves to ride a motorcycle, yah!" He said it with a huge smile while pointing toward the pig. The doctor appeared to be very proud of the little play with names.

A thought occurred to Gene. *"Is Doctor Joseph Klein slightly unstable?"* He wondered if they were all slightly unstable.

"Now look, Gene. Can you see it? Do you zee dee scar around dee neck." He kept pointing at Harley while still squatting, his arm around Gene's shoulders in a fatherly fashion. He felt very proud to show someone his babies.

Gene could vaguely see it, his eyes becoming more adjusted. He noticed several windows had been covered over with heavy black curtains eliminating any outside light.

He tried to focus on the pig. *What was his name?* He caught himself, thinking, it didn't matter what the pig's name was. He shouldn't be worried about offending him by calling him the wrong name. Hurting the pig's feelings was the least of his worries. He focused a little harder. It looked like a scar, an ugly red scar that completely surrounded the neck.

"Yes, I can see it." He was surprised with the sound of his voice. It was weak.

"Good, dat is where vee operated, yah? Dey are healing so nicely. It has only been a few months, yah? You can see dat both pigs have small tremors in some of dair legs." Doctor Klein was bursting with pride.

Gene noticed that not only Harley had tremors in two legs, but Farley's right front leg had a slight tremor as well.

Doctor Klein continued to whisper while still pointing. "Doze tremors are great signs of spinal regeneration and attachment. In fact, dis is now week twelve since dee operation and both pigs are slowly becoming physically better. We have had Harley up on his legs last week and noticed dat his front legs can move slightly. He also has feelings in his rear legs as well and, only a few days ago, vee noticed he twitched his tail! Doze are all wonderful signs, Gene. Both Doctor Morin and I consider dee operations a success!"

His voice rose with excitement, making Harley squeal. It wasn't quite a squeal but more of a moan, a sorrowful moan. The moan grew louder. Now Farley was moaning as well. Doctor Morin kept trying to soothe them. Doctor Klein mentioned it was best they leave. The pigs were becoming too agitated.

Gene tried to nod. *What is so shocking about that? They operated on two pigs and did some kind of spinal procedure. This is wonderful!* He was hopeful they could do the same for him.

As they began to leave, he whispered, "Did they have a spinal injury at one time, Doctor?"

Doctor Klein answered, "No. No. No!" He was smiling, shaking his head as he spoke, looking at Gene as if he had asked the most stupid question.

"Vee transplanted dee heads, yah?"

Chapter 24

"They're sick fucks. All of them!" He was lying on a bed, in a recovery room at Bosch, talking to no one in particular.

"I can't even begin to find the right fucking words to describe them and what they're doing. And Doctor Klein thought it was so clever they called one of them 'Harley,' named after a motorcycle. He had the most stupid grin on his face when he said it. I can't believe Doctor Klein! Klein … Klein … hmm … Frankenstein. Yeah, that's what he should be called. Frankenstein! And how about Doctor Morin … hmm, wasn't there a science fiction character called something like that? Oh yeah, the 'Island of Doctor Moreau.' Right, close enough."

He lay there, thinking. He couldn't believe what he had just seen. They transplanted heads. Fucking heads! He never dreamed it were possible. He thought they were only going to repair his spinal cord.

He muttered, "And why can't they repair my spinal cord? Maybe they will. Maybe what they were doing to the pigs was only a preliminary test to see if they could regenerate spinal cords. That's probably what it was."

He couldn't think. No, he didn't want to think. Any more speculation would make him throw up. The small room was dark, the shades drawn. He could see a closet. He tried to look past the foot of the bed toward the door but his neck was still too sore. He heard voices. They were in the hallway talking about him—Frankenstein and Moreau.

He closed his eyes but couldn't rest. He had too much nervous energy. A few minutes later he heard someone singing. He suddenly realized it was him who had been singing, chanting 'Ee-eye-ee-eye-oh.'

He stopped just as the door opened, the light hurting his eyes. Bruce stepped in. He had heard the singing, becoming concerned.

"Hey, how are you doing?"

Gene didn't answer. He knew he was losing his mind. Bruce was acting as if nothing had happened. There was silence. Gene couldn't look at him.

"I know how you feel, bud. I nearly did the same thing when I first saw them." Bruce decided the best tactic was to try and treat what Gene had witnessed in a rather dismissive fashion. He tried toning down the visit to the McDonald Room they had made only an hour earlier.

"You've got to admit I was right when I told you it was a shocker." He smiled as he leaned over the bed. There was a glass of water with a straw on the bedside table. He helped Gene take a sip.

Gene finally looked at him, shaking his head from side to side. It hurt but he didn't care. He was beyond feeling pain. Gene asked, "Do you hate animals?"

"No. No. No!" He had his hands up in a defensive fashion. "I love animals. I don't hate them. I was disturbed as much as you were in seeing those pigs. No, it's terrible they were operated on like that, but do you know what?"

Gene looked at him, waiting for the answer.

"It's terrible what happened to you with your accident. It's terrible there are thousands of people like you. It's terrible that, until now, no one had a chance. No one! That's what's terrible."

Bruce began to pace back and forth beside the bed as he got himself worked up. "Life is not fair! You know that better than anyone. What's the old saying—'Only the good die young?' It used to be in a song, right?"

Gene smiled a little.

"Here's another song you might remember." He began to sing.

"If you don't like what you've got then change it. If you don't like who you are then re-arrange it ... Raise a little hell, raise a little hell ... Raise a little Hell!" He was pretending to play the guitar.

Gene chuckled a little. He needed the release.

"Hey, you know something, Gene? I'm here for you. We're all here for you, okay?"

Gene tried to nod but his neck was too sore.

Bruce thought, *"Good, he's coming around. It's a typical reaction to what he's witnessed. He needs to be with a friend. I'm glad I've got him laughing again."*

"Yeah. I love animals. I had a dog once. She was a lab. We called her 'Kali.' She was a great dog and one day—"

"Uh, Bruce?"

"Yeah?"

"Please tell me those pigs were sick and needed to be operated on like that to be saved."

Bruce nodded as he proceeded to lie. "Yes! That's right, Gene. They were dying and the doctors did what they could and they saved them."

"Thank you, Bruce. Thank you for telling me that. Now I'm ready to talk to the doctors again."

"Sure, Gene. I'll get them."

Chapter 25

They came into the room, one by one, looking as if they had done something wrong, wanting his forgiveness. Gene had the upper part of his bed raised so he could see them better.

"Vee hope you are okay, Gene." Doctor Klein felt awkward. It was as if Gene had found out about a sin they had committed. Perhaps that was true.

Gene nodded with a frown.

Doctor Morin spoke next. "We couldn't do anything else, Gene. We knew we had to show you what has been developing over the past several months. We could have talked to you about it but we decided the best thing to do was be open and honest. We showed you because we trust you and we want to help you. Do you understand?"

Gene nodded and then asked in a very weak voice, "What are you going to do ... to me?" It was a child's voice, a frightened child.

Doctor Klein's heart went out to him. For a moment Gene sounded like Sarah to him, his beloved Sarah. His young daughter was never far from his thoughts. He spoke next.

"We vant to help you, Gene. Not only you, but soon, perhaps others as well."

"No. I mean—what are you *really* going to do to me? Are you planning on operating on me like you did with those pigs? What?"

Doctor Morin swallowed hard and then started to answer his question, at least part of it. "Before we talk about anything else, keep in mind we have been successful in one of the most radical medical procedures of all time. Also keep in mind that what we have done is not new."

Gene was listening, thinking about what he was saying, wondering about his comment about this not being new.

What did he mean by that last remark? Had they operated many times before? Transplanting fucking heads from chickens and cows and who knows what else?

Doctor Morin paused once more, getting ready for the next step. "Gene, Gene! Please listen very carefully." He had Gene's full attention. "We have a video we would like to show you. It will explain a little more, I'm sure."

Gene agreed to view it. He wasn't sure if he was ready but kept telling himself he had nothing to lose. He simply wasn't prepared for all of this. He had thought he would be getting some kind of bionic arm or legs. He had no idea what he was getting himself into.

They placed him back in his wheelchair and brought him to the boardroom. Doctor Morin asked if he was ready. Again, Gene felt he was getting deeper and deeper into—what? He wanted to say he was getting deeper and deeper into 'pig shit.' He stifled a nervous laugh. He couldn't think straight.

He said, "Yes. I'm ready."

Doctor Morin hit the play button on the DVD player. Someone turned the lights off as the screen came to life.

The images originally appeared on PBS in the mid-nineties. It showed a doctor working, with funding from the U.S. Government, on an experimental procedure for head transplants. The procedure was originally filmed in the mid-seventies, showing a monkey strapped to a chair, sitting upright.

Doctor Klein turned up the volume as they listened to the narrator.

Head transplants on animals have been attempted since 1908, but it was not until 1970 that Robert White first successfully transplanted the head of a rhesus monkey. When the monkey recovered from anesthesia White noted its aggression and also the fact that it would eat and could follow people around the room with its eyes. Monkeys lived for up to eight days in these early experiments. Since then technology has advanced but it is reported that monkeys are put down after about a week for 'humane' reasons.

Gene could see that the monkey's head was secured to the back of a chair by a halo device similar to what he had worn. It was sitting in an upright position. The doctor in the video was explaining how he and his team had severed the two heads from both monkeys and had transplanted them. As the heads were removed, they were kept alive artificially. Not only were the heads kept alive but also the bodies. One of the monkeys had died but the other one was still alive. As the doctor walked near it the monkey became very agitated, grinding its teeth. Its eyes were wide open and appeared to be very aggressive. It evidently lived for eight days. The experiments were stopped because of the Frankensteinian nature of the procedure.

Doctor Klein hit the pause button and turned the lights back on while Doctor Morin continued to speak. "Keep in mind, this occurred back in the early seventies. Since then, science has come a long way. We've addressed many issues and now are confident this procedure will work."

He pulled a small chalkboard out, drawing a rough diagram of Gene's injuries. "Your injuries are irreparable. Those are the facts. Until only a year or so ago there was nothing we could do. There was nothing anyone could do. You would live out your life as best you could, hoping for a miracle. Now there is hope." He paused, took a breath and continued.

"Now we can operate. It's as simple as that. But actually, nothing is that simple. Let me explain." He pointed to the diagram of the spinal cord, describing where Gene's injuries were.

"We cannot repair the damage. There are too many complications. The risks would be enormous. We want to reduce those risks. We want you to survive. Your only viable option is a transplant." He paused, waiting for a response. There was none. He forged on.

"The C7 vertebra, as well as your lower back, are the areas where the most damage has occurred. The C7 area is the one we need to deal with. The lower back has now become irrelevant because it is impossible to repair. Now," he paused, "C7 is close to your shoulders. In a way, that's good." He stopped again, clearing his throat. "Why is that good, you might ask? Well, to a surgeon, if we decide to do a transplant on you, it would be much easier for us to do it at the base of the neck rather than higher up.

"There are many reasons why we would prefer to work at the base. The main one is it is simply less complicated. The blood vessels are larger, the throat and breathing tube are easier to work with and we don't have to deal with the larynx. It's less restrictive." He paused, catching his breath.

"Also, there is the cosmetic aspect to this, the skin grafting and scarring. You see, Gene, we expect you to have a full and healthy life if the procedure takes place. We are concerned about the exterior of the body as well as the interior. Skin type is another issue. We are fortunate in being here, in this research laboratory where we have developed some of the best medication for skin grafting in the world. There is more!" He was excited as he continued.

"The big news is"—he took a deep breath before continuing—"we have developed a procedure that can splice the spinal cord in such a way that, yes, with the help of some new drugs we have discovered by accident, will actually grow the spinal cord back together." His face was flushed. He reached for a bottle of water, taking a long drink. No one said a word.

Gene was listening very intently. *Slice n' splice. That's what they're fucking talking about. Slice n' splice. It sounds so—what? Detached?"* He almost burst out laughing. *No, 'detached' might not be an appropriate word right now. No, I better get control here. I know my nerves are getting to me.* He smiled to himself, realizing at what he had just thought. *Yeah, right. My nerves are getting to me. That's what they're talking about right now, my nerves!* He told himself to cool it and pay attention to what the 'slice n' splice' doctors were telling him.

"Interestingly enough, Gene, nature has thrown a twist into this entire situation. The serum we are using was discovered by accident. We were looking for the magic formula where we could splice and grow the patient's damaged spinal cord back together. We tried and tried again, experimenting with animals in the lab, attempting to re-grow segments of damaged spinal cord, knowing we were getting closer but, alas, we reached a point where we couldn't go any further in our quest for the perfect drug. It simply wasn't working.

"Doctor Schultz was ready to abandon the whole idea when, finally, quite by accident, he decided to try using a healthy spinal cord instead. He added the right combination of ingredients into the serum as well." He smiled, pleased with what they had discovered. "He immediately started seeing positive results. That opened the door to new discoveries!"

Doctor Morin took another long drink and pressed on, wondering about the marvels of nature and how little they really knew about its inner workings. They were still having difficulty in understanding how the serum actually worked.

"One other thing and … it might be the most important one of all. Doctor Adams and I are two of the leading micro surgeons in North America. We have both specialized in splicing nerves and small, even microscopic, blood vessels through surgery. We also have the very best in equipment and staff."

"Let me end this," he lifted up his right hand, searching for the proper words, "spinal cord seminar by stressing to you that there is no other way. Believe me, if there were we would do it but no, unfortunately we cannot repair your spinal cord, especially in the lower back. You have two options, Gene, only two." He held up two fingers for emphasis. "You continue to live your life like you're doing now or ... you have the transplant."

It was far beyond him. He was mesmerized by the explanations and information. He had only two words to say and they weren't very technical.

"Aw, shit!"

Doctor Morin looked at him and vigorously nodded his head. He couldn't help himself. He had the largest smile on his face. He reiterated, "Yes, Gene. Aw shit!" Those two words summed it up quiet nicely. The comment certainly broke up the tension in the room.

Chapter 26

As the doctors were speaking while showing Gene the video, Mr. Lincoln entered the McDonald Room. He came there often. They were his babies. They were the result of years, no, eons of progress. Nature had slowly created the world to the way it is today, but there was one very important influence, however. Man has taken over the slow evolutionary process the past fifty or so years. Man is beginning to manipulate evolution, especially with what has been seen happening here at Bosch over the last year. Now it may be possible to fine-tune nature. Man would no longer be at her mercy when it came to certain injuries and diseases.

Mr. Lincoln parked his electric wheelchair in front of the pen and began talking to Harley and Farley. "Yes, my babies. I know you're both very upset. Shhh! It's okay now. They're gone."

The pigs were moaning. It was an unnatural sound. Mr. Lincoln wished they could speak to him. His mind drifted, thinking that perhaps they could clone a pig with a man to produce a … talking pig? He smiled at the thought, shaking his head. *Why not? It's no longer going to be science fiction. It will, some day, become a scientific fact.*

The moaning continued. He knew the babies needed peace and quiet. They needed the dark as well. It seemed to soothe them, along with soft sounds and human contact. He had to be careful and not move too quickly or make any sudden noise, especially loud noise. They could become very agitated.

Then there was the light issue. Both Harley and Farley hated light. It was as though they were in emotional pain. Of course they must be, he reasoned. There was no way of letting them know what had happened. He wondered if they sensed they were living beyond what God had planned. He stopped himself, rationalizing that if God hadn't allowed Bosch Research to make the startling discoveries that they had, this would never have happened. He would have put a stop to it because we certainly aren't more powerful than Him.

Yes, it is God's will or else we would not have been allowed to do this.

He again wished he knew what they were feeling—Harley and Farley—living in foreign bodies. Would they ever be normal again? His mind drifted back to Gene as he continued whispering soft words.

Chapter 27

Doctors Klein and Morin, as well as Bruce and Gene, were in the boardroom. Gene was still very much shaken from the experience. He couldn't stop hearing the sorrowful and tormented moans in his mind. He wondered what Farley and Harley were trying to say. *What were they thinking?* Doctor Morin must have read his thoughts.

"Gene, what we have achieved here is simply amazing. Think about it. We have overcome great obstacles with this operation. Granted, there is still a long way to go but it appears we now have the expertise and technology to perform such an operation. Any sign of spinal cord regeneration and repair is more than we had ever hoped for."

Doctor Klein looked at Gene intently while Doctor Morin continued. Gene had a fleeting thought that Doctor Morin would make a good used car salesman. He smiled, knowing he was being silly and also knowing it was nervous energy that made him want to laugh hysterically. Doctor Morin noticed his smile so smiled back, thinking Gene was enjoying all of this. They were now on-track together.

"Humans have a much better advantage undergoing this operation than animals. First, the only time we would consider an operation on a human would be in a case such as yours. You have multiple spinal cord injuries. You cannot be operated on in a conventional fashion. The damage is simply too extensive, the risks too high. You, unfortunately, have no other option than to have the operation … if you want to have feelings in the arms and legs again."

Gene noticed he hadn't said, "in *your* arms and legs."

"Secondly, you are much better prepared psychologically than Harley or Farley. They had no idea what was in store for them. One minute they were perfectly happy pigs and the next, well, their world was literally turned around. You, on the other hand, know about the procedure before it takes place. You know the risks. You have had time to weigh the alternatives and realize that this operation could be your savior."

Doctor Morin pressed the play button on the DVD once more. This time Christopher Reeve, the former Superman who had become paralyzed after an accident, was being interviewed. He expressed hope that the experiments would succeed even though they were bizarre and perhaps considered unnatural by some.

Mr. Reeve explained. "People who are trapped in their paralyzed bodies need hope that some day they will lead healthy and active lives even though their new bodies are not theirs but, instead, have been donated."

He reiterated, saying there was really no difference with someone having a foreign heart or a foreign body. One was more of a package than the other but they would both still be considered transplants.

The video ended with him being asked if he would consider having such an operation. He replied without any hesitation, "Yes, most definitely!"

That really hit home with Gene. *Here's Superman telling the world he would, if given the chance, have the operation in order to achieve a fulfilling life. I like that.* Christopher Reeve was one of his heroes.

Everyone was silent for a minute or two once the video ended. Each was deep in his own personal thoughts. Finally, Klein announced that one pig was expected to stand on its own in the very near future. Gene was half-listening, still trying to cope with the two monkeys in the video. It was unbelievable, yet, with stem cell research and cloning research advancing so quickly, perhaps nothing was impossible.

He began asking Klein questions. "Who would transplant his body with mine?" was the foremost. Klein put his hands up, stopping him after several questions were blurted out, trying to calm his young patient.

"Let's look at this as an organ transplant, shall vee?" He was speaking in a soft voice, trying to lower Gene's anxiety. "For it to take place you need to find a donor and a recipient, yah? As with, say, a heart transplant, zee donor would have to be considered legally dead.

"Vee need to find a donor dat is young and is in a coma and vill never regain consciousness, yah? Here lies dee problem, Gene. Due to dee very nature of dee operation vee cannot go public. It is vay too controversial. Vat vee need to do is sit and wait—sit and wait for the right candidate, yah? Vee need to be patient. The donor has to be young, in a coma and more importantly, a John Doe. Vee are not robbing dee grave here. I say 'vee,' because dair are many of us vorking together, vanting to make dis happen.

"You would not believe the scope of dis operation. Widtout saying much more, vee can get the right donor and still keep it quiet." He paused, waiting for all of this to sink in. Gene was both terrified and excited.

"Vee need to make sure dat de body has no family who vill come looking. Another ting dat is needed for dis to work is having dee right recipient, someone who has no friends and, please forgive me, a rather dysfunctional family. Let us look at dee facts, Gene. Your dad has abandoned you, you have no friends and vee haven't seen your mudder. It's a perfect situation."

Chapter 28

Bruce wheeled him back to his room at Edgehill. It was already mid-afternoon. Bruce asked if it was okay to hang out with him for a little while. He knew Gene would need to talk about it. Gene said that would be fine. He was still in shock.

Bruce pulled up a chair. They both sat, not speaking, for what seemed like forever. There wasn't much more to say. Gene needed to digest all of what had recently happened.

Finally, Bruce stood up. "I'm going to get something to drink. Do you want anything?" Gene told him to get him something, too.

While he was gone, Gene was able to concentrate better, going through, step-by-step, what had taken place. He didn't want to miss a thing. He kept thinking of what Superman had said; that he wouldn't hesitate to do it. He thought that on paper it seemed wonderful, but ... living with another man's body? Or would it be living *in* another man's body? That was something totally different.

He whispered several questions to no one in particular. "Would I blend with the new body? We would in time become one, wouldn't we? Okay, I've got to really think hard about this. If the operation is successful, would I be feeling my limbs again or would they be borrowed limbs from a dead man? Would I feel different inside? Would his spirit be in me? Would my spirit be in him? I would be breathing through someone else's lungs. My blood would be pumped through someone else's heart. Wait a minute. It wouldn't even be my blood, would it?

"What about having sex again? I can't even think about that! What if I died during the operation without a body. Would I still be whole in soul? Therapy would be long and hard but it already is. I have no future unless I go for it. There is nothing to lose, absolutely nothing. So what if I die? I'm ... already dead."

Bruce came back with a drink. He helped him with the straw.

Finally, Gene looked at him, wanting desperately to talk about something else for a change. "So tell me, Bruce. Tell me about the blues band you played in."

Bruce was caught off guard. He smiled. "Yeah, the blues band, the 'Strange Movies Blues Band.' We had that written on our van. I've got to admit it wasn't a very professional job, either." He chuckled at the thought.

"We were playing a gig at an art school in a city named Penticton. We had a white '59 Chevy van. This one long-haired guy came up to us just before we were getting ready to play. He asked if they could paint some art on our vehicle. We said, 'Sure man, go for it.' When we had finished playing we checked out the van." He smiled at the memory. "There were flowers and hearts and peace signs and the kind of stuff that was supposed to be cool back then."

Gene was smiling, visualizing what it must have been like playing in a band, a blues band. "Tell me about the chicks."

"What? Oh, the chicks. Yeah, right. Well, there were always a few hanging around us, you know, like they thought we were rock stars or something." He rolled his eyes as he spoke. Gene chuckled.

"We, of course, tried acting like real cool dudes, man. The chicks would love it. We'd be playing up on stage and there was always one or two of them that would look at us and smile, you know? Like, they would smile, speaking with their eyes, saying, 'Hey dude, I would love to get to know you.' Ah yes, those were fun days."

Gene wished he could have been there, back in the sixties when there was peace and love and earth shattering music, music that had a purpose, music that changed the world. Life seemed so much simpler back then. It got his mind off the events of the day.

Bruce talked a little more, Gene enjoying every bit of it, trying to picture this tiny bald man as a rock star with long hair. He smiled. He couldn't imagine it.

Finally, Bruce said, "Hey, look at the time! I gotta get goin' here. Why don't I come back later and we'll continue this conversation, okay? I've got lots to tell." He winked as he left.

Once he was gone Gene's mind fell back to the events of the day. He was thinking of the moral issues associated with the whole idea of what they were proposing. He wondered why he was the chosen one.

He quietly talked to himself. It helped. Hearing his own voice gave him reassurance. "Will I be considered divine if this works? Are they not tempting fate? What about my name? Is that an omen? Gene is so close to genetic or perhaps Genesis. Was this always meant to be? Was I pre-destined? Will God allow this to happen?"

A nurse brought him some soup. He hardly tasted it. Once done, he asked if he could be put to bed. He was tired and needed to be alone. An hour later he was both laughing and crying. He knew he was being silly but he couldn't help himself. His nerves were acting up.

Wait a minute! What about my nerves? They wouldn't be my nerves anymore, would they? I'll feel pain through someone else's nerves with my brain. Isn't all of this totally against the rules of creation? Are we not creating one whole person with two? So many questions! He realized the only way to accept the situation would be to treat it as nothing more than an organ transplant. *Hmm, what did that Doctor White call it, a body transplant? Yes, that's it. Simply a body transplant.*

Gene found himself rationalizing. He also found himself thinking of God. He needed to pray. He needed to make things right with himself and his maker.

"Please, God. I have no other choice. Please, help me. Please, show me the way. Perhaps I'm being selfish but I don't want to live like this. This is not living. My body is already dead. Was it meant to be that I would end up like this? Was that Your plan? Or, am I going against You and all rules of nature by changing Your plan and going ahead with this operation? Please help me. Please, give me strength. I know I've already made my decision without praying to You beforehand. Please, help me see that this is the right decision in Your eyes. Please forgive me."

Gene couldn't remember the last time that he had prayed.

Bruce came by later, concerned with how the young man was doing. He looked at him for a moment before quietly closing the door part way as he left the room. The kid was sound asleep. He was worried about him. He had certainly been traumatized. It was unbelievable what was going on.

He thought, *"Of all the patients I've counseled, this is by far the most bizarre case."* He remembered what his instructor had told his class years ago, to expect the unexpected. No one could have dreamed something like this would be possible. It would appear to be science fiction to anyone who was not abreast with modern scientific advancement.

Back in the seventies, when Doctor White had performed his operations, it was hard to believe that someday man would be successful. Now, close to forty years later, it appeared success was inevitable.

Bruce was wondering how they should handle Gene now that he knew about Harley and Farley. He decided to suggest to the team that they all lay low for several days. The last thing they wanted was for Gene to not be totally committed to the whole idea.

He speculated that if the operation were a success—he had to admit he had some doubts—and Gene was not totally committed, things would become difficult. Yes, difficult. Gene could very well be angry and point an accusatory finger at the team, saying he had been hoodwinked into the operation. Bruce smiled at that one.

If Gene could, in fact, point an accusatory finger then the operation would have been deemed a success, wouldn't it?

He passed the nurse in the hallway, the one that Gene had been talking to. He looked back over his shoulder as he watched her go by. She was heading toward Gene's room. He turned around and followed, keeping his distance.

He ducked into an alcove nearby as she came up to Gene's door. She had some flowers and what looked like a card in her hand. She hesitated for a moment and then entered. Bruce decided to wait, wondering what she was up to.

She came out ten minutes later, standing in the hallway, wiping her eyes with a Kleenex. A moment later she was gone.

He snuck back into the room, fully expecting Gene to be awake. No, he was still sleeping. Good. He picked up the card.

Dear Mr. Gene,
I know you're still in love with the other girl. I can understand. I only wanted to be your friend. That was all. I hope we can still at least be friends.
Love, Cynthia

He smiled at the words, thinking, *"Good, very good indeed! Let's go with that. It's best Gene doesn't tell her he is in love with the other girl. That might be too strong a tactic, especially now that Cynthia is backing off. Good. Looks like the little problem might be solved after all."*

He carefully placed the card on the small table beside the bed, making sure Gene could easily read it when he woke.

Chapter 29

He hadn't had a nightmare in over a week. This one was the granddaddy of them all. It seemed so real. He could actually smell her perfume.

She came into his room in the middle of the night, telling him he was now saved. He didn't know what she meant. "Saved from what," he wondered? She wheeled him out into the hallway, carefully looking in both directions, making sure no one saw the abduction taking place. He wanted to scream but couldn't.

"Good, Mr. Gene. The coast is clear. Let's go."

She picked up the pace as she pushed him down one hallway and then another. They went through a maze of hallways. On occasion she would jerk the wheelchair, letting him know she was in control. They heard people behind them yelling for her to stop, to leave him here. He belongs here. God wants him here. It is His will!

Gene could see her reflection in the concave mirror mounted on a corner of a hallway intersection. She had two horns on her head. It was getting warmer and warmer. She pushed him into a room, avoiding the people that were trying to stop them. It was a dark room. His eyes adjusted. He saw his dinner partner, the older lady that moaned and groaned. They had momentarily interrupted her singing when they entered. She continued, singing 'Oh Susannah.' She stopped half-way through the song and began to moan, making a deep sorrowful sound while pointing an accusing finger toward him.

She said, "You. It's you! You are now the chosen one. You are next." He didn't know what she meant by 'next.' He heard Cynthia giggling behind him as Susannah continued.

"You're next on the table, Gene. Be careful. I was healthy before they did the devil's work on me. Now look. Look at me!"

He looked. He had a good hard look. Her face was changing. It was starting to melt. He could smell her. She was dead. She had been dead for months. He smelled her putrid flesh. There was more to the smell. There was the smell of perfume. The same perfume the devil wore in order to cover up her stench of death. No, it wasn't only the stench of death. There was also something else. There was another odor that was being masked. What was it? It was familiar. He couldn't quite remember, the thought nagging in the back of his mind.

Cynthia laughed crazily as they both watched Susannah try to get out of her chair. She was still pointing at Gene but her finger was now mostly bone. Her flesh had quickly dripped off her hands and face. She was still talking. Gene could see her jaw bone move, now partially exposed.

"You … be careful. God does not want this to happen. Don't sell your soul to the devil. God will punish you like he punished me!"

It suddenly occurred to him—understanding what the odor was. It was pig manure.

He woke up terrified. If he could, he would have bolted out of bed. He was breathing hard and fast. He could smell the perfume in the room. He tried turning his head, wondering where she was.

Has she come for me? And what's that smell besides the perfume? It's manure again! Where are the fucking pigs?

As he slowly woke he realized where the smell was coming from. It was coming from him. He had done it again. He had crapped himself.

"Oh, my God. Oh, my God." He sobbed. He was terrified. He lay there, waiting to calm down. He tried to console himself, saying it was all right. He was totally disgusted, wanting to die.

Finally, his breathing became somewhat regular. He slowly turned his head, noticing the flowers and card on the table. She had been there after all.

He lay in his filth most of the night until a nurse came and got help with cleaning him. That finally convinced him. Lying in his own waste, relying on others to clean him convinced him. He would rather die than go through life like that. There was now no doubt. He would do what was needed in order to try and live a somewhat normal life. At least he would be able to take care of himself once he had the operation.

Chapter 30

All members of the L-Team were present. This was a rare event. It was also a very special time. Mr. Lincoln wanted to bring everyone up to date. They were in the boardroom at Bosch Research. He took a sip of water before speaking.

"First of all, it's nice to see everyone here again. It's been some time since we've all gotten together. A lot has transpired." He looked around the room, pausing for effect before continuing. "Now, you are all very aware of most of what's been going on but certain events took place here over the last day or so. They were so important that I decided it was time to call this meeting ... to keep you all informed."

He took another drink, suppressing a cough. "First of all, I want to let you know about the condition of Harley and Farley." There was a murmur in the audience as he continued, "They are coming along fine in some ways and not so fine in others." There were a few nervous whispers in the group. "Please, let me have your full attention. Thank you. Now, Doctor Klein will say a few words. Please, doctor, if you will?"

Joseph Klein made his way to the front of the room. He had on his white smock. Several pens were in his breast pocket. One had leaked blue ink, creating a spot the size of a quarter. He was unaware, totally focused on what he needed to say. He nervously adjusted his glasses as he turned and faced the team.

"Tank you, Mr. Lincoln. Let me begin by describing to you how dee subjects are doink physically, yah?" There was silence as he looked around the room at the familiar faces. "It appears dat," he paused before blurting out, "dee spinal cords are re-attaching very nicely."

There was instant applause. Everyone was smiling and breathing easier. Some of the team members began to stand, still clapping. He put up his hands in order to quiet the audience while he, too, smiled.

His voice rose as he tried to speak over the hum in the room. "Dey are actually beginning to have some control over dair limbs and even dair tail. You are all very aware dat, initially after dee operations, their limbs moved rather sporadically, yah?" He was referring to several incidents during and after the operations when the bodies would twitch involuntarily. This was a perfectly normal nervous system response. The twitching had continued for well over a month after the initial operations. Some of the team members were hopeful it was because of the spinal cord re-attaching itself. It proved to be otherwise, again only a normal involuntary action. At the time, there were several disappointed people.

They all knew that, if the spinal cord were to re-attach itself, it would certainly take more than one month to do so. Now, several months later, they were seeing positive results.

"Vee now have more evidence dat the healing process is hard at work. You must realize vee have been very limited in our ability to perform a psychological evaluation on dee two patients, yah? I vill turn this part over to Mr. Whitman in a few minutes so dat he can explain. Before I do, I want to inform you dat Doctor Schultz and I have done some tests and physical observations. We are firmly convinced that dee twitching is, in part, now voluntary!"

There was more applause. Everyone in the room was still smiling. Doctor Klein continued, describing some of the tests he and Doctor Schultz had performed, going over the results with the team, answering several questions. When he was finished he turned the floor over to Bruce Whitman.

"Uh, thank you, Doctor Klein." He quickly got out of his chair and bolted to the front of the room. He needed to speak. He needed to explain. He became animated as he looked at the team.

"As the doctor has alluded, performing proper and full scale psychological tests on both Harley and Farley has been difficult if non-existent. Why is that, you might ask?" He paused, holding his hands partially up as he looked at each member before continuing. "Because of unforeseen circumstances.... No. Perhaps I should rephrase that. They weren't unforeseen because the issues were discussed among all of us in a hypothetical fashion months before."

Some of the team members began to whisper, a few shifting in their seats. All wondered how bad the news really was.

"Let me explain. We are all aware that prior to the operations there was concern for the animals' mental well-being. You will recall from the video of Doctor White's, back in nineteen-seventy, that the patient was extremely agitated after the operation. We had expected and predicted this would take place with both Farley and Harley.

"I spent many days and nights with them before the operation, trying to get to know them, if you will. Now, I know that getting to know a pig might sound silly to some," —there was nervous laughter— "but it's not much different than getting to know your cat or dog or whatever. "Now, as with humans, each of the two animals has his own personality and," he put his hands up higher for emphasis, "both have similar traits. For instance, they are both male. That in itself makes it easier for them to identify with each other. They are also brothers.

"We had decided beforehand that we would try to amass as many similarities as possible between both subjects. This has certain advantages. Each patient is actually somewhat of a control group for the other. If one patient reacted in a totally unpredictable way, in such a way that was out of the realm of its previous history, then we would know there was something seriously wrong. Do you all follow me so far?"

There were several nods as he continued. No one was smiling. He had their full, undivided attention. "Well, the fact of the matter is, they are both behaving in an abnormal fashion. They are not the same pigs they were before the operation. Of course they now have different physical bodies but that's not what I mean. Their post-operative behavior is not what we had predicted."

A few hands came up in the back. Some of the members had questions. He waved his hand saying, "Let me continue, please." The hands went down. Everyone was listening intently. "First of all, from my own personal observations, and I think I speak for Mr. Lincoln and Doctor Klein as well," he looked at both of them while nodding, "it appears we have two unhappy patients. Normally, after an operation and once the anesthetic wears off, patients are depressed and melancholy. These feelings usually go away in a few hours. In some cases they linger for a few days. This, however, is not a normal operation. Farley and Harley are responding differently. They are ... out of character."

He reached for a bottle of water as he continued and noticed for the first time that his hands were shaking. He refocused on what he needed to say. "The most obvious character difference is their aggression. These guys are mean. They used to love human contact but not any more. They are simply mean. We feel that, if they could, they would not hesitate in attacking us. At first we thought they were agitated because of possible pain. We made sure they were properly medicated, even upping their dosage of painkillers. It didn't help their temperament. Interestingly, they are both equally angry. Now, we all have to realize that if an operation were performed on any of us without our permission we would be angry, too, right?" A few people smiled despite the situation.

"We also have to realize that an operation of this magnitude would take an enormous amount of time for full recovery." Several members of the team nodded, knowing full well that it would indeed take a long time before the patients could possibly get back to normal again.

"It's deeper than that. I know they can't be interviewed like a human but the three of us, Doctor Klein, Mr. Lincoln and I, have discussed this and we were unanimous. We probably know Farley and Harley better than anyone here and we all agree they have a psychological problem. It's exacerbated by the fact we cannot communicate like we can with a human. We can only observe their outside behavior. We don't know what they are thinking." He looked around the room, seeing several nods of understanding.

"The other thing we are noticing is their heightened senses. Their sense of hearing is acute. Their sensitivity to light has been elevated. We need to speak softly and move slowly when we are in the McDonald Room. The lights need to be virtually off. We had hoped this abnormal behavior would diminish with time but it's been over twelve weeks now and, if anything, it's becoming more pronounced." He took another sip of water, his hands still shaking.

"The obvious solution would be to give them more medication but we don't want to do that. This is an experiment and, unfortunately for them, Harley and Farley's comfort is being compromised for the sake of medical science. We want to monitor the subjects under natural conditions. We do not want to give them any medication that could change their behavior. They are under medical and scientific observation."

Every team member was concerned with the condition of the two patients. Questions were asked. "Do you think we'll see an improvement soon? How can we change their temperament? Can we administer a different type of medication?" Bruce did his best in being honest with the team, trying to answer as many questions as possible. He was in the hot seat and didn't like it. He finally turned the meeting over to Mr. Lincoln.

"Thank you, Mr. Whitman." Mr. Lincoln tried his best to change the subject, getting away from the uncertainty of the patients' condition by attempting to turn the meeting around to a more positive note. "Now, the good news!"

The room was again silent, everyone looking expectantly toward him, waiting for something optimistic.

"We are ready, ready to take the giant step that is necessary in achieving what we have all been striving for."

The room grew deathly quiet. Several team members still had their minds on Farley and Harley, not quite comprehending Mr. Lincoln's announcement. "We have been monitoring several individuals, someone who might fit our criteria." He looked around the room and decided to give it to them straight. "We have found a potential candidate."

Slowly, they began to applaud, one after the other, picking up the tempo. Harley and Farley were, for now, forgotten.

"Yes, it is good news." He tried to speak over the noise. "You are all aware of how hard we have worked in finding that special person." Many heads nodded in agreement. "He is a young man who has no family. We are hopeful he will participate very soon."

The room was becoming noisy with the latest news. The excitement was beginning to build. Everyone had been waiting for the next step and it now appeared to be happening. Mr. Lincoln patiently waited for the nervous energy of the team to subside.

"Now, about what Mr. Whitman has been telling us." He knew he needed to further explain. "I know you are all concerned about the character changes that have occurred in our patients and how it might affect our human candidate. I emphasize the word 'might,' ladies and gentlemen, because we still are not sure what will happen. Anyhow, we have a very big advantage in working with a human simply because we can communicate. We can find out what he is feeling. We can observe his mood much more precisely and we now have the specific medication that we can eventually administer in order to facilitate things."

He talked for over an hour about the procedure and how they were slowly preparing the subject for his transfer to Bosch. Several members had questions that were answered. Finally, near the end of the meeting, Mr. Lincoln had one last announcement to make.

"I have some news that will no doubt disturb all of you." The room went silent. "Doctor Klein received a death threat a few days ago and," the noise grew as everyone tried to speak at once. Irvine was becoming a hot bed for fanatics, or so it seemed.

"Please, please! May I have your attention? Thank you. Now, as I was saying, Doctor Klein received a death threat a few days ago and it was suggested that he stay here at Bosch indefinitely. We are hoping it is only a hoax but in view of what has happened recently, we want to use extreme caution. Be very careful out there. If you hear of anything that might cause concern please don't hesitate to call me. My door is always open. Agreed?"

Everyone nodded. The meeting was quickly adjourned. It had gone over the allotted time frame. There was now much preparation to be done.

Chapter 31

Thursday passed by quickly. Gene went through the motions of eating. He visited the woodworking shop and continued making model airplanes but his mind was elsewhere. After supper he was back in his room listening to music on his headphones when Cynthia walked in.

He was wondering when she would show up. He had wanted to tell her Lindsey was his girlfriend, but after reading the card that said she only wanted to be friends, well, that changed things. He thought he would see what her mood would be like the next time they met.

"Hey, Cynthia, thank you for the flowers and card." She blushed as she lowered her eyes.

"You're welcome."

"Can you take off these headphones for me, please?"

She leaned over. Her breasts were almost in his face.

"Come over and sit." He felt like he was calling his puppy dog.

She looked at him and smiled as she sat in the chair, hoping he had gotten a good view. "So, how have you been, Mr. Gene?"

"Good, I guess. And you?"

"Lonely. I miss you."

"Look, Cynthia." He was becoming angry. "I thought that you wanted to just be friends."

"I do. There's nothing wrong in missing a friend, is there?"

He didn't answer.

"Gene?"

"Huh?"

"Is everything all right? I mean, you look … tired. What's going on?"

"Uh, no. Everything is fine."

She didn't press it any further. He had answered too quickly, almost as if he'd been jabbed with a needle. He did look tired. He had circles under his eyes. She wondered what they were doing to him. Was he getting enough sleep?

They talked for over an hour about all kinds of things. He was glad for that, feeling the need to get his mind away from the procedure. The room was darkening as night crept in. The only light came from the hallway beyond the partially closed door.

He found out she was an only child who had grown up on a farm. She, too, had never been close to her parents. He was intrigued, slowly realizing they both had a lot in common. He knew she really did want to be his friend. He was becoming comfortable with her again. In a way, he felt sorry for her. She felt sorry for him as well. She bent over and gave him a kiss on the forehead, saying she would come by the next day. He enjoyed talking to someone who he thought really wanted to be his friend.

A minute later he was sitting alone in the dark, wondering why Bruce or anyone else hadn't come by to speak to him. Was that their plan, to leave him alone so he could squirm? He had news for them. He'd already made his decision. He was going to do it.

Chapter 32

For three days Gene went through the motions of being a patient at Edgehill. Although he had decided to go ahead with the procedure, deep down he still wasn't totally convinced. He had expected Bruce to visit him daily but he never showed. This concerned him. He wondered if they had lost interest in him, perhaps thinking twice about choosing him.

The more he thought about it, the more he wanted to be operated on. His life was a dead end. He didn't want to make model airplanes and have lunch with a drooling mental case anymore. He wished he could get it over with as soon as possible.

He hated the waiting, the anxiety. He wasn't getting a restful sleep. He was given medication. It dulled his senses. That was good. It was designed to make things easier, to mask the problems of the real world. It made him sleepy and it clogged his brain. He tried to think clearly, finally talking out loud, noticing a slur in his voice.

"What *ish* my problem? Well, the main one, of course, ish, I can't fucking walk. Nah, that's not a problem, dude. Yeah, right. Of course it's a problem, a big fucking problem, but that ishn't it. Oh yeah, Harley and Farley, the brothers from hell. Ish that the problem that I can't shake? Yeah, that ish a problem all right. I can't get over that one. I keep sheeing them in my mind. I keep hearing them moan. But … there is shtill one more problem in that brain of mine. What ish it?"

He had blocked something out. He kept thinking he had a problem and couldn't solve it because he wasn't sure what the problem was. It would come and go. He was at a crossroads in life. He needed to make a choice. He knew that. He had to decide—to decide if he really wanted to be saved.

"Yesh, saved. It's the operation," he told himself. "What about the operation? They were planning on an organ transplant. Yesh, that's it! An organ transplant, that's all. It's done all the time. There are heart transplants, kidney transplants, lung transplants. They even did a face transplant. It's a normal thing to do now, right?" He desperately wanted to convince himself that it was a typical procedure.

"No, don't fucking kid yourshelf, my friend. This ish not normal. This ish the big enchilada." He tried to reason with himself but had difficulty thinking straight. "What ish it that you are exactly thinking of getting done? Tell me. Make it clear! What ish it that you are thinking of getting done?" He paused, feeling sweat form on his brow.

"A body transplant." He heard himself croak those three words. He could feel the sweat running down his cheeks. His bowels loosened. He swore that if he could shake he would have fallen off the bed. The very idea sickened him.

Just when he thought he had made his decision to go ahead, he would back out. He needed to talk to someone, someone other than Bruce or a doctor. This was too big for him to decide alone. "Wait a minute," he reasoned, "I've already decided, haven't I? Look at the alternatives."

Again he would go back and forth, not being able to come to a decision. He desperately needed to open up—to talk to someone, to explain what he was about to do. There was only one person he could think of, one person that was an outsider to all of this.

It was Monday, five days after he had been introduced to Harley and Farley. He couldn't get over what they had done to those poor creatures, the way they had experimented on them. They were in his mind almost every minute of the day. He needed to visit with them. He wanted to see how they were healing, hoping that he could accept the whole idea better if he at least saw them once more. He was deep in thought, his emotions stretched to the limit, when Cynthia walked in.

They chatted for a little while. She sat on a chair across from him. He was in his wheelchair. Finally, she pulled closer as she spoke. "Gene, you seem so ... preoccupied. What is bothering you?" She noticed his voice was slightly slurred.

"Uh, nothing." He had become so indecisive over the past few days he wasn't sure if he wanted to tell her anything.

"Yes there is. Please, tell me. I'm your friend. I love—I mean I *like* you. I don't want to see you this way. For the past week you've been going around like you've seen a ghost. Please, tell me, okay?" She leaned slightly closer.

He looked into her eyes. She was the only person he could talk to that was fairly neutral to all of this. She did care for him and his well-being. He knew that. He felt he could trust her. He had no one else to talk to. He knew she would listen to what he had been going through. He cleared his throat.

"Look, Cynthia, can you keep a secret? I mean, really keep a secret?" He lowered his voice as he spoke. The sun had already set. They were sitting in the dark.

"Of course I can. What is it?" She pulled her chair closer, almost knee to knee.

He hesitated, finally deciding he had to unload. He couldn't keep it within him any longer. It was too damn big to carry in his heart, in his soul! He had to tell her at least part of the story. He whispered, "Cynthia, pleash swear on your mother's grave you will not tell a soul about thish."

She leaned even closer, close enough to kiss. Normally she would be thinking about kissing him, but not now. This whole scene was frightening her.

What could be so horrible, so much of a secret? She needed to know. "I swear I will not tell another living soul." Her voice was shaky.

He looked at her for a moment, tears in his eyes. She decided to be patient, waiting for him to speak when he was good and ready. It didn't take long.

"I ... wash taken ... to the lab lash week." His voice trailed off.

"To *where*? She raised her voice. Did you say the ... lab?" She quickly thought, *"Oh my God! They took him to the lab here at Edgehill and found out he has inoperable cancer."*

"Shhh. Pleash, keep it down, okay?" He cleared his throat. "Yeah, you know, the lab." He looked at the door and then back at her, whispering even lower. "The fucking lab ... at Bosch!" He was clearly frustrated, having little patience with her.

"Yes, go on." She was squirming in her chair, hands on his knees.

"Well, I shaw things that frightened me." He was talking very softly as he continued looking into her eyes. The room was now black, the door completely closed. All he could see, in his drug induced state, were two small points of reflective light that went off and on as she blinked.

"Things? What do you mean 'things'? " She was getting impatient. *Kripes, Gene! What are you talking about?* She wanted to shake the information out of him. She didn't realize how hard she was squeezing his knees, wanting more details. Gene was totally unaware.

"I shaw—. Look, do you promise you won't tell anyone thish? Ish just between you and me, you know? I've got to get thish off my chest but I can't have you or anyone elsh make a big deal out of it, okay? Thish ish between you and me!" He was raising his voice, clearly tormented by the whole situation.

She was madly moving her head up and down, leaning over him, her face inches from his, still squeezing, her hands now creeping up to his lower thighs. "Yes, yes, yes! You know that. You can trust me."

"Yeah, okay. I shaw some things at the research center, Cynthia. They were unnatural, okay? Like, I don't think I can tell you more."

"Tell me!" She was clearly exasperated, almost screaming. She would not let this go. "What did you see?" She needed to know. She grabbed his hands, squeezing as hard as she could. He couldn't feel a thing.

His head lowered as he looked down at the floor, not sure on how to continue. Cynthia got down on one knee in front of him, looking up into his eyes. "Tell me, for your own good! What did you see?" She was pleading.

"Uh, I shaw—. They were teshting animals. They were teshting these pigs and they were moaning. It was terrible. It wash shocking. I have never seen anything like it!" He began to sob, drool running down his mouth. He was an emotional wreck.

She tried to pump more information out of him but couldn't. He had shut down, not able to talk anymore.

I always suspected they were using animals. How could they? And my poor Gene, he's tormented by what he's seen. I never knew he was such an animal lover. They must be torturing those poor furry guinea pigs in their laboratories!

Tears were running down his cheeks. It made her angry, seeing her poor man in so much pain. She slowly let go of his hands, backing away. She took a deep breath, trying to pull herself together. She wanted to call that girl she had met. *What was her name? Oh yes, Sheila, the animal activist.* Yes, she wanted to call her and let her know what they were doing but she had made a promise. Maybe she could talk to Gene some more and find out exactly what was going on. She knew it wouldn't be tonight. He'd had enough. It broke her heart, seeing him sob like that.

She left him there weeping. She tried to comfort him but he didn't respond. She called the floor nurse. Minutes later Gene was medicated and back in bed.

Chapter 33

He woke up refreshed. He had finally gotten a good night's sleep. He thought about the previous night and what he had said. He was angry with himself and also with her.

She took advantage of me. That's what she had gone and done. That conniving bitch! As soon as I began to show any weakness she was there taking advantage. How fucking stupid of me for telling her anything!

A big part of him was relieved. He knew he had needed to talk to someone. He couldn't quite remember exactly what he had said. He thought he told her about animals at Bosch. He hoped he hadn't said too much. Should he try to contact her and do damage control? No, it was too late. She promised she wouldn't tell. She said they were friends. Would she say something? It wouldn't matter if she did. Who would she tell, another nurse? Harold? And so what if she did say something. As far as he was concerned it would be hearsay.

He was feeling better. Somewhere in the night he had made a firm and final decision. He hoped it wasn't too late.

Connie, his nurse, came into his room and gave him a quick wash over his upper body and face and then told him to "take these." Her hand held two pills.

"Connie?"

"Uh huh?"

"I want to see Mr. Whitman, please. I don't want to take those little purple things anymore."

Connie had suspected Gene had gone into a depressed state several days ago. She knew that was why Doctor Klein prescribed the pills. Now Gene wanted to see his counselor. That was a good sign.

"Okay, Gene. I'll see if I can contact him. Now, what would you like for breakfast?"

Bruce was listening intently when his pager went off. Doctor Klein was there as well, his face ashen. It looked as if he had seen a ghost. Mr. Lincoln was giving them some bad news.

"There wasn't too much damage, Joseph. The Fire Department responded rather quickly."

Doctor Klein couldn't believe it. Someone had thrown a Molotov cocktail through his living room window. Part of his carpet had burned and there was smoke damage. "Should vee tell dee police about dee death tret?" His voice was shaky.

"No, Joseph, I don't think it would be a good idea. Let's leave it at that. We'll tell them you haven't been home these past few days because of your work here. I'll call the maintenance department, if you like, and see that they board up the window."

Doctor Klein slowly nodded, still in shock. Mr. Lincoln smiled inwardly, thinking, *"No matter how smart Doctor Klein thinks he is, he still has trouble tying his shoes."*

Joseph looked at the floor, deeply disturbed, as he spoke. "I still vant to review dee damage."

"Of course. Why don't you take Emil, our security guard, with you? I'll call him and see if he's available." Mr. Lincoln thought Emil would be the perfect choice. He usually didn't come in for his shift until six p.m. He knew Emil would like the overtime.

Doctor Klein agreed. He was very much shaken by the incident. He needed to file a police report as well as contact his insurance agent. He left Mr. Lincoln and made a few phone calls. Bruce left a minute later, telling Mr. Lincoln he needed to visit the patient.

As soon as they were gone, Mr. Lincoln reached down into a pocket of the wheelchair, pulling out the revolver. He spun the cylinder, making sure everything was in working order before placing it back under his blanket. He wheeled down the hall, once again making his way to the McDonald Room. He was feeling very protective of his babies, now, more so than ever.

Chapter 34

"Good morning, Gene."

"Hi, Bruce."

"It looks like you had a good night's sleep."

Gene nodded as he sat in his wheelchair, his nightgown just above his knees.

Bruce glanced down, noticing several bruise marks on Gene's legs, not knowing they were the result of Cynthia's squeezing only two days before. He wondering what had happened. He quickly brought his eyes up to meet Gene's, asking him, "So ... you wanted to see me?"

"Yes, I guess I did."

"You mean, you're not sure?"

"Look, Bruce. Can we talk for a little while?"

"Of course."

Bruce had decided on playing hardball with him. Gene had had several days to think about it and now it was time for him to make a decision. It would still take a while to prepare the necessary paper work in order to have him moved from Edgehill. Most of it was already done, but they still needed a few days once the decision was made. He was checking things off in his mind as he sat with Gene, giving him time to think about what he wanted to say.

The team had to be careful how they would handle Gene's extraction if he decided he wanted to go through with the operation. That was only one of the problems. They had already agreed on a partial plan several months earlier, before Gene was even in the picture.

The prospective patient would be quickly moved from Edgehill to live with his so-called grandmother back east. They had even set up a phone number in Boston which would be call-forwarded to a special phone number back here at the lab. The caller would think they were speaking to someone in Boston, unaware that the call was rerouted back to Bosch. The line also had voice mail. Whoever wanted to call and check on the patient would initially need to leave a message. This would give the team time to come up with an appropriate response.

There was also a mailing address that had been set up. Any mail sent to the address was forwarded back to Bosch in care of Mr. Lincoln. Again, anyone who seriously wanted to contact the patient simply couldn't.

"Uh, I just needed to talk a little, you know?"

Bruce was still wondering about the bruises. He focused back on Gene, nodding. "I understand."

"So, tell me. Being a counselor, what to you think about all of this?"

He looked into Gene's eyes for a moment, thinking hard, forcing a smile. "I would jump at the chance."

Gene looked back at him, smiling as well. "But Bruce, I can't jump."

Bruce found the joke rather lame. He suddenly became tired of the whole situation. His smile quickly faded—his nerves on edge. "Okay, bad choice of words. I would take it. I don't think there would be too many people who wouldn't. It's a gift. There are no guarantees. You'd be the first. It's a very serious operation but it can be done. You've seen the results."

"Yeah, I have. I was wondering. Could I go and visit them again? You know, I want to spend some time with them in the McDonald room. We would all have something in common and I only want to be with them for a while."

"Now," he paused, still looking at Gene, "you could probably go and see them but only after you agree to the operation. You have to make that choice, Gene, and you have to make it now." His voice was firm. So were his eyes.

Gene was silent. He had hoped he could see Harley and Farley once more before his final decision.

Bruce continued. "We can't have you coming and going in the research lab. People would start to notice and wonder. We can't take any more chances. We took a very big risk the other day in showing you what we did. We are out on a limb here. We won't give out anything more. You have got to make your decision and make it now.

"That's why I came here. I was hoping that you were ready. It appears that you're still undecided. Well, we can't have that." He held up his hands in surrender as he quickly got up, still looking at Gene. "I'm sorry that you're not prepared, Gene. We gave you a wonderful opportunity but you're not ready for it. Good luck and all the best to you."

He quickly turned and walked out the door.

"Bruce. Please, Bruce! Come back!"

He was in the hallway just outside Gene's door when he heard the pleading voice. He smiled to himself before going back into the room. He was good. He knew how to shake people up.

"Yes?" He was all business.

"I'm ...," Gene gulped, "ready."

Chapter 35

The phone in her office rang once more. It was one of those mornings. For some reason, Tuesday always seemed to be bad.

"Good morning. Karol from Administration. How may I help you?"

"Yes? Hello?" The woman caller sounded as if she were far away. She also sounded rather old.

"Yes, how may I help you?"

"Oh, yes. My name is Beatrice."

Karol smiled. She was right. The woman was probably in her sixties with a name like 'Beatrice.'

The lady identified herself as Gene's grandmother from Boston. She had learned that Gene was in their care and wanted to know how he was doing.

"Yes, Beatrice, he's here!" Karol was surprised. This came right out of the blue.

"Can I speak to his doctor, please? I want to know how he is."

"Of course, I'll page him for you. Please hang on."

Doctor Klein heard his page and picked up a house phone in a hallway at Edgehill. He was quickly connected to Bea. "Hello, Doctor Klein speaking."

"Is this line secure?"

"Yes, I believe it is." It took him a second or two to catch on. He had been told to expect the call from a team member.

She explained. "It's all set. Things are in motion. We'll prepare the required forms over the next few days. We will have him released by the end of next week and then we'll get two of our guys to pick him up in an ambulance and bring him to the airport. Of course he won't really go there. Everything sound good so far?"

A nurse walked by while he was on the phone. He spoke a little louder so she could hear. "Thank you for calling! I'm sure Gene will be very happy with dee good news. He never told us about his grandmother. I'm sure he will love to live widt you, yah? I'll be visiting him in a few minutes and let him know. You take care, too. Bye for now."

The nurse looked at him over her shoulder. He smiled. News traveled fast here at Edgehill.

He hung up the phone, thinking about the call. A moment later he picked up the handset and made another call, this one to Bruce. He would meet him in Gene's room in a few minutes.

He made his way to his small office, still deep in thought. He found his briefcase, checking to make sure all the necessary papers were in order. He was both excited and apprehensive. Things were starting to happen.

He thought about what needed to be done next as he made his way to C-7. They would be sending a fax with a copy of Bea's birth certificate to Administration by early next week. Also included would be a signed patient transfer form requesting that Gene be moved to a new location—Bea's home.

Gene would need to sign another form stating Edgehill Care Facility would not be held responsible for his well-being after he left the building. Bea also needed to send in a 'Statement of Income' form showing that she was financially capable of looking after him.

One other form was needed, an inspection form done by a registered nurse back in Boston verifying that Gene's new location met and exceeded minimum requirements for patient care at home. Mr. Lincoln had fixed everything.

All that was now required was Gene's signature on their agreement that gave Bosch Research Inc. permission to do what they deemed necessary to improve his physical abilities. The agreement also stated he was doing it voluntarily and in the interests of both his well-being and medical science.

He was waiting in his wheelchair when Doctor Klein walked in. It had only been a half-hour since Bruce had last visited. Doctor Klein closed the door behind him, smiling, not noticing the bruises on his young patient's legs. He was totally focused on what he needed to say and do. He tried to make the smile appear reassuring. Gene smiled back.

He walked over and sat down beside him, his stomach now churning. "Bruce said you had some good news, yah?"

"Yeah, I've come to a decision. I want a better life, Doctor. I would kick myself the rest of my life if I didn't agree to this now while I still have the chance." He thought again about what he had said, that he would 'kick' himself. This time it wasn't funny.

"Good, Gene. I can assure you that you are not making a mistake."

"Doctor?"

"Yes?"

"Can you tell me a little about what will be taking place? You know … the procedure?"

"Of course, I vill tell you vat you need to know after you sign dee papers and are transferred, yah?"

"Yeah and … Doctor?"

"Yes, Gene, vat is it?" He was peering over his glasses as he spoke. He had his briefcase on his knees, fumbling inside, trying to find the papers, his stomach still upset.

"Can I visit Harley and Farley when I move over?"

"Vee vill talk about dat later, yah? It's important for you to understand dat they are still recovering and are very sensitive to certain tings. Dey require a lot of, how would you say, quiet time? Yah, quiet time but … vee shall see what vee can do."

They both looked up as the door opened. It was Bruce.

The papers were quickly signed. Gene requested a copy. Bruce looked at Joseph and then back at Gene. "Look, Gene. We can't give you a copy. If we gave you a copy of this agreement it would incriminate us and also let anyone who read it know that you moved to Bosch. We are going to great lengths in order to have your move undetected."

Gene nodded, "I understand. I guess that's fair." He knew they wouldn't give him a copy. After all, where would he keep it? What would he do with it if he later decided things had not worked out? He'd be in seclusion by then. Incognito.

He had a question he needed to ask. "What do you need to do in order to move me?"

Bruce again looked at Doctor Klein and then back at Gene. "Well, first of all, now that you've signed the agreement, you are officially on the team!" He smiled and stuck out his hand for Gene to shake. He paused, realizing what he had done. He ended up by patting him on the shoulder instead. Bruce had a tear in his eye. "One day soon, if things go as planned, we *will* shake hands." He was very much relieved.

"Yes, Gene. Congratulations! Vee are very proud of you. It will be all good, yah?" Doctor Klein was smiling as well. It looked as if he, too, was becoming sentimental, his stomach now settling.

Gene was feeling better than he had ever felt since his accident. A giant load had been lifted off his shoulders. He was now officially on the team.

"Okay, here is what needs to be done, yah?" Joseph's voice lowered as he spoke. Both Bruce and he looked toward the door, making sure it was still closed. "Now vee are setting tings in motion." He was rubbing his hands together.

"There has been a call placed to Administration here at Edgehill from your long lost grandmother." He winked as he said it. Doctor Klein was enjoying himself, also relieved that the agreement had been signed. "She lives back in Boston and vill be faxing us all dee necessary paper work so dat you can be out of here sometime near dee end of next week." He winked again.

Gene was excited. "Next week! Why do I have to wait a week?" He knew he sounded like he was whining but he was ready to get going now!

"Vell, Grandma Bea, bless her heart, needs time to get dee various forms plus her income statement together. Vee have to be realistic and not rouse anyone's suspicions, yah? So, to make it plausible, it vill take until the end of next week. Plus, vee have to book a flight for you as well." He winked again.

"Then, Doctor Klein, how soon until you operate?" He was becoming annoyed with the winking. *Come on, Doc. You winked once and I got it, okay? Stop with that and give me more information.* He tried to be patient as Klein went through his spiel.

"Vell, it could still take some time, Gene. Vee are now on the lookout for a candidate. He needs to fulfill certain qualifications. Vee will discuss dat later at your new home, yah? But I can tell you dat vee have a vast network vee can use. Vee have already entered your blood type, age, skin color, height, weight, tings of that nature, into dee database. Vee just need to wait until the right donor appears."

Bruce outlined who this 'Bea' was. She would be Gene's grandmother on his mother's side. She had visited on occasion and always felt Gene was her favorite. His grandfather had died years ago. She lived in Boston and was financially well off so had the resources to care for him. She was only fifty-nine years old.

They went through it together, making sure all loose ends were covered if there were any questions.

For the first time, Doctor Klein noticed the bruising on Gene's knees and lower thighs. "Vat has happened to your legs, Gene? Dair are marks, hand marks!"

"Uh, what? I don't know." Gene hadn't been aware of them until now, still not realizing Cynthia had been tightly squeezing his legs two nights ago.

Doctor Klein raised the night gown, closely examining his patient. "Gene, are you sure you don't know vat has happened?" He was always concerned with patient abuse from the staff at Edgehill. On occasion it did occur.

"Uh, no!" Gene stammered, not sure what to say.

Doctor Klein didn't push it any further, knowing he would need to talk to Gene's physiotherapist. Obviously Harold had been applying far too much pressure on his legs when they were exercising. That wasn't the first time he had done that sort of thing. They left his room a few minutes later, Gene still puzzled as to how he had gotten the bruises.

Doctor Klein phoned Karol from Administration, letting her know that it appeared Gene's grandmother lived in Boston, was wealthy and wanted to take care of him.

"That's wonderful, Doctor! How commendable of her. I wonder why she never tracked him down sooner."

"Vell, you know Karol, the poor young man comes from a very dysfunctional family, yah? In fact, his father doesn't want to have anyting to do with him. Vat a shame. He is lucky to have a kind soul like Bea, yah? Someone in dee family probably contacted her or perhaps a neighbor." Without missing a beat, he continued. "I shall find out for you, yah?"

"Oh no, that's okay—I was just wondering, that's all. I'm so happy for him!" She hung up, thinking how miracles could sometimes happen. She had seen far too many cases where there was no family. Many patients had been put on a shelf, left in care of the state. Of course they were in good hands but no one could give them better treatment and love than a caring family member. *Yes, today is turning into a very good day ... for a Tuesday.*

Chapter 36

The day went by very slowly for him. The only thing planned was more exercises with Harold. Later, he had supper in the main dining area. He looked across at Susannah, wondering what she would think if she knew what they had planned for him. It brought back the terrible nightmare with Cynthia and her devil horns. He would never forget Susannah in his dream, sitting across from him, pointing at him and saying, "Don't sell your soul to the devil."

He was back in his room, listening to 'devil's music' when Cynthia appeared at his bedside. He was startled, not hearing her come in.

She took charge and quickly removed his headphones. "Here, these are for you." She had a box of chocolates. As usual, she had a big smile on her face.

He was touched. His guard went down. No one had ever given him anything before. "Cynthia, you didn't have to do that!"

"Oh, I know, but I wanted to. You looked like you could use some cheering up, especially after the last time I saw you."

He spoke quickly. "Oh yeah, I was a bit of a mess. You know, I wanted to talk to you about that."

"You did? What did you want to tell me?" She was dying to get more information. Since she had seen him last, all she had thought about were rabbits and guinea pigs being subjected to needles and stuff.

He needed to downplay what he had told her, especially now that he had made his decision to go ahead with the operation. "Well, I've been taking these pills and they"—he shook his head as much as he possibly could—"made me real dopey, you know?"

She took a long hard look at him, considering what he said. *If he's trying to deny it, I don't believe him. He was far too upset the other night. He did see something at Bosch and now he's having second thoughts about telling me.* She tried to reassure him by saying, "You don't have to be afraid, Gene. I won't tell anyone. I promise. I told you that the other night. Remember? You know you can trust me."

"Oh, I know, Cynthia, I know! It's just that I might have exaggerated a little, that's all."

She looked at him. *Bull poop! Someone's got to him. Maybe he was threatened.* "That's okay, Mr. Gene. Let's talk about something else, all right? Let me tell you about my job here." She figured if she didn't make a big deal out of it he would open up to her a little more.

She spent at least a half-hour talking about silly things she had done, blah, blah, blah. She fed him chocolates, taking one or two for herself as she talked, all the while wondering about what he had really seen at Bosch. He enjoyed her visit and finally felt relaxed. He decided it was nice to have company, someone who talked about other things rather than the operation, although it was never far from his mind.

Chapter 37

It could have been worse. There was a fair amount of smoke damage plus a broken window. The insurance adjuster had met Doctor Klein at his home. They reviewed the damage together and talked about policy coverage and deductibles while watching the hospital maintenance men place plywood over the window.

Seeing the damage first hand had made the doctor feel vulnerable. Emil, one of the security men, finally arrived at the scene making Doctor Klein somewhat more comfortable. Emil had been a long time employee at Bosch and was now in charge of security, being very familiar with the building wing that housed the research center. He considered himself a bit of a handyman. He tried to ease the tension, changing the mood to something more positive.

"You know, Doctor Klein, I'm a bit of an accomplished cook."

Doctor Klein couldn't help but smile. He got a lot of that. Some people felt inferior in a doctor's company, treating them with reverence, trying to prove to them that they, too, had their own achievements to talk about. He looked over at Emil. He suspected that, yes, he was probably a good cook, judging by his waist size. He was happy to listen to him talk about his famous 'Burritos' instead of 'deductibles.'

Later, Doctor Klein went down to the police station and spoke with the desk sergeant, Frank Morgan. He was asked routine questions. "Are you suspicious of anyone? Do you have any enemies? Why do you think you were targeted?"

He told him that, as far as he knew, he had no enemies and perhaps he was targeted simply because he was a doctor at Irvine General. The sergeant nodded in agreement, telling him to be careful. He suggested he find another place to live for the time being. Doctor Klein told him he was rarely home because he worked long hours but would certainly heed his advice.

The officer mentioned they would continue with the investigation and get back to him if they found out anything more. Doctor Klein gave him his cell phone number before leaving.

Several minutes later he was back at Bosch. Joseph decided to get down to business as he took out his access card and ran it through the card swipe on the door leading to the restricted area. He needed to focus on their project more than ever, trying to pull his mind away from the recent attack on his house. He was very much upset with the incident. He didn't handle violence very well, easily becoming unnerved.

He headed straight to a computer terminal in the boardroom. He wanted to access their database, wondering how things were going with the search for a donor. Were there any possible hits? He keyed in his password on the computer screen and began going through the list. He knew there were thousands of men across the country close to Gene's age that had been in a coma ranging from several days to several years. The L-Team had deliberately filtered out most of those people mainly because of location. It was difficult to transport a coma victim hundreds or thousands of miles without being noticed. There needed to be at least one, and in some cases two, medical attendants with the patient at all times. It was far more convenient to transport a possible donor by ambulance, away from prying eyes.

Then there was the issue of immediate family and friends. Again, they had to filter out those victims who had family ties. The general health of the individual had to be assessed as well. They wanted a healthy candidate. Most of the coma victims had either suffered a stroke, a heart attack or a serious accident. Stroke victims were no good because they usually suffered from clogged arteries and poor circulation. Heart attack victims wouldn't do for obvious reasons.

That left accident victims, the majority being in motor vehicle accidents. Of those, a very high percentage had major bodily injuries as well as head trauma. There were also gunshot victims, drowning victims, as well as many others who had met with various types of injuries. If need be, they could also access the armed forces data base on war victims. They didn't think that would be necessary.

There was a list of criteria that needed to be followed. One was the proximity of the donor. He had to be relatively close to Bosch. Ideally within two hours by ambulance. Another was the donor's general health—it had to be good. There could be no alcohol or drug addiction, obesity or things of that nature. He needed to be free and clear of any health issues.

Compatibility was also essential for the perfect match. There was a long list they had to address ranging from the blood type, skin type, age, body size, up to and including ethnic background. They surmised that the more similar the victim was to the recipient, the less chance of any unforeseen issues arising later.

Another big concern was social ties. He could not have any. He had to be single, independent, unemployed and have no children—essentially a loner.

That last one, 'Social Ties,' is probably more difficult than the others. Hmmm, let's see what we can find.

Doctor Klein knew the vast majority of people were social animals. They had family, partners and usually children. The plus side to this was the age group. The L-Team wanted someone close to Gene's age, ideally slightly older. A young man near twenty years old would be perfect because the odds were he might not have a career job, wife or children. The down side was most men that age still had living parents and siblings.

He noticed three possibilities. One was seventeen years old who had been in a car accident. He suffered from severe head wounds, had been in a coma for over a week and the next of kin had not yet been located. The problem was the young man had stolen a car for a joy ride, was chased by the police and then had the accident. He had no identification on him which made it difficult to track down his medical history.

The other two possibilities also had issues. One was twenty-eight years old. The team suggested that age compatibility would be a problem. The closer the donor was to the recipient's age, the better. A few years either way would not be too much of a problem. The ideal ages were between seventeen and twenty-three years old.

The reason for a limited age spread was the biological clock mechanism. They were dealing with a thousand possible problems, one of them being the human aging process. Since conception, the body's internal clock begins to tick. This clock tells it when to trigger certain functions at certain times. For example, the clock would determine when to grow teeth, hair, enclose the skull completely to protect the brain, things of that nature.

What they had to be careful of was correctly matching the clocks. They did not need to be synchronized, but they still needed to be relatively close. Seven years was the decided criterion, one year younger and up to five years older. If they went any younger than seventeen they predicted there could be developmental problems since a sixteen-year-old might possibly still be growing. The growing process needed to essentially be over.

The last candidate was closer in age but had an aunt that wanted to take care of him. If it came down to the wire, Doctor Klein knew Mr. Lincoln wouldn't hesitate in using that donor if need be. He could have his contacts tell the aunt her nephew had unfortunately died of his injuries, meanwhile transporting him here to Bosch.

No, there was nothing in the database that was perfect, at least right now. He knew it would only be a matter of time before they hit pay dirt.

Chapter 38

Mr. Lincoln was in the McDonald Room looking at Harley. Harley looked back. On occasion he would grunt at Mr. Lincoln. Mr. Lincoln would grunt back, smiling. He wanted to connect as much as possible with them. That seemed to satisfy Harley. He had a drink of water and sucked on another cough drop as he studied his babies. He had to be careful about his coughing. That would set them off into fits of moaning.

Each pig was several hundred pounds. They were in adjacent pens and could see, smell and hear each other. It seemed to Mr. Lincoln that Harley was overcoming his hardship slightly faster than Farley. That was this week. Last week it appeared to be the opposite.

Lincoln was very pleased that both operations were successful. It was nice, no, it was essential, to have both of them alive. The team had two subjects they could compare. He only wished they would come to life more. They had no zest. He swore they didn't want to live. They didn't want to be here. Who could blame them? The poor creatures had no idea of what had been in store for them. They never needed the operations. They were both healthy to begin with.

Mr. Lincoln felt responsible for their pain. Of course he was. He and the L-Team sacrificed the pigs so mankind could benefit. It was an unfortunate circumstance. He rationalized, again telling himself the experiments were needed in order to move forward.

He looked at Harley again. Harley lifted his head an inch or two off the straw and grunted. To Lincoln, it sounded like it had threatening undertones. With that grunt he could have been saying, "Don't you dare come near me you son-of-a-bitch!" Maybe it was the guilt plus the responsibility that Lincoln felt. He wasn't sure. What he was sure of was that everything else appeared fine with them. It seemed as though the spinal cord was re-attaching itself.

His babies were given a daily dose of a serum Bosch Research had discovered by accident. That was one of the keys to the success of the operations. He chuckled remembering the day nearly a year ago, when Doctor Schultz announced the discovery to the L-Team. He was the kind of scientist who focused more on the small picture than the large. Some people called him slightly 'anal.'

He had first talked to Mr. Lincoln about what he had discovered. A meeting with the L-Team was quickly scheduled in the boardroom. Doctor Schultz stood in front of the group, describing the process. He had gone into great detail, explaining how he had achieved this milestone. It was an excellent presentation until he wrote down the acronym in large letters on the blackboard. It was an

Anti-rejection Spinal Enhancement Serum, or ARSES. The group laughed, embarrassing him immensely. He finally composed himself enough to laugh along with them. He decided on calling it 'SES'—short for Spinal Enhancement Serum—instead.

It seemed to be proving itself now. It had the ability of coaxing the spinal cord into splicing itself as well as having an anti-organ rejection capability. The problem was the thousands of different nerves comprising the cord. Splicing all of them through microsurgery was impossible but splicing the major ones and using the serum to stimulate nerve growth and attachment of the smaller ones was possible.

Since SES had been discovered, Doctor Schultz found several derivatives. He realized that mixing certain ingredients in a particular fashion would enhance the healing and splicing process of different nerves in the spinal cord. He and other members of the L-Team developed a timeline on doses. At certain times of the day a different mix of SES would be injected into the neck area to stimulate a particular group of nerves. Doing this with the right cocktail and at the right time increased the chance of all nerve types re-attaching.

The question was would the different nerves attach themselves to the proper recipients or would there be major circuit crosses resulting in sporadic muscle movements and coordination? It was theorized that, although cross splicing would inevitably occur with the number of nerve endings involved, the brain would have the ability to eventually sort those signals out. They all knew the human brain was remarkable. For example, eyes view images in an upside down fashion. The brain automatically corrects those images by immediately flipping them right side up subconsciously.

He quickly came out of his thoughts as his cell phone chirped in his lap. "Damn! I forgot to turn it off."

Immediately, both Harley and Fraley started moaning. He tried to hush them up as best he could as he answered the phone. He hated disturbing them. What was he thinking! He always turned it off when in the room. He quickly wheeled himself out, the phone stuck to his ear.

Chapter 39

"What! What is it?" He was clearly annoyed as he barked into the phone. He could still hear Harley and Farley moaning from the hallway.

"Sorry to bother you, Mr. Lincoln. It's Doctor Adams."

"Yes, yes! What is it, Doctor? Do you have a problem?" It was rare for the doctor to call. He wondered what could be wrong.

"No," he paused. "No, there's no problem. On the contrary, things are actually very good. We might have a package available soon." He was speaking in code, afraid the phone line might not be secure.

"Yes, go ahead!" Mr. Lincoln was excited, taking another cough drop as he listened, momentarily forgetting about his babies.

"Well, I can't tell you much more right now. We need to meet. Can I see you in an hour?"

"I'll be in my office."

He hung up, thinking how sometimes things seemed to fall into place. He put the phone under his blanket and wheeled himself back to the office. He wanted Doctors Klein and Morin with him if possible. He knew Doctor Schultz was in the lab, busy as usual, tweaking and fixing his latest mixtures.

He made his way down the hallway, noticing Doctor Klein in the boardroom. He went in to meet him. He was at the computer terminal checking out hopeful candidates from the database.

"Ah, Mr. Lincoln! I was going through the database one more time." A look of concern came over him as he studied Mr. Lincoln's face. He quickly asked, "Are you all right? You seem disturbed."

"No. No!" He waved his hand in a dismissive fashion. "Quite the opposite, we might have a package." He explained the phone call, telling Joseph to meet him in his office within the hour.

He called Doctor Morin. He was at home finishing supper. He had a bit of a social life and had been seeing a lady friend. They were finishing a glass of wine. "Henry, can you come down here to meet with Joseph and me?" Before Henry had a chance to answer, Lincoln blurted, "Doctor Adams called from Irvine General. He says we might have a package! He'll be meeting with us within the hour."

"Yes, yes, by all means. I can be there. I'll see you soon."

Doctor Morin hung up the phone, thinking about the call. Doctor Adams was working at Irvine General and probably had an accident victim who had recently been admitted. He smiled, thinking along the same lines as Mr. Lincoln as he whispered, "Sometimes things just seem to fall into place."

Chapter 40

Gene was on the Internet after he had finished supper. He was curious and wanted to get more information. He used the peripheral touch pad and keyboard to learn more about the human neck and, in particular, the spinal cord. He had navigated to several sites, trying to find one that would describe the topic in layman's terms. It was all very interesting. He knew how the cord ran down through the vertebrae but he found out it was protected by something called cerable spinal fluid. He hadn't known that the cord itself was composed of millions of nerve fibers. Then there were the nerve roots that came off the spinal cord, passing through the vertebrae, carrying information to the rest of the body.

He stopped reading, wondering how they were ever going to do it. If there were millions of tiny nerve fibers in the cord, how could they possibly attach all or even some? The more he read, the more he understood how daunting the task would be. And yet, they managed with Farley and Harley hadn't they? His stomach churned. He felt he was living a dream. Several weeks ago all he had to worry about was … what? He tried to remember.

What was the biggest thing on my mind back then? Oh yes, showing off to Lindsey. Why? Because I felt I had to. Why? Because I was fucking short, that's why. If I thought I was fucking short back then, look at me now. He tried focusing on what it would be like to live in another man's body. *That's what I would be doing. I would be using another man's body, a dead man's body. Everything but the head. Would I sense the other person's body with my brain? Would the blood flowing through my new body carry any memory of Mr. X?*

He decided that, when the time came, he wanted to know everything about this Mr. X, what he liked and didn't like, how he spoke, carried himself, everything. He wanted to know who this man really was. The most important question he had right now was how tall was he going to be? He knew it was stupid and that he should be thankful he had a chance at walking again but he could not stop thinking about it. How tall was he going to be?

Could he choose the donor? He wondered about that. What would it be like to go through a database picking and choosing what or who he wanted to be? He had his own mental list made up. Number one was definitely height.

"At least six fucking feet," he whispered. "Then … what? A body-builder, that's what! That would be number two on the list. Then, well, number three would be—"

He was lost in thought when a nurse came by asking if there was anything wrong. She had heard him talking to himself. He asked if she could wheel him back to his room. She obliged, concerned that the patient might be losing it.

He sat, listening to music, again wondering how he would change with a new body. Would that be possible? Why should he be much different after the operation? He still had the same brain. That was where the memory banks were. He concluded that, yes, he would still be the same person with the same likes and dislikes. They were only blending bodies, not souls.

While he was lost in his thoughts he didn't see her come in. His eyes were closed and he had headphones on. She looked at him adoringly. She simply could not help herself.

This poor man has been through hell. From what he's told me, he doesn't have any parents to speak of. He told me about his girlfriend. Well, guess what? She's never here. I can help him so much. We can be together. I can take him home. Maybe we could get married. I don't mind working to support both of us.

Suddenly he could smell her. He sensed she was staring at him. He kept his eyes closed, feeling invaded. *That fucking perfume is so powerful.* He breathed through his mouth, trying to avoid the smell. He didn't want to see her again. She annoyed him last night when she had put him on the defense. Besides, he didn't need her anymore. He was going to have a healthy body, probably better than what he once had. He sure wouldn't want her hanging around when that happened.

He calmed himself, thinking it would only be a few more days and then he'd be gone. He would probably never see her again. He wondered if he should mention his grandmother. What was her name again? Oh yes, Bea. He wondered if he should tell Cynthia about her but decided he wouldn't until the last minute. That way there would be no awkward moments. He was actually frightened that she might flip out and do something violent. He suspected she was very capable of that. No, he wouldn't tell her … yet.

He opened his eyes, pretending he was startled at seeing her. She stood ten feet away, clasping her hands in front of her, staring at him as if he were some kind of god. "Oh. Hi, Cynthia. When did you come in?"

"Oh, just a few minutes ago, Mr. Perfect. I didn't want to disturb you so I stood here, enjoying the view."

Oh my God. Here we go again with that kind of shit. What ever happened to us just being friends? He smiled sweetly, asking her to come and visit, hoping she would decline the invite.

Chapter 41

Doctors Klein, Adams and Morin met in Mr. Lincoln's office. Doctor Adams' brow was wet from perspiration as he opened up his briefcase, handing each of them a report. He was all business.

Doctor Klein noticed the heading. It was a police report. He began to read in earnest. So did the others. There were three victims involved in a motor vehicle accident. They were a family. The daughter was only three years old. Doctor Klein could not help but think of his beloved Sarah. He continued to read on.

Evidently, the car veered off the road late last night and plunged into the lake. All three passengers were submerged for several minutes while a Good Samaritan tried to rescue them. The male driver was pulled out first, followed by the female adult. The rescuer hadn't realized the daughter was still in the car. Paramedics found her body several minutes later.

He focused on the lone male:

Victim (1)
Name: DeGroot, William James
Male. Caucasian. Age: 23

He continued to read, noting the only next of kin was an aunt in Bangor, Maine. The police report indicated that the officer on duty had tried to contact the aunt, Mrs. Margaret Mitchell, with no success. A message was left on her answering machine asking her to contact the state police as soon as possible.

The officer had also done a search through the police database and found that the couple had been married a little over two years. The daughter was their biological child. Neither of the adults had a criminal record.

Doctor Klein looked at the next sheet. This one was the general medical report on the three victims. His pulse quickened as his interest grew. Mr. William James DeGroot and his wife had suffered severe head injuries and asphyxiation due to both the trauma of the accident and the result of being submerged under water for several minutes. He had also sustained several cracked ribs and face lacerations. All other injuries were minor except for the head area. He was in a coma. His chances of surviving were slim. His wife's chances were even less.

Doctor Klein went through the statistic sheet in the medical report, his interest growing, as he read on. The blood type was right but the medical history was still incomplete. There was no record of Mr. DeGroot's medical past at this time. Hopefully Mr. DeGroot's aunt would provide the police and hospital with answers.

Doctor Klein read the last page. It was the autopsy report on the young girl. Cause of death was due to drowning. His heart skipped a beat. She had died the same way as Sarah.

Doctor Adams could see they were almost finished reading. It was time for him to say a few words. "One of the reasons I became excited was because of the next of kin or should I say 'lack of?' I contacted the police before calling you and found out a little more about the victims. The aunt had called the police two hours ago and was told about the tragedy. She was asked if she knew of anyone else who should be notified, such as friends, family or co-workers. She told the police that, as far as she was aware, her nephew and his wife were very private people. They were self-employed. Their main source of income was from the sale of their artwork, mostly paintings.

"She was given the Irvine General Hospital number to call so she could be updated on the status of the victims. She's already called once and has been told that the attending physician would get back to her as soon as possible. Before I do, I wanted to meet with you so we could decide on what to do next."

Mr. Lincoln quickly spoke. "We need to keep our options open. This is going to hinge on you, Doctor Adams. You need to call"—he looked at the report— "Margaret, as soon as possible and let her know the condition of the patients. We also need to get more information on their backgrounds."

"Exactly. That's what I was intending on doing. I was hoping you could pick up a phone extension and listen in while we talked."

Doctor Klein spoke next. "Tell me, what is the medical state of the victim now?"

"He's stabilized. Again, as the medical report has indicated, he's suffered severe head injuries but no neck injuries. It appears his head hit the windshield, knocking him unconscious. Then, to make matters worse, he was submerged underwater for several minutes. It is my opinion he will never come out of a coma. He has a few minor injuries on his upper body, otherwise ... he seems to be in good physical health."

"Good. That's good!"

It was now close to midnight. It would be three a.m. in Maine. They would re-convene at nine the following morning, noon in Bangor. Doctor Adams would make the call then.

Chapter 42

She left the room, wondering about his change in attitude. They were getting along so well last night and now he seemed to once again be annoyed. She told herself, "Of course he's annoyed. You can't expect a patient to just forget about his paralysis and be happy all the time. Gene still needs to accept his condition. I can help. We can talk about it whenever he wants. I need to be patient with him."

Her mind lingered for a few seconds. She was contemplating, thinking there was something else. *He was ... what? He was not in tune with me. He tried to pretend. That's what it was. Why was he pretending to be happy to see me?* Again, she smiled. *Oh Cyn, Cyn, Cyn! You're such a worrywart. He had a hard day and was tired, that's all.*

Still, there was something wrong. He wasn't telling her the whole story. She had a nagging feeling that he was keeping something from her. She thought of what he had said several nights ago about the animals and what he said he had seen, and then pretend that he had exaggerated about the whole incident.

She supposed he could have been very tired. He seemed to have been drugged. They were giving him stress medication. She had seen it on his chart. She decided she needed to let him talk about it some more. She needed to be patient and let him open up to her. If what he said about animal testing were true, someone should be notified and soon.

There was one more thing that bothered her. She kept wondering why they would show Gene anything! *Why would Bosch Research take him into their laboratories or whatever they have and show him stuff? Was it because they thought they could help him? Did they develop a new type of medication that would make him better?*

That bothered her immensely. She told herself she loved him and wanted him to get better. That was partly true. She knew that the more his quality of life improved, the less of a connection she would have with him. She reasoned they were together because of only one thing. He needed her or someone like her to look after him the rest of his life. She needed him as well. She needed to care for someone because she had no one.

She could not admit her life was a failure when it came to men. Sure, there were men that wanted her but they were the likes of Harold. She would never be with that kind of man. How dare someone touch her when she wasn't ready! She hated being touched on other people's terms. With Gene, well, that wouldn't happen. That was what she loved about it. He was helpless and she could look after him forever.

No. If they took him to Bosch and showed him stuff it had to be for a reason. They have something planned. They're planning on helping him. She started feeling panicky.

Chapter 43

Margaret hardly slept a wink. She could not believe what had happened. They were in a car accident. William, Laurie and poor little Amy! She cried in bed, whispering, "Poor little Amy. Bless her heart. If William and Laurie ever regain consciousness, they'll—." Her voice rose as she panicked. "I don't know what they would do if they found out!"

The police had told her they were in a coma and the doctors were doing all they could. She was advised not to come down at this time, that the officiating doctor would be calling her as soon as he could, a Doctor Adams.

She looked at her clock on the nightstand. It was three-thirty in the morning. She wondered if she should take another one of those pills to make her sleep better. Her doctor had prescribed them to her after she had received the call. She hesitated, thinking she wanted to be sharp when Doctor Adams called.

She lay back down on the bed. She could hear the clock in the living room tick. It never bothered her until now. She closed her eyes, thinking of when she had first met them two months ago at Logan Airport in Boston. Amy looked so sweet, a strong resemblance to her mother. Her short brown hair brushed across her forehead in a boyish sort of fashion. There was a bit of her dad in her, too. She had his nose and brown eyes.

It was their first time in the States. Margaret's sister, Nancy, had given William up for adoption when he was only three months old. She had gotten into a bit of trouble when she was younger. She had originally gone for a visit to see their mother, ending up getting a job as a substitute teacher. One thing had led to another and she became pregnant. The father left, never to be seen again. Nancy stayed with her mom, thinking they could both support the child, but her mother died soon after, leaving Nancy alone once more—alone with her new baby. She did what she thought was right at the time. She gave the child up for adoption.

William was in and out of different orphanages and homes throughout his early years. He never found the right family. He had met Laurie five years ago when he was eighteen. She was a year younger. She, too, was an orphan. They waited until she was of legal age before living together. They were both artists. In fact, they had much in common. It was around that time when Margaret had gotten a call from him.

She lay there thinking. It was one of those moments when you knew exactly where you were and what you were doing, similar to when JFK was assassinated, or John Lennon. It had been just before suppertime on a cold fall day. She had invited Steve from next door to join her. She had taken pity on him. He came over the odd time to help with some things that she couldn't do on her own. They became friends, neither interested in anything more. That suited her just fine.

Steve was due to arrive for supper at any moment when the phone rang. It was William, her sister's long lost child. He explained he had tried to track down his mother, Nancy, via the Internet but had reached a dead end. He did, however, find Margaret's number in Bangor so decided to call and see if she knew where Nancy was.

Margaret was stunned. This came out of nowhere. Nancy had told her years ago about giving up her baby boy for adoption. They had never spoken of it since. Now, her sister's son was calling, looking for his natural mother. She felt faint and needed to sit down.

She heard him talking but couldn't quite understand what he was saying. It was the combination of his Dutch accent, the poor long distance phone connection and her mental state. She finally told him Nancy had died last year of cancer. She could still remember the silence on the other end of the line, thousands of miles away.

He said he was sorry he had never gotten to meet his natural mother. He had wanted to get to know her and her family. Did he have any brothers or sisters? Margaret told him he had no other family except for her. She was a widow and lived alone. Before hanging up she asked him for his phone number so they could stay in touch. They had talked back and forth a few times since.

Several months later she received a call from him. He and his wife and child were coming to Boston to check things out. They had several paintings they wanted to sell. They had a Web site set up and had made some art contacts in the United States. They were only allowed in the country for six months as visitors. If things went well they would consider immigration.

They stayed with her in Bangor for a few weeks until they found a home of their own nearby. Margaret accepted them with open arms although she thought William's wife was a bitch. She found Laurie to be very difficult at times. She had an arrogance that Margaret did not like. She didn't like the way she treated William, either.

He, on the other hand, was very easy to get along with, considering his past. He had told her he could not keep track of the many foster homes he had lived in as a child.

Then, there was little Amy. She was so sweet. She called Margaret 'Nana.' Margaret began to cry. She looked at the clock. It was four-fifteen. She decided to get up and make coffee. She washed her face while the coffee brewed and thought she wouldn't take a shower just yet. She was still sleepy and hoped that she could have a little nap later in the morning. The shower would only make her more alert. She knew the coffee would keep her awake, but she needed her daily dose of caffeine now more than ever. She was confused and in shock.

She sat out on the porch, rocking in her chair, sipping her coffee. The early morning dawn was approaching. It was going to be another warm day, even for Bangor. She sat with a blanket over her legs, holding her saucer and coffee cup, thinking back.

They had brought paintings with them. From the moment she first saw their art she was impressed, especially with Laurie's. She eventually called an old friend out west, telling her about their work. She explained how Laurie, in particular, could capture that special moment of Mother Nature. Usually, the theme was the coming together of sky and earth.

One painting illustrated giant dark rain clouds building on the horizon at dusk. The view was from a porch at a farmhouse. You could see the rocking chair to the right and an old wicker chair to the left. An old woman occupied the rocker. The impression was she had seen many a storm in the past but this one would be the best. In the background was a small shed surrounded by chickens and pigs.

Laurie had captured the wheat blowing in the distance as well as leaves swirling in the disturbed air. The whole scene was painted in an almost surreal array of colors, both natural and electric. You could almost feel the full force of an upcoming storm. Laurie claimed it was from a childhood memory.

Margaret's friend owned an art gallery and had checked out William's and Laurie's Web site. She wanted them to visit her so she could get to know them. She thought that perhaps she might have the right connections for them. That was when they had the accident near Irvine.

She began to cry again. She remembered volunteering to look after Amy while they went to visit her friend. They declined, wanting to take little Amy with them. William even asked if Margaret would care to join them. She had decided against it. She knew that if she had to sit in the car for hours with Laurie there would be hell to pay. She could sense that Laurie felt the same way about her.

In retrospect, they should have left Amy with her. Now, it was too late. She prayed they would come out of their comas but wondered how they could live without their daughter.

"Poor, poor little Amy. I'll miss her so much."

Chapter 44

Doctor Klein and Mr. Lincoln were having breakfast in the staff cafeteria. Doctor Klein decided on pancakes and sausages. He knew today would be busy for him. He might not have a chance to eat for several hours. Pancakes were the answer. They would stick to your stomach and keep you full longer than mere eggs and bacon.

Mr. Lincoln ate only toast, his face gaunt. Joseph had mentioned he should be eating more. They both knew his health was failing but there was nothing they could do except carefully monitor his condition. They hardly spoke because Mr. Lincoln needed to keep drinking to stifle his cough. Also, what they wanted to talk about could not be said in public.

Once finished, they went back to Bosch to meet with Bruce Whitman, Doctor Morin and Doctor Adams. They talked a little, waiting for Doctor Adams to get down to business. He was nervous about making the phone call, not wanting to deal with Margaret. He knew he couldn't put it off much longer and finally asked, "Okay, is everyone ready?" There were several nods.

They went into the boardroom, ready to listen to the conversation over the speakerphone. They could see Doctor Adams look at them through the window in Mr. Lincoln's office. They had stressed the importance of keeping the initial conversation short without elaboration and being careful of what was said. Of course, sometimes things just fell into place. They would wait and see.

"Uh, hello? Mrs. Mitchell?" She had answered on the first ring.

"Yes?"

"This is Doctor Adams from Irvine General Hospital. I'm sorry that I didn't call you sooner, Mrs. Mitchell, but I've been very busy."

"Yes, yes! Doctor, do you have some news for me on William and Laurie? I understand that Amy has died."

"Yes, I'm sorry, Mrs. Mitchell. Amy died at the scene by drowning. The car was submerged in the lake. They could not save her."

"Yes, and how about William and Laurie?"

"Well, Mrs. Mitchell, their condition has not improved," he sighed as he spoke.

"Please ..., call me Margaret. Tell me. What *is* their condition?" She was terribly concerned.

"They are in a coma. They had ingested a large amount of water plus they both suffered severe head injuries. I'm sorry, Mrs.—, uh, Margaret, but it doesn't look good right now."

There was a pause on the other end of the line. Doctor Adams looked toward the window. Everyone in the boardroom was nodding. He was doing just fine.

"Margaret, are you still there?"

"Yes, Doctor. I was just thinking about Amy and what needs to be done with her … remains. You know—her body." She began to cry.

"Margaret, please. Don't worry. Rest assured we can take care of everything from here, okay?"

"Thank you, Doctor. Should I … should I come down there?"

He quickly responded, "No, there is no need right now. I want you to know there is nothing you can do at this time. I promise I will call if there is any change in their condition."

"Yes, I understand. Thank you, Doctor."

"Now, Margaret, may I ask you a few questions?"

"Of course."

"Okay. I understand that the patients were visiting the States. Do you know if there are any close relatives that need to be notified?"

"Oh, no. William told me they kept to themselves. Laurie and he didn't have many friends and they were both orphans so they have no living parents."

Doctor Adams looked at the group through the window. They all nodded their approval. "Margaret, do you know of any pre-existing medical issues with any of the victims?"

"Yes, as a matter of fact I do."

Mr. Lincoln muttered under his breath.

"Could you elaborate please, Margaret?" Doctor Adams was momentarily distracted, wondering what Mr. Lincoln had just said.

"Well, there was the heart condition. They didn't tell me at first but I saw all the pills on the bedside table."

Doctor Klein was puzzled, thinking, *"Surely Doctor Adams would have been aware of the heart condition when he was trying to stabilize them. Perhaps not?"*

She kept talking, "He denied it at first. Then he said it wasn't serious. I told him it looked serious to me. My late husband died from a heart condition, Doctor. I know what *that's* all about."

"Yes, Margaret, go on. He denied it?" He wanted answers.

"Yes, he sure did. I knew he was lying so I persisted. Anyhow, that's when I got into it with his wife, Laurie. She overheard the conversation and came into the room. She told me it was none of my dammed business. You know, I've always had problems with her. We never saw eye to eye. She had this attitude. I swear it was about men. I thought she was a bit of a—"

"Yes, yes, Margaret. Please, about the heart condition." He was becoming annoyed with her, shaking his head, looking at the group, indicating he was sorry. He never suspected anything like this. Everyone was disappointed. Bruce sighed. This was not what they had wanted to hear.

"Well, I suppose I shouldn't talk ill of her you know, especially now."

"Yes, Margaret, so did he eventually tell you about his problem?"

"His problem? What problem?"

"Well, his heart problem, of course." Doctor Adams was ready to scream.

"He doesn't *have* a heart problem, Doctor."

"Well then"—he tried to remain calm while everyone in the room stopped breathing—"who *has* the problem?"

"It was Amy, Doctor. I thought I already mentioned that to you. She was born with a heart defect. They were afraid that if they came here she might not be covered by medical insurance. They didn't want to tell me about it—William because he didn't want me to worry; Laurie, because she simply did not like me and felt it was none of my business."

Doctor Adams gave a thumbs up. They were all sighing with relief. He asked her again if there were any other medical problems with any of them and she answered, "No."

He assured her he would get back to her if anything changed and in the meantime she should stay home as he might need to call back soon.

"Thank you, Doctor Adams. I am so relieved to know they are in good hands and you will do everything possible to help them."

"Yes, Margaret, I will. Good-bye for now." He was anxious to get off the phone. He didn't like lying.

Chapter 45

"Everyone, please! May I have your attention?" It was noisy in the boardroom with all members of the L-Team present. Mr. Lincoln had his hands up, trying to bring order. The noise finally subsided. There was an air of excitement all around. "Thank you. Now," he cleared his throat, "let me quash any rumors that might have begun amongst you. Here are the facts so far." He reached for a bottle of water.

"As you all know, three days ago Doctor Adams notified me about an accident victim that might have the right criteria for"—he was choosing his words very carefully—"making our dreams come true. When I say 'our dreams,' I am referring to us as a team as well as the young man, Gene, who is willing to go forward in making this event history. History for the betterment of mankind." He was grandstanding and knew it. The team knew it too, but didn't seem to mind. Several clapped.

"As the information came through, we found out the accident victim was fulfilling our criteria more than we had initially hoped for." There was some more applause as he continued to speak. "Now, the time has come to let you all know where we stand. Well, we're on the threshold, ladies and gentlemen. On the threshold! We are ready to launch the human race to a new level!" Everyone was now standing with broad grins, applauding.

"Good, good!" Mr. Lincoln was also smiling. He took a drink from his bottle. "Please. Please!" He held up his arms, motioning for them to sit while he continued. "Before I continue any further I want to let you all know that Harley and Farley are still in relatively good health and seem to be adjusting quite well." That was a lie but he needed to keep the momentum going. He knew they were suffering from severe stress even though it appeared they were physically getting better. Bruce gave him a questioning look.

There was more applause, "Please. Let me continue." Finally, silence. "Let me get back to the accident victim. His name is William James DeGroot. He and his wife suffered severe head injuries. They were submerged under water for a critical amount of time along with their three-year-old. She, unfortunately, drowned." He could hear a few of them sigh.

"Like I said before, Mr. DeGroot seems to fit the criteria very well. His prognosis is grim." He paused, taking a drink of water, smacking his lips. It was becoming warm in the room. "Yes, it's very grim. In fact, Doctor Adams predicts that he will surely die within a few weeks." That was another lie. William DeGroot could, in fact, live several more years, but more than likely would never come out of a coma.

"So, we have obtained all the necessary medical files on Mr. DeGroot from his doctor and find that, yes indeed, he is a perfect candidate. Having said that, I am asking all of you here today to vote. All in favor of transferring Mr. DeGroot to Bosch Research please raise your hand." It was unanimous. Everyone was ready to move on to Phase Two.

"Good, good! Please. Please! Let me continue." He waited for a few moments, letting the team settle down. He was very pleased, trying to keep the excitement out of his voice. "We have plans that have to be followed in order to move him here. We need to contact his next of kin back east and explain to her that her nephew took a turn for the worse and never survived the accident. In doing so, we take a giant step forward. There is no going back!" He emphasized the last sentence.

They all knew what he was saying. This was the turning point. This was the point where they would break the law. Once the next of kin was told that her nephew had died, there would be no turning back. He paused for a moment, letting them reflect on his last sentence about no going back. The L-Team was silent.

"Next, we are going ahead with Gene's move to Bosch Research. We managed to have all the necessary paper work done so he could be here as early as this evening. So, unless you need to discuss anything more amongst yourselves or with me, we are ready to go!"

Everyone was ready. This was the moment they had all been waiting for.

PART III

Chapter 1

It had been several days since Gene last spoke with Bruce or Doctor Klein. He knew they were preparing to move him to his Grandma Bea as soon as they could. He didn't want to think about it. He didn't want to think about much. He knew his life was going to change drastically once more. He should have been thankful. That was one thing he had trouble with, being thankful.

No, it was more like God owed him this. God owed him big. God should never have allowed the accident. Never! Now it was time for Him to set the record straight. Besides, God should never have done Gene wrong. He should have had better parents. He should have been taller. He should have been more popular with the girls. Instead, he was everything he didn't want to be. It was time for a change. It was time to be a taller person, a more important person, someone to be respected. He deserved it.

He couldn't help but think about life after the operation. He would eventually be famous. Some people would consider him a freak, others would think of him as divine. He closed his eyes, thinking of all the women who would want to be with him, a real man that had defied the odds, coming out ahead, being a success.

He would be reborn. Maybe he could write a book or do television interviews. Maybe be on 'Oprah,' talking to the audience, mostly female, telling them how he had defied the odds, becoming an icon, a hero! He would make history. Maybe he would be a millionaire. Yes, he liked that. He felt confident that, with the right combination, he could be a success.

He needed to be sure of the right combination. The donor—he convinced himself that it would be easier for him if he used the word 'donor'—had to be perfect. He vowed he would make the doctors tell him everything about this man. If it wasn't right he'd make them stop. He didn't know how he could do that. He didn't give it much thought because he had complete confidence in the team. There was no question in his mind.

The bitch came into his room for a visit a few minutes later. He was growing tired of her. He studied her, thinking she really thought highly of herself. He was now seeing her differently, as a slightly overweight loser. She had no friends, a definite loner. She was actually rather simple. He could play her a little but had to be careful. She had anger just below the surface. Yes, he had to be careful.

She looked at him with adoration as she came in and quickly noticed he was slipping back into himself. She could see anger in his eyes. It seemed like part of a cycle with him. He'd be good for a few days and then he would fall back into a depressed state. She thought she could see it in his eyes.

He keeps looking away from me, into the distance, dreaming of whatever. Poor, Mr. Gene. He needs patience and understanding. I'll be here for him whether he likes it or not. He needs someone like me.

They talked for a little while. She kept prompting him, asking what he was thinking and if he would share it. He finally told her he thought she should leave. He was tired and wanted to be alone. She leaned over to kiss him but he shook his head.

Gene wanted to tell her to get the fuck out and never come back and that he didn't need her anymore. It would only be a few more days until he was moved. He couldn't wait to get out of the hellhole he was in, away from the droolers and moaners, away from the smell of shit in the hallway. He felt he was better than that. He wanted the bitch to leave him alone. Soon he could choose the bitch he wanted to be with. There would be all kinds of choices.

After she left him, Cynthia went into the restroom. She wondered what was going on. He seemed so agitated, on edge. It was as if he were waiting for something. She knew his doctor hadn't seen him in several days. That was almost too long. Why wasn't he visiting him anymore? It was strange.

As she walked out of the restroom, she saw Bruce Whitman hurrying toward Gene's room. He looked over his shoulder. She quickly ducked back, away from his field of view. He seemed nervous. He didn't see her.

She decided to wait a few minutes and then make her way over to his room, to see what was going on. She peeked down the hall and saw Bruce look both ways before entering, as if to make sure the coast was clear.

A minute later she walked up to his door. It was partially closed. She could make out some voices but she couldn't quite hear. She waited outside the room, being careful, not wanting to be noticed. She had a piece of paper in her hands and pretended she was reading an important medical report. After all, she was a nurse here.

She heard Gene excitedly say, "Okay. Okay, I'm ready!" She couldn't hear much more until Gene spoke again, exclaiming, "Tomorrow?" She heard Bruce tell him to keep it down. A few moments later she caught a whisper, something about Bosch Research. She saw a staff member walking down the hallway toward her so moved on.

Chapter 2

She hardly slept. She cuddled with Kaleb and Savannah, trying to figure out what was going on. She went through it again and again, looking at all the angles. She suspected he was telling the truth about what he had seen at Bosch Research. She knew they had experimented on animals before. He had mentioned animals moaning. Why would they show him?

There was only one answer. They were ready to work on him, to do something that would conceivably make him better. She wasn't sure what it was. She supposed there were several possibilities.

They might have some kind of drug that could cure his paralysis. If they did, why were they so secretive about it? Wouldn't they want to tell the world? No. That wasn't it. She surmised that they might have some bionic attachment he would be fitted with. If that were the case, why were they testing animals? Why not simply test the attachment on humans? She didn't know. There was one thing that she knew for sure. He was perfect just the way he was. She decided she needed to do something to stop them.

She waited until eight the next morning. She looked in the phone book and found the listing for an 'S. Stringer.' She dialed the first few digits but then hung up. She had to think this through. If she called and told Sheila she knew Bosch was experimenting with small animals, Sheila would probably say the law had already ruled in Bosch's favor. Research centers were allowed to use lab rats and probably other small animals. She sat there, looking at the phone. What could she say? Finally, she picked it up and dialed again.

"Yeah, hello?"

"Oh hi, is this Sheila?"

"Yeah?"

"Hi. My name is Cynthia. We met at the SPCA a while back. I'm Kaleb's mother. Do you remember?"

"Uh, not really. What's your name again?" Sheila was wondering who she was. She was trying to think back, trying to remember this 'Kaleb.'

"I was a nurse at Irvine General. Remember, we talked about my dog, Kaleb?"

It came back to her. Oh yes, she remembered Cynthia. She seemed like a bit of a weirdo but whatever. She wondered what she wanted. "Oh yes, now I remember. How are you?"

"Well, I'm not doing so well. I was wondering if I could talk to you face-to-face ... today."

Sheila had her guard up. She wondered what was going on. *What did this woman want to talk about?* "Can you tell me what this is all about, Cynthia?"

"I prefer to talk to you privately. Can I come over tonight?"

Sheila didn't like the idea. She didn't know this woman and she certainly wasn't going to talk to her in her own home. Besides, she was busy tonight. "Look, Cynthia, I break for lunch around noon. Would you like to join me?"

Cynthia said that would be fine. They made arrangements to meet at a small diner only a few blocks from the Edgehill Clinic.

Chapter 3

The fax machine was spitting out one sheet of paper after another when she came in to work Thursday morning. Karol picked one up to see what it was about. It was from Boston. They were the papers needed for the release of Gene. Everything was there, his grandmother's statement of income form, Registered Nurse inspection form, birth certificate, a patient transfer form as well as a few other items. Karol looked at them, thinking it was strange.

It's strange to get all of this only two days after talking to Gene's grandmother on the phone. For one thing, it's very unusual to have a registered nurse evaluate a home so quickly. She suspected Gene's grandmother had connections. She smiled. *Good for him. It looks like he is going to be in wonderful hands.*

Things were all set to go at Irvine General Hospital. They were ready. Sally, the head nurse, also belonged to the L-Team. She was there with Rose, an assistant. They were at the nurses' station when Doctor Morin walked by and decided to chat it up a little. Rose thought it a bit unusual. Doctor Morin was usually not one to stop and make small talk.

A minute or so later an alarm went off on the monitor system at their station. It came from Mr. DeGroot's room. Things didn't look good. They had a 'situation.' According to the display on their screen it appeared he was in cardiac arrest.

Sally and Rose both jumped up off their chairs, getting ready to run over to his room. Doctor Morin put up his hand, stopping Rose, telling her to stay where she was at the nurses' station. She needed to monitor the equipment. He and Sally would go to the room instead. Rose agreed. She knew there would be help soon enough. Too many staff members would only make matters worse.

As Sally and Doctor Morin entered the room, Doctor Adams was already there. He had the bed sheets pulled down, rubbing the patient's chest. Sally knew the drill. She went back out the hallway to get the paddles. She closed the door behind her as she did.

A few seconds later another doctor came into the room. Doctor Adams told him it was okay. They had things under control. The doctor nodded and left. He had other patients to tend to.

Sally came back, wheeling a tray with equipment and heart paddles. She closed the door once more, standing over the bed with the two doctors. They stood there over William DeGroot, going through the motions of trying to revive him. The trouble was, he wasn't dead. He hadn't suffered a heart attack. The plan was to wait a few more minutes, pronounce him dead, and then wheel him down to the morgue. No one would be the wiser. All the required paper work would be completed by the attending doctors explaining in detail how he had died. Of course, this would all be fabricated.

The L-team achieved two things by staging his death. They could now have their donor secretly moved to Bosch without any questions being raised and, because he was now considered dead, they could use his body for the transplant. Of course they would still need to deal with William's aunt, Margaret, explaining to her how he had supposedly died.

A half-hour later Sally went back to her station, telling Rose the sad news. The doctors couldn't revive the patient. Rose commented that it was perhaps a blessing. Sally nodded in agreement as she began to prepare the necessary paper work.

Chapter 4

They met for lunch at Winkie's Diner just after noon. Cynthia would have been there sooner if she could but didn't want to arouse any suspicions. She was excited when she walked into the restaurant. She saw Sheila at a booth by the window. She quickly walked over and introduced herself again.

Sheila remembered her now. She was a bit of a strange one, but then again, she figured people would consider her strange as well.

Cynthia noticed Sheila had put on a few more pounds since she had last seen her. She had forgotten how short and round she was. There wasn't much to indicate she was a woman. She was one of those people you really had to look hard at to figure out what gender they were.

"So, Cynthia. What's going on?"

"Well, I was wondering if you could help me." Immediately Cynthia wanted to retract that. "*No. No. No,*" she thought. "*Now Sheila will know this is personal. I can't have that.*"

"Help you with what?"

Cynthia tried to cover up her mistake by saying, "Well, actually it's not me you'd be helping."

"Yes, go on."

"You see," she looked around and lowered her voice, "I work at Edgehill Clinic."

Sheila was getting annoyed. She thought, "*Come on, girl. Tell me why you're here. I'm getting hungry and I want this over with.*"

"Okay, so you work at Edgehill. So what?"

Cynthia didn't like her attitude. She thought, "*What do you mean, 'so what.' To hell with you!*"

"Well, Sheila, I didn't know who else to talk to about this but then decided that you might be the right one. Okay! That's 'So what'! "

"Okay. Okay! I'm listening."

"Good. Now, this is confidential. I don't want to get into any trouble so you'll have to promise me you won't say a thing to anyone."

"Yeah, I promise." Sheila hated the secrecy thing. She had been abrupt all her life and had no social finesse. She bit her tongue as she waited for this drama queen to spill her guts.

"Well, a patient of mine, a quadriplegic to be exact, was brought into Bosch Research a few days ago."

Sheila's interest began to perk up. She'd always had a bad taste in her mouth since she and the animal rights group attempted to raid the place a while back.

Bosch Research had made them look foolish in the public's eye, especially when no evidence was ever found regarding the abuse of animals. Her animal rights group suffered a black eye over that one. Not only did they suffer a black eye, she also felt totally responsible. She should have done more research before initiating the protest.

Cynthia could see she had struck a nerve. She kept talking, choosing her words carefully. "The patient was brought back to his room at Edgehill several hours later. He was extremely distraught."

"Well, Cynthia, that is not unusual. They probably brought him there to do tests and then told him there was no hope."

"No, that wasn't the case. I talked to him over the next few days. He told me they had shown him some of their ... test results."

Sheila leaned across the table and whispered, "First of all, why would they show him their test results? They are very secretive. There is no reason why they would do that sort of thing. Your friend was bullshitting you, Cynthia."

"Listen to me! My friend—" she caught herself, lowering her voice. "My friend, who was extremely distraught, told me he was shown animals. They were being experimented on—not only small animals but pigs as well." She could see what Sheila was thinking so continued, "And *not* guinea pigs, real farm animal pigs!"

That of course, in her mind, was an outright lie. She knew she had to be dramatic so Sheila would take the bait. If Sheila decided to act on it then they could shut down Bosch Research with their protests and negative public attention. Gene would then be back with her. She would take care of him the rest of her life, thank you very much!

Sheila leaned back in her seat. She was lost in thought. She couldn't help but think this might be very slim evidence to go on. Still, she knew in her heart that they were indeed experimenting with animals. She doubted very much there were pigs involved, though.

Her veggie burger arrived while they were staring at each other. Sheila was not a meat eater. Cynthia waited. She could see Sheila was in deep thought. Good. She had her complete attention.

Sheila took a drink from her Coke and said, "Leave it with me. I'll do a bit of checking around, okay?" As an afterthought she added, "This is between you and me, no one else, right?"

Cynthia nodded. She was happy. It appeared as if Sheila was going to act on the information.

"Cynthia, look. I think you should leave ... now. I don't want anyone to know about this meeting, okay? Here's my cell number. Call me this evening. We'll talk then."

Cynthia got up, satisfied with how things were going. She hadn't eaten anything but that was okay. She wasn't hungry.

An hour later another fax came in. Karol picked it up. It was travel information for Gene. He had been booked on a flight bound for Boston. He would be leaving at nine-thirty that evening, landing at Logan International at six a.m. local time the next day.

She picked up the phone and called Doctor Klein, explaining that the paper work was all in order and Gene had been booked on a flight leaving that night. Doctor Klein thanked her, saying he would sign the release forms as soon as he could. He also said he would call Gene's grandmother, confirming with her once more that Gene would be arriving near six a.m. and that she should make sure someone would be there to greet him.

Karol hung up, thinking about how Gene's life would be changing in a very big way once he left Edgehill.

Chapter 5

Sheila quickly finished her lunch, becoming more excited. Her mind was wandering, exploring all the possibilities. *What had Cynthia said? They'd brought this patient into their research center? Why would they do that?*

There were only two reasons she could think of. One was to show him what they were doing so they could hopefully experiment on him. Why not? After all, they were a so-called research center. And, the second reason was because ... because they wanted to ask him if he would participate in an experimental drug program. That happened on occasion.

Okay, that second one is plausible but what about the first reason? Why would they show him what they were doing to animals? And, not only lab rats, but like that weirdo said, pigs. She wondered if Cynthia misheard or misunderstood the word 'pig.' *It could still be guinea pigs. But why was the patient so upset?*

She left the restaurant and waddled over to an outside pay phone. Perry answered on the first ring. He wondered who was calling. His call display hadn't shown a known number.

"Hello?"

"Pair, this is Sheila."

"Hey, haven't talked to you in a while. Things going good?" He was glad to hear from her. Even though she wasn't his type he did have a soft spot for her. He smiled. He had a soft spot for all women.

"Well, no. I've got something to tell you. Can we meet, later?"

Perry was wondering what this was all about. He figured it might be interesting. Things had been slow in his world recently and maybe she had some information he could work on. "Yeah, sure. How about a beer at the Parrot?"

She agreed and quickly hung up. She thought the Parrot would be a good place. *The locals hang out there but usually only on the weekend. Today, after work, it might be fairly quiet. At least there won't be a band playing. Some nights they have this friggin' local band that is way too loud.*

The call reminded Perry of only a few years ago when he was hired out as a mercenary. They had made several concessions for him so he could join. He considered himself a 'gun-for-hire' for the government ... any government. He had fallen into that kind of work after finishing with the Marines. They, too, had made concessions.

Chapter 6

The driver and his assistant drove into a large warehouse. The assistant got out and pulled down the garage door once they entered. He opened up the ambulance's back doors and then guided the ambulance backwards until it butted up against the delivery van. He got back into the ambulance, helping his partner wheel the gurney with the patient out from the rear and into the back of the delivery van. Within fifteen minutes, after the transfer had been made, the delivery van pulled up to the loading dock at Bosch Research.

Less than three hours after William DeGroot's 'death,' he was carefully being tended to by Doctors Klein and Schultz in his new home, Bosch Research Incorporated.

Bruce walked up to the communal eating area at Edgehill and spotted Gene in his familiar place at the table. He looked across from him, seeing the poor woman vacantly stare out at nothing. Bruce felt badly for her but good about himself. He was glad he was part of the team, the L-Team. He knew they were doing the right thing. If mankind didn't take chances many lives would certainly be worse off. He reasoned it was because of people like him and the rest of the team that life would continue to improve.

He looked back at Gene and saw the apprehension on his face. The poor kid was worried. Of course he would be. It was time to do a little more counseling before the move. He walked over, smiling. "Looks like you're a million miles away."

"Oh, hi, Bruce. I was ... you know ... thinking."

"Of course. Hey, are you done eating? Let me take you away from here. How about a nice walk through the park?" He loved to joke. This time Gene didn't think it was very funny.

They went out to the courtyard by the fountain once more. Today it was cloudy. Gene noticed lightning in the distance.

"So today's the day, my man. Have you told anyone about you leaving, going to live with your Grandma Bea?"

Gene replied defensively, "No, who would I tell?"

"How about Cynthia?"

"Oh yeah, Cynthia."

Bruce could hear the distaste in his voice. That was good, very good. That tied up any loose ends. "Are you going to tell her?"

"Not unless I have to."

"Yeah, I know how you feel, Gene, but ... it might be wise that you do."

"I don't know. She'll be asking a million questions. I don't want to trip up at all. To be honest … I'm kind of afraid of her."

"Afraid? Afraid of what?" Bruce was getting curious.

"Well, she can be overpowering. I told her all I wanted to be was friends but she still thinks otherwise. She thinks we're maybe more than that."

"Well, the sooner you tell her, the quicker she'll get the picture, right?"

"Yeah, I suppose."

Bruce decided to change the subject a little. "So, your flight leaves at nine-thirty this evening. We should have you out of here just after supper. How does that sound?"

Suddenly, Gene didn't feel so good. He felt sweat on his forehead.

They parked by the fountain, Bruce sitting across from him. He saw the panic in Gene's eyes. "I know you're doing the right thing. You are a very brave young man. You're taking somewhat of a chance of course, but the rewards could be fantastic! This will change your life. There is no doubt about it. It will change a life that is hopeless into one that has a bright future."

Gene nodded.

"Good. Don't worry. Have no doubt that what you're doing is right. You believe that, don't you?"

There was a flash of lightning as Gene began to reply, quickly followed by a 'boom.' They decided to get back indoors. Gene felt he needed to get inside in order to hide from God.

Chapter 7

William DeGroot was being closely monitored. The move to Bosch hadn't changed his status. He was lying on a gurney in one of the recovery rooms; it was the same one Gene had been in after seeing Harley and Farley for the first time. His heartbeat was regular, so was his breathing.

Doctor Adams entered Mr. Lincoln's office. The other three doctors were already there, along with Mr. Lincoln and Bruce.

Mr. Lincoln spoke first. "Well done, you two!" He smiled, looking at both Doctors Morin and Adams. "We've already got things cleared with the morgue." He looked at the two doctors as he smiled. "Cause of death will be head trauma and drowning." He quickly moved on, not wanting to linger on what they had done—faking William's death. He was once again all business. "Now, we have got to call Margaret and tell her the sad news." He looked squarely at Doctor Adams. "Are you ready?"

Doctor Adams wasn't ready. He didn't want to call Margaret and lie to her by telling her William had died when in fact his condition had not changed. He paused for a moment, feeling Mr. Lincoln's eyes on him, waiting for his answer to the question—was he ready? He knew he had to do it, to call Margaret. There was now no choice, no turning back. He slowly nodded, his face grim, letting Mr. Lincoln know he would do it. He got up and headed toward the boardroom, feeling the weight of the world on his shoulders. The others stayed in the office and watched him get ready to put the call on speakerphone. Everyone was nervous. Doctor Adams nodded to them through the window and forced a reassuring smile as he dialed Margaret's number.

"Hello?"

"Hello, Margaret? This is Doctor Adams in Irvine."

"Yes, Doctor. What is it?"

"I have some bad news for you, Margaret."

"Oh God, no! Please tell me they didn't die!"

This was not easy for him. He struggled with what he needed to say. He felt sick to his stomach. "William passed away this morning."

"Oh, no! Oh my God. No!"

Doctor Adams felt his bowels twist and his stomach churn. "I'm sorry, Margaret. We did all that we could for him." He could hear her crying.

"Yes, I know you did." She spoke between sobs. "I know he was in good hands. Oh God! You know, Doctor Adams, it's one thing to realize it would be best for them to die, being in a coma and also having their little girl die as well, but when it actually happens ... it's just such a shock." She began to cry uncontrollably. He was very sorry it had to happen that way. She seemed like such a nice lady.

"Margaret? Hello? Are you there?"

She whispered through her sobs that she was still listening.

"Rest assured we did everything we could to save him but ... he would not have had a good life if he had survived. In fact, he wouldn't have had much of a life at all."

"Yes, I know that, Doctor, but what about the funeral? I mean ... they didn't know anyone here. What should I do?"

That was exactly the question they were all waiting for. Doctor Adams looked up into Mr. Lincoln's office, seeing him nod. "Well, we can take care of the remains here if you like, Margaret. We can have the body, actually both William and Amy, cremated here. We could even hold a small service if you like and then ship the remains back to you. Would that be all right?"

"Yes, I suppose. I mean, I don't know what else to do. Should I come there?"

"No! There is no reason for that, Margaret. We can take care of the arrangements here."

She wondered why he said 'no' so forcefully. She was also wondering about cremation. Her late husband had insisted on burial when he died. She had agreed with him. She had felt that way since childhood. She remembered having a good talk with her sister, Nancy, when they were younger.

They both believed that when someone died it took several days for their soul to leave the body. Cremation would disturb the natural course of events, forcing it to leave before its time. This could create havoc in the greater scheme of things. It was not natural to destroy someone by fire, even if his or her body were dead!

Things were happening too fast. She had been notified of her nephew's death only a few minutes ago and now they were going to cremate the body? She needed time to think. She wanted to pay her last respects before burial. Yes, that's what she wanted for both William and Amy, burial!

"I'm sorry, Doctor. What did you just say?" She hadn't been listening.

"I said we would need you to sign a standard release form for the disposal of the bodies and fax it to us as soon as you can. You can obtain those forms online."

She did not like the term 'disposal of the bodies.' Amy and William were not garbage. "Doctor Adams. Please hold off on making any arrangements for now. I need time to think about this."

Doctor Adams paused. He wasn't sure what to say next. He looked toward Lincoln's office. They were all looking back with apprehension.

"Of course, Margaret. I understand. This is all very sudden for you. Please think about this very carefully."

"Yes, Doctor. I need to decide what to do here but I don't like the idea of having them cremated. And, before I forget, how is Laurie doing? Is she still in a coma?" She was thinking she could fly out to Irvine and pay her last respects to Amy and William as well as see Laurie. Another part of her was deciding where they should be buried. She wondered if the bodies should be sent back to their country for interment or stay close to her in Bangor. She was deep in thought. *And, what about Laurie? Will she die soon or be in a coma the rest of her life?*

"Margaret? Are you still there?"

"Yes, I'm sorry, Doctor. You were saying?"

"Well, you asked about William's wife, Laurie. Her condition is stable for the moment."

He was sweating. He wasn't sure what he should say about her nephew's wife. He decided the simplest solution would be to tell the truth and see what the consequences would bring. He really had no other option. The last thing they wanted was for Margaret to come out to Irvine and see for herself.

The plan was to put it all into one neat package, telling her William had died and they would take care of the cremation. It sounded so simple. The cremation was to occur, but ... only with Amy's body. They could always add ashes from an animal, making it appear there were indeed the remains of two bodies. She must not be allowed to come out here to Irvine and yet he didn't want to sound too forceful. He had to play it smart.

He continued, "At this time there is nothing anyone can do for her, Margaret." As an afterthought he added, "Perhaps we can move her to a hospital near you in a few weeks?"

"Uh, yes that would be fine. Can I call you a little later?" She was tired, not wanting to talk about it anymore. It was all too much for her.

He didn't like that. He wanted the control. He needed to emphasize that he would call her instead. "Actually, Margaret, it might be difficult to contact me. Why don't you think about things and I'll call you back around supper?"

"Okay, Doctor, I'll be here. Please make sure you do."

Chapter 8

Cynthia was on her shift, thinking about Sheila, when she saw Karol at the end of the hallway. Karol saw her as well and waved for her to come and join her. Cynthia wondered what was up.

"Hello, Cynthia. I just wanted to tell you how good a job you're doing here." Karol was smiling. It was contagious. Cynthia couldn't help herself and smiled back.

"Why, thank you, Karol. I do enjoy it here. I love helping the patients."

"Yes, I can see that. You'll be pleased to know that one of them will be leaving us, today."

Cynthia had a questioning look on her face so Karol explained.

"Gene is going to be living with his grandmother in Boston." She had the biggest smile on her face as she told her, thinking Cynthia would be happy to hear the news.

"What?" Cynthia's mouth dropped open. She began to turn pale.

Karol looked at her with surprise as she asked, "Are you all right?"

Cynthia barely nodded.

"Here, follow me." She led her into a vacant room. "Sit on the bed. Let me get you some water." She went to the sink, wondering why Cynthia was taking the news so hard. She suspected the young nurse had acquired quite an attachment for the patient. That was normal enough. *"You sometimes hate to see people leave here,"* she thought. *"Many become friends."*

"Here, dear, drink this." Cynthia quickly drank the water.

"Now, are you feeling better?"

Cynthia nodded.

"Good. Well, I'm glad I told you. You might not have found out. After all, it happened so quickly. I mean, the forms were all faxed to me just this morning. Are you sure you're okay?"

"Yes, I'm okay. I'm sorry. I just felt faint when you told me. I was surprised."

"Yes, but the good news is that he's going to be well taken care of. His grandmother looks like she's fairly well off so he'll be in good caring hands."

"Yes, that's good." She felt sick.

Karol looked at her. She took her hands in hers and smiled. "Now, Cynthia, you know you should be happy for him, right?"

Cynthia began to cry. Karol leaned over and hugged her. She had to smile to herself. Cynthia was a good nurse. She really did care for her patients. She patted her back, saying, "There. There. It will be okay. We'll make sure he calls us sometime soon, okay?"

Cynthia was getting over her shock. *Was he ever going to tell me he was leaving or … just go?*

"Karol? When did Gene know he was going to leave?" She dabbed at her eye with Kleenex as she asked the question.

Karol was thinking she better tell a small lie. "I'm not sure, Cynthia. It happened so fast."

She knew Karol was trying to cover things up. She pretended she understood. "Thanks, Karol. It was a shock but I'm so glad he'll be okay." She was becoming very angry, wondering what to do with this new information.

She thanked Karol again and left the room to make her rounds. Her mind wasn't on the job. She kept thinking he had lied to her. He didn't care about her. He was going to leave and not tell her. She couldn't bring herself to work right then so went back into the vacant room. She thought hard and fast, wondering where he was going.

To Boston? To live with his grandmother? "He never told me a thing about her," she whispered. "Is this really true or is it something that has to do with Bosch? Is he being moved . . . there? It's really weird that all of this happened so fast. A grandmother who he never talked about now wants him to live with her? No, there's something going on here!"

It hit her just then. She was being dumped. He couldn't care less about her. He had used her. It was as simple as that. He had used her and she fell for it, hook, line and sinker. "How stupid of me," she muttered. "I don't deserve this! All I wanted to do was love him and he dumped me. The jerk dumped me! I gave up a good paying job to be with him and he doesn't care. I hate him! I hate him so much!"

She was in tears, this time not because of sadness, but because of anger. He had crossed her. He had shunned her, making her look foolish. He was so insensitive to her, thinking only of himself. She knew deep down he had been playing her all along.

Now I know what I need to do. He won't get away with this. If I can't have him, no one will! I need to do what I should have done before … when I caught him cheating on me! In her mind Gene had been cheating on her when he was with Lindsey.

She no longer had tears. She was now focused. She was going to take care of business.

Chapter 9

He was in his room listening to his iPod when she walked in. It was four-fifty in the afternoon. Her shift started at five. He immediately knew something was up. She smiled but it wasn't real. He smiled back. He could tell she knew he was leaving.

"How's it going?"

She took his headphones off before saying, "I found out you're leaving Edgehill this evening, Gene." It was said in an accusatory fashion, as if he had done something wrong. He didn't like it. No, he didn't like it at all.

"Yeah, I'm leaving. I'm leaving all of this, Cynthia!" He moved his head around slightly, indicating the room and everything beyond. "I know it's foolish of me. Why would I want to leave this, this wonderful life of sitting here day after day, not even existing?" He was getting himself worked up. She listened, trying to understand him.

"I can't wait to get the hell out of here! I hate it here! Do you hear me? I hate it here!"

"But Gene, you've got me to look after you."

"I've got a second chance, Cynthia!" He was shouting and suddenly realized that he might have gone too far.

"A second chance? What do you mean?"

He tried to recover. "I mean ... I have a new place to go to where my grandmother will look after me. That's what I mean."

Cynthia nodded, pretending to believe him while all along, thinking, *"Bull poop, Mr. Gene!"*

"Why didn't you let me know about this, before?"

"I don't have to answer to you or anybody!"

She used to love that about him. He was arrogant and obnoxious. He was like a trapped animal. You could tease him all you liked but he could never get out and bite you.

She didn't believe for one minute that he was going to live with his grandmother. She wasn't sure on how to handle this. She wanted to tell him she knew they were taking him away, but not to Boston. Would it do any good if she confronted him? No, probably not. The only way she could stop all of this would be through Sheila. If they could bring down Bosch Research then Gene would have nowhere to go. She needed to call Sheila and let her know.

She mumbled, "Good-bye" as she left his room.

He smiled, relieved that it was finally over, hoping he would never see her again.

Chapter 10

They met for a beer at the Parrot. It wasn't too noisy. At least they could hear each other. In fact, they didn't need to raise their voices.

Perry was looking at her, thinking she was the biggest animal activist he'd ever known. She was a fanatic. He liked animals as well, but not that much. She loved the cuddly, hairy things you could snuggle up to. He figured she hadn't snuggled with a man in years. He smiled. She wasn't his type but she was still sweet. She had a big heart. He liked that about her.

The waitress brought two beers over to their booth. They clicked bottles as Sheila explained what that nurse had said about animal testing at Bosch Research. He half-listened, thinking about the animals he had been near not too long ago.

His mind drifted back to Africa three years previously where he had spent many a night under the jungle sky. They were all mercenaries trained by the U.S. Government to 'suppress the insurgents.' That was the buzz term back then. Saying those words seemed to justify their covert actions. Anyhow, yes, he remembered spending many nights out in the African jungle, witnessing the giraffes and elephants in their natural habitat. No, they weren't the type of pets you would want to snuggle with.

"Are you listening to me, damn it?" She punched his shoulder, almost spilling his beer in the process.

"What? Yeah, sure." He was rubbing his arm. "So, this nurse told you her boyfriend patient saw these animals over at Bosch, right?"

"Yes, Perry! Now, please, pay attention. I know you've heard all this shit before but I really do think we've got something this time."

She explained how it was weird that this patient was brought into Bosch and then shown these animals. Evidently they were full grown farm pigs being used for experimental purposes. Perry started to listen more carefully.

"I asked her to call me later on tonight." She paused and then, finally annoyed with no response, continued. "Well, what do you think, Pair?" She knew if she used his knick-name he'd respond quicker. He had told her that his buddies used to call him 'Pair' when they were out on maneuvers because he could come down on the enemy like a cowboy with a 'pair' of .45's, blazing away. He hadn't known that some of them actually meant 'Pear' instead, considering him a bit of a fruit cake.

"What do I think? I'll tell you what I think. It's flimsy. That's what it is, flimsy. I mean, it sounds like we might have something here but I don't want to repeat our last performance at Bosch. They really humiliated us, you know. We came out with egg on our face. We had no proof that they were testing animals, Sheila. No proof! If we ever did that again I'd bring a fucking camera with me."

She nodded. He was right. They needed more to go on than what Cynthia had said. She leaned back in her chair, taking another sip of beer, thinking, when her phone chirped.

"Yeah?"

"Sheila?"

"Yeah?"

"It's Cynthia."

Sheila perked up. It sounded like Cynthia was upset. "What's up?"

"They just came into his room. They're getting ready to take him away."

"Take *who* away?" She couldn't put it together. What was Cynthia talking about?

Cynthia tried to compose herself so she could respond intelligently. She knew she was jabbering. She took a deep breath and tried to relax. "Okay. They came into his room just a few minutes ago. He's the patient I was telling you about. His name is Gene and they came into his room, several people along with his doctor, Doctor Klein."

Sheila knew who Doctor Klein was. She had heard stories about him and his group at Irvine General. He had been accused of performing abortions.

Cynthia continued, "I talked to him this afternoon, Sheila. You know what he told me?"

"No. What?"

"He said he had a second chance. He tried to cover by saying he was going to live with his grandmother in Boston. He wasn't telling the truth, Sheila. I know. He never once mentioned his grandmother before. He had told me he had no living relatives to speak of. Now, suddenly out of nowhere, he has a *grandmother?*"

"Cynthia, it's still no proof that they are taking him elsewhere."

"Let me finish." Cynthia thought, *"Damn, I'm starting to cry! Take a deep breath and get it together."* She continued. "I talked to Administration. They told me it was unusual that the paper work was faxed so quickly from Boston. Everything was too much in order."

Shelia was still not convinced. She looked at Perry and rolled her eyes. He took another swig of beer as he listened to the one side of the conversation.

"Cynthia, listen to me. Even if they did take him to Bosch, they are not committing a crime, you know. It's perfectly legal." She was standing with her hand up, palm opened.

"Yes, I know, but I need help here! I want to see where they take him, Sheila. Apparently they have him booked on a flight out at nine-thirty this evening. I checked with the airlines and there is a flight out then. All I ask is that you help me follow them. If they go to the airport and he gets on board, well then, fine, my suspicions would be unfounded, but if he never shows up at the airport then something funny is going on, right?"

"Yeah, I suppose ...."

"Can you go to the airport and check it out for me? I'd try to follow them but I might not have that much success. They might try to pull a fast one. Besides, I just started my shift." She paused, trying to sound more convincing. "Now, I know it sounds like I might be crazy. You might think that I've been watching too many spy movies but … if I don't find out now I might never know where he's going!"

"Cynthia, can you hang on a minute?" She put her hand over the phone and told Perry what was going on.

He rolled his eyes and shrugged, saying, "Why not? We've got nothing better to do."

"Cynthia?"

"Yes."

"Are you near where you can see them? Are you in Edgehill right now?"

"Yes."

"Okay, I want you to listen carefully. My partner and I will be there in a few minutes. We want you to call us as soon as you see them leave the hospital. Tell us what door they're exiting. Once you call us, just continue doing whatever it is you're doing. We don't want to have anyone get suspicious of you. Okay? It would be better if my partner and I follow them rather than you. They know who you are. Sound good?"

There was a pause. Cynthia was thinking. The logic was good but she didn't want to let Gene out of her sight. She had to trust Sheila. "Okay. I'll call you as soon as I see what door they're leaving from."

Sheila got up and paid the bill.

They jumped into Perry's Jeep and headed toward Edgehill. She quickly explained what was going on. Perry listened intently while smiling. He loved working undercover.

Chapter 11

Gene had a pair of pants and shirt on. It was a nice change for him. He was half-listening to Doctor Klein, his mind on his past life before the accident. He wondered about Lindsey. Would he ever see her again?

He dreamed of the day he would walk up to her, perhaps at the university she would be attending, putting his arms around her. She would freak! Maybe he would be there as a guest of honor, making a speech on what he had gone through, how he had endured the pain and suffering. He smiled at the idea. Who wouldn't? He would look down at her and tell her he was back, back in town.

He thought about the donor. Doctor Klein said they would talk about that later. He needed to know who he was. He couldn't wait to find out. He couldn't wait to get out of Edgehill.

"Gene?"

"Huh?"

"I want to make sure you will be ready to go in the next few minutes, yah?" Doctor Klein had been watching him closely, wondering what was going on in his mind. He had noticed a smile on Gene's face only a minute earlier. *Good, he's daydreaming, hopefully thinking it's going to work out for the best.*

"Yes, I'm more than okay, Doctor. I'm looking forward to seeing my grandmother." He winked at Doctor Klein, knowing full well he would love that.

Karol was walking down the hallway toward Gene's room, wanting to wish him all the best, when she saw part of a foot sticking out of a doorway. She wondered what that was all about and then noticed Cynthia poke her head out, looking in the opposite direction.

Karol was at first concerned but then smiled. Cynthia turned her head and saw her coming. She became all flustered as Karol approached.

"Cynthia. Here, come with me. We can see better in this room." Cynthia was puzzled. Karol knew Cynthia wanted to see her patient one last time. That was normal. She felt sorry for her, the poor, young thing with such a big heart. She wondered what Cynthia had in the paper bag.

She took her hand, leading her into a room almost across from Gene's. She put a finger up to her mouth and said, "Shhh. Let's just sit here for a minute or two, okay?"

Cynthia nodded, trying to hide the bag. She hadn't wanted anyone to see. Now that she was with Karol, anyone who did see her wouldn't think anything of it. Karol suspected Cynthia only wanted to see Gene one more time before he left. Maybe she had something to give him, perhaps a memento?

They had a view of Gene's door from where they sat. Karol began to talk. Cynthia stopped listening when she saw Doctor Klein wheel him out of the room. She was now completely focused on Gene. She jumped up off the bed when they were out of sight. Karol firmly grabbed her arm, making her know that she was to stay here with her for a minute or two. Karol did not want Cynthia to create a scene. She knew it would be easier for all involved if Cynthia kept her distance. Cynthia reluctantly sat back down, flustered.

She wanted to see him one-on-one before he left but was being held back by her boss. If she had her way he would be leaving in a body bag! It was too late now. She had missed the opportunity, the opportunity to kill him. She had wanted to grab the handle of the knife while it was still in the bag and simply stab him. Karol released her grip a minute later.

Cynthia got up off the bed, trying to compose herself, and said, "Thank you, Karol. I just wanted to see him one more time. That's all." She forced her voice to sound calm.

Karol nodded, saying, "I know exactly how you feel, my dear." She put her hands on Cynthia's shoulders while looking deep into her eyes. "You know, not that long ago I had a similar incident. Well, I suppose it was several years ago now. My, how time can—"

"Uh, thank you so much, Karol. I better get going. I've got a lot of things that need to be done." She clutched the bag, hoping Karol wouldn't notice the outline of the steak knife, and started walking out the door, down the hallway, adding over her shoulder, "And besides, I have a date this evening."

"But Cynthia, I wanted to tell you about—" Her voice trailed off. Cynthia was long gone, heading back toward the main entrance.

I'm so sorry I didn't stab that little jerk! That's exactly what he is, a jerk! She knew she was acting irrationally but couldn't help it. She was out of control, torn between wanting to kill him as well as love him.

Karol shook her head, thinking what it would be like to be young again. She wondered about Cynthia. Had she been up to something?

Cynthia was feeling panicky as she walked down the hallway. Now that she had missed the opportunity to kill him she had to get rid of the knife before going down to the main entrance. They still had the security check point there. She made her way to the kitchen where she had gotten it. She couldn't just drop it off on a tray in the hallway. It would be too suspicious. Patients were not allowed to have anything like a steak knife in their possession.

She turned a corner near the entrance to the kitchen, suddenly bumping into Harold. He had planned it that way. He knew Gene was leaving. The whole staff knew. He also knew how much she cared for him. Harold was angry with her for what she had told him, about it being none of his business and to 'fuck off.' He wanted to get even. He wanted to hurt her in a childish sort of way.

He had a bowl of tomato soup in his hands, deliberately dropping it on her front, trying to act as though it were an accident. He had hoped that, in the process, he could 'accidentally' feel her breasts. The bowl shattered on the floor as she in turn dropped the paper bag holding the knife.

She was frazzled. Harold mumbled, "Oops." They both looked at each other. She had a look of total surprise. He had a bit of a smirk. His mind was on her breasts. He had felt them during the accident. She quickly looked down at the bag on the floor. The blade of the knife was exposed. She bent down, reaching for it. He was quick and reached down as well, his hand on hers.

"What the—? What are you doing with a steak knife?" He couldn't figure it out. Why would she have a knife, a steak knife in her possession? Employees, of course, could use them but only in the staff cafeteria. Sharp objects, especially steak knives, were by no means allowed in the general patient area. Anyone caught violating any safety rules would be terminated.

They were both kneeling. She knew he had set it up. She knew he had deliberately spilt the soup all over her front. She also knew that he had touched her breasts in the process and it was no accident. No wonder she hated men.

She tried not to cry. Her front was covered in soup, soup that had been deliberately spilt by that creep! She felt violated by his groping. Her mind was off Gene for the moment, wondering how she was going to explain the knife to Harold.

He was on his knees in front of her, looking at her cleavage, thinking that he had one on her. *Yes. If I play my cards right and threaten her a little she might come across for me.* He smirked, enjoying the view.

Just then Karol came around the corner. She had been concerned with Cynthia, deciding on following her down the hallway, making sure she didn't create a scene with Gene's departure. She saw them both kneeling with tomato soup all over the floor as well as on Cynthia's white top.

"Oh my God! Is everyone okay?" She rushed over to the scene as Cynthia was getting up. Harold was still on his knees, the knife in his hand.

"Are you okay, dear?" She helped Cynthia straighten up, seeing the soup on her front. She wasn't concerned about Harold. She did not like him. He had a bad reputation. She felt sorry for Cynthia. After all she had been through, with her friend leaving and now this. She looked down at the floor again and saw the shattered soup bowl, the paper bag and Harold with the steak knife.

"What is going on here?" she demanded.

Cynthia spoke first. "I had a little gift for Gene, Karol. It was my ring. I had it in the bag to give to him. I wanted him to keep it but decided that maybe I would just keep it myself. I put it back on my finger, getting ready to trash the bag, when this man deliberately groped my breasts as he bumped into me." She pointed an accusatory finger down toward Harold. He started to sputter.

"Quiet!" Karol snapped, staring at Harold. She turned back towards Cynthia and said in a much softer tone, "Yes, go on, my dear."

"Well," Cynthia was thinking hard and fast. "He deliberately bumped into me with a bowl of hot soup and a knife. He was angry with me, Karol. I had rejected his advances only last week. I'm not sure what he was going to do with the knife." She began to cry. This time it was an act.

"Harold! What *is* going on?"

He slowly got up. "That's a lie! It was an accident! I didn't have the knife. She did! It was in the bag." He pointed toward Cynthia with a frightened look on his face, his underarms and back stained from sweat.

"First of all, Cynthia claims that you groped her. Is that true?"

"No, I mean, if I did … it was an accident. That's all it was, really!"

Karol knew his reputation. It had happened before. This time he was in serious trouble. And then, there was the knife issue. Had it been in the bag Cynthia had with her all along? Karol wasn't sure. It was difficult to see an outline but … why would Cynthia put her ring in it as she claimed? Why not take it off her finger and place it on Gene's without the bag? She heard Harold sputtering a denial. She knew he was guilty of sexual harassment. And now … assault? He tried to speak. She wouldn't allow it.

"Harold! Shut up. I want to see you in my office in ten minutes! Go! Now! Leave us alone."

He opened his mouth, trying to explain once more, but thought better of it. He turned and walked away, shaking his head, implying that they were all wrong about him.

"Now, dear," she looked at Cynthia, "I demand the truth. Did he grope you?"

"Ah—" She wasn't sure how to reply. She was new here and didn't want to make enemies. *"Besides,"* she thought, *"what about the knife?"* Would Harold make it hard for her? Would he threaten her if he got fired? She wasn't sure on what to say.

"Look, Cynthia. He's been accused of this before. I need you to press charges or else the Union will be on my butt if I go and fire him without your support."

Cynthia had had enough of men. It was time Harold got what he deserved. Gene, too! "Yes, Karol. He touched me. He touched me, deliberately spilling hot soup on me, and yes, he had a knife!"

Karol still had doubts about the knife. She had a question she needed to ask. "Cynthia, why did you have your ring in the bag? Why didn't you take the ring off your finger and give it to Gene instead. Why a bag? Was the ring really in the bag or … was it the knife?"

"Oh no, Karol! It was the ring!" She paused, trying to pull herself together. "Okay. I'll tell you the truth. I had wanted to give Gene my ring. It's not that valuable but it—I wanted him to remember me. I was afraid that if I simply pulled it off my finger to give to him, he wouldn't accept it. He can be a very stubborn man. I wanted to play it down a little, simply put the bag on his lap. That way he wouldn't know what it was until later. Maybe then he would acknowledge it as a gift from one friend to the other.

"When he left with Doctor Klein, I decided that he didn't deserve it after all. That's when I put the ring back on my finger. That's when I walked down the hall with the empty bag and that Harold guy …." She pretended to sob. "That's when Harold poured soup all over me and—"

"There, there, *there*, my dear." Karol had a tear of her own as she put her arms around the young nurse. "Everything is going to be all right. We'll take care of that Harold. Now"—she put her hands on Cynthia's shoulders as she looked her in the eye—"you go and wash up. I've got an extra blouse you can wear. I'll take care of Harold, okay?"

Cynthia nodded, wondering if it was too late to see if Gene had left the hospital. She went to the nearest payphone and put in a quarter. Her hands were shaking. She felt as though she were breaking the law. She suspected, yes indeed, she had broken the law. She had just made an attempt at murder but failed, at least for the time being. Not only had she failed but she had also come very close to getting caught, possibly losing her job. And then there was Gene. Where was he going?

Sheila answered on the first ring. They were already near the entrance and told Cynthia that they could see the ambulance. They were ready to follow.

Cynthia quickly went to the front doors near the security zone, getting odd glances from staff and patients, her white blouse covered in tomato soup. She could see the two ambulance attendants wheeling Gene into the vehicle. She didn't recognize either of them. She began to cry. She was crying out of anger and hurt. She wanted to desperately get even with him. She wanted to get even with men. Harold was going to pay big-time!

Five minutes later the ambulance left. An old Jeep followed.

Chapter 12

As he drove down the street, his mind wandered back to the jungles of Africa. *Yeah, this reminds me of the time when—*

Sheila yelled, "They turned left up ahead. I knew it! That Cynthia bitch was right. They turned off the main highway. Don't get too close!"

"Yes, Sheila. Duh! I won't get *too* close!" *She can be such a pain in the ass sometimes.*

He stayed several hundred feet behind them. They were easy to follow. Hell, the ambulance stuck out like a sore thumb. A minute later it entered a warehouse. Perry and Sheila pulled over, waiting and watching.

They stared at the building, both wondering, "*Why did they drive into the warehouse? Were they going to meet somebody?*"

Ten minutes later a delivery truck drove out through a different door. It was coming their way. They were going to duck down but Sheila was too fat. The delivery van was high enough that the driver would see them if they tried to hide. They decided to hug, pretending to kiss, neither enjoying it. It was all part of the job. Once the van passed they stopped hugging and waited for a minute or two.

"Perry!"

"Yeah?"

"Turn the jeep around."

"What?"

"Turn the fucking Jeep around! I bet you the delivery van is heading for Bosch."

"What? Do you think they did a swap?"

"What else? They dumped the ambulance and used the delivery van. Hurry up! Turn around!"

Perry did as he was told. They headed straight for Bosch Research, pulling around the back near the loading docks. Sure enough, the van was there. They saw two men in hospital garb wheel Gene in through the back door.

"Okay, I agree. It doesn't prove a thing." They were back at the Parrot, having one more beer. Sheila was talking, staring straight ahead at nothing. She was holding the beer bottle close to her lips as though she were speaking into it.

"But … you have to admit it does give credence to Cynthia's story and, if it gives credence then, what about the other part of the story, the part about the pigs being experimented on?" She turned, looked at her partner and whispered, "Perry, I think you should go in there."

"What? Are you saying I should break into Bosch Research?"

"Shhh! Keep it down would you!" She wondered where his brains were at times. She continued to explain. "Well, yeah! If we could get some evidence, some pictures of the animals, then we'd have them by the balls." She thought for a second. "Once we've got that, then we could come back and storm the building. We could notify the media. We could have our picture in the paper!" She knew he would like that. She could see him perk up a little.

"Do you understand what I'm saying, Pair? We could be heroes! I can see it now. The local headlines would read, 'Group Busts Animal Testing.' Our pictures would be featured. We could sell the photos, pictures of pigs being injected with whatever kinds of shit, maybe trapped in an undersized pen with electrodes on their heads. Who knows? We've got to follow this through, right?"

Perry was thinking about his picture in the paper. He was dreaming of how much money he would get selling the pictures to CNN. He was smiling, also holding his beer near his mouth, pretending it was a microphone. He was speaking to the media, announcing to them how much of a hero he was. He had single-handedly—

She hit him on the shoulder, quickly bringing him out of his fantasy.

"Huh? Yeah, maybe. What about your new friend? What's her name?"

"Cynthia. Good question. What about her?" She thought a little longer and then said, "Look, Pair, we've gotta tell her that we saw a swap, right? I mean, we gotta tell her we saw them swap and that she might be right. The trouble is I don't want that bitch hanging around us, knowing what we might be up to. She should definitely not meet you. You're covert!" She saw him smile. She thought, *"Perry, Perry, Perry. You're so damn predictable."*

"Yeah, you're right, Sheila. Tell her about the switch and tell her we'll see what we can do and not to tell anybody else. Okay? Tell her to call you in a few days. That should give me enough time to check things out."

He was already thinking about the layout at Bosch Research and how he could get in. He was very well acquainted with the old hospital. He had been involved in a bit of a skirmish in the building a little while back. The group had found out, through what they had thought was a reliable source, that animal testing was being performed there. They had entered the lobby area only to be met by security.

"Ha, yes, security," he thought. *"That was a joke. There were twelve of us being met by two old fucks dressed in uniform. The nurses and office staff were scrambling at the time, not knowing what to do."*

He and his friends had walked down the hall to where the alleged experiments were taking place. They pounded on a locked door leading into a lab but couldn't get in. They heard sirens in the background but didn't care. They were really doing it to alert the public about what was going on.

One of the local reporters was going to be there taking pictures. The reporter was late and the pictures had turned out shitty. Actually, the photos of him were shitty. Perry didn't like that. He had wanted his image to be the handsome 'All American Boy' fighting for what was right. It hadn't turned out that way. The story wasn't as good as it should have been.

The biggest problem was they didn't have any proof of animal testing. They had no photos. All they had succeeded in doing was make a bunch of noise in the lobby and finally getting arrested. They couldn't prove a thing. They needed evidence. They barely succeeded in letting the public know how shameful those bastards were.

If he had really wanted to get into the lab, he knew how. He had made plans a while back, suspecting that the scientists would never quit their perverse experiments. He had promised himself that, if they ever had another opportunity, he would make sure it would be done right.

He wondered, *"So, is it only experiments on pigs or is there more to it?"* He began making plans. He had first thought they should storm the building but not for a few days. It would be better during the daylight for several reasons. First, they could get in touch with the press and a few pictures could be taken outside the facility. *Yes, better lighting, better quality pictures.*

Second, the best time to do it would be again in daylight. The front entrance to Bosch would be unlocked. Perhaps the security level would be lessened. He wanted this one to be big. He had had enough of their shit experimenting with animals. Actually, he couldn't care less about the animals. He wanted to be the guy, the spokesman, the hero!

He stopped, realizing that he was getting ahead of himself. The first thing that needed to be done was gather proof. They needed proof before storming the building. Sheila's phone chirped, bringing Perry out of his daydream.

"Yeah? Hi, Cynthia."

"Did you follow them?"

"Yeah, we followed them."

"So … did they go to Bosch Research?"

"Uh … no. As a matter of fact, they went straight to the airport."

"What? That's … impossible! No, they were supposed to—" her voice faltered. She was wrong after all. He was going to Boston to live with his grandmother. She still couldn't believe it.

"Cynthia? Are you still there?"

"Ah … yes. I can't believe he left. I really thought I would see him again. I don't know what to say." She started crying again, this time in frustration. She never dreamed he would actually leave for Boston, thousands of miles away.

Perry was listening with interest. Sheila could be one cruel bitch at times, but the more he thought about it the better it was. They didn't need that broad anymore. In fact, she would only create problems. She was far too emotional. Sheila was doing a good job in blowing her off the way she did.

Chapter 13

He had the weirdest feeling when they brought him through the back door at Bosch. It was like being a criminal to mankind. He could see it all, an announcer at the circus showing him off to the public. *This is the mad doctor's secret weapon, the new GENE 2009! It's a super model, ladies and gentlemen. It can walk. It can talk. It can even shit gold nuggets.*

Bruce greeted him in the storage room, taking over from the attendants. Using his security card, they entered the building and then made their way to the boardroom. Gene noticed several people who were new to him. Bruce introduced them, explaining they were all part of the team. Someone jokingly called it the 'Humpty Dumpty' team. He wasn't sure if that was funny. Doctors Adams, Morin and Klein were also there.

Mr. Lincoln wheeled up beside Gene and introduced himself. He smiled at the young man. "I want to tell you how happy we all are that you have come to work with us." He put his hand on Gene's shoulder as he spoke, making Gene feel somewhat more comfortable.

Gene was surprised with the term 'work.' He filed the comment away while listening. Mr. Lincoln was clearly the one in charge.

"I'm sure that some of my colleagues," he looked at Bruce and Doctor Klein as he spoke, "have told you we are a very capable team. Well, yes, we are! You are in the best of care." He patted Gene's shoulder. "Now," he looked at everyone in the room while speaking, "we want you to be as comfortable as possible so don't hesitate in letting us know if there is anything you need." He looked at Gene as he finished the sentence. Gene could feel that he was sincere in what he was saying. "Okay, Gene. Let's go into my office so we can talk privately, all right?"

"Sure, it was nice to meet all of you." He felt awkward. He felt like a prized cow. They were the butchers, yet, he also felt they were sincere in wanting a better life for him. He rationalized, thinking it was his emotions playing with him.

Bruce wheeled him into the office with Mr. Lincoln and then quickly left, leaving them in private. Mr. Lincoln pulled the curtains over the window that viewed the boardroom and began speaking. Gene felt slightly intimidated by him. He seemed like an imposing man—even in the wheelchair. Gene found himself being drawn in by his stare.

"I have been watching certain scientific developments with keen interest that have evolved over the past several years. I, too, know what it's like to lose hope, Gene. I was involved in an accident many years ago. Fortunately for me,"—he looked at Gene and smiled—"I still have the use of my hands. Even though I can use them, my body has never been the same. I can't use my legs. Half of me is gone. I have sat in this wheelchair for years, asking myself, why? Why me?" He was staring at Gene as he spoke.

"I know you've asked yourself the same question. It's not fair. It's not fair that we have been reduced to only a part of what we once were." He coughed and quickly reached under his blanket for his water. Gene waited, thinking of what he had just said. Mr. Lincoln took a drink and continued.

"I made up my mind several years ago, deciding to put together a team of specialists, an elite team that would dedicate themselves in finding a procedure for repairing spinal cord injuries. I have been described by some as being obsessed with this and, yes, I have to agree, I am.

"We were, and still are, faced with all kinds of obstacles but we can overcome them." He let the statement sink in before continuing. "It's ironic that society has yet to catch up and accept the medical procedure which is now possible. If we weren't so controlled by politics and government intervention we would be doing this openly so the world could view our achievements. Unfortunately, for mankind, that won't happen for several years."

Several years! Does that mean that I have to be hidden for several years?

Mr. Lincoln continued. "We have got to maintain complete secrecy. We've seen government, radical groups, as well as society in general, interfering in our research. Do you understand what I'm saying, Gene?"

Gene was spellbound. Mr. Lincoln had his complete attention. He simply nodded.

"Good! Now, I know you have a million questions but before you ask, let's get you settled in and then we can all meet and talk about things."

Gene felt light-headed. He was breathing faster. He was terribly excited. His mouth was dry but he ignored it. Things were starting to happen.

Chapter 14

Perry finished his beer, not even tasting it, his mind miles away. Sheila knew the best thing to do was to leave him alone, let him think about things. Finally, he looked at her and smiled. "Okay, I think I know how to do it. Tell me what you think."

She listened carefully, nodding her approval as he laid out his plan.

He was driving down a back road toward Edgehill Clinic. It was almost dark as he made his way along a residential street with houses on only one side. The other side had some brush and a few trees. Just past the brush was a chain link fence. The property on the other side of the fence belonged to Edgehill. He pulled his Jeep over onto the brush side of the street and got out. He had his binoculars in his pocket as he looked around, making sure he wasn't noticed.

The street was empty. He walked into the brush until he came to the fence. He couldn't see much of anything from that vantage point so followed it a hundred feet farther until he could clearly see the building wing that housed Bosch Research.

It was several hundred yards away across a marsh area. There were a few bushes and groves of trees on the property, a few more up against the building. From where he was standing he could see lights in several windows. He took out his binoculars and scanned the area, planning on how he was going to enter. He noticed several windows that were blacked out by some kind of dark curtain.

The windows had grills covering them. In fact, all the windows on that side of the building had steel grills bolted from the outside—designed to keep patients in. He knew this had once been an asylum for the mentally unbalanced.

He tried to zoom in on the windows that were blackened but couldn't see any detail. He looked around, planning a route he could safely take to get to that part of the building. He had seen enough for tonight. He would come back tomorrow when he was better prepared.

Chapter 15

Cynthia felt cheated. Everything was now out of her hands. She was losing control of the situation and of herself. She felt miserable. There was nothing more she could do. She hugged Kaleb as she fell asleep, dreaming of Gene sitting in his wheelchair, begging her forgiveness as she brought the knife down, ending his miserable life once and for all.

While she was dreaming, so was Gene. His was a little different.

He was on the cliff, the very same cliff where he had the accident. This time, when he dove, he actually flew! He never hit the water. Instead, he swooped down toward the beach. He was free from gravity. He could go wherever he wanted. Lindsey and Dan were on the beach with several other people from his class. They all looked up and marveled. He heard someone say, "Hey, that's Gene! Remember when he was a midget? Now look at him. He can do anything he wants." They pointed and looked in awe as Gene flew down.

He spotted Lindsey and dove toward her. As he got closer he opened up his hands, extending his fingers like a hawk's claws. He grabbed her by the arms, pulling her up and away with him. She screamed in surprise and then began to giggle. He could smell her hair. It was musty and sexy. He flew higher and higher. She loved it, screaming in delight. She smiled up at him, saying, "This is so exciting! You're a powerful bird of prey even though you're so small." He gave her a malicious smile. Little did she know she had said the wrong thing. They were several hundred feet up in the air.

He chose his location perfectly. They flew over some rocks. He tried to let her go. That fucking bitch! She clung to him with one hand, shaking him, yelling his name. "Gene. Gene? Gene!"

"Gene, it's time. Wake up."

"What? Where am I?"

"Good morning, Gene. It's time to wake up. We've got a busy day ahead of us." Doctor Morin waited a few minutes while Gene came around and then said they were all going to be meeting in an hour so he needed to get ready. He left while Gene was being washed by Charlene, a registered nurse he had met the night before.

All members of the L-Team, except for Charlene, were present in the boardroom. She was tending to William DeGroot. Mr. Lincoln called the meeting early, before Gene would join them. There were certain things that needed to be discussed without his knowledge.

"Okay, everyone. Things have happened very quickly over the past twenty-four hours and you all need to be updated." He pulled his hands from under his blanket as he spoke, waving them for emphasis.

"Both patients are now here at Bosch Research." He paused again, unsure on how to continue. "There has been a bit of a 'fly in the ointment' with regards to our situation." He looked around the room, making eye contact with each one of them. "It seems that Mr. DeGroot's next of kin, his Aunt Margaret, may want to come here to Irvine to view his body as well as the little girl's."

There was dead silence. Everyone was on edge. After all, they were prepared to commit murder. That's what it was. They were going to be accomplices in the demise of William DeGroot. They did not want to hear about any 'fly in the ointment' shit. Things weren't going according to plan.

Mr. Lincoln had his hand on his chin, implying that he was in deep thought. He wasn't. He had already planned this whole event out previously. He continued, "Well, Doctor Adams had tried his best to talk her out of it, but when he called her again last night, she was convinced she would be coming to visit in the next few days. It reached a point where the more Doctor Adams tried to persuade her not to come, the more stubborn she became." He raised his hands, palms facing out toward the room.

"Rather than make her suspicious, he decided to use reverse psychology and welcome her instead." He smiled. "That didn't work either. She seems to be very shrewd so we have had to change our plans. I'm telling you this now, before we meet with Gene, so you know what we are dealing with. Anyhow, while on the phone with her, Doctor Adams asked a few more questions about William DeGroot, general things—things that would help us with Gene. She was a wealth of information.

"I guess she felt she had talked enough about dying and wanted to talk about the family while they were alive. At least that part of the conversation was beneficial. Anyhow, we need to discuss the problems and possible solutions with all of you." He turned and looked at Doctor Morin.

"Yes, Mr. Lincoln. Thank you. We have come up with a plan that we need to vote on. Remember, this is a team and we all have equal input." Several people nodded. "Good! Now the problem is, Aunt Margaret is coming to view the bodies, but at this point in time, there are no bodies, only one body and that belongs to Amy, so"—he held up his hands and paused before blurting out—"we need to begin the operation, today."

Someone exclaimed, "*What?*" The noise grew louder, everyone talking at once. No one was ready for this. Most had thought the procedure would begin in at least a week from now, certainly not today.

Doctor Morin put up his hands, forging on, "Your attention, please." There was a buzz in the crowd. It took a few minutes for everyone to settle down. Things weren't going according to plan.

"I know this has come as a complete surprise to all of us but we don't have any choice. Because of the situation with Aunt Margaret, we have to provide her with evidence that William has indeed died."

He kept talking, explaining what they needed to do—discussing all the available alternatives. After a few questions were answered they took a vote.

Charlene was quickly called in to participate. There wasn't much debate. They were caught between a rock and a hard place. It was unanimous. They would meet at five-thirty this evening to begin. There was no other way, besides, the team was ready. It was time.

Mr. Lincoln was thankful the vote went as well as it did. He knew everyone was under enormous pressure. They needed to be a cohesive group, undivided. There was a moment during the meeting when the team seemed to have come apart. *That's what it is. Everyone is stressed. It will only get worse if we wait any longer. It's the right decision. We need to go ahead with the procedure as soon as possible.*

Five-thirty was the best time to begin. The doctors and team members needed to go about their regular business during the day, not arousing any suspicions. The operations would be done after their daily routines had been completed. It would put enormous strain on all of them. Attempting an operation of that magnitude could continue well into the night but they were all experienced, used to working long hours.

Everyone left except for Mr. Lincoln, Doctor Klein and Bruce Whitman. They decided it was best if only two or three people met with Gene.

Charlene wheeled him into the boardroom and left. Gene sensed something in the air. They were looking at him rather strangely. He began to feel faint, telling himself to take a deep breath. He could do this. He needed to do this! He told himself he was ready.

Chapter 16

He, of all people, was at a loss for words. Mr. Lincoln didn't know how to begin. "Ah, how are you feeling, Gene?"

"Good, I guess."

"That's good."

Bruce knew Lincoln was struggling with the conversation so took over. "We've had a meeting with the team."

"Yeah?"

"Yes, and we're ready to go ahead." He paused, waiting for Gene to respond. Gene had no comment, waiting for them to continue, knowing full well his life was in their hands.

"Circumstances have made us move the planned date for the operation forward."

"Circumstances? What circumstances?" He was a whole mix of feelings. He was frightened, agitated, curious, puzzled, and most of all, running out of patience.

"Well, your donor is beginning to falter." He said it in a matter-of-fact voice even though it was a lie. Bruce didn't want to go into any great detail with Gene about the situation with Margaret.

Doctor Klein jumped in. "Vee have decided that vee vill begin this evening."

Gene's face turned pale. His eyes bugged out. *Holy shit! Tonight! I don't think I'm ready!*

Mr. Lincoln had regained his composure. He read Gene's expression. "I know this comes as a surprise to you, Gene."

Surprise? It's a fucking shock to me! I don't know if I can go through with this!

Mr. Lincoln continued. "We had a meeting with the team and we've voted in favor of commencing early this evening."

"What about me? Don't I get a say in this?" He heard himself pleading.

Bruce quickly replied, "Yes, of course you get a say in this." They all knew whatever he said didn't matter anymore. They were only being polite. Regardless of what Gene decided, they would be giving him a sedative soon and then, later, wheel him into the operating room. The operation would be carried out with or without his consent.

"So, what do you say? Please, keep in mind that if we don't act quickly we might never get another chance."

Gene looked at all of them, not knowing quite what to say. Finally, he asked, "Who is he? Who is this donor? Tell me all about him."

Mr. Lincoln cleared his throat. "His name is William and he's twenty-three years old. He, along with his wife and daughter, had a vehicle accident. This was a few days ago. William and his wife almost drowned. Their daughter did."

Gene listened, fascinated at what Mr. Lincoln was saying.

"William weighs one hundred and eighty pounds, is RH negative, has no drug or alcohol addictions and is in good physical shape, but … is deteriorating quickly. If we don't operate tonight he may not be healthy enough to undergo the operation later." He paused, letting Gene take in the gravity of the situation.

There was silence. Doctor Klein spoke up a few seconds later. "It is now entirely up to you." Again, they were only being polite. "Are you ready?"

Gene was thinking about a million different things. His life was at stake here. *No, my life left me when I had this accident. I have no choice but to take this chance.*

He looked at the doctor, thinking of what to say next. Things were moving too quickly for him. He couldn't help it, he vomited. Doctor Klein was quickly at his side with tissue, trying to wipe up the mess. Gene's head was shaking, tears in his eyes. Doctor Klein gave him some water, trying to calm him. Finally, in a weak voice, he asked, "Doctor Klein?"

"Yes, Gene."

"I … I want to see the donor." Doctor Klein was about to say something but Gene continued. "I want to see him. I want to know what he looks like. I need to know as much about him as possible."

Mr. Lincoln and Doctor Klein both looked at Bruce. They were wondering what the psychological ramifications would be if he saw his donor, or worse, if they denied granting him the request.

Bruce hesitated, thinking the same thing. He slowly turned back to Gene. He knew as soon as he saw the look on Gene's face that he had to say "Yes."

They brought him into William's room. As they got closer to the bed, Gene had a better look. William was lying on his back. Bruce wheeled him up to the side of the bed while Doctor Klein walked over to the opposite side. With both hands, Joseph Klein slowly turned the donor's head so Gene could see the face. It was an eerie moment for all. No one spoke. The only sound was the steady beeping of the heart monitor.

William DeGroot lay peacefully on his back in bed. A tube had been placed up his badly broken nose to aid in his breathing. He had several bandages on his swollen face. The top of his head was wrapped in gauze, covering his forehead. He had two black eyes. His breathing was shallow.

After several minutes Gene asked Doctor Klein if he could raise one of William's eyelids. Doctor Klein raised his own eyebrow, surprised with the request, but obliged.

The first thing Gene noticed was how blood-shot the eye was. He was taken aback. He hadn't expected that. He focused on the pupil, noticing William had brown eyes. He found that very interesting. His eyes were green. Something about that disturbed him. He looked deeper into the eye, wondering if he could see the man's soul. He wanted to get a sense of him. He was mesmerized.

Slowly, his eyes wandered. He looked down at the face, trying to picture what the man had looked like before the accident, before the bruising and swelling had taken place.

Doctor Klein broke the silence by saying, "I've got something better for you, Gene." He produced the victim's driver's license. Gene could see for himself what William once looked like by the photo on the license. He read the information, finding out his name and where he lived. He carefully read the description and focused on height.

Yes, six feet zero inches tall. Good! The guy is one hundred and eighty pounds, twenty-three years old and has brown hair and brown eyes.

He mouth slowly formed a smile as he realized that soon things would be much different. He was feeling better, becoming excited. He had a crazy thought of mentally talking to William, saying, "Guess what, buddy. You're going to have black hair and green eyes pretty soon." He immediately regretted thinking that. In his mind he sounded smug. He knew he should feel humbled instead.

He asked Doctor Klein to remove the bed sheet so he could see himself. *This is becoming weird. I've got to choose my words better but … it is true. I do want to see myself.*

Doctors Klein and Morin pulled the sheet off the bed and raised the nightgown up to the shoulders. They came around to both sides of Gene and lifted him out of the wheelchair so he could have a better view. He did see. He had a really good look.

The first thing he noticed was how long the legs were. He told himself, "Good, yes, very good." He then looked at the penis, thinking, "*Okay, it's shriveled now but maybe it's normal or bigger than normal under different circumstances.*" He wondered if he'd ever be able to get it up.

He looked at the hands, his new hands. They were big. The guy was bigger than him, with long arms and an average chest, a chest that had some hair on it. Tall, lean, and lanky! He wondered if he would be capable of playing football again.

Throughout all of this he couldn't help but feel uncomfortable. He felt he was a vulture picking away at another being. It wasn't right, but another part of him was excited, excited to be given a second chance.

What did the medical community call it? Harvesting? That's it. They harvest eyes or lungs or whatever from a donor. This time this will be the biggest harvest that the medical world has ever seen!

"Doctor?"

Doctor Morin spoke with a whisper. "Yes, Gene." There was an air of reverence in the room. They had come to pay homage and respect to the donor without realizing it.

"Can I please be alone for a few minutes?"

Doctor Klein looked at Doctor Morin, both understanding the need for Gene to spend some private time, time alone with his new body. Without saying a word they placed him back in the wheelchair, as close to the bed as possible.

"We'll be outside the room so call when you're ready."

Gene didn't reply. He sat, staring. He was fascinated and yet he had the strangest feeling he was on a shopping trip. He told himself that was exactly what it was. It was like going to the mall and getting new clothes, new boots, socks, pants, shorts, shirts, body. He was feeling weird.

He looked at the body, wondering what William would think if he knew what was in store for him. *Would William still be considered alive after they operate? Will I feel William's presence in me once we unite as one?*

Gene was not one for prayer but was overcome with the need to make things right. Still fixated on William, he began. "Please, God. Please help me. Help us. We will soon be one being. Please forgive me. Please forgive the doctors and team members as well. We all want to do what's best for mankind as well as ourselves. That's all. It should really be a simple matter. It's like an organ transplant. There shouldn't be any difference between this and a heart transplant, right? Amen." He felt better. Now it seemed like the right thing to do, to go ahead with the operation.

A few minutes later Doctor Klein came back into the room. He was having difficulty trying to grasp the situation, thinking along the same lines as Gene, wondering how he would feel if he were in Gene's position.

Gene blurted out, "What did he do? Where did he live?"

Doctor Klein stopped him by saying, "Dee donor is married, yah, to a pretty wife who is in vorse shape than him. He has fawdered a child—a daughter who has since died as a result of dee accident. He is an artist and has been adopted since childhood. No mudder or fawder. He only has an aunt, yah? Dee aunt has told us dat he likes dogs but not cats. He does not like green peppers but loves onions. He does not like raisins or coconut."

Gene was thinking hard about the information Doctor Klein was giving him. Did he want that kind of information? Would it help or hinder him? If the guy liked dogs would Gene naturally like dogs as well? If he knew the donor liked dogs, would that persuade him to feel the same? He didn't want to be the same. He was Gene, no one else! He was only borrowing a body for a lifetime. That's all.

He cut Doctor Klein off by saying, "Thank you, Doctor." He'd heard enough.

Chapter 17

Doctor Klein scrubbed his arms and hands in preparation for the operation. He tried to convince himself that this was not murder but merely a transformation from one life to another. He went through a mental checklist, wondering if they had done everything possible to confirm that the donor would be in a coma for the rest of his life. He knew of many cases where victims had suddenly wakened years later.

He again told himself this operation would make things better for both the donor and Gene. He reasoned that, even if the donor regained consciousness, his quality of life would still be very poor. He persuaded himself once more to believe they were doing the right thing.

There was something else that he needed to convince himself about but had trouble doing so. He didn't like the fact they had lied to Margaret and now they were lying to Gene. He knew that was wrong. He was nervous. They all were.

Doctor Morin tried to rationalize. He told himself what they were doing was all for the good of science. Every worthwhile endeavor needed a sacrificial lamb. Deep down he was not totally sure. He had rehearsed this scene hundreds of times before. He had accepted the risks and moral issues. He knew that no matter how much he tried to think otherwise, he had taken an oath to help patients, not decapitate them.

Doctor Adams had been immersed in the planning of the operation. He and Doctor Klein would be working together. He went through the procedure in his mind again and again, making sure they had covered everything before they began. He smiled, knowing full well there was always something that would be forgotten. It never seemed to fail. He tried to reassure himself that this time it would be different.

Doctor Schultz was the least experienced of the four doctors but had a textbook knowledge of the different techniques they would soon be applying. He was a surgeon, a good surgeon, but his interests had now changed from the operating theater to the laboratory and research areas. He had no doubt in what they were about to do. His only concern was with the law. He was very nervous about taking the life of one person in order to save another, especially when they were doing it for their own self-interests. He was not fooling himself with this 'for mankind' rhetoric. No, for him it was strictly for fame and glory.

He was worried about getting caught. It would be a very bizarre case indeed if it ever went to court. His career would be over. He was very nervous because he knew he was committing a crime like the rest of them. He couldn't deny it. The team was committing murder. It was as simple as that. He knew, if caught, they would all go to jail. He began to sweat. He looked down at his hands as he put the latex gloves on. There was a slight tremor to them.

All the other team members went through their own feelings as they prepared for the operation. They tried to put away the nagging thoughts and doubts that kept surfacing. They knew this needed to be done. Science had driven them to this point and if they didn't do it now it would soon be done by another team, perhaps from Canada or Germany or England. They were not alone in this.

Mr. Lincoln was also nervous. He had been told to keep out of the operating rooms. He was not a surgeon and would only get in the way, plus there was always the risk of contamination. Only the people that were vital to the operations were allowed in. He was glad he didn't have to witness the procedures. Instead, he stayed away, leaving his cell phone on in case there were any emergencies.

Chapter 18

He didn't have lunch. Even if he'd been allowed to eat he wasn't hungry. He waited in bed, trying to keep his mind on other things. Charlene came in every once in a while, asking how he was. He finally told her he was terrified. He was having panic attacks. She came back very quickly and had him swallow two pills. Fifteen minutes later he was feeling much better. Twenty minutes later he was asleep.

They came in to prepare him for surgery at four-thirty in the afternoon. Gene felt relaxed and calm as they finished scrubbing and shaving him. The sedative was still working.

They wheeled him into the operating room and placed him on an operating table. He noticed there were several people in the room ready to go to work. They all had their operating scrubs and masks on. Gene wondered about the masks. He knew it was a medical requirement but he couldn't help but think they were wearing them to help hide their faces as well. Were they ashamed at what they were about to do? He mentally shrugged, telling himself he was over-reacting.

An anesthesiologist asked how he was feeling.

"Sick."

"Yes, that's normal, Gene. Just try to relax."

He was given another sedative intravenously. He began to feel better, trying to focus on the positive side. He kept telling himself he had nothing to lose and that he was far better off than his donor, William DeGroot.

Moments later Doctors Klein and Morin came in. They slowly administered the SES serum. All his bodily functions were monitored. He heard the steady 'beep-beep-beep' of his heart on one of the many devices.

A few minutes later the anesthesiologist began administering the general anesthetic. Gene's eyes were slowly closing. He could barely see the harsh operating lights through his eyelids. He felt wonderful. He began drifting away, thinking about getting a second chance. *A second chance*!

He mumbled incoherently, "Yes, this time I'll be taller. They won't call me midget anymore. Those fucking – bitches – will pay – more – atten—"

He tried to fight it but couldn't. The anesthetic had taken over. Patient 'A' was now under.

Chapter 19

She had thought about it all night, what this Doctor Adams had told her, about not coming and then … finally telling her to come if she wanted. She needed to be there. There was no doubt in her mind. She knew the doctor meant well and wanted to spare her pain and suffering, but she didn't like the way he had said 'disposing of the bodies.' That didn't sit well with her.

That's why she was on her way, flying into Denver and then on to Irvine two hours later. She would be arriving very late, close to midnight. She had booked a motel for three nights.

Her mind kept going back to Amy and William. Poor Amy! She never did have a chance at life. And, poor William, he never did either, dying at the age of twenty-three. What a terrible shame. She pictured them lying in the morgue on a stainless steel table similar to what she saw on those detective shows. The body covered in a white sheet, a name tag on his big toe. It was so cold and impersonal. At least they hadn't suffered.

She thought again about the bodies and funeral arrangements. She had several friends in the neighborhood who had gotten to know the DeGroot family a little. She was sure they would attend the funeral. She knew Pastor Tim could be called in for the service. She liked him. She had gotten to know him under some bad circumstances, attending five funerals in the past year, all of them being friends and neighbors who had simply grown old.

William certainly wasn't given a chance to grow old. She dabbed at her eye with Kleenex, trying not to break down again. *And then … Amy. Poor, poor Amy. She was only a child.*

Doctor Adams had mentioned they would be making arrangements with the local funeral home to prepare the bodies for the funeral back east. She was thankful for that. She didn't want to see them under a white sheet on a steel table. No, she would be able to view them resting in peace at the funeral home as soon as the necessary—. What did Doctor Adams tell her? She remembered him saying she could view the two bodies as soon as the 'necessary steps' were taken. She presumed that paper work needed to be completed as well as whatever they did at the funeral home. She hoped she would be home with them within three or four days.

And, what about Laurie? Well, quite frankly, I couldn't care less about her but she is Amy's mother. I'll have to talk to Doctor Adams when I meet with him. Should she stay in Irvine or be flown back to Bangor with us?

PART IV

Chapter 1

It was exactly five-thirty when all four surgeons were ready to begin. The rooms were labeled One and Two, respectively. Doctors Klein and Adams occupied operating room One with Gene while Doctors Morin and Schultz were with William in the second operating room. There were several nurses as well as an anesthesiologist in each room. There was a large window separating the operating theatres. Both teams could communicate with each other via an intercom system.

Gene was lying on his back, his head and face shaved, with an intravenous tube in his right arm. They had begun to inject him with a derivative of SES, the Spinal Enhancement Serum. This mix, called SES-3B, was highly experimental, designed to enhance the body's natural immune system, giving it an anti-organ rejection capability. It was considered highly experimental because it had never been thoroughly tested. In fact, the only test subjects had been animals, the largest being pigs.

There would likely be side effects. Every new medication had some. That didn't matter. What did matter was the end result. The main concern was what SES appeared to do—having the capability of coaxing nerve endings into a rough form of re-attachment. This was a phenomenal discovery. They could not follow the FDA required guidelines for testing and re-testing. No, if they didn't act quickly, another research group would.

They were confident SES-3B had the characteristics they were looking for in spinal cord re-attachment, the ability to help nature in nerve ending growth and repair, at least with pigs. Test results suggested it should be capable of roughly re-attaching severed nerve endings, not individually at this time but rather in micro-clusters, in humans.

They knew they were on the leading edge. Completing a successful operation on a human would change the course of medical history. One giant leap for mankind, akin to landing on the moon.

The same procedure was being done in room Two. William was lying on his back with an intravenous tube inserted in his right arm. He was being given

SES-3B. Each patient had monitors attached to various sensors on his head and body.

A mechanical breathing device and defibrillator were nearby. Two blood transfusion devices along with many units of blood were also present, ready to be hooked up. The vital signs of each patient were satisfactory. Pulse activity was normal. Blood pressure and respiration were good.

Doctor Adams began by taking out a marker pen and, with the help of Doctor Klein, traced where the initial incisions would take place. They wanted to make sure the natural creases of the neck would hide the scarring, at least partially.

They made a V shaped mark just below the neck on the front of Gene's body. The point of the V dipped down six inches toward the chest area. The upper ends of the V stopped on either side of the neck on top of the shoulders. They continued the line from the upper part of the V around the base of the neck, dipping down slightly in a semi-circular fashion at the back, and then came up the other side, making a complete loop.

Doctor Klein looked through the window toward Doctors Morin and Schultz. They appeared ready. He asked the anesthesiologist in each of the operating rooms, "Gentlemen, are we ready to begin?" He spoke toward the intercom mounted on the wall beside the window. His voice was slightly muffled by his surgical mask. They replied that the patients were stable. There were no complications. The operations could commence.

The two doctors in the other room looked at Doctor Klein through the dividing window. "Yes, we are ready as well," they replied, complete with a thumbs up.

Doctor Adams looked at Doctor Klein and nodded. He took out a scalpel and made the first of many delicate incisions.

Chapter 2

Emil walked into Bosch at 6 p.m. The first thing he did was lock the front doors. Justin, his young assistant, was to do the same with the doors at the loading dock as well as the side door leading out to the meadow beyond.

Emil was deep in thought, thinking about Justin, as he let himself in. The kid was getting on his nerves. Emil figured him to be a fucking know-it-all. He tried to give him some slack, thinking what he was like when he was that age. He shook his head, doing the math. Hell, that was forty years ago. This was the year he had planned on retiring but he wasn't ready. He wondered if he ever would be.

He went into the security office directly across from Mr. Lincoln's and signed in. Greg and Mark were there finishing up their day shift. They told him all was well. Emil quickly scanned the monitors and alarm system. Yes, all was well. He could see Justin on the closed-circuit TV at the loading dock.

Once Greg and Mark left the building, Emil put his lunch bucket down on the desk. Today he was going to compare Manuel's burritos with his own and see who really made the hottest.

Perry looked up at the clock, realizing it was finally time to get ready. He was glad things were slow in the construction business. His boss had told him he would call if he needed his help. That was two weeks ago. Perry didn't mind. He had a few dollars saved up and he liked the idea of taking the summer off, lying on the beach by the lake, looking at all those hot bodies in their bathing suits.

His boots were already polished and his fatigues lay over the chair. He was pretty much ready to do battle, making sure his weapon was loaded, ready to shoot. In this case it was a small digital camera. He hummed an old marching song as he dressed. Once in uniform, he packed several items into his duffle bag that he knew he would need.

His mind was back in Africa, remembering the time they were preparing to regain control of a small village. The insurgents had been occupying it for several hours. Perry and his group had driven a few miles nearby. They hiked through the dense foliage in the dark until they came to the outskirts.

There were ten of them, broken down into five two-man units. Each unit would go from hut to hut making sure the enemy was gone. He and Jeff entered the first one, surprising everyone. There were twelve people all huddled together. The oldest appeared to be around ten years. Two of them began to cry. He could not imagine what they must have thought, seeing two Americans with weapons drawn, busting into their home. Hell, he remembered even Jeff being scary to him. His friend had towered over him.

His thoughts were so far away that he didn't remember putting his camouflage paint on or darkening his blond hair. He was thankful it was dreary outside. He was out the door by eight, prepared for the mission, still humming his marching song. The sun would be set within a half-hour at this time of year.

He got into his Jeep and headed down the back roads, trying to get as close as possible to the facility without being detected. He was wearing a large brimmed hat so it would partially cover his face, hiding his camouflage paint. He also had a full-length coat over the fatigues. He hoped he wouldn't be noticed by anyone while driving.

Chapter 3

It had been close to three hours since the operation began. Team A, comprised of Doctors Klein and Adams, along with several nurses and the anesthesiologist, was totally in its element. Team B, Doctors Morin and Schultz and their group, was in the other room, equally immersed.

Each team had rested the back of its patient's head in a plastic mold to give it stability. The operating table had a removable section that would expose the shoulders and upper neck. The body was positioned in such a way that the shoulders were slightly over the edge on the removable section of the table. With the head resting in the mold, the doctors could remove the one section of table to facilitate in operating around to the back of the neck, without moving the body. The hospital bed could also be raised several feet, as well as rotated, so the doctors would have an easier time working on the backside of the patient without needing to stoop.

Doctor Adams had begun the operation by making an incision along the marker line they had previously drawn. He started at the point of the V, cutting upwards on Gene's left side toward the base of the neck. The anesthesiologist relayed their progress to Team B via the intercom. Both teams could view each other's progress through closed-circuit television. Team B followed, making the same incision on the donor, patient B. Thus, the pattern was established. Team A would proceed with team B closely following. In this way, one team would not get too far behind or ahead of the other.

Once the incision was complete Doctor Adams made another, starting at the point of the V and up the middle to just below the larynx. Doctor Klein tried to control the bleeding as well as hold on to the edge of skin that had been cut and pulled back. He gently kept pulling while Doctor Adams chiseled, separating it from the underlying muscle and tissue. Charlene, one of the nurses, was ready with suction.

Another incision was made, this time from the point of the V along Gene's right side, following the line the felt pen had made, up towards Gene's shoulders. As soon as the skin had been pulled back several inches, Doctor Klein used retractors, holding the skin flaps that were now on both sides of Patient A's neck. This enabled Doctor Adams to begin cutting into muscle and tendon at the base of the neck, being careful to avoid the jugular vein as well as the carotid and subclavian arteries.

They continued by cutting the sternohyoideus muscle and its affiliated muscles near the front portion of the neck, using retractors where needed. Next, they worked their way to one of the largest muscles of the neck, the sternocleidomastoid.

As the work progressed, they began cutting into a network of minor veins and small arteries. The plan was to leave the major arteries and veins intact until the last possible moment.

Now they were coming to a crucial part of the operation. Blood loss was becoming a factor. Clamps were used to stem the flow from the larger blood vessels while sutures temporarily closed some of the smaller ones. Doctor Klein maneuvered a suction tube, busily trying to clear the area of blood, making Doctor Adams field of view unobstructed. It was becoming somewhat of a challenge. The bleeding was now an issue. Of course, this was to be expected.

Doctor Adams pried at the under part of the skin around the sides of the neck while the retractors gently pulled back the flaps.

The anesthesiologist monitored the vital signs while communicating with the doctors in Team B. They, in turn, relayed that they were now at the same stage as Team A. Outside of the bleeding, all was well.

Each team was ready to make an incision into the trachea, preparing to insert a breathing tube. It was partially exposed just below the thyroid gland. Again, they were careful to not disturb the arteries and veins that wrapped around the immediate area.

Doctor Adams slowly made an incision and inserted the breathing tube several inches toward the lungs. Doctor Klein clamped the trachea onto the tube making it airtight. They wanted to make sure no blood or debris would be drawn into the lungs along with the patient's airflow.

The gentle whoosh of air slowly being pumped into the lungs could be heard over the steady beep of the monitoring equipment.

Chapter 4

Perry drove down a side street close to where he had parked the night before and slowly pulled over. He parked the Jeep off the road and quickly scanned the area, making sure no one noticed him. The sun was almost set. It was quickly becoming dark. He decided he'd better hurry while there was still a little light.

He took off his hat and coat while in the vehicle, placing them on the back seat. It was a hot evening—he was already sweating. He leaned over, grabbed the black duffle bag and collapsible ladder, and exited out the passenger door. He looked around once more. There was no one.

He quickly walked into the bush until he came up against the chain-link fence. He put the duffle bag and ladder down. When folded in half, the aluminum ladder was only three feet in length. He was glad he had painted it black.

He made his way along the fence until he could clearly see Edgehill and Bosch Research. It was still light enough to see the white building. It appeared there was going to be a bit of a moon out tonight. He reached for the binoculars and focused on the blackened windows at Bosch. There were three of them. Each was covered with a steel grill like the rest of the windows in the wing. He wondered how difficult it would be to remove the metal framework. He was glad for being fairly slim and in good shape.

He tried to estimate the height of the windowsills. They looked to be around six feet off the ground, at least eight inches higher than him. He would need a ladder to stand on in order to work the bottom bolts. The outside dimensions of the window frames appeared to be around three feet high by two feet wide. He knew he'd have to stand near the top of the ladder in order to loosen the top bolts. He hoped they could be easily removed.

He looked at the six windowpanes in each window. He figured the windows were probably locked and alarmed. He would have to cut out at least two panes and be careful of the cut glass when he slipped through. He wondered about the black covering. Was it only paint or was there a curtain covering it as well? He needed to get closer to find out.

He again looked at the path he planned on taking through the trees and marsh area leading to Bosch Research. Once near the building he still had to make a run for it over a lawn area. Fortunately, there were some decorative bushes every hundred feet alongside the building. That would provide some much needed cover if anything went wrong.

The chain-link fence would be no problem. He had wire cutters. He would cut the softer wires that held the fence to the posts and lift up the bottom so he could slide under. No one would notice.

He walked back toward the duffle bag and ladder, looking along the bottom of the fence, trying to find a dip in the ground. He chose a spot nearby. He brought the bag and ladder to the location he had chosen. He took out the wire cutters and cut three of the wraps that held the fence to a post. He bent down and began pulling at the bottom of the fence, slowly stretching it off the ground. It didn't take long for him to make an opening large enough to slide his body, ladder and duffle bag through. The sun had completely set by now, the moon peeking out behind some clouds.

He suddenly heard rustling in the bush to his right. He was already in a crouched position, getting ready to shimmy under the fence. He turned his head toward the sound. He stopped what he was doing and listened intently. His heart was racing. He smiled, loving that sort of stuff. He waited for a moment, finally deciding it was probably a small bird or animal.

As he began to slide the duffle bag under the fence he heard voices coming from the street about a hundred yards away. It sounded like women, two women. They were making their way down the road toward him. He heard a dog bark. They were walking a dog. It barked again.

He pushed the duffle bag and ladder under the fence and quickly scrambled behind. Just as he pulled himself through to the other side he again heard rustling in the bush. This time it was the dog. It was quickly running toward him. He pulled the fence closed just as the German shepherd reached it, growling, desperately wanting to get at him. Perry was still on his knees, looking at the dog face-to-face only inches away on the other side of the fence. He could smell and feel the warmth of the shepherd's breath. He was shaking as he very quickly crawled backward into the dark, dragging the duffle bag and ladder along with him.

He heard voices yelling, "Kobi!" Footsteps came closer. The dog wouldn't leave. He kept growling, trying to dig his way under the fence at the same location Perry had gotten through.

Perry quickly slid behind a bush and created a cloud of dust in the process. He was thirty or so feet from the fence. He saw light from a flashlight. He heard voices. This time they were very close. He was sweating profusely and his nose was filled with dust. The dog had his head under the fence, trying to pull his body through to Perry's side.

"Kobi, what do you have there, boy?" She quickly reached under and grabbed his collar. He struggled, trying to get through to Perry, but she was stronger, pulling him back to her side of the fence.

A light swept across the area passing directly over him. He was on his stomach, his head down. He tried to suppress a sneeze. He was dead still, hoping they would leave, glad he was camouflaged.

Finally, after what seemed like forever, he heard her yell back to her partner. "It looks like he might have spotted a rabbit. I'm putting his leash back on."

He couldn't help it. He sneezed into his sleeve, trying to muffle the sound. The flashlight quickly scanned over his location once more.

A voice from the street yelled out, "Connie, are you okay?"

"Ah, yeah ... I just heard something on the other side of the fence. It sounded ... weird." She wasn't sure what she had heard and tried to convince herself that it was only a small animal not too far away, noticing the dust in the air.

Perry kept his head down, not sure what Connie was going to do. The light went off. He could hear the dog whimpering on the other side of the fence. They were still there. He waited, not moving a muscle.

"Connie? Connie, what is it?" The other woman on the street was becoming concerned.

"Uh, nothing. Nothing at all." Connie waited another moment before turning back to her friend.

The voices and sounds of footsteps soon became distant. Perry found himself breathing quickly. His heart was racing as he told himself, "That was way too fucking close!" He lifted his head and did a quick scan before moving farther back, finally sitting up behind some brush sixty feet from the fence. He was both smiling and shaking, trying to stifle another sneeze. He was dripping in sweat. He loved this sort of stuff.

He slowly calmed down, his mind drifting as he took a swig of water and quietly blew his nose. He thought about the time he was a mercenary soldier back in Africa. He caught himself, quickly getting back to the business at hand. There was no time for daydreaming. He had a mission to accomplish.

Chapter 5

"Shit!" Emil shook his head in exasperation. The red heat and air warning light blinked on the control panel. Justin was sitting beside him in the security office thumbing through a girlie magazine. He had decided it was time for a coffee break.

"What's up?"

Emil looked at the blinking light, knowing full well what the trouble was. "It looks like we've got a problem with the electrical circuit for the air-conditioning … again."

"I thought Manuel convinced the powers above to get it taken care of. Just because they're doctors doesn't mean they can't listen to us."

Emil looked at the kid, trying to suppress a comment. *What's with this 'us' shit? As if the kid has any say in the matter. The fucker always has a comment.*

"What are you going to do, call Manuel?"

Emil thought about it. "No, it looks like I'll have to get into the utility room and open the hatch to the crawl space. I'll check things there first. If resetting the breaker doesn't work, then I'll call Manuel."

He slowly made his way with the ladder and duffle bag, crouching under trees and bush, until he was only several hundred feet from the white, institutional building. He squatted, catching his breath, as he took out the binoculars. He focused on the three windows. This time they were at an angle from his point of view. He could see that the grilles were bolted from the outside onto the cement blocks of the building. He knew they had been there for many years. This might make things difficult. It would be hard to undo any of the bolts, especially if they were rusted and painted over several times.

He rested for a few more minutes to cool off. *Fuck, is it hot!* There was no rush. He could take all night if necessary. He took out the bottle of water, noticing his hands were trembling. He took a long drink. He was still shaken from the dog and woman.

He was concerned with the moonlight. It was a little too bright. He had to make his way over several hundred feet of lawn to get to the side of the building near the windows. He decided to wait a little longer, thinking the clouds would soon blow over, masking the moonlight at least temporarily.

He closed his eyes and slowly drifted back to a time not too long ago, a time when he was in the thick of things, a time when he was a hero!

It had taken him a while to get over the incident back in Angola. It was times like these, sitting in the dark, preparing for action, that made him think back to when he had been in the 'Special Forces' with the Marines. Yes, life should have been simpler then. He had been solid muscle, in the best shape of his life.

He had always wanted to travel to Africa and finally got his wish. They had done several weeks of training deep in the jungle. It was survival training. Each of them was to spend a week alone with only the bare necessities. He had seen the jungle very differently than most.

The official stand was that they were there to fight for freedom and abolish terror. It should have been easy. Perry was well trained like the rest of his group. He was eager and cocky. He was a true patriot, feeling he was doing his country a service … until the incident.

They had been under fire. The whole operation was going sour. No one should have known they were there. They had been ambushed. Jeff, his long time partner, was crouched beside him. They were hiding inside a concrete building, terrified, ready to shoot at anything that came their way. Several in his group had already been killed.

They thought they were safe in the room, waiting for the opportunity to shoot some of those bastards. They heard noises coming from the hall so crouched lower, behind some rubble, waiting for over an hour. Jeff told him to stay put while he checked it out. He saw him crawl, slowly making his way across the room, peeking out around the doorway.

Perry heard a 'boom' as a spray of blood, brain and hair flew off the back of Jeff's head. He presumed the bullet had hit him between the eyes. He had no time to take a closer look. He knew Jeff was dead.

He bolted. He jumped out of a window and landed in an alley, badly spraining his ankle. He heard another 'boom' and, thinking it came from behind a pile of garbage, fired his weapon. He heard a thump and thought, *"Good you son-of-a-bitch. Gotcha!"*

He peered over the garbage and saw her, a young woman, pregnant. He had shot her right in the mid-section. She looked like she was almost due to have the baby. She lay there dying. She was terrified, the dark pool of blood spreading beneath her as her breath became shallower. She looked up at him, at first in terror, then in anger. She began to lose her focus. She had never been any threat. He told himself it was an accident as he knelt down in front of her, seeing the pain and disbelief in her eyes.

Other locals began to come out of hiding. They ran up and, seeing he wasn't a threat any longer, tried to help her. He was bent over in shock. He'd completely forgotten about his sprained ankle. He couldn't believe it. Why did he have to shoot so quickly? He got sick, bending over, throwing up. He had tears in his eyes. He hated it there, hating what he had done.

Someone threw a rock, hitting him on the back of the neck. He turned, this time with his rifle pointing toward the ground. He was hit again. The locals were beginning to stone him. He could see the hatred in their eyes. He was alone, trying to hold up his hands, shaking his head, telling them he was sorry. No one listened or cared.

He made his way down the street, limping, threatening anybody in his path with his rifle. The gathering crowd followed, throwing everything they could get their hands on at him. He was hit on the head by a large rock. Blood ran down the side of his face. He could feel it ooze down his neck under his shirt, becoming sticky. He could smell it. He was becoming dizzy, starting to fade. He turned back toward the crowd, firing several warning shots over their heads. That stopped them, but only for a few seconds.

He was losing consciousness as he turned a corner and stumbled into his commanding officer. They had heard the shooting. He asked Perry what had happened. Perry couldn't speak. They quickly drove off.

Later, the Marines did a full investigative report. He was dismissed from duty partly because of stress but mainly because of the incident. He knew he had made a mistake. He knew he had killed two innocent people with one bullet. He had over-reacted, had not been professional.

He felt something hit his back and, for a moment, thought he was still in Angola. A pinecone had fallen from the tree above.

He sat for several minutes, his mind soon wandering once more, thinking about some of his close buddies and how tight a group they had become, especially when under fire.

Suddenly clouds blew in, covering the moon, bringing him out of his daydream. It was now as dark as it was ever going to get. He looked around. Deciding it was safe, he picked up the bag and ladder and made a dash for the building several hundred feet away. He reached his destination in less than a minute. He crouched against the white structure behind some shrubs. He tried to slow his breathing.

Chapter 6

Medical tubes were nearby, ready for them to use as they focused on Gene's jugular vein and carotid artery. The tubes would eventually be clamped on both ends of each vessel, enabling the circulatory pump to partially bypass the heart.

Using two clamps, they quickly stemmed the flow of blood in the jugular. Doctor Adams expertly severed the vein between the clamps, trying to minimized blood loss. Within a minute he had inserted the circulatory shunt tubes into both ends of the vessel, bringing it in-line with the heart pump. There was now a pool of blood surrounding the area. That wasn't a surprise. It couldn't be helped. They did their best to control the bleeding now more than ever.

Both operating theatres were becoming warmer as the air conditioning unit struggled. The hot lights they were working under didn't help matters. Doctors Adams and Klein were sweating profusely. They all were. The nurses tried wiping their brows under their face masks as much as possible. The doctors wanted to take a breather, to relax for a minute, especially after shunting the jugular vein but there was no time. They needed to press on.

The next step was the carotid artery, one of the largest in the body. There was no way around blood loss with that one. As soon as a small incision was made blood began squirting several feet into the air. Doctor Adams quickly continued, trying to stem the flow. He finally secured a shunt tube between both ends of the severed artery, similar to what he had done with the jugular. It, too, was now in-line with the circulatory pump.

One of the nurses, Sally, was kept busy sponging up the excess blood. It was quickly becoming a gory scene. There was now an array of clamps and tubes around the base of the neck. Charlene was helping with suction. Two other nurses were preparing more gauze and sponges. The anesthesiologist was closely monitoring blood loss. They were replenishing the transfusion bags at a faster pace.

Patient A's blood pressure dropped to a dangerous level. They had done everything they could to prevent that from happening. They had to wait and see, hoping the pressure would soon increase. While waiting, they reviewed the plan for the final portion of the first stage in the operation, the severing of the spinal cord.

Team Two performed the identical procedure in the next room but was now experiencing trouble with its patient. The bleeding was worse. The surgeons were having difficulty controlling it. Doctor Schultz suspected they hadn't given the donor's body enough time to eliminate some of the medication that had been administered to him while he was in the hospital—drugs that had made William's blood thinner. They had no choice but to press on.

Several minutes went by. Gene's blood pressure slowly began to climb to a healthier level. For the moment everyone felt relieved. So far so good.

Doctors Adams and Klein knew they were at a critical stage in the operation. They could see for themselves, by looking in the opened wound, where the spinal damage actually was in the neck area. The cord needed to be severed just above the injury. Doctor Adams had to be very careful in removing the surrounding bone.

They needed to cut the cord slightly longer than necessary to prevent it from retracting too far up the neck. There was tension, not only with the cord, but also with the team. Doctor Adams began to drill, saw and grind at the bone, being very careful not to damage the spinal cord. He was totally focused on his work.

Doctor Schultz was doing the same in the other room. They conversed via intercom. Each team kept the other posted at all times, the anesthesiologists carefully monitoring the operations. Doctor Morin could hear the high-pitched sound of the drill Doctor Adams was using. Doctor Schultz exclaimed to Doctor Adams that the bleeding was increasing. They were having trouble.

Doctor Klein knew it was only a matter of time. If they could keep on schedule, things would work out. They pressed on.

Chapter 7

Perry moved out from behind some shrubs next to the building, carrying the duffle bag and ladder. He quickly made his way to the three darkened windows and checked each one very closely. He settled on the middle one. The bottom of the metal grill that covered it was at eye level. He looked at the corner hex bolt that secured it to the cement wall. There were a total of six. Two were on the bottom, two on the top and one on either side of the three foot by two foot metal framework. The bolts appeared rusted and had indeed been painted over several times throughout the years.

He crouched against the building for several minutes, listening intently for any noise behind the window. All was silent. He decided to get to work, putting on his gloves and spraying the two bottom bolts with a concentration of paint remover and penetrating oil. Waiting for the mix to work, he unfolded the six foot collapsible ladder and placed it up against the building next to the grill. He climbed up several steps so he could spray each of the remaining bolts.

Once done, he quickly climbed down and got out the socket set. After finding the right socket and coaxing it over the painted bolt head, he tried to loosen the bottom corner one first. It wouldn't budge. He tried the one above it. Again, it didn't move. He picked up the ladder and duffle bag and headed back into the bush next to the building. He needed to give the oil and paint stripper more time to do their jobs.

He waited ten more minutes and then tried again. This time he would put every ounce of muscle into it. He put the ladder back up and got into position with the socket wrench once more. He heaved with all his might. For a moment it wouldn't budge, but then there was a snapping sound. The bolt broke. The force he'd exerted made him flip off the ladder. Fortunately, he was only two feet off the ground. He quickly got up and looked around. The coast was still clear.

He climbed up once more and looked at what he had done. The head of the hex bolt had indeed broken off the shank. That was good, very good. The next bolt started to back out with a squeak. He stopped what he was doing, listening for any sign of someone nearby. He heard a low moaning. He cocked his ear against the window and heard it again.

It sounds like a pig moaning, two pigs moaning on the other side of the wall. Good! He was excited. He knew he was on the right track. That weirdo woman knew what she was talking about after all.

He continued to turn the bolt. This time there was no squeaking. It came out easily enough. He knew he would need to remove all the bolts. The grill was far too strong to bend. He tried removing the third bolt but again it screeched in protest. He stopped and listened. The pigs were still moaning, this time a little louder. He sprayed the bolts with penetrating oil once more.

Chapter 8

Emil entered the utility room and quickly closed the door behind him. He could hear the condenser fan struggling in the crawl space. He went over to the main electrical panel and checked the breaker. It was hot to the touch. Part of the air conditioning circuit appeared to have shut down. Manuel had told him that the first thing to do was to flick off the 220 volt breaker and then snap it back on. When over-heated, it would switch itself into the 'off' position.

Justin was in the security room monitoring the closed-circuit TV screens. He was getting hungry. He had eaten a salad at his mom's house over three hours ago and had forgotten to bring his lunch. He peeked in Emil's lunch box, quickly taking out a burrito.

Both teams were busy in each of their separate operating rooms. Everything was barely under control. Doctors Schultz and Morin, along with their team, were experiencing heavy bleeding from the donor, William DeGroot. They were still adjusting and adding clamps, desperately trying to control the problem.

The anesthesiologist in room One was closely monitoring Gene's blood pressure. It appeared to be improving. Doctor Adams cleaned the neck area of any remaining muscle and tendon, completely exposing the vertebrae. He used a small drill to cut into a tiny portion of a vertebra. He slowly and expertly moved the drill, applying pressure to the delicate area. The high-pitched whine overpowered the other sounds in the room. There was a noticeable smell of heated bone. He worked for several minutes until finally it came loose.

Now, only the spinal cord connected the body to the neck. Doctor Adams looked at Doctor Klein. He paused for only a second, giving him a look that said, "Here we go!" He quickly placed a clamp on the lower part of the cord slightly above the damaged area. There was just enough room below the clamp enabling the cord to be snipped at an approximate 45-degree angle. This would ensure a more successful graft and the clamp would provide a few extra millimeters of cord they could work with when they later began to do the reverse, splice the cord on the donor.

The artificial respirator and heart pump were working smoothly for both the body and head. It had been decided beforehand that they would try to keep Gene's body alive as long as possible, just in case. After all, the operation was highly experimental.

Doctor Klein conferred with Doctor Shultz and his team. "Are you ready to remove dee head completely?" There was a pause and then a muffled voice came from the anesthesiologist over the intercom.

"Yes, Doctor Klein, we are ready but I'm concerned with the bleeding."

"Vee must act quickly now, Doctor! Dair is no time for delay. Can we continue, yah?"

There was a pause before permission was granted. Team B severed William's spinal cord. Both heads were now completely separated from the bodies. All four body parts were being kept artificially alive.

Chapter 9

Perry climbed back up the ladder, trying to loosen the two remaining bolts. As he worked, there was a screech from the protesting bolt followed by more moaning from the pigs inside. He had no other option. He kept turning the squeaky bolt until it came loose. The penetrating oil mix had done all it was going to do in lubricating and breaking up the rust. He quickly moved to the last bolt and, again, it squeaked before finally coming free.

The pigs were becoming perturbed. Perry decided not to wait for them to calm down. He needed to act fast, knowing someone would soon be alerted to their moaning. He quickly pried the grill off the window. He fumbled around in his pocket and found the glasscutter. He took the suction cup out of the duffle bag and stuck it on the corner pane closest to him. He easily cut out the glass, gently pulling it toward him.

He reached in and ran his hand around the inside perimeter of the window, feeling an alarm sensor just as he had suspected. It would only be activated if there were any attempt in opening the window frame. He cut out the other pane next to the first one. Once done, he cut the thin wood sash separating the two, giving himself more than enough room to slip through.

A heavy black curtain hung on the inside of the window, blocking any view. He paused before sliding through the window, listening carefully. All he could hear was the moaning of those damned pigs. He wished they would shut up. It was giving him the creeps. There was something about the sound that wasn't quite right.

He waited for several moments, still wondering if anyone was in the room. Satisfied that the pigs were alone, he squeezed through the opening. The pigs heard him and became even more agitated. He couldn't stop now. He had to take a chance, hoping no one would come to investigate. He slid inside, his eyes trying to adjust to the dark.

He pulled the curtain back, hoping to bring more light into the room. That didn't help much; the moon was still behind clouds. He slowly felt his way along the wall, moving towards the sound of the pigs. He stumbled onto his knees into straw and what smelled like pig manure. The pigs were moaning louder, clearly upset with his presence, the sound becoming almost painful.

He still couldn't see so decided to use his flashlight, a heavy-duty model designed for experienced campers and hikers. His eyes finally made out both of them. He aimed his light down onto the one closest to him as he stood up, the moaning now loud squeals.

He looked down and noticed the trembling legs of both pigs. The poor animals; it looked as if they were trying to run but couldn't get up. He didn't want to disturb them any more than he already had but he still needed to take pictures. He stood up, moving in closer, trying to get a better look, the flashlight now focused on their heads.

His mouth dropped open. "What the fuck? It looks like a scar that goes all around the neck!" He took a closer look. One pig was staring back at him, its eyes rolling back in its head, saliva dripping out of its mouth. Perry was stunned ... not believing what he was seeing.

It looks like they have transplanted heads for God's sake! Yes, the skin color of the body doesn't quite match that of the head.

He felt sick, dropping to his knees again. He yelled to no one in particular, looking up at the ceiling. "For God's sake! Why did they have to go and do *that*? Those sick, miserable, bastards!"

He heard a noise from outside the door, quickly becoming aware of what had to be done. He needed to take as many pictures as possible before leaving. He put the flashlight down and grabbed for his camera, turning on the flash mode. He began taking pictures, one after the other.

Mr. Lincoln wheeled himself into the room. He had heard Harley and Farley screaming from down the hall. He saw a crazed man in battle fatigues taking pictures, flash after flash, of his babies, screaming about how those sick sons of bitches were going to pay for this.

He yelled at the mad man to stop while fumbling for his gun. "Stop it. Stop it! You're alarming my babies with those damned flashes. What are you doing? Leave my babies alone! They're terrified. Stop it. Stop it. Stop it!"

Perry looked over to where the voice was coming from. He couldn't quite make out Mr. Lincoln because the flash from the camera had momentarily blinded him. He quickly got up off his knees, half-yelling, half-stumbling in straw. He grabbed the flashlight while lunging toward the voice, screaming how they'd all pay for this terrible sin.

"You fucking ... Frankenstein!" He didn't know what else to say, how to describe what he had just seen. He threw the flashlight as hard as he could toward where he thought the voice was coming from.

Mr. Lincoln had his gun out, his hand shaking, as he tried to aim it at the intruder, hoping to shoot him in a spot that wasn't life-threatening. The spinning light from the flashlight momentarily distracted him. In an instant the flashlight hit him on the temple making his hand jerk upward as he squeezed off a shot.

For the third time in five minutes Perry dropped to his knees. This would be the last as he fell over on his side. The bullet from the small .22 caliber pistol entered his head slightly above the left eye. The bullet fragments scattered just behind the skull, some entering the brain. Perry's left eye popped out of its cavity as a result of the head wound, leaving it partially hanging by a string of optic nerve. Farley and Harley were lying on their sides, moaning crazily, their legs twitching. Perry was moaning as well, his legs were also twitching.

Mr. Lincoln momentarily blacked out. The flashlight had hit him squarely on the temple. His head drooped forward, his eyes out of focus. He slowly regained his senses, noticing blood dripping onto his lap from his head wound. The flashlight had produced a large gash on his head. For a moment he didn't quite know who or where he was. The smell of gunpowder coupled with the excitement made him cough. He slowly lifted his head, his ears now ringing from both the shot and the impact from the flashlight that was now on the floor. The light beam angled crazily up toward the ceiling. Through it he could see a cloud of blue smoke. Still not sure of where he was, he had a fleeting thought that he was having a near-death experience, expecting to see angels at any moment. He blinked, beginning to understand what had happened, knowing he could easily black out. He needed to get some control.

He took a deep breath and slowly managed a drink of water. The coughing stopped momentarily. He tried not to get dizzy. He focused on the pigs. He looked over at his two babies and for the first time noticed the crazed man lying between them. That didn't matter to him. What mattered to him were his babies. He was very much concerned with them, trying to talk soothingly despite feeling weak.

He groaned, "There, there, my pretty ones. Everything is going to be all right. Daddy has taken care of business. He'll protect you. Shhh, it's okay now. No one will harm you."

He slowly turned his head toward the broken window. He could see the curtain blow slightly inwards and was concerned that someone else might be out there, ready to break in. He focused on trying to stay conscious, clutching his gun, deciding he'd shoot anyone who attempted to enter from that direction. His mind was not far from the death threat that had been made earlier to Doctor Klein. He momentarily wondered if the security guards had heard anything. He hoped they hadn't.

Harley and Farley were slowly calming down. Perry no longer groaned although his feet still twitched. Mr. Lincoln's vision was blurred and his head ached. He knew it was only a matter of time before he passed out. He needed help and he needed it now. The wall phone seemed miles away. He asked himself, could he make his way to it—and call for help?

Chapter 10

Emil was in the crawlspace next to the condenser fan. He could hardly hear himself think—the fan was making a loud racket. He took out his flashlight and tried to find the sub-panel, going to step 'two' in resetting the circuit.

He sees lights, clouds and old men beckoning him onwards, upwards towards … heaven? He feels at peace. He's having an out-of-body experience. He can see the operation from the upper corner of the room. It's a grotesque scene. He sees Doctor Adams cutting and drilling into his neck. He can see Doctor Klein standing behind his head, holding it with both hands as Doctor Adams continues. He watches Doctor Klein gently and carefully remove his head from his body. He sees his body lying like a lump on the operating table, tubes and clamps sticking out from many different places. What was once professionalism is now panic. Chaos has entered the room.

He leaves, floating into a serene and indescribable space. He knows all the answers to all the questions. He feels God but cannot touch him. He has no worries for he has put himself into the hands of Him. And yet … it appears God does not want him. He is stuck between the living and the dead.

He drifts farther and farther away, thinking he will never come back. He can hear Klein shouting. He can hear people moving about in panic. He senses Klein looking at him, at his face. He wants to open his eyes and stare back, letting him know that he feels lost. He wants to let Klein know he is missing part of what, his soul? *Yes, that's it.* He is missing part of his soul. He cannot go anywhere without it. He pleads, "Please put me back together. I don't care if I ever walk again. I need my wholeness, my completeness, my soul!" He senses he is spiritually in two.

He's again diving into the lake. He knows he can break his neck if he's not careful. As he falls toward the water with his arms stretched out in front of him, he is in slow-motion, seeing the rocks more clearly now. *Yes, there had been a drought and, yes, the lake is low.* He hits his neck on a rock and blacks out.

He asks himself, "Has it been days, weeks, perhaps months or has it been merely hours?" He doesn't know. Time moves quickly and time stands still. He's in a world of contradictions. *Am I drifting in and out of consciousness or is it one dream after another? Perhaps that's all it is, simply dreams.*

He's been given a lot of drugs. He's not sure where he is. He can't open his eyes. He feels nothing. He has no body. He dreams of water and drowning. He's confused. He feels different. He feels torn. He is not at peace. He is terribly angry. He is being nagged like his fucking mother had nagged dad all his life.

He's tired and only wants to die. Perhaps he is already dead. If he *is* dead, shouldn't he be at peace?

A long forgotten prayer enters his mind. *If I should die before I wake, I pray the Lord, my soul to take.*

Chapter 11

Doctors Klein and Adams were both very stressed. The severing of the head was a major task to say the least. Making sure all blood vessels, nerves and muscles were cut at proper lengths and angles was very difficult to do—all the while trying to ensure that the patient remained stable.

They had come to a major point in the operation. The head was completely severed from the body. A ten inch gap now separated the two body parts. Numerous clamps and hoses were attached to both. There were several bloody sponges and towels on the operating table and floor.

The same was true in the second operating room. They, too, had sponges and gauzes filled with blood that was on the floor and table. The nurses assisting Doctors Morin and Schultz were kept busy helping with the bleeding. The anesthesiologist was busy as well—monitoring the various data on the screens. Both surgeons looked like they had come out of a butcher shop. Their pale green operating gowns were covered with blood, including part of their surgical masks and head covers.

Patient B had developed a serious bleeding problem. They had plenty of units of blood on hand and, so far, were maintaining stability. The head of patient B was also completely severed. It, too, had tubes coming in and going out.

Team A was in a somewhat similar situation. Even though the plan was to attach their patient's head onto the body of patient B, they still wanted to keep Gene's body alive temporarily, hoping they wouldn't need to reattach it if a problem developed with the procedure. They heard a voice over the intercom. It sounded rather weak and shaky.

"Doctor Klein? Joseph? Please. Please help me."

"Mr. Lincoln? Vair are you? Vat is wrong?" Doctor Klein could feel sweat running down his back as he yelled in the direction of the wall phone. He heard Harley and Farley moaning and squealing in the background. Something was seriously wrong.

"Joseph, listen to me." Mr. Lincoln sounded weak.

"Yah? Vot?"

"I'm calling from the McDonald Room."

Doctor Adams yelled from the background, "What in hell is going on?"

Doctors Morin and Schultz both looked up through the dividing window. They could hear the commotion in the next room.

Doctor Klein pictured Mr. Lincoln speaking to the wall phone, facing Farley and Harley. Normally it was used for monitoring. This time it sounded like it was being used for an emergency.

"Something serious has happened. I'll tell you when you get here. Can you come ... now?"

He couldn't believe it. It was Mr. Lincoln and he wanted him to drop everything and go and help him. Whatever for? And he sounded so weak and what ... desperate? He needed to see what was going on but not until it was absolutely safe for him to do so. He couldn't just leave in the middle of an operation, especially one like this!

Doctor Klein looked at his partner with puzzlement. Doctor Adams looked back. Joseph was concerned. The whole team was. They had never heard Mr. Lincoln sound like that before. He was always so in control. Now he sounded shaky. Something was seriously wrong.

Joseph began to speak to the anesthesiologist, wanting to ask if it was okay if he left, only for a few minutes. "Doctor, I tink I vill go and—"

Doctor Adams jumped in. "No, Joseph! I know what you're thinking but come on, man! Don't be ridiculous. You can't just get up and go see what's going on. I need you here!"

"Please!" It was Lincoln over the intercom again. "This is very serious. I need your ... help!"

It was both a command and plea. Lincoln needed him. Doctor Klein didn't know what to say. He blurted out, "Vee are close to ending dee first part of dee surgery. I vill come as soon as I can, yah?" There was no response. "Mr. Lincoln! Can you hear me?"

"I .... Come .... I need ...." Mr. Lincoln was incoherent. He glanced over at Perry's twitching body. He wasn't sure he could manage until help arrived.

Doctor Klein was looking at the floor, puzzled, when he heard Doctor Adams call his name.

"Joseph!"

"Yah?"

They looked at each other. Both knew Lincoln was in serious trouble. Nonetheless, the team needed Joseph, at least until the situation became stable. Adams barked, "We need you ... here!

Joseph was stunned, trying to make sense of things. He felt torn. He slowly got back to work, helping as best he could. Several long minutes passed while the team worked hard, finally finishing with the first phase of the surgery. They monitored the many sensors and instruments, satisfied with the results. Everyone felt slightly relieved; so far things were moving smoothly.

Doctor Adams looked at each member of the team with his eyebrows raised, asking the silent question. They all nodded in agreement, knowing what he meant.

"Joseph!"

"Huh! Vot?"

"Go!"

"Vot?"

"I said, go!" Doctor Adams was as curious as he was. "Go and check things out. We can handle this for now. Use the intercom and keep us posted." As he quickly began to leave, Doctor Adams shouted once more. "Doctor!"

"Yah?" Doctor Klein was perplexed, feeling he was losing control.

"Put on one of the lab suits before you leave."

"Yes, yes, of course. Vat vas I tinking? Good. Good!"

The lab suit was airtight—used for research. It would completely cover him from head to toe. Putting it on while leaving the room would keep Doctor Klein relatively sterile although he would need to scrub again before continuing with the surgery. Joseph took off his bloody operating gown and surgical mask, removed his operating slippers and quickly got into the lab suit. Armed with only his security clearance card, he made his way to the McDonald room.

Chapter 12

Justin had his feet up on the security desk, drinking another glass of water. Emil's burrito had gone down smoothly enough. It hadn't seemed too hot at the time. He had eaten it quickly. It was good. Now, after several minutes, he was sweating. It wasn't because of the air conditioning problem either. It was that fucking fireball burrito! His stomach was beginning to churn. He hoped Emil would get back to the security office within the next few minutes. He didn't think he could hold out much longer. He took another gulp of water.

Doctor Adams was agitated. He couldn't blame anyone for the interruption. He was certain there must be a major problem or else Mr. Lincoln would never have bothered to call, especially now. He looked at the monitors once more. Things were still okay. He glanced at Gene's face noticing a twitch above his left eye. He wondered if Gene was having some kind of dream or was this simply a reflex action.

The blood pressure was low but stable. They had gone through several units of blood. Charlene operated the suction while he stood back to stretch. He had been bent over for several hours. Another nurse, Sally, handed him a bottle of water. He took a deep swallow and looked through the window into operating room Two. He could see Doctors Morin and Schultz huddled over their patient. Doctor Adams looked at the video monitor, getting a better view of what they were doing.

The scene was similar to the operating room he was working in. A nurse was using a suction tube to clean up the excess blood while another used gauze and towels to clean the surrounding area. Their anesthesiologist was also closely monitoring the patient's vital signs.

Doctor Adams spoke into the intercom. "Doctors, do you need help?" He knew they had everything under control. He would only get in the way and yet he wanted to let them know he was free for at least a few minutes.

Doctor Morin replied in a worried and frustrated tone. "We are trying to get a handle on this. Please stand by in case we need you."

"Okay, Doctor. I'll be waiting." He looked back at Gene's face. It was serene.

Chapter 13

Doctor Klein half-ran, half-walked in his lab suit toward the McDonald Room. It was only two hundred feet away. He was telling himself, "Dis is bad! Very bad! For Mr. Lincoln to call undt sound dee way he did is disturbing, yah!" He quickly swiped the door lock and entered.

His eyes tried to adjust to the darkness as he peered through his face shield. It had a little condensation on it from his exertions. He heard Farley and Harley moaning and screeching. Something had happened to them. He couldn't imagine why Mr. Lincoln would have called him during the operation. *What has happened? What has gone wrong?* He saw Mr. Lincoln stooped in his wheelchair where he normally parked when visiting his babies.

"Vat is happening? Vhy did you call, yah?" He tried to whisper but couldn't. It didn't seem to matter. The babies were extremely agitated. He yelled instead, still not being able to see clearly.

Mr. Lincoln slowly lifted his head and pointed to the man lying in the straw. Doctor Klein took a moment to adjust to the darkness. He couldn't believe his eyes. "Oh, my God, vat has happened to dis boy?"

He quickly opened the pen, his doctor's instincts taking over. He needed to help this young man who appeared to be unconscious. He noticed a blue haze that hung in the air.

"I had no choice. He was ranting and raving. He was disturbing the babies. He was going to lunge at me. I had to … shoot him." Mr. Lincoln was speaking in a slurred and defensive tone toward Doctor Klein's back as Joseph bent over the victim. He couldn't quite hear all of what Mr. Lincoln had said.

Doctor Klein checked the pulse then realized that this was not a young boy after all but, instead, a young man. He looked at the head wound, shaking his own head, wondering how this could have happened. He was half-listening to Mr. Lincoln and his explanations while he studied the victim. "He is still alive! Vee must get him into dee operating room as soon as possible."

"Yes, we've got to get him out of here, Joseph." He took a gulp of air and continued. "And we've got to remove any evidence that he was ever here. Do you hear me? If anyone ever finds out about this—" He began coughing.

Doctor Klein slowly nodded his understanding. He, of all people, knew the predicament they were in. If the police or security guards investigated then the whole operation could possibly be found out. He began to panic, thinking things were getting out of control. One minute he was assisting in an operation that would make history and the next minute, well, he was involved in a possible homicide. He knew they needed to act fast. He looked in the direction of the window and saw the curtains move in the breeze as he asked Mr. Lincoln again what had happened. He still wasn't clear.

"I heard Harley and Farley moaning and screaming. I have never heard them so agitated. I quickly came in and saw him." He was trying to point at Perry, seeing him twitch in the straw, but he couldn't raise his arm. He was too weak. He mumbled, "This crazed son-of-a-bitch was in the pen, taking picture after picture with a ... flash camera." His voice was shaking. "I told him. I told him to stop. I had my hand on my gun ..." His voice trailed off.

"Your gun? Vat gun?" Joseph didn't quite believe his ears as he turned toward Mr. Lincoln for the first time. "And ... my God! Vat has happened to your head?" He quickly moved toward him, examining the head wound, wondering how bad it was.

Lincoln ignored Klein's second question about his head. "I've been carrying the gun since the death threat. I didn't want to tell anyone for fear it would only frighten people." He spoke defensively while Doctor Klein tended to his wound.

"You have been carrying a loaded firearm widt you all dis time?" He spoke slowly and emphatically. He was astonished. He hated violence and weapons. To have this man, whom he looked up to, carry a loaded weapon around with him was ... unthinkable! Doctor Klein's emotions were high.

"Listen to me, Joseph." His voice was now firm. "I carried the weapon purely for defense. Remember, *we* didn't initiate this violence that's been going on here in Irvine. We needed to take precautions. You have to agree."

Doctor Klein turned his head toward the twitching man lying in the hay as he listened to Mr. Lincoln. He knew he was right. *Who knows what this man might have done if Mr. Lincoln wasn't here*? *He could have—.* He didn't want to think about it. He opened up a first-aid kit that was mounted on a nearby wall while Mr. Lincoln kept talking.

"Only you and I know about this, Doctor. We might have to tell a few select members of the team later but right now you need to remove any evidence he was ever here." He was now all business, forgetting about his injury for the time being. "We need to put something over the window so it's secure. Then, and *only* then, can we start trying to save his life. Do you hear me?"

Doctor Klein was shaking, staring at nothing while holding a bandage from the first-aid kit.

"Do you hear me?"

Doctor Klein slowly nodded as he placed the bandage on Mr. Lincoln's head. He was speechless.

"Good! Get busy. Check outside and see how he got in. I'll see if I can find something that we can use to cover that window. Go. Go. Go!" As an afterthought he yelled out, "And, keep an eye out for the security guards! We don't want them to know about this."

Doctor Klein quickly closed the first-aid kit, still not able to speak. He made his way over to Perry and found the wrench and bolts that were in his pockets. Perry had his one good eye opened, his legs still twitching. There was a gurgling sound, along with drool, coming out of his mouth.

Doctor Klein checked his pulse. He couldn't help it. He was first a doctor then a … what? He wondered, *"Then an accomplice?"*

He left the room, completely stunned. He saw the overhead exit sign and ran toward it. He pushed the lock bar on the outside door, trying to open it. In his haste he set off the security alarm. He rarely swore but this time he couldn't help himself. "Sheet! Vot have I done!"

The alarm sounded throughout the entire wing at Bosch Research. Mr. Lincoln was still in the McDonald Room when he heard it. He shook his damaged head, cursing Joseph. "Sometimes doctors can be so damned stupid! Why did he go and do that for?"

Emil was still in the crawl space trying to reset the last breaker. The condenser fan was making one hell of a noise.

Meanwhile, Justin was becoming desperate. "Aw man. Where is that stupid old fuck? I can't wait any longer!" He took his legs off the table and stood up, feeling one cramp after another hit his stomach. He had to move—and move quickly. He shuffled out of the security room, making his way as fast as he dared to the men's room down the hall. He wasn't sure if he was going to make it. He opened up the restroom door just as the alarm started to blare. All he could think of was getting into a stall as quickly as possible.

The alarm made Farley and Harley moan and screech even louder. Harley had his mouth open only a few inches from Perry's hand, trying desperately to get at the human.

The team in each operating room could also hear the alarm. Everyone was concerned and wondered what had happened, why it went off. Doctor Adams had been checking the monitors when the alarm sounded. He noticed a quick spike on the screen. He was surprised and pleased. Gene had also, no doubt, heard the sound.

The situation in the operating room seemed to have stabilized despite the alarm. Doctor Adams was very much disturbed, wondering what was going on with Mr. Lincoln. He left the room after explaining to the anesthesiologist where he was going. The anesthesiologist had a questioning look on his face. Doctor Adams told him he would only be gone a minute or two and to call him on his cell phone if anything developed. He also told Doctors Shultz and Morin he was heading out to investigate, to see why the alarm was activated, and would be back as soon as possible. They hardly heard him. They were preoccupied with stabilizing William.

Doctor Klein propped the exit door open and quickly made his way outside along the building toward the window. He noticed the ladder and window grill against the outside wall. He spent a few minutes fumbling, trying to re-attach it. He was not a mechanic. The situation was exacerbated by the sterile lab suit, gloves and face shield.

Mr. Lincoln was also busy trying to find something that would do the job of covering the vacant panes. The alarm was deafening. He hoped someone in the operating room would go to the control panel and reset it. He felt faint and his head ached.

And, where are those security guards? He wished they were here and yet he was glad they hadn't made any surprise appearances. He cursed again, thinking about doctors and how they could sometimes be so stupid. They had no mechanical or electrical sense.

Doctor Klein was in the middle of trying to secure the grill back over the window when he heard the police sirens. "Oh, my God." he whispered, "Dair coming to get me!" He tried to calm himself and become rational. He was terrified. The adrenaline had kicked in and sweat ran down his face. He worked faster as he heard the sirens approach, all the while wondering if someone had witnessed the shooting and had called the police. *No, this cannot be happening.*

He felt sick to his stomach. If they caught him, he would be found guilty of assisting with the crime and covering up the evidence. He stopped working, deciding to leave it, to leave everything the way it was, not to touch the ladder and grill, thinking it was already too late. He was sure.

He headed back toward the exit door, terrified. He stopped halfway. *Dey can't find my fingerprints on dee bolts and ladder can dey? I do have dee suit and gloves on.* That was a break in his favor. He decided to at least take the ladder and duffel bag into the building with him. He got busy again. "Yes," he whispered, "take it in and hide it." He asked himself, "Do you have time? Yes, yes. Do it! Do it quickly!"

The sirens stopped as police cars pulled up around the corner in front of the main entrance to Bosch. Joseph could see the reflection of their lights blinking off the trees near the front doors. It was time to get inside.

Chapter 14

There were two police cars with flashing lights at the entrance to Bosch Research. Mr. Lincoln made his way to the front doors, trying to remain calm. Doctor Adams appeared in the hallway in his lab suit as Mr. Lincoln wheeled by. Mr. Lincoln tried yelling to him over the deafening sound of the alarm system but ended up waving instead, indicating to Doctor Adams to get back in the operating room. He'd handle the police. Doctor Adams wondered what had happened. He noticed blood on the side of Lincoln's head as well as the bandage.

There were three officers standing outside the glass doors, waiting to be let in. Mr. Lincoln couldn't help but think they knew about the shooting. He suspected someone else was with that man when he was shot. He must have been the one that had called the police. And where were those damned security guys? He decided to let the police do the talking as he unlocked the front doors.

"Is everything okay?" One of them had a flashlight in hand as he shouted. All three quickly entered the building, the alarm still blaring.

"Yes, of course," he yelled back. "Why did you come?"

"We were called." Two of the officers began to make their way down the hallway, deeper into Bosch, while the third looked at Mr. Lincoln suspiciously.

Mr. Lincoln felt sick. His nerves were stretched to the limit. He needed to explain that he had shot the intruder in self-defense. He didn't know what the intruder's intentions were, especially with the death threat to Doctor Klein. And, how were Farley and Harley to be explained?

"Look, officer, I didn't know what was going on, okay? It just happened! I was in this room when—"

He heard a voice interrupting him from behind. It was Joseph Klein yelling, running down the hallway toward them, fiercely waving his arms, his face shield still on.

"Vee are sorry officers but it vos me, Mr. Lincoln! I am dee one to blame."

Mr. Lincoln looked at him incredulously, wondering what Joseph was thinking. *Don't take the blame for me, Joseph. Besides, my fingerprints are all over the gun.*

All three officers looked at Doctor Klein questioningly as he continued to shout through his face shield.

"Yah, it was me dat accidentally opened dee rear door, setting off dee alarm."

"Is everything okay now?" The officers were very curious. They wondered why this man, dressed the way he was, opened an outside door late at night, setting off the alarm. They also wondered about the other man, the one in the wheelchair. He had, what appeared to be, a fairly recent head wound.

Emil had finally made his way back into the utility room and heard the alarm for the first time. He pressed the appropriate buttons to disable it.

"Yah, vee—" The alarm turned off, enabling them to speak easier.

"Vee are sorry dat you were called, yah? Vee had forgotten dat dee alarm automatically alerts dee police vhen it is activated." He had slowly realized what had happened as he was hiding the evidence. At least he hoped that was why the police were there, being called automatically by the alarm rather than by a witness to the shooting.

Mr. Lincoln tried to let out a sigh of relief without being detected, mentally taking back all he had said about the doctor being stupid. The police were looking at both of them with curiosity, especially Mr. Lincoln, again wondering how he had gotten the head wound.

"Well, do you mind if we look around while we're here?" Before they had a chance to answer, one officer began walking down the hallway, ready to investigate further.

Lincoln spoke quickly. "Actually, we do, Officer. We are busy here tonight doing more research and, in this line of business, well, we need to be careful of contaminants. Let me assure you that everything is fine and I want to thank all three of you for coming out so quickly." He made an attempt to chuckle as he spoke.

Doctor Klein said, "I'm sorry, gentlemen. I have to get back to dee lab. Tank you vonce again for comink so quickly."

The officer in charge questioned what was really going on. He thought both guys looked like they were caught with their hands in the cookie jar. Still, there was nothing they could do. No crime had been committed.

"Okay, just make sure you lock up and reset the alarm. Have a good evening." They turned and walked out the doors, one of them shaking his head, still not convinced.

A minute later Justin shuffled out of the men's room, looking as pale as a ghost.

Mr. Lincoln tried to convince both Emil and Justin that it must have indeed been a faulty alarm circuit. Emil finally agreed thinking that perhaps the condenser fan had overloaded the electrical panel causing the alarm to go off on its own. Justin didn't really care. He was still trying to recover from stomach cramps.

Emil asked Doctor Klein about Mr. Lincoln. What had happened? It appeared he had been hit on the head. Joseph fumbled with an explanation, claiming it was a minor accident. Mr. Lincoln had somehow fallen out of his wheelchair.

Chapter 15

It seemed like an eternity but Doctor Klein finally made it back into the operating room. He quickly took off the lab suit and scrubbed before joining Doctor Adams and the other members.

"Joseph! What's going on?"

"Vee had problems but everyting is now under control." He saw the nurses nearby as he spoke so needed to be careful with what he said. He tried to instill calm in the room.

"It vos a faulty circuit widt dee burglar alarm, yah!" He tried to smile as if nothing were wrong. He turned to Doctor Adams, giving him a look that said, "We'll talk about this later." He continued, "How are vee doink, here?"

"There might be some serious problems with William. We are having trouble controlling the blood loss. So far, the patient's blood pressure is stable. When you're ready … we'll move the organ to the donor."

He called the head an 'organ.' This made him feel a little better. Doctor Adams tried to convince himself and others that this was only an organ transplant. The nurses, as well as the rest of the team members, had discussed this situation many times previously, agreeing that the use of proper terminology would de-sensitize the nature of the operations.

Doctors Adams and Klein carefully prepared the head and associated life support equipment, getting ready to move into operating room Two where it would be matched with the donor. The concern was to move the head and attach it as quickly as possible.

Doctor Schultz and his team in room Two went through the final stages of the operation, essentially a mop up. They had controlled most of the bleeding from William's headless body but there were still issues. In such a procedure, any stoppage in bleeding was only temporary. They tried various techniques in trying to arrest it. It seemed to work … for a few minutes.

Doctors Adams and Klein were in the process of delivering Gene's head into operating room Two while Doctors Morin and Shultz were taking a bit of a breather. Things seemed to be under control.

Doctor Morin looked down at what used to be William DeGroot and thought it was indeed a scene from 'Frankenstein.' There was no longer a head or neck, simply limbs—limbs with a torso that appeared to be breathing on its own. The respirator blew air down the lower esophagus, making the chest rise and fall. There was a wet, floppy sound to it.

The surgeons in Team B thought they had the bleeding under control. It was slowing. Things looked good. They began to relax. Doctor Morin was at the foot of the table with Doctor Shultz standing beside him. Their anesthesiologist was at a nearby table closely studying the vital signs.

The implications of what was being done hit both doctors once more. Doctor Morin was not sure whether he should smile or cry. He felt as though he had sinned. Over and over, in his mind, he tried to justify the end result, telling himself, "This is for the good of all humanity." It wasn't convincing, at least not for him. Even though he had a strong desire for this to work, something deeper told him it was wrong. Perhaps that was why he hesitated when the body lurched upright.

It wasn't a big lurch, really, only the nervous system reacting, perhaps similar to a chicken that had just been decapitated. Both Doctors Schultz and Morin jumped back, startled. Maybe this was a sign from God after all—telling them to stop with this nonsense.

The legs twitched and kicked, causing some of the clamps on the respiratory tube to come loose. The bleeding began again. Everyone had been taken by surprise. All were having trouble reacting. They did not expect this to happen. Someone screamed.

Doctor Morin came out of his trance and grabbed the legs while Doctor Schultz tried to do damage control with the loose clamps. The anesthesiologist produced a strap, wrapping it over the lower legs and under the operating table, tying them down securely. Doctor Morin placed another clamp on one of the locations that caused them trouble. Doctor Schultz tried to re-adjust the respiratory tube. He was clearly shaken. He barked at the nurses, telling them to strap the rest of the body down immediately so this would not occur again. The bleeding continued.

Doctor Klein appeared somewhat distressed as they delivered Gene's head into operating room Two. The rest of Gene's body was still on the operating table in room One, artificially being kept alive with hoses and clamps.

He couldn't keep his eyes off the head, now being wheeled on a hospital gurney along with associated medical equipment and tubes. He wondered if he was playing God, not sure if this was right. He had pondered the ethics of this very situation for many years and was still tormented. Yet, the scientist in him thought differently. He wished that he could have been given a second chance at life, just like Gene was now getting.

He snapped back to reality by the tone of Doctor Morin's voice as they entered room Two. Doctor Morin was usually a very calm individual but not today. There was panic in his voice. "We're having a serious problem. We need more help. Please, hurry!"

They left Gene's head on the gurney just inside the doors to room Two as they rushed to Doctors Morin and Schultz's aid. They tried everything. It wasn't right. William's head was still alive only because they wanted to do tests on it. It had no other value. What had value was now essentially failing. What had happened?

Dr. Schultz told them about the bleeding and the lurching. Doctor Adams made a mental note. As soon as they had the situation under control they, too, would strap Gene's body down.

They worked furiously to stabilize William's body. The defibrillator paddles were standing by in case the heart failed. It seemed that things were changing for the better. William was slowly improving. They were getting the situation under control once more.

After several more minutes of closely monitoring the patient, Doctors Klein and Adams turned their attention back to Gene's head on the hospital gurney just inside the operating room. Gene's face looked slightly tormented, his eyelids twitching. There was a funny kind of expression on the face. Klein tried to read it—wondering what Gene was thinking. *Never mind Gene's expressions for now. Get back to reality.* He was still shaken by the incident with William.

What to do! It's a dilemma! He looked at the clock. It was already past midnight. Somehow he had to get through this. *First the police and now the lurching. Oh my God! And then, what about that young man that was shot. He needs to be stabilized. He needs medical attention.*

Doctor Adams began to speak. "We need to quickly strap—"

Mr. Lincoln's voice blared over the intercom. He had no idea what the circumstances were in the operating room and interrupted what Doctor Adams was trying to say. "Doctor Klein, would you please report to me as soon as possible. There are some things that need to be addressed."

Doctor Klein turned and faced the wall phone, his back to Doctor Adams and Gene. He knew that the young man who had been shot desperately needed a doctor. As he began to reply, he heard a scream from room One where Gene's body was being monitored. There was utter chaos. All hell broke loose.

Chapter 16

Gene's headless body had also jerked itself into a sitting position. The clamps that fastened the tube onto the carotid artery became partially dislodged resulting in a steady stream of blood that was now crazily shooting toward the ceiling. Another side stream squirted directly onto the operating mask of Sally, the nurse who had screamed. She raised her hands, trying to shield herself from the spray. The body twitched, the streams of blood squirting wildly around the room. The in-line heart pump kept doing its job, mechanically pushing blood out of the detached tubes in a rhythmical fashion. Everyone was stunned.

Doctors Adams and Klein scrambled back. The anesthesiologist yelled, hoping to be heard over the nurse's screams. He needed help in pushing the body down onto the operating table. They each grabbed an arm, trying to bend the body into a prostrate position. It refused. As they forced the upper torso down, the legs came up. It was all too much for Sally. She was becoming faint, desperately clutching to the side of the operating table, trying to regain some stability. No one could blame her. The whole scene was both bizarre and gory.

The sound from the heart monitor became sporadic. The beeps were no longer rhythmical. The breathing tube that had been inserted into the windpipe was now loose. The whooshing sound, coupled with a gurgling noise, steadily grew louder. The team had trouble in getting control of the situation.

Doctor Adams shouted. He needed help. He needed clamps. He needed the breathing and blood tubes re-inserted. He needed the body strapped down so there would be no more involuntary muscle spasms.

Team A was scrambling, trying to regain control. Doctor Klein helped in reinserting the breathing tubes. Sally produced several more clamps. Doctor Adams tried to stem the bleeding. Two other nurses were busy attempting to strap the body down.

They worked hard to stabilize the situation. It was all too much for their young patient. Gene's heart suddenly stopped. They tried in desperation to keep his body alive. They placed the defibrillation paddles on the chest and charged them again and again, hoping the heart would start. They worked feverishly, the minutes slipping by, the heart still not beating. No one said a word. All were focused on trying to save the young man's body. Doctor Adams stopped first, realizing there was nothing more to be done. They had lost the battle. He stepped away from the body while Doctor Klein kept working, trying to revive their patient. A few seconds later, Joseph Klein also stopped. He, too, realized the patient's body was, indeed, dead—there was no longer any hope.

Even though Gene's head was still alive, everyone felt a terrible loss with the death of his body.

The doctors looked at each other, not believing the stupid and bizarre series of events that had taken place only minutes ago. It was almost comical. No, it was far from being funny. They had wanted to keep the body alive. If the rejection process started they could have at least attempted to re-attach Gene's body back on his head. Now, that option was lost forever.

Chapter 17

Everyone tried to relax, to take a breather. At least the head was still functioning. In fact, the facial expressions showed a more than normal amount of brain activity. Doctor Klein wondered what was going on inside Gene's mind at that moment. Was he dreaming, and, if he was, what could it possibly be about? What if he were touching the outer reaches of the after-life. Perhaps he was having a near death experience.

He had heard many stories about people who knew they were close to death and had unexplainably drifted to the edge, to the fine line that divided life from death. People reported being beckoned by perhaps an angel, some type of being dressed in a white robe, telling them it was not the right time and to go back to the living. This experience made them feel at peace. More than that, it gave them spirituality, a purpose in life. It changed their whole outlook.

Doctor Klein thought about what he had taken as an expression of torment on Gene's face. He wondered if Gene was indeed at peace or … was the expression only an involuntary muscle spasm.

Doctor Adams was reassuring Sally, telling her everything would still be all right. It was not a sign from God. If God indeed wanted them to stop they would never have discovered the various medications and procedures needed in order to make this possible. God was with them. In fact, he wanted to help them.

She calmed down, whispering she could not go back into the operating room. She felt disgusted and sick. He told her not to worry. They had more than enough help. He suggested she perhaps go and take a long shower. He could see blood in her hair. It was beginning to clot.

Doctor Klein suddenly remembered the intercom call from Mr. Lincoln as Doctor Adams came out of the recovery room. "Doctor, vee need to leave for a few minutes, yah?"

Doctor Adams looked at him, getting the message. "Yes, I understand. Let me see if we can get one of the doctors next door to monitor our patient."

"Yah, you go ahead. I vill put on dee lab suit again and meet you in dee hallway."

Chapter 18

He feels himself dying. He senses the life in his body leaving him. He tries desperately to grab it back. He's partially successful. He still has a portion of it. He knows he has been torn apart. He has been split. One part is dying, the other already has. He's drifting upward toward … he's not sure. He has come to a spiritual fork in the road. He stops wandering and waits. He can't decide on which road he should take.

It doesn't matter for he has no choice. It is beyond him. It is far beyond him. He is simply a vessel. No, he is actually two vessels traveling … somewhere. He panics. He knows this is not right. He needs to be complete, to be whole before he travels any farther. He feels he has put one foot into the sea of death. He wants to fall in but cannot. Death won't accept him. He is being forced back to life. He doesn't want to live. All he wants is to be whole and complete. He wishes he could die as one.

Doctor Klein was in the hallway just outside the operating room. He noticed more condensation on his face mask. He knew it was because of his heavy breathing. He told himself to calm down. He paced back and forth. He tried to think of what they could do to cover up the shooting.

And then, there is the loss of Gene's body, and now—. His mind went blank. He was on overload. Five minutes later Doctor Adams came out with his suit on, wanting to know what was going on.

"Okay, tell me!" He had to raise his voice a little so Joseph could hear him. He was also shaken by the death of Gene's body.

"Der vas an intruder dat got in dee McDonald Room. He attacked Mr. Lincoln. He vas taking flash pictures! Farley and Harley are deeply disturbed. Mr. Lincoln shot him."

"He shot him?" Doctor Adams' face went white, not believing what he had just heard. He had never been under so much stress. He spoke quickly. "What about the police? Why did they show up? Was it because of the shooting? Are they coming back?"

"No. No. No. Everytink is all right in dat department, yah?" Doctor Klein put up his hands, trying to calm him. "Dee police came as a result of an alarm dat I had inadvertently set off widt an outside door. Everytink is fine, now."

"What about the shooting victim?" Doctor Adams was still unnerved.

"Yah, Mr. Lincoln called again. It seems dat dee victim is getting vorse. Vee need to see how bad dee damage is but my initial inspection told me dat he vos in serious trouble." He added, "It vos a head shot, Doctor." He studied Doctor Adams' reaction as he said the last sentence.

"Joseph?" He grasped Klein's sleeve as he spoke. "What can we do?" He was still in shock with the news—not quite understanding.

"Vee half to try and save dee man's life, if vee can, yah?"

Doctor Adams slowly nodded, trying to compose himself. They turned toward the McDonald Room. As an afterthought, Doctor Adams asked, "Who is this guy?"

"Vee haf no idea! He came in through a vindow in battle fatigues, yah."

Doctor Adams was now deep in thought, thinking about the situation. He was busy re-evaluating their options.

Chapter 19

The doctors were monitoring Gene around the clock. It had been eighteen hours since they had begun the operations. It was now noon the following day. The surgery was finally finished.

Things hadn't gone according to plan. Murphy's Law was strongly involved with the events of yesterday. What could go wrong did indeed go wrong. They had been continually fighting an uphill battle.

Doctor Klein was with Gene on this shift, sitting in the recovery room. Doctor Morin and the others were getting a well deserved rest. Doctors Schultz and Adams were stressed the most. Complications had caused their team to work harder than expected.

Doctor Klein was sitting beside Gene's bed, reflecting on what had happened. It was unbelievable to him. The operation was one thing but to have an intruder come in, especially at that particular time during the operation, well, it was simply ridiculous.

And … what about Mr. Lincoln shooting that young man? That was bad to say the least. He lingered on the last thought, on Mr. Lincoln shooting this person. They still had no idea who he was. All they knew, from Mr. Lincoln's explanations, was a man in battle fatigues broke into the research center and attacked a helpless invalid in a wheelchair. This, after all the death threats that had been going on. And then there was the police arriving. He remembered Mr. Lincoln being in shock, almost telling the officers the truth. Joseph breathed a sigh of relief, thinking, *"What a night!"*

He looked at his patient. Gene had a halo strapped on his head, not unlike the one he had when he originally came into the Irvine General Hospital many weeks before.

They had worked for hours, trying to re-attach hundreds of blood vessels, some of them so tiny it was impossible. They had tried their best in stitching the spinal cord together. The cuts were perfectly matched. Now it was up to the body to do the rest.

The muscles would eventually splice together. The tiny nerve endings that branched out from the spinal cord were another matter. The Spinal Enhancement Serum they had been using on Farley and Harley had proven itself, at least on animals. They would soon find out if it worked on humans.

He looked at Gene's face. It appeared to be serene. He wondered what Gene was dreaming.

Doctor Adams had finished showering, getting ready to dress and head home. He was exhausted. He needed a good eight hours of sleep. He noticed his cell phone for the first time since the operation as he put on his pants. He checked for messages. There were four of them.

He listened to the first one. Administration from Irvine General needed him to come in and sign some papers concerning a recent death at the hospital. The next message was from an old friend, another from his bank and the last one was from Margaret. She was in town.

He didn't want to talk to her, not right now. He was too tired. He found himself thinking of what he should tell her when the time did come. It was coming soon. He would talk to her after he had rested.

He reconsidered. Maybe he should talk to her now. That would buy them some time until they could get things better arranged. He picked up his cell phone and called her number at the motel. She wasn't in. He left a message.

"Hello, Margaret. This is Doctor Adams returning your call. I'm sorry that I didn't get back to you sooner but I've been very busy. Things have … changed since you and I last talked. Please call me back as soon as you can. Thank you."

He stood there, with only his pants on, holding the cell phone, wondering where she was. If she were planning on coming to Irvine General they might all be in serious trouble. *Maybe we can still get out of this in one piece.* He dialed Mr. Lincoln's number next.

Chapter 20

Mr. Lincoln was more than tired, he was exhausted, his head still aching from the attack. He hung up the phone, thinking about what Doctor Adams had said. He wondered how it would play out. They had to be prepared for Margaret and all eventualities.

He called Doctors Klein and Schultz, telling them what they would need to do if Margaret paid an unexpected visit to the hospital. He then called Doctor Morin and, after explaining about Margaret, asked what he had found.

"I'm glad you suggested I check things out." Doctor Morin was excited. "I walked back to the perimeter fence as soon as possible and found the location where he had crawled through. I came back and drove my car to the breached area of the fence. I noticed a Jeep parked along the side of the road not too far away. It was parked on the fence side of the street.

"It seemed suspicious to me. I thought that, if I were going to do a break-and-enter in fatigues, a Jeep would be the perfect vehicle to use. I checked it out and found a large brimmed hat and overcoat in the backseat. It appeared to me that the perpetrator used the hat and coat to cover his clothing and identity so I took down the license number."

"Yes, yes. Go on." Despite himself, Mr. Lincoln could not stop smiling. Doctor Morin sounded like a detective, a 'Harry Bosch,' from one of those Michael Connelly books.

"I called our contact." He paused, waiting for Mr. Lincoln's prompt.

"Yes. Go on."

"He did a vehicle license check. The guy who owns the Jeep is an unemployed construction worker who was once a mercenary. Our contact is trying to dig out more information but, at this time, it appears he lives alone."

"Yes. Good! Did you get the vehicle moved?"

"They're doing so as we speak."

He could hear Mr. Lincoln exhale in relief.

Chapter 21

He's walking down a country road far from home. He can feel his muscles work his legs as he swings his arms, the sun on his face. He looks down and marvels. Each foot is being lifted and moved forward in perfect rhythm. His body is being carried along in a nice easy motion by his legs. He can feel himself smiling, appreciating the simple process of walking. He can walk and not think of what has to be done in order to achieve it. His brain automatically sends the proper messages to his legs, feet, muscles and nerves.

As he looks down, he notices his feet are no longer on the ground. He is beginning to float down the road. He doesn't like it. It's frightening. He has no control. He continues to float higher, still moving his legs in a walking fashion. He's now above the trees. He's afraid the spell will be broken and he'll come crashing down. Instead, he floats higher still. He senses the air cooling as he floats farther away from the country road. He's now thousands of feet above the earth. He's shivering. He can't stop his legs from walking.

He doesn't want his feet to move. He doesn't want his arms to move. He tries to stop them but can't. They seem to belong to a foreign body. His entire body is moving against his will.

He begins to tumble ... slowly at first. He falls forward, head over heals, picking up momentum. As he spins, he sees the earth and then, a moment or two later, he sees the sun. He tries to yell but can't make any sound. His body is creating a whipping effect on his head. The body tries to use centrifugal force to rip his head off. He can feel the skin on his neck stretch from the force of the spin. He can feel his spinal cord stretch, his neck muscles aching. All he can do is close his eyes.

The spinning increases. The tears from his eyes are being pressed against his face. His neck is getting longer. The skin around his neck is too tight. It feels ready to split. The top of his head is about to burst, his brain ready to fly out of his skull. His vertebrae begin to crack and break. He hears each one snap, like a dry twig, while his spinal cord stretches taut.

Then, just when he thinks he'll be torn apart, the spinning slows. He notices his head move slightly closer to his body. He senses the tension in his spine begin to diminish. His skin slackens ever so slightly.

He feels sick to his stomach. He has no control over his bowels. Those aren't his bowels. Those bowels belong to the monster. The body that is attached to his head belongs to the monster. The monster wants to get rid of him, to separate. He, in turn, wants to get rid of the body. They are opposing forces.

Chapter 22

Sheila tried calling Perry one more time. She heard his cell phone ring at the other end of the line and then the call-answer kick in. "Hi. This is Pair. If it's important, you know what to do."

This time she hung up. She had already left two messages. One was last night around eleven, the other this morning at ten. He did say he would get back to her and let her know what he had found out. She decided to drive by his place to see if the Jeep was parked in his yard.

She got into her Ford Explorer and backed out of her driveway, wondering why he hadn't called. She had to admit it was so typical of him. He had done it to her numerous times before, not returning her calls. This time it didn't seem right. She knew they were on to something. Bosch Research had been caught red handed in the switcheroo when they moved Cynthia's friend from Edgehill to Bosch.

What about the animal testing with real live barnyard pigs? If Cynthia were telling the truth, maybe Perry was caught when he went sneaking into the lab. Is that why he hasn't called me?

She drove by his place. His Jeep wasn't there. That still didn't prove anything. *He could have gone out for breakfast or something but why didn't he answer his fucking phone?*

She drove down near Bosch Research to see for herself if his Jeep was parked nearby. She came up empty handed. There was no sign of him.

She returned home, still wondering what was going on. She walked into her kitchen to call the police. Maybe they had a report of something. At least she could find out. Just as she was picking up her house phone, her cell phone rang.

"Oh good, that's him." She got ready to give him hell. She looked down at the call display but didn't recognize the number.

"Hello?"

"Sheila? It's Cynthia."

"Hi!"

"Hi. Did you find anything else out?" Cynthia's voice sounded desperate.

"Uh, no." There was silence on the other end. Sheila thought she had lost the connection. "Hello. Are you still there, Cynthia?"

"Yes." She sounded sad.

"Look, Cynthia, I gotta go. All I can suggest is that you get his grandmother's phone number and call. Maybe you can talk to him, all right? Maybe he'll want you to come and visit him."

"Yeah, it's just that something happened at Bosch last night."

Sheila was immediately interested. "Yes! Go on."

"One of the nurses here at Edgehill told me the cops came by last night. A burglar alarm was set off. I was wondering if maybe Gene ... did something." She faltered, still hoping Gene was nearby, perhaps trying to send some sort of signal to her. She still couldn't accept that he had gotten on a plane bound for Boston. She was also wondering if Sheila had been telling her the truth. Had they really seen him get on the plane?

She suspected, by the tone of Sheila's voice when she had told her the news about the burglar alarm, that something funny was going on. *It's just too much of a coincidence that the dog-gone alarm went off one day after Gene left Edgehill. It had never gone off before.*

"Sheila?"

"Yes?"

"There was something else." She baited Sheila with the last phrase, wondering how quickly she would respond.

Sheila blurted, "Yes! What?"

There it is. Sheila is far too excited. Something is going on. She was sure Sheila had been lying all along. "The nurse at Edgehill also said it was around midnight when the alarm went off."

"Yes?"

"Well, apparently almost everyone that works at Bosch was working there last night ... at midnight."

"At midnight? What the fuck were they doing there at that time of night?"

Cynthia did not like that kind of language. "That's why I called. I know darn well you were lying to me, Sheila. He's there, isn't he?"

There was no answer.

"Isn't he? You lied to me! Your friend got caught sneaking in. *That's* what happened. He went in to check things out because you both suspected something was up when you saw them take Gene back to Bosch."

"Cynthia, get a grip. Listen to me!" She had to think this through. The weirdo was far too smart. She decided to tell her a half-truth.

"Cynthia, I don't know what went on at Bosch last night." That was true. She didn't know what *really* went on.

"Your friend broke in, didn't he?"

"I have no idea. That is the honest-to-God truth. I haven't heard from him since last night. I don't know where he is."

"And ... what about Gene, where is he?"

"I don't know, Cynthia. I really don't know."

There was a pause and then Cynthia blurted out, "I'm so angry with him, Sheila. I'm so angry with him. I trusted him. I gave up a good paying position for him. He used me." She began to cry.

"Cynthia. Pull yourself together, okay? We don't know what's going on so we can't jump to conclusions."

"I know, Sheila. I know, but ... something weird is going on. I know that for a fact."

"What do you mean?" Sheila wondered what else Cynthia knew.

"I called. I got the number of this so-called grandmother in Boston and I called it. Do you know what I got? I got an answering machine. I'm not surprised. I didn't leave a message. I called again two hours later and the same thing! I called again and again and again, over the last twenty hours, Sheila, and nothing. Nothing! Just a message saying 'You've reached this number and we can't come to the phone right now. Please leave a message.'

"You know, I started thinking. If I were them that's how I'd do it, too! Set up a phone number back east with a voice mailbox. Check the mailbox periodically. If you have a message, get your lady friend to reply saying she's grandma and that he's sleeping or he's gone to the hospital for testing or he doesn't want to be disturbed or whatever!"

She kept talking, convincing herself more and more. "I know he's not there. He doesn't have a grandmother. I wanted to see if I could get some more information when I called the number. No, sir! They've got it all covered."

Sheila was listening carefully, taking in the news. "Yes, maybe you're right. Listen, let's stay in touch and if anything comes up we'll call each other, okay?"

That seemed to pacify Cynthia a little. Sheila could tell she was at her wits end.

Chapter 23

"Hey, Frank! What are you laughing at?" Joey was walking by the desk sergeant and noticed him chuckling, shaking his head. He knew Frank Morgan had a good sense of humor so wanted in on the joke. Besides, he was in no hurry. Things at the Irvine Precinct had finally slowed down since the shooting of that pro-choice guy. They had a suspect but didn't have proof. They had had trouble with him before but could never lock him up. The suspect knew they knew so he was keeping a very low profile.

Then there was the fire-bombing at that doctor's house. That seemed to be a dead end. There were no prints, no witnesses. Those pro-lifers were becoming smarter and smarter. Joey knew he shouldn't lump all pro-lifers into the same group but it seemed to him that the more radical members gravitated in that direction.

"Frank? What? What's so friggin funny?"

Frank continued to chuckle as he looked up at Joey. "Ya know, Joey, the public never ceases to amaze me. I just got a call from this lady. Of course the caller ID is blocked, right?" Joey smiled.

"So, I asked her, 'How can I help you,' and she says she wants to report a missing person. I say, 'Okay, who is this person?' She says, 'I don't know if I should tell you his name.' I say, 'Okay, ma'am, let me try something else. How long has he been missing?' "

Joey's smile broadened as he saw the smirk appear on Frank's face. He knew what he was talking about. They sometimes received ridiculous calls.

"She says, 'Well, he's been missing about sixteen hours now.' I say, 'You know, we usually don't do anything until the person has been missing at least forty-eight hours, unless, of course, it's a child. How old is this person?' "

He looked at Joey, rolling his eyes as he kept up the one-way dialogue. "She says, 'He's in his early twenties.'

"So, Joey, I decided to have a little fun with this one. Ya know what I mean?" He winked. Joey knew exactly what he meant.

"So I ask her, 'Okay, lady, he's in his twenties, and may I ask how old *you* are?' There was silence for a minute and she finally says to me, 'What's that got to do with it?'

"I don't want her to hang up so I ask the normal questions. 'Okay, he's in his early twenties. Caucasian?' She says, 'Yes.' I ask, 'How tall?' She says, 'Around five feet five inches.' Finally, I ask, 'Do you have any idea where he might be?' Again she pauses and then says, 'Yes. I think …, I think they took him!' I didn't know what to think, Joey."

Frank began to laugh along with Joey as he made a 'doo-doo doo-doo' sound—pretending aliens were coming to abduct someone.

"Okay. Let me continue." He had tears in his eyes from laughing so hard.

"So … you think they took him? She says, 'Yes, that's right! They took him.'

"Ma'am … *who* took him?"

Frank's eyes were bulging out as he continued. Joey was laughing, thinking, *"This guy is a master at story telling."*

"So, she says to me, 'Bosch Research took him!' I ask, 'Why would they take him.' There was a pause, Joey, like she was thinking real hard. Finally she says, 'Well, because he was probably breaking into their place.'

"Joey, can you believe this? Someone calls to report a missing person who has been abducted by Bosch Research 'cause he was breaking into their premises. But wait!" He held up his hand to continue.

" 'So, lady, are you calling here because you think that we have a police report on this?' She says, 'Well, I don't know why I'm calling because he should have called me by now. I mean, he did say he would call once he was finished.'

" 'Uh, lady, are you telling me that you're an accomplice to all of this?' I'm waiting for an answer and she hangs up, Joey. Can you believe how stupid people can be?" Joey was shaking his head while smiling.

"So, just to be on the safe side, I called Bosch Research and asked if there had been any report of an attempted break-and-enter. I was put through to the director or whoever. Anyhow, I talked to this Lincoln guy and he questioned me what this was all about. I had to tell him about the goofy phone call. You know what, Joey? He was laughing just as hard as we are."

Chapter 24

Doctor Klein walked into the room after having a restful sleep, wanting to know how the patient was. He was thankful the ordeal was over. He quietly stood beside the bed. The monitors showed a stable situation. He smiled, thinking of what they had pulled off. They had managed to manipulate nature once again.

He and Bruce Whitman had both been standing guard for several days now. They took turns eating and sleeping in the recovery room. They would not let their young patient out of sight, each for a different reason but both with the same goal. Doctor Klein wanted to be on top of any physical problems that might have occurred since the operation and Bruce wanted to be on top of any psychological problems.

Doctor Klein leaned over the bed, becoming concerned with the recovery. There was some indication of organ rejection. Gene needed to be monitored very closely. He lifted the eyelids, looking deep into his patient's eyes. He was concerned about the brain activity. It was becoming too intense. He considered administering more medication.

Bruce and he had talked about the unusual activity. They both had different theories. Doctor Klein believed most of the brainwave patterns had to do with shock. Bruce tended to believe a little of the shock theory but also felt Gene was facing a psychological rejection, an inner turmoil perhaps?

Doctor Klein turned on a powerful lamp as he re-examined the neck.

He saw the sun. He felt his face being touched. He felt feathers touching his face. Was it an angel's wing? He wanted to reach out and touch the angel but he couldn't. There seemed to be an invisible barrier between them. He also felt warmth on his face. He reasoned that it must be the sun after all.

He removed the gauze and again checked the wounds. The neck diameter of both the donor and Gene hadn't matched as well as they had hoped. The doctors had needed to stretch tissue and muscle. The skin pigment wasn't quite right, either. That was a small issue for now. He was much more concerned with infection and rejection. Both problems were occurring. Gene had an angry red band on either side of the wound.

Doctor Klein made a mental note, promising he would check the wound every few hours. If needed, they would increase the amount of SES-3B serum to combat the infection.

Strangely, when Doctor Klein took Gene's temperature orally, it was somewhat above normal. When he took the temperature rectally, it was lower than normal. There were two different people with two different body thermostats involved here.

Doctor Klein wondered what else was so different between them. What else was so different that he couldn't see or measure? Maybe Bruce was right. He was beginning to suspect that there might be an inner conflict taking place in their patient.

Chapter 25

Several weeks had gone by since the operation. Doctor Klein spent as much time as possible with Gene. If he could spend more he would but he had other patients to tend to. He was now back and forth between Irvine General and Bosch Research, determined that he would not be held hostage by the death threat any longer.

Doctor Morin had also been visiting Gene's room several times a day. Doctor Adams came in when he could. He was still very busy at Irvine General. Doctor Schultz visited four times a day, busily administering the serum. He was still very bothered by the whole situation, especially with what they had decided to do to make the operation a success.

Bruce Whitman knew, more than anyone, that Gene needed peace and quiet. He convinced them to keep the visits short, very short.

The doctors congratulated each other. All indications showed that the operation was going to be a success. The rejection process seemed to have halted. The infections were clearing.

He is lying on water. He's floating, a lifeless body floating face up. This has become a typical scenario for him. This time he knows it's a dream and only a dream. He's in the ocean, drifting closer and closer to shore. It feels good. As he gets near the shore he notices he's now slowly being pulled back toward the open water.

He wants to go to shore. He needs to go to shore in order to survive but the current is too strong. Frantically, he tries to swim but realizes he's powerless, not being able to move his arms or legs. He wills himself instead, desperately trying to move his body closer to the shoreline. The power of his mind is slowly taking him closer but the current strengthens and pulls him back out to sea.

He panics. It takes every ounce of energy to move his body to shore. It is a tug-of-war between the underlying current and his mind, both opposing forces. He feels his body stretch. He is now very close to shore. He tries harder, getting closer still, aware that his body is now stretched to the limit. Suddenly he hears a ripping sound. He sees blood in the water, blood all around him—his blood. His head has been torn from his body. He screams.

Doctors Klein and Morin were in the darkened room when Gene's eyes opened. Outside of the SES serum, they had been trying to wean their patient off all medication as soon as possible. It had been several hours since the last dosage. They wanted Gene to come out of the drug-induced coma.

Gene stared at a white ceiling; wondering if it was fog—fog from the ocean. He didn't know where he was. He thought he was outside somewhere, floating on his back, looking at the sky. He heard a whoosh sound just to his left as well as a beep sound. It was beeping about twice every second. He tried to calm himself.

He heard excited voices. Two male voices were becoming louder. One had a thick accent. He saw a face appear. It belonged to a man who looked vaguely familiar. He wasn't sure. The man was calling his name. *Yes, that's right. My name is Gene.*

He remembered bits and pieces of who he was. He was a young man. He was sure of it. There was some kind of strange and bizarre relationship between him and the man with the thick accent. He couldn't quite understand what it was.

He saw another face, another man that looked vaguely familiar. Perhaps they were brothers, maybe his brothers. No, they looked too old. They were in their fifties. Was one of them his father? No, he was sure he didn't have a father.

He tried to concentrate on what they were saying. It was difficult to do. He could hear the words but couldn't understand. He knew they were words and not just gibberish but still couldn't make any sense of their meaning.

Doctors Klein and Morin were at his bedside. They were both very excited. This was a historical moment. They needed to talk, to find out what and how their young patient felt.

Doctor Klein leaned over, Doctor Morin slightly behind and to his left. He spoke in a slow soft voice despite his excitement. "Gene. I'm Doctor Klein. Do you remember me, yah?"

Gene's eyes were vacant. Doctor Klein continued to speak, leaning closer. "Dis is Doctor Morin beside me. You remember him, yah? You have been in a coma for several weeks, Gene. Vee have operated on you, yah? Do you understand, Gene?"

Gene remembered his own name. He also remembered he was a young man and vaguely recognized the two faces in front of him. He tried to make sense of what this man was saying. He couldn't do it. He lay there, staring back.

The doctors could see a lack of comprehension on their patient's face. They knew from past experience with Harley and Farley that they needed to do things slowly. They wanted to bring Gene back to reality at a comfortable pace. They made sure the drapes were closed, keeping the lights down to a minimum. They hoped this would make Gene feel more relaxed. Recovery would be faster with little light and noise.

They left the room. Gene could hear excited voices as they walked down the hall. He heard a soft thud. *Is that a door closing? Yes.* He slowly became aware that he was in a room with a door and that two older men had come and talked to him.

He closed his eyes and then realized he could open and close them whenever he wanted to. He opened the right eye and blinked. He opened the other eye and blinked again. He was thrilled with this discovery. He had control over his eyes. He felt tears run down his cheeks as he again closed both eyes.

Chapter 26

He was in medieval England, captured by the King's army due to his own negligence. He had dived into shallow water when he shouldn't have. They brought him to the town square, threw him on the brick road and shackled his arms and legs.

The crowd was jeering. Someone threw a small stone, hitting him on the neck. He quickly realized it wasn't a small stone that was thrown. Oh no, it was a large rock. Others in the crowd began throwing rocks at him as well.

He could feel blood run down his face, around his neck. His neck was being targeted. The pain was becoming unbearable. Just when he thought he would pass out, someone in the King's army shouted at the crowd, telling them to stop. They did. There was silence. Everyone waited.

He was on his back, bleeding on the red brick. He needed time to recuperate but time had run out. He heard horses approach. He looked up, smelling all five of them. A horse was positioned near each one of his arms and legs. A chain was attached to his left leg and looped around the saddle. They did the same to his right leg with another horse.

Before long, there were chains attached to two horses for each of his arms. His body slowly lifted as the horses moved away from him. In a few seconds he was suspended. He could hear the noise the horse's hooves made—a 'clop-clop' sound on the brick. He bent his head back and saw the fifth horse backing toward him. This time they made a noose with the chain, placing it around his neck, the other end attached to the last horse.

There were two teams. Team 'A' was at his arms and head, team 'B' at his feet. He was going to be drawn and quartered as well as have his head ripped from his body.

He could hear the sound of hooves as all five horses were being readied by five tall women. Each woman had a whip in her right hand. Several of the King's men were laughing and joking. They were enjoying the sport. The crowd jeered, pointing at him. He had been negligent with his body. He had committed the worst crime. He had injured himself deliberately. He deserved to be torn to pieces.

All five women stared at Gene as they raised the whips while trying to hold back the horses. The horses were nervous, ready to bolt. The women continued, slowly raising the whips in unison until their arms were high above their heads. They held that position ... waiting. Everyone was waiting. The crowd was silent, the horses, jittery.

Finally, the command was given from a man somewhere behind him, sounding strangely like his father. He heard the crack of the whips as the women quickly brought them down. The horses bolted. The crowd cheered. He could feel his arms and legs being ripped from his body. He screamed. God, how he screamed! He couldn't hear himself above the roar of the crowd. Blood sprayed everywhere.

He was still alive as his head was torn from his neck, tumbling down the cobbled street. He could clearly see the crowd as the horse pulled his bouncing head behind it. He desperately wanted to die.

He thought he had wakened from a terrible nightmare but wasn't sure. He wondered if perhaps he really was awake. Was he still alive? He could still smell the horses. He was terrified. He heard rustling near his feet, thinking it was one of them, getting ready to continue pulling him apart. He tried to look toward the sound but his head wouldn't move.

Slowly he settled down, hearing the steady whoosh and constant beep. He assumed the sounds were from some kind of equipment that helped him. He heard someone cough. The coughing continued for several minutes. Then he heard a voice, a strangely familiar voice.

Mr. Lincoln cleared his throat. He suspected that Gene had awakened from another terrible dream. He had thought about what had happened during and after the operation, how everyone on the team had sacrificed something in order for this to work. He understood he had sacrificed the most and felt that he had the most to lose.

He wheeled himself to the side of the bed. He'd been watching over Gene more than Doctor Klein. Gene was now his baby. He was terribly disappointed with what had happened to Harley and Farley. Ever since the mad man in fatigues had come storming into their pens taking flash pictures, the pigs had regressed.

It only took one jerk to screw up an experiment that seemed so promising. Never mind, Perry got what he deserved. He paid a huge price for what he did.

Mr. Lincoln felt like he had experienced a death in the family when Harley and Farley were traumatized the way they were. He knew it could take months or even years, if they lived that long, before they could get back to the condition they were in before the incident.

"Nonetheless," he whispered, "it was a valuable lesson for all involved. Things have got to be done carefully and slowly in order to make progress, especially with Gene. I cannot let my baby get upset. Gene cannot have a psychological breakdown. Gene needs human contact as much as possible."

Chapter 27

Doctor Klein busily made his rounds at Irvine General Hospital. He got back into his old routine so things wouldn't look too suspicious, still spending the majority of his time at Bosch. He had heard nothing more about the death threat although it was still very much on his mind. Now, he had other things to worry about. There were far more serious issues to consider than a mere death threat. His mind was never far from Gene.

He was visiting one of his patients, Derek, a young man who had been in a serious vehicle accident, when a nurse walked in. It was the young nurse he used to work with. He tried to remember her name. *What is her name? Gloria? No. Cynthia, that's it.*

She marched up to him without smiling. He knew something was wrong.

"Hello, Cynthia. How are you?" He smiled as he looked her way, wondering what she was doing here at Irvine General.

She didn't look happy. He wondered if she were depressed. It appeared as though she hadn't slept in a while. There were dark circles under her eyes. He felt a little frightened by her.

"You took him, didn't you?" Her face was flushed with anger, her eyes firmly focused on his, waiting for an answer.

"Vat are you talkink about?" He could feel himself flush as well. He hated that. He admitted his guilt by the way he acted. She was brash and aggressive, putting him off guard.

"You know what I'm talking about, Doctor!" She raised her voice. She had been thinking of Gene constantly over the past several weeks, going over and over again what had happened—how her man had been taken from her. She needed to at least talk to Gene, to set things straight. If he didn't see things her way, well, she decided, she would take matters into her own hands. She vowed she would never be used by a man again.

"Please, keep it down, yah? Dis man is recovering from a serious injury undt needs his rest."

"I don't give a doggie-doo about *this* man, Doctor Klein! What have you done with him?" She glanced at Derek and then back at the doctor, again focusing on him.

Doctor Klein was sweating. A nurse walked into the room, wondering what was going on. Joseph wasn't sure how to handle the situation. He wasn't a very good liar. "Uh, please, come widt me. Vee can talk in my office, yah."

Cynthia was ready to tell him she was calling the police but knew that wouldn't help. No, the best thing, she decided, would be to see if she could get more information. "Okay, but you better not lie to me!"

She shook her finger at him. Doctor Klein was becoming angry with this display of insubordination. His anger brought back his composure.

They went into his office at Irvine General. He closed the door for privacy. He would need it.

"Cynthia, please sit. I know you are upset but please realize dis is not as bad as you might tink, okay? Please sit und I vill explain."

She walked toward the chair, across from his desk, glancing at the diplomas and family picture on the wall. She slowly sat down, wondering about the lady and little girl in the photo.

He sat down behind his desk, clasping his hands, speculating on what she knew. "Okay, can you give me your vord you vill not tell anyone about dis?"

"I don't know, Doctor. It depends."

"Okay, den I vill give you ... a partial explanation, yah?"

"Just tell me what you've done with him!" Her voice raised several decibels.

He looked at her, contemplating on how he should handle this. There was really nothing she could do. She was no real threat to Bosch Research. She could run to the authorities and then ... what? They wouldn't believe a thing. He could talk to Mr. Lincoln and get him to arrange a transfer for her somewhere else, another city perhaps, like Kelowna. The third possibility was to tell her a partial truth. That might work. It would be the easiest solution.

"Huh, you are right, Cynthia. Yah, vee took Gene." He paused, letting it sink in. "Vee took dee young man because he *vanted* us to." He shifted in his chair. "You see, vee are involved in some very serious research, yah?"

Cynthia nodded, waiting for him to continue. She could see he was squirming. "Vee have developed a medication dat promises to be a big step forward in repairing dee human body."

Cynthia was becoming more angry. *All I want is to look after him for his own good. These darn meddlers are trying to change all of that. He's fine just the way he is. Can't they just leave him alone, alone with me?* She wanted her Gene back the way he was. She needed him back so she could look after him. He might not feel that way right now but she knew, with a little more persuasion, Gene would be happy with her. She wouldn't harm him. She simply couldn't.

She immediately questioned herself. She knew she had come very close to stabbing him the last time. Yes, very close indeed. She wondered if she would have actually murdered him. She surprised herself by knowing that, yes, it could have been very possible. He had dumped her, lying to her all along. He deserved to die. She loved him and yet she hated him. She had to control her emotions. They were getting her into too much trouble. Her heart was racing. She tried to calm down as the doctor kept talking.

"Now, dis might take months or even years, yah, undt it might not work at all." He lowered his eyes while he shook his head.

She couldn't help herself. She had to ask. "Are you experimenting with animals?"

His mouth dropped open. He was thinking that, no doubt, Gene had told her about Harley and Farley.

She continued with her cross-examination. "Are you experimenting with pigs?"

He didn't know what to say. He began to open his mouth, waiting for words to form but she interrupted him, again.

"Are you experimenting with guinea pigs?" She was now leaning across the table, only inches from his face, no longer thinking about Gene.

He couldn't believe what he was hearing. She was worried about guinea pigs, not Harley and Farley. He relaxed, realizing she was far off course.

"Let me say, Cynthia, dat in dee past, vee have been accused of doing such tings, but vee never have. Vee were cleared only a little while ago, yah? Perhaps you saw it on dee news. But let me explain, yah, because I know vat you are tinking."

He paused. Cynthia had leaned back in the chair, her arms and legs crossed, glaring at him, wondering what he was going to say next. It was his turn to lean forward. "Vee had talked to Gene and told him dat perhaps vee could help him. Again, dis might or might not vork and ... who knows how long it vould take."

He took his glasses off, cleaning them even though they didn't need it. He continued. "He vanted to see for himself vat vee could do, yah, so vee let him come into the laboratory and have a look. He vas on medication, Cynthia. He had been agitated so I had prescribed a sedative before he came to look and, yes, dair ver guinea pigs."

He continued to fabricate his explanation. He was thinking of years ago when he was in medical school. They had used a freakish looking guinea pig for dissection. It was the ugliest looking thing. He tried to remember the name of it.

"Yes, dee guinea pig dat Gene saw is a peculiar species. It is hairless und rather grotesque. It has been known to carry vermin. Ven Gene saw dis, he vos shocked. Vee had been using dis type of guinea pig for years for general experimentation. It is not against dee law, Cynthia. Dee only ting dat is against dee law is its grotesque nature. Dat is it."

She looked at him, wondering if that were true. At least part of his explanation checked out. She knew that Gene had been stressed and was on medication just like the doctor had explained. She decided to get right to the point.

"What are you going to do with Gene? Can I see him?" As she spoke, she still wasn't sure if it was such a good idea. She had to get her anger under control before she ever talked to him again.

"Gene vill be given some experimental drugs to see how he vill respond widt his condition. At dis time he needs to be quarantined so dat he is not taken ill by anyting. He needs to be isolated. If you like, I can give him a message for you, yah?"

She decided to let things go ... for now. At least she knew they weren't working on cute furry guinea pigs and anyhow, this medication that he was taking might not work. She prayed for Gene, wishing and hoping that he did *not* recover so they could be together again.

She almost felt foolish with her accusations except that she had one more question. She still wasn't sure if they tried to sneak him into Bosh or not but decided to ask, wondering what his reply would be. "Doctor? Why did you sneak Gene out of Edgehill and into Bosch? Were you breaking the law, kidnapping him?"

He stammered a little. He was going to deny the accusation but thought better of it. "Gene vanted to be treated at Bosch, yah? Vee did not kidnap him but vee had to protect ourselves, Cynthia. Dis is why it is extremely important dat vee keep dis under our hats. You see … dee business dat Bosch Research is in is very competitive. Vee are always aware of possible sabotage. Vee are dealing widt lots of money and need to take extra precautions. Dat is why, again, I emphasize to you dee importance of secrecy. Vill you keep dis conversation secret? Do vee have a deal?"

He quickly stood and extended his hand, trying to persuade her into working with him. Cynthia considered for a second or two. She shook his hand reluctantly saying, "Yes, Doctor, providing you let me know how he is making out from time to time."

"Of course, Cynthia. Of course." He wondered why she was so obsessed. *What would she do if she ever found out what really happened?*

He decided that they might be very wise to keep close tabs on her. Perhaps he could persuade her to come back to Irvine General and work with him once again.

Chapter 28

Mr. Lincoln sat beside the bed, carefully studying the patient's eyes and face, wondering if Gene were really conscious. He decided to make an attempt at communicating. "Gene, can you hear me?" He didn't expect any response. He continued.

"Gene, my name is Mr. Lincoln. I hope you remember who I am. I am part of a team that has," he was trying hard to choose the right words, "been involved in helping you." *Good. Choose your words carefully and always have a positive note to them.* "You are in wonderful hands, Gene. The best medical team possible is caring for you. I know because I chose them. Do you understand what I'm saying? If you do, perhaps you can blink your eyes."

Gene was hearing this soothing voice speak wonderful things. He liked the contact. He didn't want to be alone. He didn't want to dream again. The dreams were always dark and morbid. He couldn't take it anymore. He needed support. He didn't want this connection with another human to be broken. Unaware of what he was doing, he blinked.

Mr. Lincoln could hardly contain himself. He couldn't wait to tell the doctors. He was thrilled he was the first person to communicate with the patient. He wondered if the blink was voluntary so decided to continue.

"Good, Gene. I'm glad that you can hear and understand me. You are on the road to recovery. Every day you will grow stronger as you heal. The doctors are already agreeing that things are looking good. Isn't that marvelous? All you need to do is rest and get strong. Do you understand?" He stopped and put a hand to his mouth, trying to suppress another nagging cough.

Gene blinked again. He thought he understood the words but he wasn't quite sure. He did understand the soothing inflections. It had a strong, positive influence on his mind. He wanted to stay awake and be gently spoken to … forever.

"Good, Gene. I'm so glad you can hear and understand. That's simply wonderful. Would you like me to keep talking?" Mr. Lincoln was very excited but tried to keep his voice calm.

Gene quickly blinked, surprised he had processed a conscious thought. "Yes," he told the voice without speaking, "Yes, I want you to keep talking! Please don't stop. Please don't leave me, please, please, *please* keep talking. If you stop talking I will die. I know I will. I'll fucking die and, when I do I'll be taken to a dark and painful place for eternity. For fucking eternity! I know that will happen. I cannot die. Please, keep talking."

Mr. Lincoln could see by Gene's facial expressions that he was becoming aggravated. Gene's lips were quivering. *Damn, maybe I should leave. On second thought, Gene did blink at me when I asked the question about talking. I wish I could talk face-to-face but I'd need someone to lift me out of this wheelchair. Maybe it's best that I talk like I do with Farley and Harley.*

He decided to continue, soothing Gene with his voice, talking about nothing in particular but keeping it bright and positive. He could see the lips relax as soon as Gene heard his voice. He realized he needed to stay near his baby as much as possible.

Chapter 29

He desperately needed a glass of water. His throat and mouth were terribly dry. He woke up after what seemed like several hours of sleep. This time the sleep was blissful. He hadn't had any dreams. Excellent! He only wanted a glass of cool water to wet his dry throat. He could feel himself trying to swallow. It felt like he had a large lump in his throat, a large, sore lump. A face appeared in front of him. He was startled but then vaguely remembered who it was. It was a doctor who was trying to help him.

Doctor Klein was in a chair beside Gene's bed. Bruce Whitman was asleep in another chair at the foot of the bed. The doctor was thrilled to hear about the communication between Mr. Lincoln and the patient. *Good, very good indeed.*

He jumped up when he saw Gene's eyes open. He took a damp cloth and leaned over, placing it on Gene's forehead, looking into those eyes, smiling with adoration. He couldn't help but be so damned happy. It was like having a child, his child! He rubbed his hands together.

It appeared that Gene was trying to swallow. The doctor took the cloth and dipped it into a glass of water, slowly rubbing it on those dry and parched lips. He asked Gene if it felt good. Gene blinked.

Doctor Klein smiled. *Good, yes, very good.* He squeezed a few drops of water into the partially opened mouth. Gene blinked again. Doctor Klein asked Gene to blink if there was any pain. Gene just stared. It was no longer a fixed stare. The eyes were now able to focus and slowly move about in their sockets.

Gene could see a curtain in front of what he thought was a hospital window. The light in the room was minimal. That was good. He sensed that if the room were brighter he would feel more stress. As he became more aware, he could feel a lot of things just below the surface, anger, aggression and fear, to name a few. He was still terribly confused. He wasn't sure where he was. His short-term memory was poor but he could remember some things from his past.

He remembered his friend Dan and one of his old girlfriends, Amber. They used to do things together but he couldn't remember what. It seemed like such a long time ago. They were friends, he and Amber. No, they were more than friends. She was his first? No, maybe he was her first. He couldn't quite remember. It was all very frustrating.

He felt the cool damp cloth on his face and was instantly relieved. Just the slightest touch put him back in control. He knew how the cloth felt and where it was located.

He also had his sight. Correction, he had controlled sight. He could focus and move his eyes. He could discern depth with his vision and he could now begin to interpret what he saw.

His hearing was good. In fact, because he couldn't move his head, his hearing was accentuated. He could pinpoint things in the room from the direction of the sound. He knew someone else was in the room at the foot of the bed because he could hear him breathe. He knew where the glass of water was and where the other man was sitting, all through his hearing.

He could smell as well. He could smell the antiseptic in the air. He could smell the cologne on one man and the body odor of the other. He could smell flowers somewhere. He could smell the freshness in the sheets and pillows.

He could also taste. He could taste the water the doctor had dribbled into his mouth. He could taste the finger of the doctor as he slowly pried open his lips.

His jaw muscles ached. He tried to smile but felt as though his face were cracking. "Okay," he told himself, "a little bit each day. Just keep working on it."

The problem was he had no feeling below his neck. He could not feel his toes, fingers or anything else for that matter, except ... his face. He didn't understand.

Chapter 30

Gene's condition slowly improved. His throat wasn't as sore as it was the week before and he now felt a terrible itching around the neck area.

Doctor Klein could see his patient was becoming more aware as each day passed. Gene, on occasion, would move his mouth, trying to speak. They called in Mr. Whitman whenever there seemed to be a breakthrough in communication.

Gene had managed to produce a croaking sound from the throat area. He did this several times and would have continued if it hadn't hurt so much.

Doctor Schultz came in regularly to administer the serum, now in much smaller doses. He also wanted to visit as much as he could even though he had his hands full with his research. He was still bothered by the operation. No one had been prepared for what had happened, especially the lurching of the body after the bleeding had seemed to be under control. He had been comforted and supported by everyone else. After all, they were all part of the L-Team. No one could be blamed for the unexpected turn of events.

Today, Doctor Klein, Doctor Schultz and Bruce Whitman surrounded the bed. They could see that Gene was trying to speak. They knew their patient had a lot of questions that needed to be answered.

In order to keep Gene in a relatively peaceful state, the doctors and Bruce had agreed their patient should be given a little information every few days to gradually explain what had happened. The worst thing to do would be to give the right information at the wrong time. They did not want to anger or frustrate him so they carefully prepared statements that were to be delivered in stages. Today seemed like the perfect time to begin.

Doctor Klein had already memorized the first carefully crafted statement. Doctor Morin had jokingly dubbed them 'Press Releases.' He leaned over the bed, beginning his recital. "How are you feeling, Gene?" They wanted to include Gene's name as much as possible to reinforce a sense of identity. They had already established a communication channel with the blinking of the eyes. One blink meant yes or good. Two blinks meant no or bad. Gene blinked once. Doctor Klein continued.

"That's good, Gene. Vee all vant you to feel good, yah?"

The team had mixed opinions when it came to who should give the 'Press Releases.' Doctor Klein's accent might prove to be an obstacle because Gene could possibly find it too difficult to understand the doctor's words. On the other hand, the accent would bring back familiarity and maybe even trigger memories that could help in communicating. The majority voted in favor of Doctor Klein speaking. He continued.

"Vee have gone to great lengths to make you happy and comfortable, Gene. Vee are here to help you and keep you informed. Do you understand me, Gene?"

Gene was angry and very frustrated. He quickly blinked once, wanting to say, "Yes, you dumb shit, get on with it! What the fuck is going on?"

Doctor Klein noticed the anger flash in the eyes. He also noticed perspiration on Gene's brow. He continued with his recital.

"Some time ago, a group of expert doctors and technicians, including myself, operated on you. It vas an operation dat you had agreed to. You needed dee operation so dat you could have a much better quality of life, yah? I am very happy to report to you dat the operation vas a success and it appears dat you are vell undervay to full recovery! Do you understand me, Gene?"

Gene quickly blinked once.

"Good, Gene. I am glad dat you understand vat I've just said, yah? Now vee vant you to rest and later vee vill talk again about your condition, yah?"

Gene closed his eyes for a moment, needing to think about what this doctor had told him. He didn't like it. He had the feeling that he was being patronized. He quickly opened his eyes, wanting to say, "Who do you fuckers think I am? I don't like your attitude. Why can't I move my arms and legs? Why can't I even move my head? It seems like I've been lying here forever! I'm getting very tired of this shit."

Bruce Whitman was concerned with the look in Gene's eyes. There was too much anger in them. It reminded him of a time when he and his dad had visited an auto parts yard. The guard dog came running out, ready to attack. Luckily, the dog was chained. Bruce never forgot the look in its eyes. He appeared … wild.

He decided to leave for an hour so Gene could think about what had been said. Besides, he was deeply disturbed with the memory of the dog. He quickly exited the room, feeling a chill in the air.

Gene was angry, frustrated and sad. He closed his eyes but couldn't stop the tears. He tried to think back to before the operation. He only remembered his old girlfriend, Amber, and Dan.

What a fucking jerk! He was my best friend. He had such a big fucking ego! It's just like him to not come and visit me. Who gives a shit, anyway?

Gene was thinking very hard about when he had last seen him. He remembered the sun, the lake and … what else? He couldn't remember anything else except darkness.

Chapter 31

He fell asleep, totally exhausted. He dreamed of the lake, Dan and Amber. *Yes, Amber. Wasn't she a sweet little thing?* He loved to treat her badly and then have his way. In his dream he saw himself standing over her, telling her what to do. The bitch would do whatever he wanted. That was good. He was having a wonderful time entertaining the thought when a nagging feeling crept deep within him.

He suddenly felt that perhaps he'd been too mean to Amber when all she wanted was love. He could hear a very faint voice in the back of his mind telling him he was acting like a jerk. He became angry with the thought, mentally yelling back, "Fuck you!"

His eyes quickly opened. He didn't know where he was. He was frightened. He felt he had been invaded by … what? He wasn't sure. It was very odd to have such a weird thought come out of nowhere. He wanted to yell out, "Man, oh man, not only can't I walk, move my arms, talk, or even eat, I can't even fucking sleep! Somebody, please … give me a break." Of course, he couldn't yell out anything, at least not yet.

He heard a noise. Someone was at the foot of the bed. It was the old guy who coughed a lot. He sensed he was being observed. The old guy was annoying him. He wanted to scream, "Quit looking at me. I'm not some kind of monkey in a cage!" The word 'monkey' stirred up a creepy kind of memory that he couldn't quite understand.

He hated being studied. He tried to ignore the guy but couldn't. A moment later he heard him wheel closer to the head of the bed. He wished he could ask him what the fuck he wanted. *No, I'm just a bag of shit that everyone can come and have a look at. Isn't this fun?*

His eyes were open, waiting for the old guy to speak. Gene tried to speak first, wanting to say, "Come on you old fuck. Don't just sit there. If you want to talk then do it. Either that or leave." Instead, he heard a gargling sound come from his throat. The noise prompted Mr. Lincoln to wheel even closer.

"Hello, Gene. This is Mr. Lincoln. Can you hear me?"

Gene blinked once.

Mr. Lincoln had nothing in particular to say except that things were wonderful and everyone would be happy ever after, blah, blah, blah!

Gene found himself smiling. At least he thought he was smiling. It wasn't a happy smile even though he had to admit he was comforted by the sound of Lincoln's voice. Maybe it was the fact that he needed a connection with the human race. Maybe he felt he wasn't part of it, but a freak of nature instead. He wasn't sure what he felt. He only knew that, once the voice began, he felt better. It was a link to the real world. He wasn't quite sure what the guy was saying, but it didn't matter.

Mr. Lincoln had tears in his eyes as he spoke. He wanted to talk, to tell Gene what had happened. He needed to explain about the shooting and how things had gotten so terribly complicated and how happy he was that Gene now had a second chance. He knew Gene wouldn't understand right now. He would have to wait until the appropriate time. He continued to speak of nothing in a soothing and nurturing voice.

Gene closed his eyes, listening to the soft and reassuring sounds, slowly drifting away. He thought about part of his past. He vaguely remembered his mother and father. Why they had an only child that she wanted to abort was far beyond reason. He would never forgive that dirty fucking bitch! He hated all those dirty fucking bitches. He hated them!

He mentally clenched his hands into fists. He wanted to hit all the women he had ever known, thinking of how he could get even with them when … he started having second thoughts. There was a small flicker of doubt that crossed his mind. His subconscious mind was telling him he needed to get control of his feelings, especially for women. They weren't all bad.

Fuck you! They are all bad. Don't you dare tell me anything different. Who the fuck do you think you are? Get out of my mind. I don't need that shit. It's too confusing.

He waited. There was no reply. As he focused on his hatred for women the small and determined voice started up once more. "There are plenty of good women in this world. There are plenty of good people in this world. You have got to get a grip and consider yourself lucky for who you are and for being given a second chance. Do *you* understand?"

He was dumbfounded. He couldn't believe what he had just thought. That wasn't him thinking. No, it couldn't be. It was the complete opposite of who he was. *Where did that come from? That was not me! I know I don't think like that.* He tried to dismiss it as a drug induced side-effect but had difficulty doing so. He kept rationalizing. *God only knows what those bastards have injected into my body. They've certainly had their way with me. I'm powerless to stop them. I'm their human fucking guinea pig.* He closed his eyes, trying to relax, trying to open up his mind to wherever it wanted to take him. It was an escape. He needed to mentally get away.

As he lay there, he became more and more conscious that things weren't quite right. He couldn't put a finger on it. It might be akin to someone who felt there was something happening within his body that didn't seem normal, perhaps a cancerous growth? Whatever it was, it didn't belong. It was foreign. It was a foreign growth of some sort. It wasn't only a foreign growth. Gene was concerned it could also influence his thoughts and feelings. He felt he was being changed and altered in a most profound way.

He was aware that his whole body had become fragmented. He tried to reason, telling himself again and again it was only a side effect from the drugs that had been forced into his body, tearing him apart.

He concentrated on trying to remember, knowing he was a young man. He had memories of Dan and Amber, people from his past. He remembered going to school. He remembered reading about Africa. He remembered the glossy pictures of giraffes and monkeys. He even remembered the smell of the printing ink as he stared in fascination at the strange and exotic animals.

He was suddenly frightened. Remembering those pictures was one thing but did they start to move in his mind? Was this an actual experience he once had? Maybe something he'd seen on TV? It felt like he'd been there, standing in the jungle, looking at wild animals nearby. He could even smell them. He asked himself if he'd been there before. Maybe it was in a past life. Had he been reincarnated? He felt like two pieces that didn't quite match.

Chapter 32

Bruce was in the midst of a heated discussion. He was very concerned about Gene's lack of progress. The doctors argued that there was progress. Their patient was healing nicely and they hoped to see some very positive results soon.

"No, that's not it! I see regression happening."

Mr. Lincoln asked, "Why would you say that? There is more and more communication developing every day."

"Yes, I know, but I sense anger, a very deep anger."

Doctor Klein spoke next. "But of course there is anger, yah? Do you remember when vee first met the young man, how angry he vas then? You even wrote it in your report, yah?"

"Yes, I know. I know!" He put up his hands in exasperation. "Listen to me, please." He slowly put his hands down, trying to reason with them. "Gentlemen, I have spent many years studying the human mind. I see a pattern developing. His attitude is becoming similar to Farley and Harley's. You have to admit that we have noticed a tremendous amount of anger and frustration since the operation. There seems to be more to it than that. There's also torment. Why? Because, now this is only speculation, but I believe we are beginning to see a split-personality occur here."

There was protest as Bruce quickly continued. "Please!" He put up his hands once more, wanting order. They silenced, waiting for more of an explanation.

"Remember over a year ago when we had this very same discussion? We were in the boardroom going over and over again and again about all possible scenarios. One of them was a 'what if.' What if the donor's body retains memory. What if it retains even a small portion of memory compared to the brain. What if that memory is stored in cells. It could be cells in the lung, cells in the stomach, even cells on the bottom of the feet.

"We all know about muscle memory. That explains why you can pick up a guitar years after you've put it down and still play almost as well." Even though the discussion was serious, Bruce could see a few smiles. Everyone was well acquainted with his past by now, how he had once played in a blues band.

"What I want to emphasize is," he put his hands up, forefingers extended, "if muscles have a certain amount of memory then it's not ridiculous to theorize that perhaps bone has too, or even skin, although perhaps a different type of memory. Regardless, it's still memory!"

He looked around the room, knowing they had all heard this before. The problem was they were surgeons. They would naturally tend to concentrate on the physical part of the operation instead of the psychological part.

"So," he continued, "what if. What if this memory coming from the donor is filtering into the brain. What if it's trying to interact or even persuade or debate with the brain. What if our patient hears voices, not knowing where they are coming from. Perhaps a schizophrenic symptom is developing here." He paused, letting his explanation sink in before continuing.

"Hell, the patient is still not even aware that he has been operated on. Not only an operation but a body transplant. Listen to me!" He was pleading. "Don't dismiss the possibility. Keep your eyes and ears open for anything that appears unusual. That way, we can all understand the situation better. Until there is a full two-way communication, we have to carefully observe what's going on."

He sat down and took a deep breath. He was angry with them. This very situation had been bothering him for weeks.

Chapter 33

He decided that he had to set some goals. He wanted to speak again, to communicate with the outside world. He began exercising his facial muscles. He worked on opening and closing his mouth, raising his eyebrows, moving his eyes around in their sockets, even trying to smile. He also tried to generate some sound in his throat.

Doctor Klein was in his face as soon as he attempted to emit any sound. He was staring at Gene. Gene stared back, trying to smile. Doctor Klein smiled back.

Yes, it works! My face works. I can fucking smile. Great! That says a thousand words. That says I'm okay. I'm in no pain. I don't need any more drugs. I'm happy. I feel good.

He didn't feel good. He felt angry and mean. He figured he could fool those stupid fucks with a phony smile.

Doctor Klein was beaming. He told Gene, "I'll be right back."

Yeah, Doctor. You better hurry back because I just might not be here when you return. You know? I just might jump out of this fucking bed and run out the door and maybe play football or go jump off a fucking cliff! He suddenly realized there was something about jumping off a cliff. It was beginning to come back in waves. *Yes, I dove off a fucking cliff, didn't I? I was showing off, wasn't I? I had to be the center of attention. I had to be the fucking hero! The big male ego got me into this mess.*

Doctor Klein was excited as he headed toward his office and read the next 'Press Release.' He had already memorized it but still wanted to make sure the delivery was perfect.

He was back beside Gene's bed a few minutes later, puzzled with the look on Gene's face. He noticed tears appearing in his young patient's eyes. He smiled reassuringly but Gene didn't smile back. He wondered if he should hold off with his speech but then decided he'd continue as planned.

"Hello, Gene. It looks as if you are feeling better, yah? You are getting stronger by the day, yah?"

Gene blinked twice. Doctor Klein didn't notice.

"Good, Gene. You are in very good hands and vee are here to help you as much as possible. You are recovering very nicely, yah?"

Gene looked at him, becoming very annoyed with the dumb fucker who always ended his sentences with 'yah.'

"It is time to let you know dat you are in a special facility, Gene. Vee are all vorking together with you so dat you can get well. You have been in a bad accident but now dat is over widt and vee are all looking forward to a full recovery. Isn't dat marvelous?"

Gene blinked twice and uttered a moan. Doctor Klein was startled. The moan sounded exactly like Harley and Farley's.

"Gene, I vant to ask you a question, yah?" He caught his breath, still thinking of the moan. "Vee vant to know how comfortable you are. Vee vant to know if vee can slowly turn up dee lights and open dee curtains, perhaps a little bit at a time, so vee can all see better, yah?"

Gene thought about all of that. He liked the room dark but he didn't know why. Perhaps he felt he could hide better, but hide from what? He felt ashamed, like a freak of nature. That's exactly what it was. He felt like a freak of nature.

Gene did not respond to Doctor Klein's question. To turn up the lights and open the curtains would make him feel exposed. It made him feel very uncomfortable. He wanted to stay under his rock where he felt he belonged.

Doctor Klein continued. "Gene, vee don't have to keep the lights on for long, yah? Perhaps we can turn them up a little for a few minutes, Gene? Would dat be all right with you, Gene? You can blink ven you want it dark again, yah?"

Gene still didn't respond. *"Why the fuck does he keep calling me by my name? The dumb fucker should realize I know my own name by now!"*

The doctor pressed on. "Perhaps you can vair dees sunglasses, yah? Can I put dees on you?" Gene considered and then finally blinked once.

"Ah yes, dey look good on you, Gene."

Gene wanted to see for himself. He needed to see himself in the mirror. He needed a lot of things but first he needed to learn how to talk again. He moaned. This time it was the doctor's turn to blink.

"Yes, Gene, I understand dat you vant to talk, yah?"

Doctor Klein could see Gene blink once through the glasses.

"Dat is good. Vee have you scheduled for dat very ting starting tomorrow. Vee have dee best speech therapist dat will come here daily to assist you. Her name is Mona and I tink you vill like her, yah?" There was no response. Doctor Klein decided to leave it at that. They had both covered a lot of territory. It was time for Gene to rest.

Gene closed his eyes, thinking of all the things he wanted to say once he got his voice back. He wanted to know, in detail, what had happened to him. He remembered the dive into the cool lake and then blackness.

He woke up feeling his entire body covered in sweat. *Wait a minute. I feel my entire body? I can't believe it! I haven't felt my body sweat for how long, since the accident?*

He could feel it. He felt a chill from the sweat on his back. He felt it. Oh, God, how he felt it. He focused on the new sensation, asking himself, "Is this really true or just another illusion?" He'd been on such an emotional roller coaster ride that he had learned not to trust even himself. *But, no, I do feel the sensation of sweat, especially near my lower back. I'm sure of it!*

He wanted to call the doctor over but couldn't. *And where is that Lincoln guy when you need him?* He hadn't seen him for several days. He wondered about Lincoln, what his role was in all of this. He was too confused and tried not to think about anything, yet ... it troubled him. There was something that had happened. What was it? They showed him things—their secrets. He couldn't quite remember.

Chapter 34

Bruce sat in his office deep in thought. He knew they would soon need to explain things to Gene. It would be best to wait until Gene could communicate better before they talked about what had happened several months ago. He was confident that Mona would have Gene speaking soon. He was also very much aware there were things going on within Gene that he needed to understand so the team could better deal with the situation. It had long been speculated that attaching foreign body parts could create conflicts, not only medical conflicts but possibly mental and spiritual conflicts as well.

He had confided with the other members of the team that he was planning on doing a word association test while Gene was in a deep sleep. He wanted to know if he could get any insight into what Gene was feeling and dreaming. Having an EEG set up while saying key words would give him more clues as to what was going on within. He knew it was important that they find out as soon as possible. Everyone was in favor. He looked at his watch. He was going to be late for the meeting. He hurriedly made his way down the hall.

They were all sitting in the boardroom when he walked in. The meeting had begun without him. He wondered if that was an omen. Were they dismissing him and his concerns, preoccupied with their own medical achievements instead?

Doctor Klein was at the blackboard reviewing Gene's condition. He was writing as he spoke. "It has been several months since we performed what appears to be a very successful operation, yah? As with any complicated procedure, such as vat we have accomplished so far, there are always problems to be addressed. Dat is why we are here today. I vant to give you a status report on dee patient." He paused while looking around, acknowledging Bruce in the process. He noticed everyone was listening intently so continued.

"At present, dee patient is healing beautifully. Initially dair ver signs of organ rejection but vee used dee right combination of drugs to combat dee problem and dey performed marvelously. I vant to tank all of you who are responsible in making dat part of the operation a success. As you all know, it was a major concern and it now appears dee situation is under control."

He wrote 'Organ Rejection' on the board, placing a check mark beside it. "In particular, I vant to tank Doctor Schultz for his brilliant work in dat department." There was applause as Doctor Schultz stood up and nodded.

Doctor Klein took a deep breath, paused, and then slowly continued, his accent steadily growing stronger. "Dee exciting part of all of dis is it appears dee patient is beginning to feel certain zenzations in dee body, yah?" He had written 'Feelings' on the blackboard and was startled when some of the team members began to applaud. He looked up at the group, seeing their smiles. He couldn't help but smile back. It was contagious.

"Dis vas vat vee had all been hoping for, spinal cord healing. It seems to be starting. Yes, no matter vat dee outcome, dee operation is definitely a success!"

There was more applause. They were all standing. Some members hugged each other while others shook hands. This was the moment they had all been waiting for. Bruce wondered about Joseph Klein's last sentence, what he had meant by it. The part about 'no matter what the outcome' concerned him.

Doctor Morin was shaking Doctor Klein's hand. Doctor Schultz had his arms around both of them. Doctor Adams and Mr. Lincoln were shaking hands as well, patting each other on the back. Someone brought out several bottles of champagne and glasses. Everyone was smiling, everyone except Bruce. They were getting ready to do a toast when Doctor Klein put up his hands, trying to bring order to the room.

As the applause died down, he continued. This part of the status report would be harder to deal with. "Unfortunately, all is not vell with dee patient, my friends." They looked up at him expectantly, confused as to what was really going on. "Dair is grave concern dat dee healing process is only vorking in dee physical sense."

He wrote the word 'Blending' on the board, placing an 'X' beside it. They waited patiently for more of an explanation. He continued, trying to do his best, still not sure if what he was saying was correct. "It is von ting to do a successful body transplant in a medical fashion but it is another ting to have dee spirit, as it were, to be whole as vell. I have to admit dat, as a doctor, my main focus, as vell as widt many of you in dis room, is on the physical side of the operation. Vee all had discussed dee moral implications over and over. Vat vee didn't discuss fully vas vat I have called dee 'spiritual' issues or perhaps, 'blending' issues dat have arisen."

They were mesmerized, trying to comprehend the full implications. Doctor Klein needed help with his attempt at explaining. He looked at Bruce as he continued. "As Mr. Whitman has predicted, vee are dealing vit two distinct individuals in our patient. After all, our patient is now comprised of two different people. Vee had strongly felt dee patient's brain vould take complete control of dee new being."

He stood in front of the blackboard with chalk in hand, not quite sure how to continue. This was new territory for him. It was new territory for everyone. He paused, took a deep breath and pressed on. Everyone was silent, waiting for answers.

"Vee felt dee brain vas dee complete source of," he began to write and underline the words as he spoke, "physical feelings, memory, emotions, thought processes, sexual urges, physical urges, bodily functions, to name a few. By understandink dee EEG patterns of dee patient's brain vee are slowly becoming aware dat it might not be dee entire truth anymore." He paused, seeing several puzzled looks.

"Vee have noticed strong brain activity. It is beyond vat vee vould consider as normal and probably indicates agitation, aggression and fear. In short, vee are beginning to understand dat inner forces are tormenting dee patient. Yes, tormenting, because dee patient cannot come to terms widt both forces vich are now making up one body." The team couldn't stay quiet any longer. Whispers were becoming louder.

He raised his voice to compensate. "Vee can control dee spiking in two vays. Vee can administer more tranquilizers, vich vee do not vant to do. Vee vant to communicate with dee patient. Vee vant to find out vat is going on inside dee body. Vee need to keep dee patient alert."

He put up his hands, trying to again lower the noise level in the room. "Dee second way is widt better communication. Dee patient has had extreme difficulty in tryink to speak, yah? Dair vos some damage widt dee larynx ven vee operated plus dee heavy medication dat had been administered has clouded dee mind."

He stopped, suddenly tired, wishing he were a million miles away. He looked at Bruce, asking him with his eyes. Could he please take over and talk about the patient's progress or lack of it?

Bruce quickly stood, making his way to the front of the room. He was energized, needing to speak, wanting to explain his theories.

"Thank you, Doctor Klein." He turned toward the team members.

"This is now becoming a critical issue as Doctor Klein has mentioned. It is something that was unforeseen when we planned this entire project only two years ago. As you are all aware, things did not go as planned."

They all nodded, understanding what he was getting at.

"We are dealing with more complications than we had ever realized."

More nods from the group.

"In order for us to help Gene we need to have some feedback. As Doctor Klein has pointed out, we can control the patient's agitation in two ways. One, we can administer more medication. Or two, we can try to communicate better. We don't want to administer any more medication unless absolutely necessary so therefore we need to have a better form of communication. We cannot expect to get the full picture from blinking eyes and an EEG hookup." His hands were extended, emphasizing the problem.

"Our next step is to get our patient to speak. It has been difficult so far because of the tube that has been inserted into the windpipe as well as the minor damage to the larynx. The tube has now been removed and Mona here," he pointed toward a short and plump lady sitting at the table, "is a leading specialist in speech therapy." She smiled as he continued.

"She will be working aggressively with the patient so we can all benefit from this. Once we get a handle on the situation we can use the appropriate therapy and medication to make life better for ... everyone."

For the moment there would be no celebrating. The champagne was put away.

Chapter 35

Bruce and Mona walked into the dark room, quietly closing the door behind them. They looked at each other for a moment, each taking in a deep breath. Slowly, they made their way to the side of the bed.

"Hello, Gene."

Gene wanted to say, "Hello, Doctor. Wait a minute. You're not a doctor. You must have flunked medical school, right? You're just a counselor."

He blinked once.

"This is Mona. She will be your speech therapist."

He blinked again. *Mona! Looks like you've been eating too many fucking donuts.*

"Hi, Gene." She smiled as she leaned over.

He blinked, noticing she had a booger stuck up her fat fucking nose.

"I'm hoping that we can get you speaking in no time. Would you like that?"

He glared at her. *Don't be fucking talking to me like I'm a little child, bitch! You just love this shit, don't you? You love the control, especially over a man. Hey, let me ask you something you fat dumpy bitch! When was the last time you got laid? And, I'm not talking about you with another dyke but ... with a real man.*

He finally blinked, "Yes."

She was beginning to sense something seriously wrong with the patient. She needed to choose her words more carefully.

Gene was very agitated. *There they go again. Trying to get me to do this or to do that! There's always something with these people. Why can't they leave me alone?*

A voice, in his mind, yelled at him. "Shut up!"

He couldn't believe what he'd just heard. This voice told him to shut up. It was an aggressive voice. He didn't know what to think. He was completely startled. *Where did that come from? Who is in my mind? Why would I say that to myself?* Shocked with the unknown voice, his mind did indeed shut up. He listened instead.

Mona spoke in a soft tone. "Can you make a high pitched sound in your throat for me?"

He decided to chill out a little, trying to do what she'd asked.

"Good, that's good." She knew that the safest sounds for Gene to make, without damaging the surrounding tissue and larynx, were higher pitched sounds requiring less air movement than a lower pitch.

"Okay. Can you make the sound a little lower this time?"

They continued for several more minutes. She was trying to get a feel for the voice range—to decide what would be the best way to get it extended and improved.

Bruce stood back, watching and listening closely. He looked at how the mouth tried to move and, in particular, he looked at the eyes, trying to read anything in them. He needed to know more about the inner workings of the patient's mind. He needed to know who they were now dealing with because this was not the same person. No, it was someone different, someone who made him feel very uncomfortable. He decided to do word association later in the evening once the patient was in a deep sleep.

Chapter 36

The EEG was being closely monitored. Bruce had waited beside Gene's bed until sleep was in the rapid eye movement stage before beginning the word association experiment. Now he was ready. He began by softly speaking the word 'mother.'

Gene is having the recurring dream of floating on his back on the ocean. The current is strong. He has no control in getting back to shore. He's trying to paddle with his legs and arms but they won't move. Suddenly, his mind is filled with the vision of a woman that he both loves and hates. He wants to reach out to her, and … and what? Hug her or slap her? He's unsure, feeling very uncomfortable.

She keeps telling him, "An apple a day keeps the doctor away." He wants to eat a ton of apples.

Bruce saw a spike associated with 'mother.' He continued. He softly spoke the word 'father' as he viewed the response on the display.

Gene is reaching for the woman who he thinks is his mother when, in reality, it's his father that he sees. His father tells him he's got a job out of town so, "Good-bye, it's been nice knowing you." Gene wants to cry. He is no longer floating. Now he's drowning. He's sinking just under the waves. He can't keep his head above water. His lungs are filling with salt water. As he drowns, he realizes he has never known his mother or his father. He has lived his whole life not knowing who they are.

The EEG spiked with the word 'father.' Bruce carefully looked at the facial expressions as he continued, this time whispering the word 'Africa.'

Suddenly, everything is peaceful as he travels down a jungle road. He's in a truck. He's in the back of the truck with several people. The sun is hot. He feels safe and warm. He's wondering how he has suddenly been transported from the ocean to the jungle.

He sees children, small African children. They are huddled together, laughing. He feels the hot sun on his face. He looks away from the village toward the jungle. He can smell the jungle. He looks to his left and sees the brush land. It's getting hotter. He sees animals—giraffes, elephants, water buffalo and beautiful birds. He misses not being there. It was a home for him. No … wait! He never had a home there! He's confused.

The EEG patterns leveled out to a more peaceful reading. Bruce was pleased. Just this simple sub-conscious experiment showed him where the 'ouch' lines were. He continued with the word 'school.'

There's a group of children in the back of the truck, traveling through the dense jungle. They enter a clearing and eventually arrive at a small village. People are smiling and waving. Everyone is happy to see them.

They stop in front of a big white building. He looks up and sees the national flag blowing in the breeze. The sun is now too hot. They're all anxious to get into the coolness of the building. He runs in with the children. As he enters, everything turns black. He thinks it must be because of the strong contrast from bright sun to dark shadow. He loves the darkness. He feels the coolness of the air as he hears the laughter of the children. He is at peace.

Then suddenly, Chad, the bully he had punched out at school, appears from nowhere, holding up some shoes. He wonders how he knows this 'Chad' guy and why he has shoes in his hand, holding them up at eye level. And he's all the while snickering, pointing to them, telling all the children in the classroom that they are not normal shoes. No indeed! They are not normal. They are, in fact, elevator shoes. Chad asks the class, "Do you know why these are called 'elevator' shoes, children?" Everyone has a blank look.

He carried on with the experiment for several more minutes, not wanting to overdo it. Bruce's sole purpose in the exercise was to see if he could get any insight into the mental turmoil that the patient seemed to be exhibiting. He needed to determine if the new body was playing a significant role in bringing back memories and past experiences. Did it influence the brain because it had its own memories and experiences? If it did, to what degree? Did the brain have complete control over the new being or did the body control part of it as well? There were many questions that needed to be answered.

Chapter 37

Mona came by for an hour every day and taught Gene how to move the mouth and form words with the lips. He could remember how to speak but he wasn't sure how far he could stretch his throat without hurting it anymore than it had been. It did feel better and she was helping. They were making progress. They had removed the tubes that had been placed in the throat and windpipe. He was finally eating solid foods.

His memory had also slowly been coming back, some of it he just couldn't figure out. He had unexpected flashbacks. For example, when he ate a banana, the taste of it triggered a distant memory. He could have sworn he was crouched in the jungle, hiding from something. He wasn't sure. A while later, when he was being cleaned, the scent of the soap reminded him of his mother. The funny thing was he couldn't remember her ever using that type of soap. He wanted to tell the doctors all of this so focused more and more on being able to speak.

Gene experimented with sounds from his throat. Mona had been coaching him to produce both low and high pitches. It seemed that the sounds he made were rather high. He could not get down to a lower pitch.

Mona explained that the vocal chords had probably tightened up since the operation and therefore the frequencies were higher. She compared it to guitar strings—the tighter the string, the higher the pitch. He thought of a guitar. *Somewhere, someone had played a guitar?*

He could still feel and, on occasion, hear a voice within him during waking and sleeping hours. It was bizarre. The voice was becoming stronger each day, tearing him apart. Not only did it show up unexpectedly but it was also beginning to creep into his deep emotional self, influencing him.

For example, he sensed a strong grief for another person, his lover perhaps? He kept going from one extreme to another. It made no sense. He didn't *have* a lover. The closest person who would fit that description would be Amber and all he wanted to do was use and control her.

He and Lindsey were never lovers. He had feelings for her, but he also had feelings for other people he had never met. A male figure crept into his subconscious self periodically. His father must be worried about him. No, that wasn't his father he saw. Fuck his father for abandoning him. Fuck his mother, too.

He tried to silence his mind. He could somewhat control the foreign feelings and the voice but he feared it would only get stronger. He forced himself into thinking of other things instead, pleasant things. He tried to concentrate on his voice therapy. Mona had him do facial exercises until it hurt. She also made him concentrate on opening and closing his mouth. Each day after she left, his throat and mouth would ache. It was a good healthy ache.

His memory was coming back in waves. He could now remember the diving accident and the first time he had met Doctor Klein who told him the news— that he would never walk again. He also remembered losing all hope, spinning farther and farther downward into the deepest hole he had ever been in.

He remembered something else, that fucking nurse that drove him bat shit. As he thought about her, he began to feel sorry, forgiving her for being who she was. He quickly caught himself, wondering why he had sympathy for her. He thought, *"It's not her fault. She is who she is, right?"*

That's wrong. What I just thought was wrong!

He defended himself by saying, "Fuck you! It is her stupid ass fault."

Doubt came into his mind. *Are you sure about that?*

He was becoming angry for being doubted, "I said fuck you! She's a fucking idiot!"

Again, a thought that was definitely not his crept into his mind, arguing, *"No, she's just a young woman who thinks she's in love with you."*

He had to agree a little. "Okay, maybe you are right … just a little. I'll cut her some slack, okay?"

He got a mental reply. *"Okay."*

He decided to be firm so said, "Good, now leave me alone. I've got to think."

The voice replied, *"I'll be quiet for the time being but don't start thinking those thoughts again or I'll be back."* It was threatening.

He caught himself, realizing what had just occurred in his mind. It was unbelievable! He had an entire conversation with someone else in his own fucking head! He was becoming very troubled, again feeling out of control. It just happened. There was no warning. All of a sudden an unknown voice would speak to him, usually arguing and questioning him.

He took a deep breath, trying to calm down, knowing there was no sense to what had just happened. He wondered if he was having a breakdown of some sort.

He tried to think back. *Where was I? Oh yes, the accident and how they came in and told me I had a second chance. A second chance?* He repeated himself, wondering about this second chance.

It was coming back. They showed him things. He couldn't quite remember what they were. He had blocked them out of his mind. They told him they could operate and it might correct his problem.

That's right. He was getting excited. *They corrected my problem. I'll be getting better! But why am I having these flashbacks—flashbacks that I can't remember being involved in? Who am I?*

He thought for a few more minutes, slowly smiling. He knew he'd been given a second chance at life and he was alive. Yes, alive! Not only was he alive, but he was also beginning to get some tingling in his lower back and left foot. He was also very close to being able to speak. *Yes, now I know what happened. I remember seeing the donor before the operation. He was a few years older than me. He was in an accident. He was six feet tall!*

Chapter 38

Doctors Klein and Adams came into the room as if on cue. It was rare to see both of them at the same time. Each had his own very busy schedule.

"Hello, Gene. I hope you're doing well, yah?"

Gene blinked. He was doing well. He was still alive and now he finally figured out he was taller. He was fucking taller. He was seven inches taller! This would make all the difference in the world, coming from five feet five inches to six feet. Seven inches taller! He could look down at women and, more importantly, they could now look up to him. Yes, he was happy.

"Good, dat's good! Doctor Adams and I vant to do some testing with you. We think that you might be having some feeling in your extremities by now." He winked good-naturedly. Gene winked back. He knew he was smiling. He could feel his face muscles stretch.

Doctor Adams was thinking about the decision to administer a small amount of medication to help the patient's mental state. It appeared to be working. He got down to business, explaining what they were planning on doing.

"We're going to do an experiment. We want to see where you are experiencing feeling. We're going to place a hoop over your torso and have the top bed sheet cover it. Now, there are several reasons for this. One is because we don't want you to see what part of the body we are stimulating. We need you to tell us where you think the feeling is coming from, okay?" Gene blinked once. Doctor Adams continued. "Another reason is because ... because we don't want you to try moving your head down for a look. We are afraid you might put too much strain on your injury." That second reason was only partially true.

"When we operated, we tried to do as much micro-surgery as possible but it was a daunting task. It was an impossible undertaking, trying to re-attach all the nerve endings. That's where the serum comes into play. It's designed to stimulate nerve re-attachment and appears to be doing just that, but ... the nerve endings have no way of knowing who their companion nerves are. They don't know what nerve to match up to so, it's random. That means the brain has to figure this all out. Do you understand?"

Gene blinked again.

"Good, so are you ready for the test?" He smiled as he asked the question. Gene could see Doctor Adams was as excited as he was.

He blinked once.

Gene's head was firmly fastened with the halo device. Even though his eyes focused on the ceiling he could still see a little of his surroundings. He noticed them place a hoop over his torso and then lift up the bed sheet that was covering him, placing it over the hoop and back down around his neck.

The experiment was going to be a simple hot and cold procedure. Doctor Klein reached into a bowl and took out some ice. He applied the ice to the bottom of Gene's left foot.

Doctor Adams saw Gene's eyes flinch. *Good, better than we had hoped.*

"I'll ask you a series of questions and I want you to blink your response."

Gene blinked once.

"Okay, did you feel anything?"

Gene blinked once.

"Was it hot?"

Gene blinked twice.

"Was it below your waist?"

Gene blinked twice.

Doctor Adams thought that perhaps Gene blinked twice unknowingly.

He asked again. "Was it below your waist?"

Gene blinked twice, again.

Doctor Adams looked at Doctor Klein and then back at Gene.

He was going to ask once more when Gene croaked, "Elbow!"

Chapter 39

He made an attempt at raising his head so he could see his body but the halo apparatus prevented him from doing so. He tried to wriggle his toes and fingers. He thought they were moving but he was still not sure. It could be wishful thinking. He had tried with the doctor just last week but there hadn't seemed to be any evidence of movement, only a slight tingling, as though a nerve in his arm was asleep.

They had continued with the hot and cold experiment on a daily basis, realizing that, even though the nerves were crossed, there were some sensations in different parts of the body. It was only a matter of time before Gene would be able to move and control the body after having to re-learn things—similar to a recovering stroke victim.

Now that most of his memory had come back, he was trying harder and harder to heal. He couldn't wait to get out of bed. He was thankful his old body was now gone. He wondered what they had done with it. He had so many questions. He kept working on his jaw and throat muscles. He could hear the moans and raspy sounds he was creating. They were much more controlled now, almost sounding human. He fell into a deep, dreamless sleep.

A voice awakened him. It was Doctor Klein. "Good morning, Gene."

Gene automatically replied, "Good morning, Doctor," but it didn't quite sound that way. It sounded more like 'Goah ornin Ock tor.' They both smiled. Doctor Klein was totally impressed with what Gene had just said. He couldn't help himself, beginning to talk excitedly.

"Gene, Gene, Gene! Dat is marvelous. You can now speak, yah! It's coming, yah? Soon you vill be able to talk! That is vonderful, yah? I vant you to tell me all your thoughts as soon as you can, yah? Vee have a lot of catching up to do. I have a lot to tell you as well, yah? Good. Good. Good! Oh yes, Gene, I almost forgot. Merry Christmas!" He quickly left, wanting to share the good news with the rest of the team.

Gene felt the happiest he had ever been. It was Christmas and he had been given the best gift ever, the gift of life! He felt good. He was on the road to recovery and he knew he'd soon be ready to play football. He would also be able to take out all those little bitches that didn't want to have anything to do with him in the past because he had been too fucking short. He had been too fucking short! Not anymore.

He was waiting for the voice to begin talking to him again, but instead there was silence. *Good. I don't need to listen to your shit!*

He couldn't wait to get out of the hospital. He was planning on getting a job and working out at the gym. Maybe … he might even take out that cute little Marcy. Yes, maybe he just might ask her out. She was the little piece of work that wanted all the boys to stare at her wonderful and sexy body and then pretend she was disgusted with them. The more they looked, the skimpier the outfits.

He was getting angrier by the minute. He had a lot to prove to everyone, especially himself. As he was thinking about all of this he became increasingly distracted by a nagging itch on the bottom of his left foot. He was hoping it would go away so he could continue daydreaming and then it hit him.

"Wait a minute," he exclaimed, "it's an itch! It's an itch on the bottom of my foot! I can feel it. Yes, Yes, Yes! I can feel it! It's Christmas everybody and I feel an itch!"

In his mind it was all coming together. He was healing. He would no longer be paralyzed. He would become a real man. The man he had always wanted to be, the man who would teach all the women in his life a lesson. A good hard lesson!

Bruce came into the room wearing a Santa hat, ringing some bells.

"Ho! Ho! Ho! Merry Christmas." He quickly pulled out a guitar he was hiding from behind his back.

Gene smiled, thinking, "Cool!"

Bruce had met with the rest of the team the previous day. They had discussed the best way to tell Gene the truth about what exactly went on the night of the operation months ago. They had agreed that they needed to play things down as best they could. Bruce had suggested that the guitar might be just the ticket in making things a little easier.

"Hey, I know you like the rap stuff but I can't play that."

Gene smiled and said, "Ohhkaay."

Bruce made an attempt at smiling back, saying, "The closest I can come to rap is maybe … jeeze, Gene, I don't know. How about some blues instead? No, wait a minute, how about some Rolling Stones?" His heart wasn't into it. He knew what was coming, what needed to be explained.

Bruce sat on the edge of the bed, getting ready to sing. He began with 'Satisfaction.' Before too long he was on his feet, shuffling, singing, "I can't get no, I can't get no … satisfactioon!" He was puffing up his lips just like Mick.

Gene kept smiling. He was so happy.

Bruce stopped a minute later, not knowing what to do next. He was beginning to feel awkward.

"Moooorrrre."

"What? Okay, sure. More Stones?"

Gene blinked.

"Okay, how about—" He stood up, trying to think of another good Stones song that he knew. He didn't know too many but then … it came to him.

"Yoooou kaaant always get whaaatt you waaahannnnt. I said, yoooo kaunnnnt always get whaatttt yoooou waaahaannt." His lips were sticking out again as he got up and danced.

Just then Doctor Klein came into the room. Gene was laughing, remembering the last time Bruce had been surprised by the doctor.

This time it was different. Bruce's voice trailed off. He strummed half-heartedly, hitting a few bad notes before finally stopping. He looked at Doctor Klein. They seemed to be speaking to each other with their eyes. Something was wrong. What was it? The way the doctor and Bruce looked at each other was suspicious. Gene felt a chill run down his spine. His mouth went dry, his smile quickly faded.

Doctor Klein broke the stare and made his way to the side of the bed. Bruce put the guitar down and stood beside him. Doctor Klein smiled reassuringly but Gene wouldn't buy any of it. There was something that the doctor needed to say and it wouldn't be good.

Gene thought, *"Come on, Doc. Tell me now and get it over with. It's the spinal cord, right? It's not fucking healing, right? All this was done for absolutely nothing, right? Tell me! Tell me everything. Now!"*

Doctor Klein cleared his throat. "Gene, der verr some very interesting developments dat occurred durink dee operation vee had performed on both you and dee donor. Some tings have … changed, yah?"

Gene wondered, *"What fucking 'tings' have changed? Give it to me straight!"*

Doctor Klein paused, seeing the look of alarm appear on his young patient's face. The team had expected this reaction. Of course! Who wouldn't be upset when a doctor tells a patient the major operation that would change his life forever had not gone as planned. Doctor Klein remembered the orchestrated words by heart, waiting and dreading to recite them, but … now the moment had come.

"Gene, you need to know dat dee donor vee had chosen for you—" His voice faltered. He looked into Gene's eyes, seeing fear and apprehension. He took a deep breath before continuing. "He died in dee operating room, Gene, after vee had removed dee head from … dee body …." His voice lowered to a whisper as he finished the sentence.

Gene tried to comprehend all of this, thinking, *"Let me see. The guy who was a perfect match for me fucking died on the operating table? So now do I even have a fucking body? Yes, I do. I know. I can feel it. In fact, I can feel a slight churning in my fucking stomach. Maybe I should say I feel a fucking churning in 'our' stomach. Who the fuck am I? Keep talking, Doctor. You've got a lot of 'splainin' to do!"*

Doctor Klein sighed before trying to continue. It had been decided that it would be best for all concerned to dole out a little information at a time so the shock would be lessened. He forced a smile while trying to follow the prepared statement.

"Gene, do not be alarmed by dis now because dair is still good news, yah?"

Gene was listening very intently.

"Because of dee circumstances dat happened, vee ver very fortunate dat vee"—he paused for a split-second and then blurted—"vee had a backup donor. Dee donor had dee same blood type and also had a healthy body dat we could use as a substitute." This was not easy for Doctor Klein. He found himself shaking. His voice was weak. He took another breath, trying to compose himself.

"You must realize how lucky you are. For us to have a donor, widt dee same blood type, available vhen needed is truly a miracle, yah?" He continued, trying to emphasize how lucky Gene really was. "Vee are even more fortunate dat you do not appear to have any medical complications widt your new body. It seems to be functioning fine. Vee are trilled widt your progress, Gene."

He re-emphasized Gene's good fortune by saying, "Please remember dat you are a very lucky individual and have been given not only a second chance but now it appears you have been given a turd chance, yah?"

Gene's emotions were all over the map. He laughed at the 'turd' chance. Maybe the word 'turd' was appropriate. He also thought Doctor Klein's talk was a prepared speech, sensing the rest of the team's input. He suspected they had met previously and discussed what they should and should not tell him.

Gene was stunned with the news. He quickly tried to grasp the positives. He rationalized, thinking, *"It's not all bad, is it? In fact, I really don't see anything negative. The main and most important thing is that I am getting better. I do have a body that is still a good match. I've been given a 'turd' chance. It's almost like God decided he would bless the operation and make me a whole and happy person again. I deserve it. I demand it! I've put my life on the line for this and it's still working out. Good. Good. Good! I can deal with this change. Yes, I'm still happy about all of this."*

He smiled at the doctor. Klein smiled back. The doctor was relieved that this was going far better than he had hoped. He told Gene they would talk again in a few days. He would explain more later. They'd both had enough for one day.

Doctor Klein again said, "Merry Christmas."

As he left the room, Gene returned the greeting. "Air ee is ass Ock ore!"

Chapter 40

Later on Christmas Day Doctors Klein, Morin, Adams, Shultz and Mr. Lincoln came into the room to wish Gene a Merry Christmas. He was given more medication and then, once they made sure Gene's sunglasses were on, opened up the curtains and began singing several Christmas carols.

Once done, they lifted Mr. Lincoln onto the bed. For the first time since the operation Gene could see him. He remembered him as being younger looking, not as sickly as he now appeared. They all sang, 'We wish you a Merry Christmas' with Gene trying to sing along.

Doctor Klein said he had a Christmas surprise. Gene looked at the doctor, wondering what it was. He could feel the soothing effect of the pills he had been given as he listened. Doctor Morin took pity and divulged the secret, saying they planned on removing the halo apparatus around the head early the next morning.

Gene said, "Ank oo" and smiled.

They all left a few minutes later except for Mr. Lincoln. He wanted to have a face-to-face talk with Gene. He had been bothered by what had taken place over the past few months. He needed to talk. He needed to explain. The doctors gave them their privacy, closing the curtains before leaving the room.

Mr. Lincoln began by saying how very proud he was of Gene and the team. He emphasized how dedicated they all were and how happy he was that they had taken a chance and stuck their necks out.

Gene giggled at what Mr. Lincoln had said, thinking, *"Stuck their necks out? No, no, no, Mr. Lincoln, I'm the one who 'stuck' his neck out."*

He couldn't help himself. He felt giddy. He smiled and laughed. The sound of the laughter was rather high-pitched, making him laugh even harder. He was just so damned happy. He wanted to hug all the doctors. The pills were doing their job.

Gene's giddiness made Mr. Lincoln somewhat sad. He wished things had worked out differently. He had been tormented by what had happened the night of the operation. He wanted to let Gene know what kinds of sacrifices were made in order to be here, smiling, today. The others had no idea he needed to tell Gene the full story.

They would probably disapprove of what he was about to say but he didn't care what they thought. All that mattered right now was for him to clear his conscience because he was totally concerned with himself.

"I want you to know that, during the operation, an intruder broke into Bosch Research. He came through a window, ending up on some straw between Harley and Farley. Do you remember them?"

Gene nodded.

"The intruder was a mad man, screaming and yelling, while taking several flash photos of my babies. He attacked me, throwing a flashlight at my head, hitting me! I had no other option. I shot him. I accidentally shot him in the head, Gene."

Gene was listening with amazement. *Holy shit! Mr. Lincoln shot someone trying to break in? Well, good for him, I suppose. Why did that bastard break in?*

Mr. Lincoln was sensing Gene's questions so continued to explain. "The intruder, a guy named Perry, broke in to take pictures of what we were doing. It was all planned and carefully coordinated. He trespassed and paid the price. I did some research and found out he had been dishonorably discharged from the Special Forces unit of the Marines. Evidently he had shot and killed an unarmed pregnant woman. There is confusion as to what really happened. The Marines decided to dismiss him because of other incidents leading up to the killing."

Gene listened intently, wondering how this Perry guy ever got into a situation where he shot a pregnant woman. He waited for only a few more seconds before he got his answer.

Mr. Lincoln cleared his throat and then kept on talking, trying to let Gene know that this Perry guy was a rotten bastard and needed to be shot. As he spoke, Mr. Lincoln realized he was not only speaking to Gene but also to his own conscience. He needed to get this off his chest.

"Perry, along with his group, was assigned to eliminate uprisings that were developing in a small African town. They had done several weeks of training deep in the jungle and were ready to quickly go into the village, surgically remove the troublemakers, and leave. Something went wrong. Something went terribly wrong. The insurgents were tipped off. The Marines were ambushed. Perry barely escaped. The question was did Perry shoot the defenseless woman out of anger or error? I personally believe he was a killer and did it deliberately." He was trying to convince Gene as well as himself with the last sentence.

Gene's mind was spinning with this new information. He wondered where Perry was now. *Is he okay? Is that why I've been having these dreams about Africa? Do I have his fucking body? Tell me, Lincoln. Tell me!*

Gene's eyes were wide open, perspiration on his brow, attempting to speak despite the sore throat. Mr. Lincoln leaned forward so he could understand what Gene was asking.

Gene spoke again, this time louder, with a high pitched voice. "Haw taw is Pair ee?"

Gene looked at Mr. Lincoln, waiting for an answer. Mr. Lincoln understood the question perfectly, surprised by it. He didn't answer. Instead, he leaned back and looked at Gene in a disgusted sort of way for a second or two. There was a moment of silence between them. Mr. Lincoln finally yelled for Doctors Klein and Morin who were waiting in the hallway. He told them that he was ready to leave. He didn't want to talk to Gene anymore. He was very disappointed with the question. After all they had done, giving their patient a second chance. Gene was only concerned with being tall. There were so many other things that were important with living besides just being tall. *No, Gene doesn't see it. We've wasted our efforts on someone that is so terribly shallow. What a shame. What a terrible shame.*

The doctors very quickly came back into the room and picked him up off Gene's bed. Mr. Lincoln was all the while staring at Gene as they placed him back in the wheelchair. He kept asking himself, "How can a person be so selfish? Nothing matters to Gene except for being tall. After all that we tried to do, nothing else matters."

Gene stared back, thinking, *"The fucker won't answer! The son-of-a-bitch will not answer me! He will not answer me! How tall am I?"*

Chapter 41

He was left alone and glad for it. He thought about his dreams, the other voice and the connection with Africa.

This Perry guy was shot by Mr. Lincoln. Was he near death and did the doctors operate to save him or transplant him? It was all falling into place. Of course! The original donor died on the operating table. At the same time, Mr. Lincoln shot this Perry guy in the head. The docs brought him in and voila, they made a combo. Gene and Perry! Hmm, Gene and Perry, Gene and Perry ....

"Hey, Perry. How are you doing? I hope you have a decent body, Perry. Right? I sure hope you like women. You *do* like women, don't you? Come on, you've been talking to me on and off for weeks and now that I know who you are you've shut up? Gimme a fucking break!

"Perry? Perry? I understand you're a bit of a he-man, right? Being in the Marines and all, right? Being in the Special Forces and training in the jungle must take a real man to do that. That's good, Perry. You know, I'm a real man, too. I am! I know how to handle women, Perry. Hey, I know you shot that pregnant lady and killed her. Lincoln is telling us that you did it deliberately. I don't buy that shit. What was it like shooting her, Perry? Was she calling you names?

"Hey, Perry, I've got a question for you. How tall *are* you? I know that you can't be a fucking midget to join the Marines, right? So come on, if you're such a big fucking he-man, talk to me!"

Gene realized he'd been rambling. It was only nervous energy. He waited for Perry to speak. He tried to clear his mind. He couldn't do it. He was far too excited. He had the fucking body of a Special Forces Marine for God's sake. *Unbelievable! This will work out great!*

Gene knew Perry would eventually talk to him. It was only a matter of time. He supposed Perry was probably in shock more than him right now. It was all very bizarre for both of them.

Poor Perry has gotten himself into a predicament that no one in their wildest dreams could think up! He smiled at the thought.

He was beginning to feel smug again. He felt he'd finally gotten what he deserved. All his past dreams were now going to be fulfilled. He couldn't wait to actually put on a uniform and walk into the gym. Better yet, have the uniform on and walk, no, *march* up to Dan and look him in the eye, saying, "Hey, you little fucker! Who's the midget now, Dickface?"

Yes. Yes. Yes, and ... how about Mom and Dad? That would be good, too. Just walk up to Dad and give him a little nudge. When he tries to shove back, give him a slap on the face and tell him that he better not fuck with a Marine, a Special Forces Marine! Yes. Yes. Yes! Gene was smiling.

What about my mother? What would she do when I walk up to her in my uniform? His mind went blank with that one. He stopped smiling.

He tried talking to Perry once more. "Hey, Perry, I hope we're friends, right? I mean, it would be pretty shitty if we weren't. I've got to ask you, Perry. How many medals do you have? You know? How many medals have you gotten for serving our country? I guess I should ask you, how many medals do *we* have, right?"

He was beginning to feel stupid. He thought he might be pushing the envelope a little too far. Perry was no doubt in shock. Maybe he needed time before he could talk to Gene again. There was nothing Gene could do about it but wait and see.

He was so excited about what had been happening that he had trouble sleeping. This was the best Christmas ever! He closed his eyes and began singing in his mind. It wasn't Christmas carols, it was the Rolling Stones.

You kaaaant alwayyys gettttt whaaaat yoooou waaHannt!

EPILOGUE

Derek was deep in thought. In the real world people played for keeps. At least that's what a reliable source had once told him many years ago. In his mind she used to be a reliable source back then, back when he didn't know any better, when he was only six years old. He had come home from his first day of school, crying because the other boys had taken his marbles. He couldn't understand why they would win his marbles and not give them back. His mother told him to be prepared for life. In the real world, people played for keeps.

He clutched the steering wheel while thinking back fifteen years ago. He looked through the rain-streaked windshield and stared at the blinking red lights ahead of him. He heard an angry horn blast behind him. He quickly put the car back into drive to follow the three other vehicles ahead of him.

He felt like he was in a parade and, in a sense, he was. He was coming home after the weekly doctor's visit, having the bad luck of getting behind a school bus which made the thirty minute journey home last even longer. At each stop the bus would flash its red warning lights as another group of young children disembarked into the waiting arms of their mothers.

The rain, coupled with the stronger medication his doctor had prescribed, made things appear surreal. The red flashing lights and bright yellow rain slickers the children and parents wore mesmerized him. He should have heeded the prescription warning.

What did it say? *Dispense date: March 13/09. Take two every four hours. Do not operate heavy equipment.* His Caprice was certainly not heavy equipment. He had a chuckle over that one.

Yet another stop and another group of young children getting off the school bus, some not much older than he had been when he was told that, in the real world, people played for keeps.

Derek needed to focus, to make sure his driving was safe. It was difficult. The painkillers made him feel euphoric. He giggled, partly because of the wonderful feeling the drug produced and partly because the pain had momentarily subsided. He knew it would be back again soon. There was no escaping it. Doctor Klein had told him it was all part of the package. He would have to accept and deal with it.

It was easy for the doctor to say. He didn't have to suffer night after night, day after day. But then again, he was playing for keeps when he decided to have the operation, wasn't he? Outside of the pain, there was some good news—Cynthia. She was certainly interesting.

He smiled, sitting in the car with the wipers flapping, waiting for the school bus to move on. Yes, she certainly was interesting. He had been a little afraid of her at first. She seemed far too controlling. He had felt intimidated by her until he realized she really did want to help him.

A horn blared behind him. The driver was obviously becoming frustrated with the stop-and-go traffic the school bus was creating. This time they went four blocks before the bus stopped, letting off more of its young cargo. There was only one more bus stop to go.

He was in no hurry to get home. He wondered if it really was home. No, the house in the hills on ten acres was nice but not home. It was only a staging area for both of them.

He and his roommate were simply friends. She had wanted nothing more than companionship and support. He had gladly obliged. Both were recovering from separate accidents.

Derek knew he was ready for a real relationship but not with her. There was no chemistry. That was fine. In fact, they had laughed about it. He certainly felt chemistry with Cynthia.

The bus finally pulled over, letting the long line of traffic pass. After a mile or so he made his turn onto Crawford and headed up the long winding road to the house they both shared.

He would tell her he had found someone—someone who wanted to be with him, to take care of him, to love him. He knew his new relationship was a little too fast for his liking. "But," he reasoned, "sometimes those sorts of things happen in life."

He pulled into the long muddy driveway, glad to be back in the country, away from Irvine. It was still raining. He knew the weather made the pain worse. It was coming back now in waves despite the medication.

Derek slowly got out of the car. It had become a science for him. He opened the door of the Caprice and slid his legs out, still in a partial sitting position. He grabbed the edge of the windshield with his left hand and pulled himself into a semi-standing state. He stretched his back into a straighter position, all the while trying not to move his neck. It took close to five minutes before he was completely out of the car. He knew he moved like an eighty year old man. In reality, he was only twenty-one.

He was wet from the rain when he finally closed the car door. He slowly shuffled toward the house, deciding he would tell her about Cynthia while he had a hot bath. That would do him and his neck a tremendous amount of good.

She listened to him speak from behind the bathtub curtain, explaining his feelings as he soaked in the hot water. He had been a mess when they had first met. She remembered being in a similar situation, living on her own.

Doctor Klein had introduced them, knowing they could both use a roommate. They quickly realized how much they had in common. Each helped the other with the everyday things they had trouble doing on their own. It had been a necessity at the time but lately they were both adjusting better, becoming more self-sufficient, independent.

She knew the hormone treatments and counseling had helped her considerably. The therapy would probably never end. She needed to accept that fact even though she had difficulty. She had a long battle ahead of her.

They were silent for a minute or two. He lay there, soaking in the tub, thinking about his accident, how his neck had been operated on. He wished the pain would go away for good.

She sat with him on the other side of the bath curtain, thinking about how she, too, had almost died. She remembered the painful hours of rehabilitation and realized that her world had been completely turned around. Things would never be the same. She felt ashamed of who she now was, not wanting anyone to know her secret. She thought back to the countless hours of working with professionals, learning how to walk again, to talk again. She even took a course on how to apply make-up. She remembered the day she started out on her own, trying to cope with the outside world.

She was terrified at first, not wanting to be alone. The doctors assured her that she wouldn't be alone. They would always be nearby. It was time for her to move on, no farther than a few miles from Irvine. She was given a fresh start at life.

At first the doctors carefully monitored her every move, visiting her several times a day. Once they could see she was able to cope on her own they reduced their visits to only twice a week.

She and Derek were both in their own worlds, bringing back memories that were somewhat parallel.

She thought back to when they had come into the recovery room months after the operation.

She remembered all three of them standing by the bed. She had wondered, "What? What's wrong? Is it my neck?" She tried to speak.

"What?"

One finally sat on the bed, the other two standing behind him. She was frightened, not sure what was going on.

The one on her bed spoke while looking down at the floor, not being able to meet her eyes. "We need to talk. There was a glitch. There was a glitch during the operation." Tears began to well in his eyes.

She wanted to say, "Glitch? What are you talking about, a 'glitch?' A glitch happens in computer software, *not* in an operation." She couldn't speak. Even if she were capable of speaking clearly, she wouldn't have been able to find the right words.

Derek moved lower in the tub, hearing her breathe on the other side of the curtain. He knew she was a wonderful person but ... only a friend. They had talked about sex. She explained that she simply wasn't interested. She told him it was because of her injuries. He suspected otherwise, thinking there was something strange about her. She was different. He couldn't explain what it was.

He soaped himself, getting ready to let her know that he'd met someone. The arrangement they now had would be changing.

She remembered the doctor struggling, trying to explain, still not looking in her direction. "There were unforeseen circumstances—too many complications. The original donor died. He died on the operating table."

The doctor pressed on, finally having the nerve to look up. "We were stuck. We scrambled and finally realized that there was only one plausible solution to this whole event." He had let the sentence hang, not knowing how to continue.

Derek turned the hot water on, heating the bath a little more. His neck was killing him. He had needed the operation in order to save his life. The doctors had told him he was lucky he hadn't been decapitated in the car accident. He should have been using his seat belt. He had gone through the windshield.

She remembered being dazed, not understanding what Doctor Morin was saying.

"I'm trying to explain to you. There was only *one* other possible solution. Do you understand? We had to attach your head to the only other recipient that was available, the original donor's wife!"

Things began to swim in Jean's head. She remembered moaning, "No, no, no! I'm Perry!" She assumed that Mr. Lincoln had told her, in so many words, that Perry was the new donor. She never dreamed it would be William DeGroot's wife, Laurie.

Derek turned the hot water off, still thinking about his past operation. He knew he had been fortunate. Doctor Adams was one of the best surgeons in North America. Who would have thought he would be here in Irvine when he needed him the most?

She vaguely remembered Bruce grabbing her hand, pleading.

"Jean, *please*. Listen to us. I know you have a lot of questions. Let me try to explain."

Jean remembered crying, thinking, "*A lot of questions? Do I have a lot of questions? Yes, you fucking moron, I have a hell of a lot of questions. I mean, I've heard of sex change operations but … this is ridiculous!*"

Derek had been in recovery for months. Throughout the many days in Irvine General his nurse was there, always beside him, finally telling him she loved him, that he was the only one. He had found her unnerving and overpowering at first—vaguely remembering how she had stormed into his room at the hospital months before, putting Doctor Klein off guard.

Jean remembered Bruce being persistent, needing to explain as best he could.

"During the operation, Doctors Schultz and Morin had an unexpected situation. William's body had lurched and, in the process, tubes and clamps became dislodged. The blood loss was just too extensive. He died. Your original donor, William, died on the table, Jean."

She remembered the tears in his eyes as he tried to explain what had happened. Doctor Klein was standing behind them, looking down at the floor, not wanting to face her.

He completely submerged his head in the bath water while thinking of Cynthia, how she hadn't been interested in him at first, not until he had mentioned living in the country with a friend, a woman friend. Her name was Jean. Doctor Joseph Klein had treated her at Irvine two years ago. Did Cynthia remember her? That's when she began to get interested.

Jean played back the events, trying to make sense of the explanation.

Bruce continued. "When Mr. Lincoln heard a commotion in the McDonald Room he came in to investigate. This mad man was ranting and raving." Bruce had his arms up over his head to emphasize what he was saying.

"He lunged at Mr. Lincoln. Mr. Lincoln had no other choice. He shot him in self-defense." His arms were now extended outward, palms up, hoping she understood the situation Mr. Lincoln had unwittingly been put in.

Doctor Klein couldn't bear it any longer. She remembered him stepping up to the bed, meeting her eyes.

"Vee considered using him as a donor but dee blood type vas all wrong. Vee vere stuck. Stuck widtout a solution until … Doctor Adams came up widt a brilliant idea. He suggested vee use dee only udder available donor dat vould fit dee criteria. If he hadn't suggested it, you vould have died!"

Derek decided he would have Cynthia come over tomorrow. She wanted to meet his friend. He had felt uncomfortable with her heightened interest in Jean's life but suspected that perhaps Cynthia was only jealous of the other woman. He smiled at what Cynthia had suggested.

Jean was half-listening at Derek splashing in the tub. Her mind was still in the recovery room at Bosch.

She remembered Bruce Whitman talking excitedly. His voice becoming elevated as he tried to explain, continually pacing back and forth beside her bed.

"We took this Perry guy's Jeep and parked it in an alley near the downtown core with Perry in the driver's seat. We wanted to do a cover up, making it look like an attempted murder. He had a murky past, Jean. The police have several suspects in mind. He's in Irvine General but will soon end up in Edgehill."

Jean remembered trying to nod her understanding as Bruce kept talking, waving his hands up and down as he spoke.

"You have the body of the original donor's wife, Jean. Her name was Laurie. She was the perfect match for you except for the X and Y chromosome thing, but we're slowly dealing with that. Her body was healthy but unfortunately she was going to die very shortly from head injuries."

Doctor Morin added, "The next of kin was a lone aunt back east. Laurie and William had no other relatives. You see, they were from South Africa. The aunt came to Irvine to view the bodies. William, the original donor, died on the operating table. We told the aunt that Laurie had also passed away but … that was only partially true. She was in a coma and would never recover. Her body is now transplanted onto you, Jean. You're both recovering very nicely. "

Doctor Klein stepped in, continuing with the explanation. "Vee arranged a funeral service for Laurie because she vos witoudt a body, yah? Vell, dat is not totally correct. Vee buried your *old* body vidt Laurie's head, makink it complete, yah?" He had a bittersweet smile on his face, thinking how very clever they all were. "*Yes,*" he thought, "*we covered all the loose ends.*"

Doctor Klein was already thinking about the next project they were planning. Unfortunately Mr. Lincoln had passed away so would not be there to lead the L-Team. They would miss him. They had made a pledge, both to Mr. Lincoln and themselves. They would continue to move forward and learn from their previous mistakes. They already had a patient in mind, a young man who came from a dysfunctional family. It was only a matter of time before they found the right donor. They were sure that this time nothing would go wrong.

Doctor Klein had been puzzled with the only person on the L-Team who hadn't made the pledge, who decided he had had enough and wouldn't continue with anymore procedures. The doctor shrugged, thinking they could replace Bruce Whitman quickly enough, perhaps with someone that actually held a doctor's degree.

Derek soaped himself, thinking of what Cynthia had said—that perhaps she could move in with the two of them. At first he thought it was crazy but Cynthia kept trying to change his mind saying, this 'Jean' sounded interesting and she would like to get to know her. They could be friends. Besides, her dog and cat would love to live in the country.

Jean remembered how she had tried to sort things out, thinking, "*I can't believe this. I'm a woman. I'm a woman? No. No. No! Let me get this straight! William died on the operating table so … they were stuck with what to do. Then, the fuckers decide to use his wife's body, Laurie, and attach it to me! I can't do this. You call the organization 'Bosch Research?' That's a fucking laugh! It should be called 'Botched Research' instead! It's too crazy. Then, what happened? Oh yeah, they buried my body with her fucking head! Oh my God, now she and I are locked in death, buried together and … we're also locked in life, attached together! Oh my God! Oh my God! I can't be a woman. Aren't women the weaker sex? Don't they sit and nag all day?*"

An inner voice had replied, "No, they don't. They're loving and caring."

No, they're not!

"Yes, they are!"

Jean took a deep breath, slowly realizing that she had been given another chance—another chance at living.

Okay, let me come half-way here. I guess they can be nice. I know I can do this. I might have beautiful long legs.

Derek decided he would ask her. Actually, he would tell her about Cynthia. He was sure she would understand. After all, he and Jean were only friends—

roommates. And yes, he decided he wanted Cynthia to move in with them. It would help with the rent and besides, Cynthia was a nurse, someone who could take care of both of them. He smiled, thinking that Cynthia was a sexy looking woman with nice big breasts. He was ready for a real relationship.

Jean remembered looking up at Bruce as she tried to speak.

Bruce heard a mumble so leaned over and asked "Yes? What is it?" He didn't quite hear. Doctor Klein had gotten up, too, along with Doctor Morin. All three were leaning over her bed—listening closely to what Jean was struggling to say.

"Doctor?" She was looking at Doctor Klein as she tried to speak. "Howwww t … tt … tt … tahhhllll ammmm I?"

"Jean. Jean? Are you still behind the bath curtain?"

"Yeah, I was thinking, why?"

"Well, I was just thinking, too. I've decided I want you to meet someone, someone very special."

AUTHOR'S NOTE

April 26, 2009

Back in the early eighties I saw a remarkable documentary on PBS. Doctor White was performing head transplants. How bizarre was that? I watched with fascination, seeing a monkey strapped to a chair, having the body of another attached at the neck. It was hard to accept ... so Frankensteinian! I was torn, ready to turn off the television in disgust and yet glued to it, wondering where this was all going.

My feelings changed when I saw Christopher Reeve being interviewed on the same program. He was asked, while in his wheelchair, if given the opportunity, would he do it? Would he risk his life to be somewhat normal again? He replied without any hesitation that, yes, he would.

That simple and yet complex question, coupled with the quickness of his reply, convinced me. If I were paralyzed and were asked the same question I would answer the way my hero, Superman, did. With a resounding yes!

I began to wonder. What if I were in Gene's predicament and accepted the odds, getting ready for the procedure. How would I feel, sitting and waiting, thinking about the donor, wondering about my life. Would it be worth it? Of course it would.

The years flew by. My younger sister came over one day, explaining how she had trouble getting up off her hands and knees. We had just returned from the beautiful island of Bali a few months previously. I suspected that perhaps she had caught a virus. No, Jeannette hadn't caught a virus. It was much worse that a mere virus. She was sentenced to a slow death, death with the help of ALS, commonly called Lou Gehrig's disease. How could that be? She was only forty-eight years old. She had her whole life to live.

I visited her several times a week, seeing the disease take its toll. Every few days she would lose another faculty, her body slowly shriveling until she was reduced to virtually nothing, eventually dying of starvation.

Her family and friends patiently waited for the moment of death, all of us mystified, all of us feeling helpless. This wasn't fair to her. It wasn't fair to me!

Somewhere in my mind I needed to speak out. I needed to open up and release what was inside. The idea of writing a book on being helplessly trapped in one's body with no hope of recovery never occurred to me, or had it?

I dabbled, writing notes, slowly becoming excited, enjoying the idea of writing a story. My reasons were purely selfish and yet, perhaps honorable. I did it for Jeannette as well as for myself. I know she might think me a little crazy but I also know she's very proud.

As I immersed myself into a task that I had no idea would be so time consuming and rewarding, I couldn't help but think of another story I had read in college and how it helped influence my writing. The story is called 'Johnny Got His Gun' by Dalton Trumbo. You might have heard of it.

Johnny is a young war victim. He has lost all his limbs as well as part of his face. He cannot speak. He is trapped inside his body. The sad part is that he still has his mind just like Jeannette did when she passed on.

Perhaps there is hope for the many patients who are paralyzed. Maybe scientists will come up with a far less radical technique to give people back their lives. They could possibly have a second chance. I pray that will happen very soon. We, as humans, need to be very careful in what we wish for because, sometimes, "You can't always get what you want ..."

Gerald Deshayes
gerrydeshayes@hotmail.com